THE BIOLOGY OF HORROR

THE

BIOLOGY OF HORROR

Gothic Literature and Film

Jack Morgan

Southern Illinois University Press

Carbondale and Edwardsville

Library of Congress Cataloging-in-Publication Data

Morgan, Jack, date.
The biology of horror : Gothic literature and film / Jack Morgan.
    p. cm.
Includes bibliographical references and index.
1. Horror tales—History and criticism. 2. Horror films—History
and criticism. 3. Gothic revival (Literature)—History and criticism. I. Title.

PN3435 .M67 2002
809.3'8738—dc21
ISBN 0-8093-2470-9 (cloth : alk. paper)
ISBN 0-8093-2471-7 (pbk. : alk. paper)   2002018761

Printed on recycled paper. ♻

The paper used in this publication meets the minimum requirements of
American National Standard for Information Sciences—Permanence of
Paper for Printed Library Materials, ANSI Z39.48-1992. ∞

For Brendan and Jennifer and for Griffin

He comes, pale Vampire, through storm his eyes, his bat sails
bloodying the sea. . . . Darkness in our souls do you not think?

—JAMES JOYCE, *Ulysses*

Already the dark and endless ocean of the end
is washing through the breaches of our wounds,
already the flood is upon us.

—D. H. LAWRENCE, "The Ship of Death"

CONTENTS

ACKNOWLEDGMENTS

This book began as conversations with my then colleagues Margaret Sinex and Dennis Perry, who set my feet upon a gothic path that led to some years of considerable labor. I will try to choose my friends more carefully from now on. Thanks are due also to Karl Kageff for his faith in the project, and I must thank as well Kris Swenson, Anne Matthews, Jenny Olson, Nick Knight, Ann Peterson, Gene Doty, Charles Grimes, Jim Wise, Ellen Aramburu, Michelle Sweeney, Gilberto Perez, Lou Renza, Michael Molino, Trent Watts, and Steven Schneider. My appreciation is extended to Malcolm Hays for lending his technical and literary acumen to this task, and to Michael McKean and Mary Reynolds of University of Missouri-Rolla Technical Editing, who rescued the manuscript from a software funk I could not have begun to fathom.

A previous version of chapter 1 first appeared in the *Journal of Popular Culture* 32.2 (Winter 1998): 59–80. The *Journal of Popular Culture* was also kind enough to present the essay its Louis B. Nye article award for 1998–1999. A version of chapter 7 was published in *Post Script: Essays in Film and the Humanities* (Summer 2002). Thanks to the editors of both of these journals.

THE BIOLOGY OF HORROR

INTRODUCTION

"The Body Is His Book"

THE WORD *LIFE*, ASIDE FROM MEANING THE TOTALITY of what is happening, can be taken to signify mainly two different things: the complex memory image that constitutes one's story folded into the collective history; secondly, the autonomic biological dynamic that is ongoing—the vital process in which one's body, brain included, is an entirely dependent participant—Life, with a capital *L*. The first, the psychological, goes to who one is in the ego sense; the second, the physiological, goes to *what* one is as an organism. And the second is indeed secondary in human reckoning, a reality we realize will trump ego-life one day but which for now, we think, can be bracketed. Mentality meanwhile is off on its quasi-independent career as if our physical organism were, except in the case of eating and sex perhaps, a vestigial evolutionary nuisance. Thought tends to regard itself as essentially above the biological; the brain appears to it as a package of electrified tissue to which,

I

it must begrudgingly acknowledge, thinking is somehow embarrassingly indebted. But physical life, as Henri Bergson notes, has created thought, and "in
definite circumstances, to act on definite things." How then, he asks, can
thought embrace that life "of which it is only an emanation or an aspect?"
(*Evolution* x). Owen Barfield similarly refers to "primordial tensions and events
which were not produced by, but which produced, the physical organism itself as well as the consciousness that is correlative to a physical organism"
(*Rediscovery* 25). Ours is a psychology correlative to and defined by our biological character, but the human psyche is not comfortably at home in this
biological landscape it cannot fathom, in a nature everywhere characterized
by perishableness. Victor Frankenstein, for example, seeks to acquire dominion precisely over this elemental exigency of the human organic context and
to that end resolves to apply himself "to those branches of natural philosophy which relate to *physiology*" (italics added, 30).

There are of course contemporary scientific interrogations of organic life;
fractal geometry, for example, attempts to suggest the mathematical archetypes implicit in the seemingly whimsical generation of organic forms in nature—"the frolic architecture of the snow," to use Emerson's phrase (34). And,
along somewhat the same track as Bergson and Barfield previously, George
Lakoff and Mark Johnson in their cognitive study *Philosophy in the Flesh* (1999)
have constructed matters, as other cognitive scientists are now doing, not in
terms of the mind in the body but of the body in the mind, seeing mentality
as fundamentally incarnated. They have pointed to the extraordinary quantity of embodied material and activity implicit in the unconsciously metaphoric
dimension of our thought-language—"the hidden hand that shapes conscious
thought" (12–13). The claim of these researchers is not simply that the body
is indispensable since it situates the neural wherewithal by which "higher"
thought is achieved. They assert, beyond that, that the nature of perception
and conceptualization is defined by our physical movement in space, our object manipulation, and all the other characteristics of bodiliness (37–38). D. H.
Lawrence of course insistently affirmed the "physical mind" as well, and
Susanne Langer noted decades ago that physical organs such as the eye and
ear involve what Coleridge called "primary imagination"—they are discrimi-
nating, active, and intelligent organs, not receptors of material to later be pro-
cessed by an autonomous rational faculty—mental life "begins with our
physiological constitution" (*New Key* 83). This book will suggest that the horror literature tradition is an aspect of our mental life in which our physiologi-

cal constitution is most notably implicit, that horror is essentially bio-horror and involves the tenuous negotiations between rationality and a looming biological plenum that defies rational mapping. Emily Dickinson notes the *physical* jeopardy in which the brain is situated—that while it runs evenly and true all is well, "but let a splinter swerve . . ." (270). If a vein breaks or a piece of plaque becomes jammed, then, her grim ellipsis implies, all is lost; rational thought is an extinguished privilege. However ignored and repressed it is, physicality situates an uncanny dimension that intrudes upon routine life in the form of stroke, coronary, dream and nightmare, the menstrual cycle, childbirth, menopause, and so on.[1] In recent decades, physicality has dramatically come to the fore in headlines that center on genetic research, cloning, stem cells, and so on. And our neglected, marginalized organic life, it will be argued here, also finds symbolic expression in the atavistic, demonic images conjured by macabre literature. Body horror, pain, death, and dismemberment are facts of everyday physical life on the one hand and phantoms of our dreams and imagining at the same time. Cancer is a distinct reality in the world, and anxiety regarding it constitutes another kind of reality, the reality in which horror literature is situated. Though they intertwine, pain is one thing, the fear of pain another, and fictive dramas of pain yet another.

Even the new attention to embodiment and the body evident in contemporary literary criticism, psychology, and philosophy, however, have not begun to bridge the division between thought and the vital dimension of organic livingness. And this attention has tended to err, one might argue, in reifying the body and affording it a "misplaced concreteness," to use Whitehead's term, as though the body were the end of the story, as though it did not extend out into the farthest reaches of nature, into endless and mysterious patterns of relationship to other expressions of existence—"other regions of space and other durations of time" (Whitehead 58). "When I have a beautiful woman's body as a model," Rodin remarked, "the drawings I make of it also give me pictures of insects, birds, and fishes" (qtd. in Hartman 304)—testimony, surely, to the physical nature of mentality, the biomorphic character of perception. Walt Whitman writes: "I find I incorporate gneiss, coal, long-threaded moss, fruits, / grains, esculent roots, / And am stucco'd with quadrupeds and birds all over" (*Collected* 88). Our bodies are not hardwired structures unto themselves; rather they situate a nexus of life, an intimate experience of the natural order. It is always worth reminding ourselves of the reciprocity involved in our breathing, for instance, that the atmosphere *insists* on our breathing, that is, inspires us, rather than that *we* breathe. Breath is inside us and outside us, and, quite beyond our control, "it is entering and leaving us all day and all night from the day we are born until the moment we cease to breathe" (Barfield 72).

An earlier draft of this book was subtitled "Toward an Organic Theory of the Gothic," and another, "Toward a Poetics of the Macabre." Both titles, either of which could have been retained, suggest the project's current direction. The "toward" would remain appropriate too, intended as it was to characterize the book as an investigative discussion, limited groundwork having been laid in the specific area dealt with here despite energized literary-critical attention to horror fiction in recent years. This study, then, represents a reconnoitering, a literary investigation of, to use a phrase of Freud's, "certain things which fall within the class of what is frightening." It proceeds for the most part inductively, working as much as possible from examples, and follows from my impression that a case might be made that horror invention, loosely designated as "gothic" over the past two and a half centuries or so, merits, even demands, consideration as a primary fictional form.[2] It is true that horror literature is much more respected than when Anna Barbauld wrote in 1810 that "this species of composition is entitled to a higher rank than has been generally assigned it" (qtd. in Varma 1), but its acceptance is still on the whole very provisional. However crude any given occurrence of horror literature might seem, I think there is much to indicate that the horror mythos emerges from "the dark backward and abysm of time" and reflects particular aspects of our bio-existential situation; it emanates, that is, from the agonies and exigencies of physical life. As H. P. Lovecraft observed in his *Supernatural Horror in Literature,* involved in macabre fiction is

> psychological pattern or tradition as real and as deeply grounded in
> mental experience as any other pattern or tradition of mankind; co-
> eval with the religious feeling and closely related to many aspects of
> it, and too much a part of our innermost biological heritage . . . to lose
> potency over a very important minority of our species. (13)

Of interest here in terms of the present study's emphasis is Lovecraft's recognition of a biological heritage nourishing the genre, whereas most analysis of the gothic tradition has tended to look past the physiological, privileging the psychological instead, as if the latter were a disembodied dimension. The least "psychological" of humans, the most primitive, primordial, and biological, is the baby, but is it in its polymorphous perverse world free of the darkness that later fuels the horror imagination? The human infant's radical bodiliness is arguably raw psyche. Wittgenstein observes in this regard that "[a]nyone who listens to a child's crying and understands what he hears will know that it harbours dormant psychic forces, terrible forces different from anything commonly assumed. Profound rage, pain and lust for destruction" (2).

"There is no extended analysis," Stephen Bruhm writes, "that attempts to locate *physicality* . . . as a concern for the Romantics" (xvii). I take him to be referring to the fact that Romanticism sought to relocate the spiritual in the framework of physical life, to rediscover spirit in the things of the earth, to establish a new realization of what in its own way the pagan past seems to have realized and perhaps folk consciousness to some extent retained—a sense of our continuity with other things in a mysterious physical matrix. In this respect, the Dark Romantic tale of terror would seem to have taken the same path Romanticism more broadly did, situating those aspects of the marvelous with which it dealt not in an ethereal otherworldly location but in the elemental realities of the natural world, in the strange spirals of organic life. Classic "high" literary gothicism, with its assertive physicalness, may then be viewed as a modality within the historical Romantic project, though grotesque imagining was alive of course well before the Romantic sensibility took it up and has continued to flourish well after Romanticism's heyday. Through its particular narrative strategies, horror awakens thought shockingly to its intimate and inescapable connectedness to the flesh and to pain, to the kind of recognition Astrid, the narrator of Janet Fitch's recent novel *White Oleander,* experiences while trying to comfort a friend in a maternity ward:

> I couldn't stop thinking about the body, what a hard fact it was. The philosopher who said we think, therefore we are, should have spent an hour in the maternity ward of Waite Memorial Hospital. . . . The mind was so thin, barely a spider web, with all its fine thoughts, aspirations, and belief in its own importance. Watch how it evaporates under the first lick of pain. (420)

Macabre literary invention addressed the "embodied mind" long before such phrases, thanks to Merleau-Ponty and other more recent analysts, had currency.[3] Symbols themselves are coming to be recognized as issuing from and circling back to physical embodiment—"meanings arise through body and brain" (Lakoff 495). While there are obviously other dimensions involved in horror, the present book proposes the primacy of this one, positing bio-morphic imagination as critically underlying gothic fiction's Dark Romantic project and of macabre literature in general, and to a degree and depth that goes beyond the conscious, thematic level. One of M. H. Abrams's studies of the Romantic tradition was titled *Natural Supernaturalism;* in the gothic, the nexus of the supernatural and the natural is corporeality. Films such as *The Exorcist, Rosemary's Baby, The Stand, 'Salem's Lot,* and *Stigmata,* for example, all imag-ine diabolical assertions upon the physical body of a young woman, suggest-ing an arch assault on the wellsprings of human life. In the film *Seven* (1995), the human monster's obsession with souls stained by the seven deadly sins is enacted in grotesque torture dramas played out on his victims bodies, and sig-nificantly, his ultimate prey is a pregnant young woman. Our "psychological" fears are realized in very physical terms. What John Donne wrote in "The Ec-stasy" of love might be said appropriately of horror as well: Its "mysteries in souls do grow / But yet the body is his book" (132).

Most studies of horror do somewhere reference its bodily focus, of course; feminist criticism almost invariably remarks it, but the concern of most criti-cism is rarely principally that.[4] The over-psychologizing of the horror mode in critical analysis may in part reflect the fallacy earlier noted in terms of which thinking is regarded as functioning "in some ghostly realm independent of the body." Consciousness, E. W. F. Tomlin argues, thereby is viewed as having no compelling connection with the organism of the person thinking (17). The gothic perception, on the contrary, is characteristically carnal, reflecting the embodied context of fearful thoughts. Sue, in Stephen King's *'Salem's Lot,* for example, attempts to rationalize and thereby deflect evidence of vampiric activity in her town: "Her mind was clear, still unimpressed with this talk of bloodsuckers and the undead." But terror takes hold of her at a more atavis-tic and undeniable level: "It was from her spinal cord, a much older network of nerves and ganglia, that the black dread emanated in waves" (305). One might point as well to a certain convergence of King's rhetoric here and that of Mark Johnson in his study *The Body in the Mind: The Bodily Basis of Mean-ing, Imagination, and Reason.* King's network of nerves and ganglia may be equated with Johnson's structures of bodily experience, which "work their way up into abstract meanings and patterns of inference" (xix) but do not neces-sarily lose their biological definition in the process. Traces of the older physi-cal-psychological networking King references, of meaning's organic ground-ing, arguably survive in gothic-relevant words such as *revulsion, panic, disgusting,* or *gross* and in idioms such as "I can't *stomach* that attitude," or that whatever, in all of which cases the meaning is biomorphic, carrying an at once mental and physical tenor.[5] Horror is similarly bio-psychological. When King, in *'Salem's Lot,* describes the atmosphere of a place that "took the heart out of you and made you no good" (140), would anyone argue that the sense of the phrase is "psychological" and merely delivered by way of a physiological metaphor? The horror imagination is somatic; its fears, for all their "mental" manifestations, are deeply situated in the ungraspable bio-logic of hormone chemistry and nerve synapses and in the reciprocity between those and the "exterior" organic environment of which humans are protein variations. To modify a phrase from Bergson, the brain is part of the organic world; the organic world is not part of the brain (*Matter and Memory* 19).[6]

This study began, at far as I am aware at least, with my puzzling—still unresolved—over Herman Melville's enigmatic "Benito Cereno," that dark tale of a slave mutiny on a Spanish ship off the coast of Chile in 1799. To the extent it was read at all before the revival of Melville's literary reputation, the story had been taken as a work of pure imagination. The American literary scholar Harold Scudder, however, browsing in a used book store one day in the late 1920s, came across a copy of Captain Amasa Delano's *Narrative of Voyages and Travels in the Northern and Southern Hemispheres* (1817) and discovered that the events narrated in "Benito Cereno" were factual—Melville had not even changed the names of the people involved. What he *had* done apparently was to gothicize Delano's nonfiction narrative, arguably creating an odd amalgam of it and Poe's "The Fall of the House of Usher." Comparing the Delano original to Melville's end result seemed to me to offer a rare, almost forensic opportunity to view the hand of the gothic author at its work— the base narrative and the Poesque overlay could be distinguished from one another; one could note what Melville retained or discarded, what he heightened or diminished in order to transform Captain Delano's nonfiction text into a tale of the grotesque. This interest carried over to my reading and rereading of other gothic works, books, and motion pictures that I tended to view in the light of "Benito Cereno" in the hope of gaining some insight into the nature and function of horror invention generally and its particular rhetorical pathways.

Rereading a book outside the gothic field at the same time, C. L. Barber's *Shakespeare's Festive Comedies,* I was struck by Barber's reference to the fact that those late medieval factions opposed to the Dionysian spirit of spring holiday tended to emphasize *"the mortality implicit in vitality"* (10). The phrase seemed to situate a critical opposition, one that brought the horror sensibility and logic into focus over against the comic. Barber's book as a whole in fact seemed to shed light on the matter of horror though it never broached the subject as such. In its treatment of holiday and summer festival as enduring rituals of natural vitality and fertility, it seemed to me to suggest a binary dynamic between comedy and horror—evident, for example, in an early English holiday couplet he quotes: "Wormes woweth under cloude, / Wymmen waxeth wounder proud" (21). What was referenced here was the body not in an individualistic sense but as part of the larger life schema—diurnal, seasonal, agricultural, all of which, as Barber shows, were bound up in traditional premodern and early modern holiday and festival. An ancient ritual synthesis seemed to suggest itself: the conjunction, as in the couplet quoted, of Thanatos and Eros, the implications of worms and morbidity on the one hand and of women walking delightfully alive and majestic on the other. They are the farthest apart images imaginable, and at the same time they are part of an intimate continuity. One thought of Bergson's identifying an essential upward and downward movement in life, the ascent characterized by ripening and creating—traditionally that would be seen as phallic, fertile, comic. He does not offer adjectives to characterize the descending path, perhaps because it is a negative, but one might supply them—exhaustion, infirmity, and decay, a falling toward the worms. This descending path, I would argue, represents the track of horror. The more I considered it, the more Barber's cogent remark suggesting the oneness of the mortality/vitality opposition seemed propitious; so much so that, in a way, *The Biology of Horror* seems to me now largely a gloss or attempted elaboration upon Barber's phrase in terms of comedy and horror, fertility and its antagonist. His book, which in many respects anticipated the work of Mikhail Bakhtin, which was not to appear in translation until 1968, led me to return to others of a complementary perspective, notably Susanne Langer's *Feeling and Form* (1953), which had appeared the same year as Barber's study, as well as to Bakhtin's *Rabelais and His World* itself.

I think that horror can be productively analyzed in terms of the kind of model Langer proposes for comedy; horror indeed embodies a dark foil for comic regeneration, subverting Eros and all it implies. If the quest romance, as Northrop Frye argues, represents ritually the victory of fertility over the Waste Land, horror situates dark romance's inversion of those terms and the privileging of various sinister elements antagonistic to the quest project; Frye notes, for instance, giants, ogres, witches, and magicians (*Anatomy* 193). Horror, despite its often obscene depravity, is driven by an antierotic, and fertility-adversarial perspective. Though the Dark Romantic impulse shares the broader Romantic concern with physicality, it is with the menacing aspects of physicality. Increasing freedom in publication has in fact drawn the gothic's aversion to the organic out to the point of such over-the-top vileness that one hesitates to quote hard-core examples—the loathsome necromancy experiments in Brian Lumley's *Necroscope,* for instance. Here, however, is a passage from Clive Barker's *The Damnation Game.* If for grossness it outdoes horror films such as *Suspiria* or *Rabid,* or some of the more repulsive passages of *Silence of the Lambs,* or even some graphic episodes of *The X-Files,* it is really not by very much. The evil Mamoulian is conjuring abominations to subdue Carys, the recalcitrant daughter of Joseph Whitehead, who has locked herself in a bathroom.

> A gruel of filth had started to seep over the lip of the toilet and dribble onto the floor. Wormy shapes moved in it. . . . The water splashed more loudly as the flood rose, and in the stream she heard wet heavy things flopping onto the bathroom floor. . . . The dribbles from the toilet had become a heavy stream, as if the sewers had backed up and were discharging their contents at her feet. Not simply excrement and water; the soup of hot dirt had bred monsters. Creatures that could be found in no sane zoology; things that had been fish once, crabs once; fetuses flushed down clinic drains before their mothers could wake and scream. . . . Everywhere in the silt forsaken stuff, offal and dregs, raised itself on queasy limbs and flapped and paddled toward her. (211–12)

The scatological extravagance of this surpasses even *Grand Guignol* reach and is, to be sure, a long way from the restrained subtlety of Henry James's *The Turn of the Screw,* say, but one is not deploring literary decline here; Barker's writing, in this early novel at least, is of an exemplary elegance for that matter. His work is in a line distinct, however, from that of the genteel ghost story cultivated by writers such as James and Edith Wharton; the menace in Barker's stories does not take the form of shadows on mansion walls and eerie revenant forms crossing aristocratic lawns in the moonlight. His novel is a contemporary *Melmoth the Wanderer, Dracula,* or *The Monk*—visceral, excessive, bloody, and obscene. The macabre author's study is, like Frankenstein's laboratory, "a workshop of filthy creation" (32).

Nor is the Barker paragraph, I would argue, mere pandering to a vulgar audience; rather it goes to the nature of the gothic horror modality, its interrogation of the most abhorrent implications of the flesh and of physical life, their most pathological possibilities. The excerpt quoted represents an instance of the pure—that is to say impure—horror practice. The cloacal vocabulary in the passage reflects its bio-pathological bias: "dribble," "seep," "wormy," "discharged," occur in conjunction with "gruel" and "soup" in conscious violation of a primitive hygienic imperative that all things sewer related be kept distinct from food. We would as soon that mental images of the two kinds also be kept apart. Deformed fetuses are conjured—offal, dregs, biological mistakes that flop and flap on the tiles—signifiers of horror literature's engrossment with things that are contra naturam, physiologically aberrant and monstrous.

Barker's passage inscribes the human anxiety of organism, as did Mary Shelley's *Frankenstein,* if Ellen Moers's thesis is correct—that the novel reflects Shelley's anxieties regarding giving birth, which she had done as early as eighteen. Other recent gender-oriented literary criticism comes round to similar physiological conclusions. Joan Copjec, in her *Read My Desire: Lacan against the Historicists,* discussing the rise of vampire fiction, argues that it reflected eighteenth-century breast-feeding anxieties (118–39). And Moers's birth dread hypothesis is perhaps reinforced by the nightmarish organic images that assail the postpartum young woman in Charlotte Gilman's "The Yellow Wallpaper." Forms in the wallpaper "loll like a broken neck" and "stare at you upside down"—the fetal arrival position—"up and down and sideways they crawl, and those absurd, unblinking eyes are everywhere" (91). Moers has in fact been one of the few critics—Linda Badley is another—to emphatically note gothic fiction's biological emanation. The genre seeks, she recognizes, "not to reach down into the depths of the soul and purge it with pity and terror (as we say tragedy does), but to get to the body itself, its glands, epidermis, muscles and circulatory system" (214).

The chapters in *The Biology of Horror* discuss different thematic elements of the horror invention rubric—malevolent locale, pestilence, lethargy, infertility, and so forth—in terms of their broad biological implications. It is important to emphasize, however, that these elements intercontextualize and reinforce one another; horror categories bleed into one another as it were. The book's concluding chapter considers the matter of horror's possible therapeutic function, related to the question of what accounts for the esoteric pleasure we take in reading this species of literature and viewing the analogous cinematic works. (Though the traditional usage, "pleasure" may not be the best word—Emily Dickinson notes, I think more precisely, the tendency of horror to *captivate* [129]. The question might better be put in terms of why horror does captivate and fascinate, why it can be so hypnotic, seductive, and intriguing). What would lead Sir Walter Scott, for instance, to praise the *beneficial* qualities of Mrs. Radcliffe's—for its time—morbid work? He remarks the pleasure it produces, its "blessed power in those moments of pain and languor, when the whole head is sore and the whole heart sick" (qtd. in Moers 215). What is Thomas Ligotti getting at in similarly suggesting that artistic horror "can be a comfort. . . . it may confer—if briefly—a sense of power, wisdom, and transcendence" (*Nightmare* xi)? Do such observations apply to a novel like Clive Barker's quoted above? I would say so, and the author's great and growing popularity would tend to suggest so. The nature of the gothic's possibly wholesome function, however, is a consideration I have for the most part delayed until the final chapter, letting the question hang above the text all along because that seemed a fertilizing strategy. Readers who want everything up front may wish to read the conclusion first.

I would mention finally that this book casts a wide speculative net and ranges around and about a good deal in space and time; it is not intended to be a narrowly focused literary critical monograph. My main justification for that is the fact that, as Lovecraft notes, some of the most significant horror work is found outside what is usually viewed as the gothic or horror literature canon, in scattered fragments set in contexts not always definable as literary gothic (*Supernatural* 16). The notorious Nazi documentary film *The Eternal Jew,* for example, makes use of the repulsion triggers perfected in landmarks of macabre German expressionism such as F. W. Murnau's 1922 *Nosferatu* and Fritz Lang's 1931 *M* and manipulates the camera-technical horror savvy such films pioneered.[7] It employs the defining gothic strategy discussed earlier— that of bypassing the rational and addressing the visceral instead—and points up the dangerous political and totalitarian possibilities of manipulated horror imagination. The film's strategy is to go to the heart of elemental dread—the fear of contamination, the central theme of Lovecraft's classic *The Shadow over Innsmouth,* for example. Images of healthy, outdoor German life—grazing lambs and so on—are juxtaposed to dreadful scenes of kosher animal slaughter by rabbis, images of cockroaches, and especially—shades of *Nosferatu*—of rats swarming and scavenging en masse. *The Eternal Jew* may even have been consciously conceived to be viewed in a mental montage with, and thereby

to capitalize on, the lingering horror images the German public retained from
Murnau's film of almost twenty years earlier. That the producers of *The Eternal Jew* had such associational strategies in mind is suggested by their use of
actual footage from *M,* a terribly disquieting film that, like *Nosferatu,* had made
a deep impression on the public. The famous scene in which Peter Lori ("the
Jew Peter Lori" the voice-over says) pleads grotesquely for understanding of
the heinous child murders he has committed is included in *The Eternal Jew.* In
the film, the Jew is a vampire, sucking the blood of Aryan Europe, and like
the vampire of Murnau's film, the "Jews" in the 1940 film are meant to evoke
rodents and the medieval epidemic associations still vivid in the European
imagination. The latter connection is in fact explicitly made in the voice-over.
Like Nosferatu, the haunted "Jewish" figures are meant to suggest slippage to
a lower order of life—they are drawn as stooped and skulking, sliding along
the walls of sordid, sinister places, their eyes derelict and resentful. In fact, the
following description of Murnau's vampire Nosferatu by Gilberto Perez, if one
didn't know better, could be taken as descriptive of the "Jews" in the Nazi
production: They are "loomingly thin" presenting a "skeletal aspect" and
"monstrously suggest a cross between a human skeleton and a rat." Their re-
semblance to rats "makes more pronounced [their] association with pestilence"
(Perez 124). By cutting from the haggard "Jews" to teeming rats, and back, the
Nazi film suggests their association in squalor—the two are equated with vile,
contaminating conditions into which, it is implied, the film viewers, be they
less than vigilant (read *vigilantes*), may slide. The insinuation in *The Eternal Jew*
is that the Jew is like Nosferatu: "rats he carries with him."[8]

The present book also references writing in nonfictional epidemic, mar-
tyrological, and execution accounts, Frederick Douglass's slavery narrative,
Catherine Williams's early-nineteenth-century true crime narrative, and other
literature remote from the standard gothic canon. The bricolage character of
the modality itself leads to critical traveling as well. Maggie Kilgour, in *The Rise
of the Gothic Novel,* notes that gothic fiction "feeds upon and mixes a wide range
of literary sources out of which it emerges and from which it never fully disentangles itself. . . . The form is itself a Frankenstein's monster, assembled out
of bits and pieces of the past" (4). The emergence of an energetic film branch
of horror invention has further complicated the genre's profile so that by now
discussion of salient horror tropics occasions a knitting together of many sun-
dry strings, often from dissimilar historical locations, which may sometimes
need to be discussed in close proximity. Ezra Pound's observation that all ages

are contemporaneous is perhaps especially true of horror; he added that in terms of literature, "many dead men are our grandchildren's contemporaries" (6). Recent movie history would seem to bear this out; thanks to the influence of film, exorcism and stigmata, for example, are arguably more a part of the American popular cultural imagination today than they were one hundred years ago, and the currently popular television "crossing over" genre, purporting to contact the dead, recapitulates Victorian theosophy. And cloning research provokes much the same trepidation that informed Mary Shelley's *Frankenstein*. Clive Barker may have had this sort of irony in mind when he appended the following lines epigraphically to his horror novel *The Great and Secret Show:* "Memory, prophecy and fantasy— / The past, the future and— / The dreaming moment between— / Are all one country." And part of that one country, this book will argue beginning with chapter 1, are the comic and horror literary modalities, which would seem remote from one another indeed. But we may perhaps set out with Samuel Taylor Coleridge's favorite precept in mind: "Extremes meet."

Mortal Coils:
The Comic-Horror Double Helix

I am running from the breath
Of the vaporing coves of death.
I have seen our failure in
Tibia, tarsal, skull, and shin.

—JOHN CIARDI, "Elegy for a Cave Full of Bones"

Battalions of the accursed . . . will march . . . some of them livid
and some of them fiery and some of them rotten. Some of them
corpses, skeletons, mummies, twitching, tottering. . . . Here and
there will flit little harlots. Many are clowns . . . some are assassins.
There are pale stenches and gaunt superstitions and mere shadows.

—CHARLES FORT, *The Book of the Damned*

I reason, earth is short,
. . . .
The best Vitality
Cannot excel decay.

—EMILY DICKINSON

SOMETHING EDITH WHARTON DESCRIBES IN HER AUTO-
biography suggests the uncanny currents that run from body chemistry to the
literary horror sensibility and its expression. When she was nine and living in
Germany with her family, Wharton contracted typhoid and lay near death for
weeks. This experience, in which her body was in effect violated and overrun
by an alien force, left her, she notes, "prey to *an internal and unreasoning physical timidity*. . . . It was like some dark, indefinable menace, forever dogging my
steps, lurking and threatening . . . and at night it made sleep impossible" (italics added, *Ghost Stories* 301–2).[1] The disease episode apparently brought home
to her the realization from which horror invention flows, that she was a physiological creature and thus subject to physical assault and even overthrow at
any time, and that this takeover would be an occult matter occurring on a level
other than that of her quotidian concerns and awareness; she could be

blindsided at any moment. Wharton's body would frequently remember and revisit its experience of biological peril, the fear, "internal and unreasoning." She notes that the sense of menace was most severe when she was returning home from walks with her father or governess and had to pause liminally at the entrance of the house and wait for the door to be opened: "I could feel it behind me, upon me; and if there was any delay in opening the door I was seized by a choking agony of terror" (301–3). This suggests the workings of biomorphic imagination, and the translation process whereby the experience of traumatic physical jeopardy may achieve later symbolic form.

While tragedy has traditionally been regarded as preoccupied with fate, horror, it might be argued, is driven by the recognition Camille Paglia articulates, that *"biology* is . . . Fate" (italics added, *Personae* 104). She writes of Melville's weird tale "The Tartarus of Maids" that it is "grotesque with biomorphic allegories" (590). Any extensive review of *The X-Files* television episodes will confirm that a similarly physiological disposition shapes its plots, the emphasis frequently being on postmortem work, for example, a field in which Scully has expertise, having done a post-M.D. residency in forensic pathology. The introduction to the *Frankenstein* 1818 edition noted that Mary Shelley had not merely woven "a series of supernatural terrors" but that the kind of event at the heart of the novel had been judged credible by "some of the *physiological* writers of Germany" (italics added, 5). But it would be surprising of course if such an elemental reality as our biological peril were *not* prominently represented in art and ritual. The central myth of Christianity involves Christ's choice to participate in the adventure of incarnation and the dark earthly consequences that unfolded from that choice, culminating in a drama of bodily torture and blood atonement unique in the literature of religions. Our own faces lightly veil the classic memento mori, the skull. John Donne recognizes this in the *Devotions,* noting the redundant nature of medieval religious articles such as skulls set in rings as reminders of mortality: "Need I look upon a death's head in a ring," he asks, "that have one in my face?" Tracing the continuity of biomorphic imagination in literature, this line of Donne's is used by Thomas Harris as an epigraph to his extraordinarily macabre novel *The Silence of the Lambs* (1988).

The gruesome implications of human mortality are of course much more disturbing than the neat term *death* implies. It is characteristic of horror fiction that in it mortality is played out graphically. It is one thing to concede in the abstract that "we all owe God a death"; it is quite another to address "the bitter hug of mortality," to entertain, as horror literature and film do, scenarios in which Death's servants—Wasting, Sickness, Pain, and Decay—carry out his projects. Such literature privileges tropes going to the physical repulsion and pain associated with dying. Indeed pain as such may involve as primal a repression and fear as any, including the Freudian castration one—no wonder that only very recently has the contemporary medical care establishment begun to address what would seem to have been forever the most obvious of urgencies, pain management. And the ancient idioms of pain connect us with the remote biological past. In pain, as Emily Dickinson notes, "Ages coil within / The minute circumference / Of a single brain" (452). We ordinarily avoid this and other loathsome implications of mortality by any number of sublimating strategies, including word choice. Dickinson muses regarding the word *death:*

> It don't sound so terrible—quite—as it did—
> I run it over—"Dead", Brain, "Dead."
> Put it in Latin—left of my school—
> Seems it don't shriek so—under rule.
>
> (203)[2]

Macabre literature works in reverse of the strategy Dickinson considers ironically here, however, foregrounding the very grim realities that *do* shriek. Organic apprehension is a privileged theme in fairy tales and children's rhyme as well. "Humpty Dumpty" recites a narrative of the body's fall and irredeemable fragmentation; "Ring Around the Rosy" recites the relentless course of bubonic plague concluding in bodily collapse. "Little Red Riding Hood," "Jack and the Beanstalk," and "Hansel and Gretel" evoke Hannibal Lecterish nightmares of being eaten. The literature of terror insinuates itself physically—its implications get under one's skin, in parallel with the fate of its characters who are biologically assailed.[3] Ellen Moers notes that in general, "the earliest tributes to the Gothic writers tended to emphasize the physiological" (214). And Victor Frankenstein's own presumptuous aspirations, as pointed out earlier, are biocentric; his investigations are not in the realm of physics or astronomy but narrow to an obsession with biochemistry and physiology, notably with the study of bodily deterioration. His proto-cloning adventures steer him along the gothic mortuary track: "Now was I led to study the cause and progress of . . . decay, and forced to spend days and nights in vaults and charnel houses" (30).[4]

Despite the designation *morbid* tale, rarely is a fine point put on the sick preoccupation of horror literature in the way Noel Carroll does in his *Philoso-*

phy of Horror, for example, noting that the genre's monsters are "impure and unclean. They are putrid or moldering things, or they hail from oozing places, or they are made of dead or rotting flesh . . . or are associated with vermin, disease" (23). Those associations arguably apply not only to monsters from Grendel to Godzilla but to the horror genre's whole inspiration. The cloying associations of the Black Lagoon are finally the disturbing thing, not the after all rather pathetic creature that serves to figure forth the slimy atmosphere of the stagnant organic recesses that have bred him. Focus upon the vile and abhorrent things of gothic imagination raises the familiar question of why people are attracted to such subject matter at all and, as I mentioned in the introduction, what it is they get from it. In actuality, it is inconceivable that organic affliction, the body's loss of its physical integrity, could be of anything other than clinical interest. A focus upon sickness for other than medical purposes is considered aberrant in ordinary life; it is essentially and understandably taboo. The distinction between disease and decay on the one hand and their employment in art is all important to the question of horror's function and appeal. It must of course be recognized regarding repulsive subject matter that it is not repulsive things as such that literature and film address but those things symbolically realized. No sane person, that is, is drawn to real world instances of rot, corruption, and putrefaction. We can probe our aversions and their implications, however, through the mediation of art, through what Kenneth Burke calls "symbolic enactment," wherein our fears and repulsions are materialized in a virtual form (20). The death of Christ enacted in the Catholic mass is not literal carnage; it is a framed ritual pageant for the purpose of contemplation and meditation.

A ritual hunt-dance, similarly, is not to be confused with the hunt in fact— the ritual is art and has its own energy, function, and potency. The *danse macabre* is thought to have developed as street performance reflecting medieval plagues, but as art, it becomes a thing in itself, a mainstay of later weird literary conjuring long after the literal contagion that begot it has passed. The dance has served lately, for example, as the title of Stephen King's valuable treatise on horror literature *Danse Macabre* (1983). Literary and filmic horror is not horror itself; as Ernst Cassirer emphasizes, "the image of a passion is not the passion itself. . . . At a Shakespeare play we are not infected with the ambition of Macbeth, with the cruelty of Richard III, or with the jealousy of Othello" (*Essay* 147). Viewers of *The Blair Witch Project* participate in a ritual summoning of terror—they are "aware" that the film's horrors are virtual just as they are aware that this "documentary" is actually not one at all. That [awareness] is bracketed, however, so that the illusion may work its way. When Wendy, in *The Shining*, looking out on the breathtaking vista at the turnoff just short of the Overlook Hotel, literally loses her breath in reaction to the awesome beauty of the Rockies, the reader does not lose his or her breath (King 75). Nor does horror literature in truth provoke adrenalin production in the body or fight-flight reaction. If there are even traces of those things involved in reading *Dracula,* for instance, it is in an aesthetic version distinct from the emotions that would attach to real life horror—the reader's or film viewer's reactions are more in the nature of emotion *about* emotion. When Frederick Shroyer refers to the "peculiar nervous pleasure" horror fiction affords (ix), he is referring to an emotion aroused by a *literature* of a certain kind. The concern with horror throughout the present book represents an aesthetic interrogation therefore, one addressed to the experience of the virtual morbid—a form of essential play or performance in literary space and time.[5]

Horror texts, literary or cinematic, address organic states of siege, whether the organic unit under siege is the cell, the house, the city, or some other expression of the human biological matrix. Given the modality's essentially somatic coding, it is not surprising that the medically grounded best-sellers of Robin Cook, for instance, whatever their literary shortcomings, provide one of the popular contemporary versions of horror invention and are part of a medical pathology subgenre that may well become a major gothic branch in time as it becomes evident that the viral and bacterial menace medical science thought it had virtually banished has in fact turned and counterattacked, auguring neomedieval plague scenarios, pandemics, exotic contagions, and draconian quarantines. Not only the formidable danger posed by these elements through their own agency threatens these days, but human agency has been added—conscious plague agents may enter cities carrying God-knows-what horrors in aerosol form. Given bio-terrorism, the image of National Guard troops medievally digging long burial trenches on the outskirts of American cities unfortunately seems not quite the far-fetched thing it would have forty years ago.

Medical research may be sliding into the pattern of the transgressive quest prefigured in horror works such as *Frankenstein* and Hawthorne's "Rappaccini's Daughter," as efforts to conquer a given medical scourge trigger more virulent iatrogenic versions of that scourge or a near neighbor to it and as we lose track of our poisons. The gothic nightmare of scientific overreach endures, current optimism regarding genome research notwithstanding. Films such as

Mimic, The Stand, and *Outbreak* are part of a growing genre of contagion horror. The Centers for Disease Control in Atlanta and the World Health Organization in Geneva may become mainstays of contemporary macabre literature in the way earlier horror fiction had its ghostly, superannuated mansion on a forsaken hill. Werewolf and vampire narratives are of course themselves versions of contagion horror. David Cronenberg's *Rabid* (1977) typifies the way in which the macabre possibilities of the contagion theme may be played out in a contemporary setting as rabies carriers, suddenly seized, leap on and bite Montreal pedestrians, subway riders, mall shoppers, and so on.[6]

Current genetic mapping meanwhile re-enables the "horror of heredity" theme, which, in a nurture-oriented psychology was, until recently, beginning to be regarded as folkloric. It is becoming increasingly possible to discover, not unlike the narrator of "The Shadow over Innsmouth," the cryptic and possibly dreadful fate implicit in one's chromosomes. *Jurassic Park, The X-Files, Millennium,* and so on, tap fears of errant cloning experiments, and disastrous genetic tampering shapes plots like that of Cook's novel *Mortal Fear* (1989). Richard Preston's nonfiction *The Hot Zone* (1994) is a chilling profile of Ebola, the viral monster that, Preston notes, "flashed its colors, fed, and subsided into the forest. It will be back" (411). Anorexia nervosa, at the same time, represents a contemporary malady of likewise gothic-biological implications: one's daughter, seemingly possessed, turns daily, inexplicably, more skeletal and cadaverous, as if she were being courted nightly by a vampire. And psychology becomes evermore neuropsychology, a matter of biochemistry, neurotransmitters, and so forth, rather than one of autobiographical analysis. Elaine Scarry, remarking the way in which Renaissance medical texts narrate the track of sickness through various body parts until the whole is devastated, notes:

> Dangerous diseases in the twentieth century also elicit from us a ritual recitation of body parts . . . cancer of the bone, cancer of the lungs, cancer of the throat, of the mouth, of the prostate, of the pancreas. . . . AIDS has reoccasioned this same reanatomization of the body: over the course of several years, our collective attention has moved relentlessly from body part to body part—genitals, anus, blood, veins, lungs, saliva . . . even tears. (102–3 n22)

Such a focus touches upon the vital sources of the horror mode, its prevalent organicism. It is deeply, and it would seem transhistorically, significant that we are perishable, that disease may come and rains and harvests may not, that slaughtering enemies raid, that community coherence wanes and formerly settled, assured populations may become wanderers in desolation.[7] All expressions of vitality have their opposing possibilities to provoke dreadful imaginings. Lazarus, raised from the dead, merely resumed his journey deathward. The passage of time has not altered the fact of our contingent corporeality, our organic realization and its prescribed extinction. Ultimately, "all fall down."

★ ★ ★

There have been many recent books written on the literature of horror, not so many on the aesthetics or theory of the mode. Aiken and Barbauld's essay "On the Pleasure Derived from Objects of Terror" (1775) was an early example of the latter; John Ruskin's chapter on the gothic in *The Stones of Venice* (1851) is a Victorian example; Edith Birkhead's *The Tale of Terror* appeared in the 1920s, as did H. P. Lovecraft's *Supernatural Horror in Literature*. David R. Saliba's *A Psychology of Fear* (1980), Stephen King's *Danse Macabre* (1983), Terry Heller's *The Delights of Terror* (1987), Noel Carroll's *The Philosophy of Horror* (1990), Stephen Bruhm's *Gothic Bodies* (1994), and Linda Badley's *Film, Horror, and the Body Fantastic* (1995) are some more recent ones. In addition, a number of untraditional studies such as Julia Kristeva's *Powers of Horror,* Terry Castle's *Masquerade and Civilization,* Mary Douglas's *Purity and Danger,* Peter Stallybrass and Allon White's *The Politics and Poetics of Transgression,* and Camille Paglia's *Sexual Personae* have contributed valuable supplementary insights useful in the study of horror fiction. Nevertheless, a poetics of horror remains to be constructed, and the modality has only in recent years come to be acknowledged as having its own raison d'etre and its own place in the literary landscape. The macabre's undeniable literary, cinematic, and popular-cultural appeal hardly needs elucidation—the undiminished attraction of Poe's work, the cult status of Lovecraft, the fabulous popularity of Stephen King, the rich film corpus from *Phantom of the Opera, Nosferatu,* and *Frankenstein* to *Rosemary's Baby, Night of the Living Dead, The Exorcist, Angel Heart, The Shining, The Howling,* and so forth. At the same time, a vital line of European horror literature is evident in the dark-fantastical narratives of British writers: Anthony Burgess, J. G. Ballard, Patrick McGrath, Clive Barker, and Brian Lumley, the last two of whom have become increasingly popular figures for American horror fiction audiences. We have in fact for a number of decades been living in the context of a ubiquitous, bizarre, and frenetic popular cultural carnography, a visceral discourse of the terrifying, in which *Psycho* seems to have become the defining icon. Besides the thriving "goth" element evident in current youth culture, there has recently been, as Marina Warner remarks, a curious resurgence of interest in Halloween in the United States and Britain, an interest, she observes, that seems to grow annually and to more and more include adults:

> [A]irline clerks now dress as ghouls for the day, a ball and chain shackled to their ankle; young executives go to work with axes through their skulls and bloody eyeballs. The range of costumes for children encompasses the full cast of hell servants, as well as random figures from later Gothic invention. (110)

This popular cultural gothicism and its outrageous physicality runs counter to, and is arguably not unrelated to, a contemporary intellectual stream bound in the opposite direction. Granting some recent exceptions already noted, the present information age's constructions of intelligence, for example, are radically disembodied, positing a cyber-reality in which signifiers function freed from significant connectedness to biological life. The current spike in the popularity of gothic's virtual horror arguably constitutes one aspect of the demonic return of corporeality, its mythic insistences against the particular repressions implicit in the prevalent informatic paradigms. But this must be left for the moment to be taken up at greater length later.

In *Love and Death in the American Novel* (1960), Leslie Fiedler refers to "the archetypal function of the basic gothic story; for such a function it must have or it could not have persisted as it did" (128). But horror's popularity is often too readily accounted for by reference to mere "escapism." Frederick Shroyer, for instance, in his otherwise very useful introduction to Le Fanu's *Uncle Silas*, refers to the modern reader who "living in a routine, drab IBM world seeks to escape into calendarless, clockless places where it always is midnight and winter, and where frightened girls tiptoe fearfully down haunted corridors of lightless, decaying, moor-surrounded castles and mansions" (xi–xii). Such melodrama is indeed, for better or worse, macabre literature's usual vehicle, but underscoring classic gothic's prevalent artifices explains little in and of itself, and the "escape" characterization does nothing to rehabilitate the genre's still slightly disreputable image owing to, among other things, its undeniable sensational elements, its frisson of sadomasochism, and its often uncritical popular acceptance. But while the horror tradition includes much that is common, cheap, and salacious, it may be pointed out that those adjectives are frequently and justly applied to the comic as well.

Another factor in horror literature's having been critically slighted until recently was the continuing hesitation to acknowledge the gothicism prominent in canonical works ranging from *Macbeth* to the poetry of Emily Dickinson and to the works of writers such as Melville, Faulkner, Ambrose Bierce, and even Tennessee Williams in the case of *Suddenly Last Summer,* to mention only a few American examples. Of the work Faulkner produced in the 1930s, only the gothic-excessive *Sanctuary* remained in print continuously. And Toni Morrison's most popularly esteemed novel remains her gothic *Beloved.* The often fierce corporeality of Emily Dickinson's work, her eerie anatomical tropes, has rarely been fully acknowledged.[8] Poems such as the one beginning "How many times have these low feet staggered" reflect Dickinson's transgressive, macabre sensibility. The poem treats a women's corpse as a public fascination, a display. The audience or, even more ghoulishly, the corpse is playfully challenged to get the casket open: "Try—can you stir the awful rivet / Try, can you lift the clasps of steel!" Viewers, contrary to the obvious taboo, are encouraged to explore the corpse as a curiosity: "Stroke the cool forehead—hot so often— / Lift if you care the listless hair— / Handle the adamantine fingers" (88). The physical-biological preoccupation here is that per se, it is not a device referencing something else. The body, Dickinson knows, is not a known quantity to be mystified; it is itself mystery incarnate, the occasion of birth, life, sexuality, and death as well as of all disease, nightmare, and terror. Despite the ubiquity of such tropes in her work, however, the word *gothic* does not appear, for example, in the index to Richard Sewall's authoritative Dickinson biography of 1974.

"When we come to deal with such forms as the masque, opera, movie, ballet, puppet play," Northrop Frye observes—and he might have added horror to the list—"we find ourselves in the position of the Renaissance doctors who refused to treat syphilis because Galen said nothing about it" (*Anatomy* 13). For our purposes, it is a question not of Galen's but of Aristotle's authority, and later neoclassical strict adherence to it, probably having prolonged horror literature's stretch as an ugly sister among literary species, and only begrudging acceptance into the standard literary canon, until the late-eighteenth century. Lovecraft, in his *Supernatural Horror in Literature,* observed of this postponement: "[I]t is . . . genuinely remarkable that weird narration as a fixed and academically recognized literary form should have been so late of final birth" (21–22).

Aristotle's familiar aesthetic paradigm, characterizing the comic dramatist as presenting people worse than they really are and the tragic dramatist presenting them as better than in reality, was overwhelmingly dominate. Tragedy portrayed the noble actions of noble personages and comedy the ignoble actions of meaner sorts. There were various other literary modalities, but tragedy and comedy constituted the two great dramatic forms. Granted the *Poetics* was not the final word on literary modes and much has been written since; in modern times, less stiffly classical-aristocratic descriptions of tragedy have been articulated, but the tragic modality has remained problematic in a way that the comic never was. There would seem to be a need, in fact, to question whether, strictly speaking, Tragedy *is* Comedy's balancing opposite in the simple and certain sense it has popularly been taken to be, or at least whether it is that any more. George Steiner analyzed this matter four decades ago in his *The Death of Tragedy* (1961), suggesting that tragedy rigorously defined was a form confined to fifth-century Attic drama and that it represented so specific a "congruence of philosophic and poetic energies, that it flourished only during a very brief period, some seventy-five years or less" (x).

In any event, there seems to be something chronically unsure about our understanding of tragedy; at the very least it is a more intellectualized and culturally specific mode than is the case with comedy. Camille Paglia views it as a gendered mode, and I think she is correct in identifying tragedy with "the agon of male will" and noting "the difficulty of grafting female protagonists onto it" (*Personae* 7). (In the gothic tradition, on the other hand, in *Dracula, The Turn of the Screw, Halloween, Friday the 13th, Silence of the Lambs,* for example, heroines are common.) When Arthur Miller's *Death of a Salesman* achieved fame in the early 1950s—another example of the tragic genre's difficult nature—critics were at pains to account for the tragic power of a play that seemed to run counter to the traditional assumptions about the nature of the form. And any of us might refer to having seen or read a great comedy last night, for instance, anything from Aristophanes to Rabelais to Woody Allen, and no one would blink; our sense of the mode is, like our sense of the horror mode, pretty assured. It would be rare, on the other hand, for someone to say he or she had watched a tragedy last night on TV or at a cinema unless the person was differentiating among a dramatist's—probably Shakespeare's—works. For someone to remark having seen a gothic horror movie last night, however, or having read a horror tale, would cause no hitch at all; we would know with considerable certainty what he or she meant. The local Blockbuster typically has sections labeled "Comedy" and "Horror" but not "Tragedy."

A step toward loosening and broadening prevailing conceptions of tragedy was taken by B. L. Reid in his *William Butler Yeats: The Lyric of Tragedy,*
which appeared the same year as Steiner's book. Reid's study privileged primitive "generic" tragedy, as opposed to the codified, Aristotelian version, emphasizing tragedy's elemental origins in pagan ritual, its source in early people's
recognition of "the physical and metaphysical rhythm in the design of their
lives, the regular march of the seasons, the inevitability of suffering and death,
the hope of resurrection." Reid questions what happened to this original
"blood knowledge," this sense of life, in the centuries when literary modes
were being defined according to "Aristotle's dry analytical prescriptions" (11).
What happened, he asks, to the original "dung and death" that refined analysis would later turn into *"Tragedia cothurnata,* fitting Kings, / Containing matter, and not common things?" (viii).[9] It might be proposed as a hypothesis that
this discarded dung and death tradition became an informal folk species, a
nascent form of what we would now call horror, and later received a certain
codification of its own when it achieved formal, written realization. Reid's
study liberates criticism from erroneously considering tragedy as an exclusively
dramatic expression and focuses instead upon its informal, primitive character. Comedy may be similarly informalized, taken as a "sense of life" rather
than as a species confined to drama. And one might posit a colloquial *horror*
sense of life as well, one which should long since have figured in a revised and
broadened critical anatomy, possibly even as a pretender to the comic-antitheti-
cal role tragedy has been viewed as filling. The horror spirit may in fact represent the true Thanatos antagonist to the comic Eros.

I think a "loose" definition of the literary gothic in fact comes closer to the
mark than does a "purist" historical one. Horror literature has arguably itself
been somewhat too codified, too identified with its high gothic expression, with
the result that its visceral, generic nature has been obscured. An alternative
view would see literary horror issuing from an informal vernacular tradition
and, as earlier suggested, greatly antedating the "high" gothic literary expression it would receive in the nineteenth century. Marginal expressions of a horror mythos might even have been traditionally misread as "tragic," since the
latter was for a long time the only anti-comic term with scholarly currency.[10]

* * *

Neither Frye nor Suzanne Langer, in their theoretical work, question the traditionally drawn comic/tragic contrast, with the result that neither takes into
account to any degree the literary significance of horror fiction, even though

Langer was intrepid enough to attempt a unified aesthetic theory encompassing painting, literature, music, drama, and even film. Frye does cite the extensive range of demonic archetypes upon which literature involving "the nightmare and the scapegoat . . . bondage and pain and confusion" draws. He cites images of ruins and catacombs, dark animal images of monsters or beasts of prey; vegetable ones of sinister forests or enchanted gardens, waste lands, forbidden trees, the tree of crucifixion, the stake of execution; organic instrumentalities of pain and death—"scaffolds, gallows, stocks, pillories, whips, and birch rods" (*Anatomy* 147–49). He nowhere, however, treats horror as in any sense a genre itself—with legs as it were. That Langer does not consider horror as a distinct literary type is unfortunate—Poe is mentioned in *Feeling and Form* only with regard to his poetic criticism—since hers is a theory of art that lends itself particularly well to an elucidation of the horror modality's character. Moreover, her critical analysis, like Reid's, questions codified theories of modes and even employs, as he would later do, the term *sense of life*. It is particularly her discussion of comedy, rather than her consideration of prose fiction, that I think can be useful toward conceptualizing literary gothicism.

Mikhail Bakhtin's work, though like Langer's largely concerned with the comic, is another source relevant to the gothic tradition. His analysis suggests comedy's biologicalness, its degradational return to "the material bodily principle" from which we issue and from which the abstractions of ordinary social, political, theological, and mercantile life tend to separate us. He tracks in carnival a return to the organic, a "transfer to the . . . sphere of earth and body in their indissoluble unity." In carnival, he argues, the element of degradation "has not only a destructive, negative, aspect, but also a regenerating one" (*Rabelais* 21). Carnival's destructive valences, that is, were balanced by revel's erotic charm evident in, for example, Rosalind's remark addressed to Orlando in *As You Like It* (4.1.68–69): "Come woo me, woo me, for I am in a holiday humor, and like enough to consent" (*Complete* 607). Here, arguably, Pagan tradition tracing back to the Comus and forward through the Saturnalia comes to inform the sophisticated comic drama of Shakespeare's England.

Horror's degradation, in contrast, is a one-way street; the elements of built-in upswing, of rejuvenation, are not there. Despite the commonplace wisdom that comedy and tragedy are kindred, it is arguable that instead, as I have implied, it is traces of horror that are more often found bound up with comedy, and the two may well have been part of an original single weave that, somewhat along the lines Bakhtin discusses in terms of medieval carnival, later became unraveled. In the old folk cultural schema, he argues, "terror was turned into something gay and comic" (*Rabelais* 39). What Langer and others have argued regarding the tragic-comic opposition might be modified and applied to the horror-comic linkage: that the two in fact cross-fertilize and inter-define each other, that they have both individual and dialectical identities. In Thomas Ligotti's contemporary horror story "The Last Feast of Harlequin" (1991), a yearly winter carnival is described as transforming a small Illinois town into "an enclave of Saturnalia." The Saturnalia, like the Comus, implied orgiastic revelry related to fertility, but as the Ligotti narrative notes, "Saturn is also the planetary symbol of melancholy and sterility, a clash of opposites contained within that single word" (*Nightmare* 214). Saturnalia would thus seem to have situated the comic-horror nexus being suggested here.

The fertility-sterility, comic-horror opposition, while subtle and deep-structural, is often apparent. On the back cover of the Scribner paperback edition of Joseph Heller's *Catch-22*, for example, this most famous of modern American comic novels is described as moving "back and forth from hilarity to horror." Why, one might ask, is this back and forth movement not unaesthetic, awkward, irksome; how can it be, as it is, in fact seamless and harmonious? How does an essentially comic novel accommodate passages like the one in which the details of tail-gunner Snowden's death at high altitude are given? The memory has haunted Yossarian in nightmares ever since but has been suggested previously in the book only in glimpses. "Dobbs had beseeched him on the intercom to help the gunner, please help the gunner." Yossarian negotiates the plane's narrow passageways to the tail section, where Snowden lies with a wound "as large and deep as a football" in his thigh. "Yossarian's stomach turned over when his eyes first beheld the macabre scene. . . ." He crawls through a cramped tunnel to get to the first-aid kit, only to discover that the twelve Syrettes of morphine that should be there are missing. He is left with two unavailing aspirins to hold to Snowden's "ashen lips unable to receive them." He works carefully applying a tourniquet; doing so gives him some sense of control. Snowden watches with "a lackluster gaze," periodically moaning, "I'm cold, I'm cold."

Yossarian proceeds dutifully with his elementary Army Air Corps first aid, loosening the tourniquet now and then lest gangrene set in and replying to Snowden's repeated "I'm cold" with a helpless, "There, there. . . . There, there." He begins to feel a little calmer and even takes some satisfaction in the bandage he has ably applied and neatly knotted. He reassures Snowden that they will shortly be on the ground and a doctor will be available: "Everything's under control."

> But Snowden kept shaking his head and pointed at last, with just the barest motion of his chin, down toward his armpit. Yossarian bent forward to peer and saw a strangely colored stain just above the arm-hole of Snowden's flak suit. Yossarian felt his heart stop, then pound so violently he found it difficult to breathe. Snowden was wounded inside his flack suit. Yossarian ripped open the snaps . . . and heard him-self scream wildly as Snowden's insides slithered down to the floor in a soggy pile and just kept dripping out. (446–49)

The abject is come upon in this body's deconstruction; we are made aware of "the subordination of all living things to biological reality" (Paglia, *Sex, Art* 104). And again, the word *death* is insufficient to cover this. The cramped laby-rinth of tunnels, turrets, and passageways in the bomber suggest a medieval fortress. The scene's graphic carnage and the gothic arabesque diction of a phrase like "when his eyes first beheld the macabre scene" hardly need to be remarked. But this horror is not an anomaly or a digression within the comic novel; rather it situates a necessary element in the comic dynamic itself. It is against such a background of terror that the novel's comic vision, and all comic vision, works and is deepened.

C. L. Barber's work, as does Langer's and Bakhtin's, assumes a fertility thematic informing comedy. Barber argues the relationship of most Shakes-pearean comedy to annual carnival or folk celebration, that traditional festi-val like the May Game, growing out of the rhythms of a seasonal/agricultural calendar, involved "the composition of experience in ways which literature and drama could [later] take over" (18). It is, as I have implied, based on the assump-tion of fertility origins, but in terms of fertility *inversion,* that horror can ar-guably be usefully examined.

"All creatures live by opportunities, in a world fraught with disasters," Langer writes, "that is the biological pattern in the most general terms" (*Feel-ing* 329). This would define an existential agon that the literary comic and horrific recapitulate from different angles. The "fraught with disasters" part of the equation arguably expresses horror's emphasis, the "opportunities," comedy's. Langer's theory of comedy is in part traditional: Fertility patterns, originally ritually expressed, underlie it, and the essence of the comic artifice is its virtual reflection of the "eternally full and undulating stream of life" (363).

Sharing the view of Ernst Cassirer, Owen Barfield, and others, she sees art as aesthetic-conceptual, an autonomous human modality serving a critical cognitive function, that of rendering tangible for us something not realizable in any other way. Bergson, for one, stressed the essential unfitness of ordinary rational thought to comprehend vital process, biological reality—as Melville observes somewhere in *Clarel,* nature vetoes all her commentators. It is Langer's hypothesis that the version of thought exercised in art creates images that do reflect and do bring us into a kind of contact with physical life—its melodic insistences, its motifs of ripening and decline, of surge and rest, vitality and fatigue. Art, she argues, and only art, can touch upon truths going to our deepest physiological existence; comedy, like music, gives us a *felt* sense of our biological being. Through comedy, for example, we experience "the lilting advance of the eternal life process indefinitely maintained or temporarily lost and restored . . . the great general vital pattern we exemplify from day to day" (351). It is not this *fact* or concept that the comic sets forth but this tension dramatically objectified and configured in artistic images that reflect the pattern of our survival and rebound in the context of biological life's constant brushes with destruction. Bakhtin notes similarly of the comic sense of life in carnival that "its categories are not *abstract thoughts* about . . . the interrelatedness of all things or the unity of opposites. No, these are concretely sensuous ritual-pageant 'thoughts' . . . played out in the form of life itself" (*Rabelais* 123).

In ritual-pageant realization, as rendered sensuously in comic art, vitality ongoing is emotionally "understood" and enjoyed. This infectious comic vitality is not thematic; it is sensuous and formal—just as a ballet's theme is distinguishable from its somatic, kinetic registration. Our argument will be that in the case of horror literature too there is a formal dynamic speaking to the audience's somatic sense of physical life. But horror privileges the peril implicit in physical life, the chronic peril and the peril of catastrophic culmination. Horror as art manifests these things in a way that is conspicuous, resonant, and formal; unlike lived horror, art horror presents macabre reality as both shocking but contemplatable—as virtually present for consideration.

There is a drama occurring in biological life in all its expressions: the processes of fatigue and refreshment, loss and restoration of balance, lethargy and revival. Tragedy perhaps presents the longer-term cadence of growth, maturity, and decline in living, addressing death in its grand, solemn, destined design. It is a commonplace, however, that this is not what we dread so much as what Sir Thomas Browne referred to as "the ignominy of our natures"—that we are material subject to decomposition, forthcoming cadavers (111). We fear as well the dissolution and exhaustion that plague everyday life and that mark the grim stations on the way to a foreordained physical destruction. Implicit in the comic rhythm is the lurking possibility of disaster as well as life's day-to-day corrosive effect upon us. Comedy takes calamity into account, but it privileges recovery, the vigorous, exhilarating rebound of living things from mishap, or their artful dodging of disaster. When Rabelais's narrator in *Gargantua and Pantagruel* addresses the murder of Abel by Cain, for instance, the infamous act is framed in the sacrificial fertility tradition, contextualized as an element in a larger comic-fertility scheme of things: "[T]he earth soaked with that righteous blood became so prodigiously fertile in all the fruits the soil offers us (and especially the medlar apple) that everyone ever after has called it the year of the giant medlar apples" (135).

Horror is the literary mode, on the other hand, that presents us with the implications of the calamity apart from any ameliorating, earth-abiding, perspective. It privileges not just the close call but the actual disaster, absent the rebound; Cain's spilling of his brother's blood begets no splendid crop of apples. The grotesque takes neither note of nor consolation from the full cycle of biological life. Danger is the foil against which we view comic dexterity and audacity with delight, but the stakes are real; dissolution and decline will prevail sooner or later: "I reason we could die" writes Dickinson, "The best Vitality / cannot excel Decay" (142). Vitality and decay define the comic-horror polarity; the *dance de vie* goes on with the *dance macabre* as its shadow counterpart. Decay is a formal reality established in the design of things. Horror reflects the inevitability of "crash's law" in Dickinson's poem 997: "Dilapidation's processes / Are organized Decays. . . . / 'Tis first a cobweb on the soul. . . ." Ruin, she observes, "is formal . . . consecutive and slow" (463). The poem traces the gothic's focus—crumbling, deterioration, decay, cobweb, dust, rust, ruin, slipping; life is a crash proceeding in very slow motion. D. H. Lawrence notes the same thing: "Piecemeal the body dies, and the timid soul / has her footing washed away" (*Poems* 718).

In the case of comedy, as earlier noted, presented with an image of life renewing itself and restoring its balance, one experiences a pleasurable recognition, a satisfying sense of the mysterious vitality that begets and sustains us. That spirit is evident, for example, in the frolic and inexplicable gladness of young mammals. In adults, its expressions are artistic, decorative, and sexual. Langer identifies the sexual as the primary expression of the life spirit:

[T]he sex impulse . . . is closely intertwined with the life impulse; in a
mature organism it is part and parcel of the whole vital impetus. . . .
Consequently the whole development of feeling, sensibility, and tem-
perament is wont to radiate from that source of vital consciousness,
sexual action, and passion. (*Feeling* 330)

Thus bawdy, for instance, the ribald jokes and double entendre of Shakespeare's comedies, like the considerably more obscene humor of Rabelais, does
not stem merely from either author's deference to the tastes of contemporary
audiences but rather is an integral part of the comic imagination, tracing back
to the genre's fertility origins, of which the Greek *Comus*—a fertility rite—was
but one expression.

Even familiar everyday jokes like the following are informed by this sense,
indeed celebration, of biological energy:

A traveling salesman is driving along back roads through the Dakotas
in the dead of winter and meets with a major winter storm—howling
winds and blinding snow. There is no shelter in sight and near zero
visibility. His heater gives out, and soon after, the car rolls to a halt,
unable to proceed through the many feet of snow. Recognizing he will
freeze to death in the car—he is already numb—he sets out through
the storm, wearing only his business suit and dress shoes, on the desperate chance he may find a homestead. After hours of aimless trek-
king, snow-blinded and all but frozen to death, he miraculously
stumbles right up against the door of a farmhouse.

The owner hears the thud and opens the door. The frostbitten salesman, unable to speak, slumps against the doorframe. The farmer, appalled at the man's condition and anxious to help, says to him: "My
friend, I can see you are in need of help—I'll be glad to give you a
change of clothes, some hot cider, a warm bed for the night, and a hot
farm breakfast in the morning. But I think it only fair to make clear
that my wife and nineteen-year-old daughter are gone to my mother-
in-law's in Sioux Falls for a week. There are no women here nor will
there be during your stay." With a trembling hand, the traveling salesman wipes away some of the ice that has frozen his lips shut and says
through chattering teeth to the farmer, "W-w-well, is there another fa-
fa-farmhouse near here?"

This is quintessentially comic whether or not it is "funny." On one level, it is a cultural artifact—a good part of the joke's character derives from the fact that it is a variation on a familiar formula. It depends on audience awareness of the plethora of once common American obscene jokes whose plot involved a traveling salesman being given a room at a farmhouse for the night and then having some kind of sexual misadventure involving the farmer's daughter. But on a deeper level, the joke is existential, provoking the kind of "surge of vital feeling" that is the essence of the comic spirit as well as the source of laughter (Langer, *Feeling* 340). The joke goes to our recognition in it of life's resilient energies, the delightful resurgence of vitality despite the vicissitudes and calamities the flesh is heir to, in this case, despite winter's terrible wrath, when death threatens if our body temperature should fall very far short of a critical 98.6 degrees. Analogously, starvation in the Klondike and having to eat one's shoe is horror material. What makes Charlie Chaplin's version of this situation comic is not that he eats a shoe, but the vivacity with which he does so; he brings the panache appropriate to banquet and the flair of fine dining to the meal.

The salesman joke and Chaplin's *Gold Rush* scene instance what C. L. Barber called "an expression of the going-on power of life" (118). They may be said to image the *charm* of the vital energy that motivates the world. Barber elsewhere speaks of the "upstarting, indomitable gesture" that characterizes the comic (129). This is the spirit Langer notes as comedy's driving force, "at once religious and ribald, knowing and defiant, social, and freakishly individual" (*Feeling* 331). The organism maintains its equilibrium by adjustment, by adaptation, by hook or by crook, despite the stresses it undergoes; and that sense of buoyancy informs comic imagination. Its equilibrium disturbed—by infection for example—the body normally recovers and reestablishes its well being. It does so repeatedly, and it is this flexibility, this pattern of lost and recovered biological poise, "the image of human vitality holding its own in the world," that defines comedy. Importantly, however, the spunky élan of living things that comedy celebrates, the dauntless life-spirit, is defined by a context of menace and hazard.

A comic novel such as *Tristram Shandy*, as Camille Paglia observes, is made up of "a series of disasters to body parts—a flattened nose, shattered knee, crushed groin bone, a penis circumcised by a falling window" (*Personae* 654). She might have added that Tristram's very conception—the transfusion of "animal spirits," he notes, was half-botched when his mother, at his father's point of sexual climax, disconcertingly inquired if he had remembered to wind the clock. Thus is Eros plagued by disconnects and detours in making its comic way. Sterne's novel concludes on a similarly biological note—the failure of Tristram's father's bull to successfully impregnate Obadiah's cow despite Mr. Shandy's high opinion of his male animal. But the novel's final sentence sounds an unabashed comic-phallic note, characterizing itself as a Cock and Bull story "and one of the best of its kind" (573). The fertility bywords *Cock* and *Bull* are significantly capitalized.

A Henny Youngman joke might further the point here:

> An old man and old woman are talking in a home for the aged. The old man remarks that he is so old he can no longer remember how old he is. The woman tells him to pull down his pants, which he does. "You're eighty-seven," she says. "How can you tell?" he asks. "You told me yesterday," she says.

An erotic rascality, an undefeated vigor, delights us here in its survival despite the ravages of age, senility, and institutionalization. "The same impulse that drove people, even in prehistoric times, to enact fertility rites and celebrate all phases of their biological existence," Langer writes, "sustains their interest in comedy. It is the nature of comedy to be erotic, risqué, and sensuous if not sensual, impious and even wicked" (*Feeling* 349).

This irrepressible vitality drives the comic even when it is not being specifically sexual. Langer discusses that comic folk personage, versions of which are the Harlequin, Pierrot, and Fool. While he appears in sophisticated literary comedy, she notes, his roots are "in the humbler theatrical forms that entertained the poor and especially the peasantry" (342). A contemporary version of the type is Wile E. Coyote, that obsessive desert dweller whose extravagant engineering exploits repeatedly explode in his face, crush him, propel him from cliffs, and so forth, but who no sooner picks himself up from one calamity before, still idea-ridden, plotting what will turn out to be another debacle in his ever-optimistic pursuit of the Road Runner. Coyote exemplifies the traditional Pierrot archetype:

> He is the personified *élan vital;* his chance adventures and misadventures, without much plot, though often with bizarre complications, his absurd expectations and disappointments, in fact his whole improvised existence

has the rhythm of primitive, savage, if not animalian life, coping with a world that is forever taking new uncalculated turns, frustrating, but exciting. He is . . . genuinely amoral . . . but in his ruefulness and dismay he is funny, because his energy is really unimpaired and each failure prepares the situation for a new fantastic move. (Langer, *Feeling* 342)

Peter Sellers's Inspector Clouseau, in the *Pink Panther* films, who sheds humiliation as a duck does water and resumes his Quixotic adventures undiminished, is another example of the type. So was George Herriman's *Krazy Kat,* a cartoon phenomenon in American newspapers of the 1920s to the 1940s. Hopelessly in unreciprocated love with Ignatz, a mouse, Krazy is undaunted by the latter's constantly braining him with bricks; the cat in fact interprets this violence as an expression of affection on the mouse's part. This premise was material for years of popular comic strips in which Krazy's charming good will, what Gilbert Seldes called his *sancta simplicitas,* withstood all of Ignatz's abuse (18). I think the essential comic point is not that Krazy, or Wile E. Coyote, or Inspector Clouseau, *refuse* to despair—which would individualize, solemnize, and sentimentalize the matter—but that they *do not* despair; it does not occur to them, so wonderfully driven are they.

In more mainline literature, this proximity of catastrophe to the comic is evident in Frank McCourt's recent best-selling memoir *Angela's Ashes,* a comic work in which elements of horror are explicitly present, as they are in *Catch-22.* Despite squalor, death, hunger, and disease, the narrator's buoyancy and indefatigable gameness register a joie de vivre beneath the pitiable surface details of his autobiography. No matter how dire the circumstances, a sense of human pluck, the kind of resilient spirit evident in the joke examples above, prevails. When he is hospitalized with typhoid and barely survives, Frank spends his time in stitches of laughter with Patricia, a dying girl in the next room. As incorrigible as he is, Patricia imitates the ward nun's pious admonishments: "Give thanks, Francis, give thanks, and say your rosary." He laughs so hard a nurse comes in and scolds the pair—"There's to be no laughing." When the reproachful nurse leaves, Patricia is quick to imitate her, too, and her Kerry accent: "No laughing, Francis, you could be doin' serious damage to your internal apparatus. Say your rosary, Francis, and pray for your internal apparatus" (194–95). Patricia dies of her diphtheria not long afterward, but the two youngsters laughing in the somber contagion ward exemplify the triumph of the vital spirit over disease and death. Again, it is not that they *refuse* to be down that registers the comic sense of life; it is that they *are* not down because they are wonderfully up, enlivened by the mysterious human capacity for delight. W. H. Auden writes: "Among those whom I like or admire, I can find no common denominator, but among those whom I love I can: all of them make me laugh" (372).

Even a scene that would suggest only the most morbid possibilities emerges as comic in McCourt's telling. It is again a scene wherein an enduring comic impetus appears in a distinctly ghastly context. Frankie visits the miserable tenement home of his friend Paddy Clohessy. Everything there would justify despondency; the outside toilet is down a flight of dangerous, broken stairs, and the small children rarely reach it in time, and so forth. Dennis Clohessy, the father, dying of tuberculosis, lies on a bed and hangs over a bucket into which he spits his coughed-up blood. But he is oddly alert and animated given his situation, an inspired talker whose colorful, Rabelaisian tropes delight Frankie. Paddy quotes his father's remark, for instance, that the British Quality "wouldn't give you the steam off their piss" (162). When Mr. Clohessy learns that Frankie is the former Angela Sheehan's son, he is elated:

> "Ah, Jaysus," he says, and he has a coughing fit which brings up all kinds of stuff from his insides and has him hanging over the bucket. When the cough passes he falls back on the pillow. "Ah Frankie, I knew your mother well. Danced with her, Mother o'Christ, I'm dying inside, danced with her I did below in Wembly Hall and a champion dancer she was too."
>
> He hangs over the bucket again. He gasps for air and reaches his arms out to get it. He suffers but he won't stop talking. (162–64)

The run-on "'I'm dying inside, danced with her I did'" is a pure expression of the comic-horror reciprocity, the two spirits, death and dancing, entangled in the scheme of physical life. Clohessy's undiminished ardor for the world, his enthusiasm for talk and reminiscence, embody the "life feeling . . . religious, ribald, knowing and defiant" (Langer, *Feeling* 331), prevailing in the face of the death principle, in fact deepened and defined by that principle.

We might finally consider briefly, in terms of this comic-horror convergence, two previously mentioned British horror novels written roughly two centuries apart: Ann Radcliffe's *The Italian* and Clive Barker's *The Damnation Game*. These novels share a landscape of things vile, delusional, transgressive, spectral, and macabre, yet they also borrow elements normally identified with the "new comic" pattern. Central to Northrop Frye's socially defined comic pattern are the young man and young woman whose romantic-erotic yearning toward one another is blocked by an obstructive—often paternal—power structure (*Anatomy* 44). In Langer's terms, this would imply an unnatural interference with healthy organic process, with natural and vital growth and adaptation. In either case, the established order is in need of cleansing and refreshment.

In *The Italian,* Vivaldi and Ellena are kept apart by a treacherous old order, a cabal of corrupt familial, legal, and ecclesiastical authority. The hindrance here, however, unlike in comic action, is central—a dire and even mortal threat possessed of and willing to employ its system of imprisonment, torture, and murder. In *The Damnation Game,* Marty attempts to save his lover Carys, as Vivaldi does Ellena, from heinous parental intrigues, in this case involving not only the horrors of imprisonment but also those of entrapment through heroin. The novels thus entail, as does the new comic drama, a situation in which an illegitimate, and in these cases demonically evil, order prevails. There is a descent into the suffocating vaults, cellars, and enclosures of the prevailing tyranny, but ultimately the life principle defined by the young lovers prevails over the death principle, and Carys and Marty, Ellena and Vivaldi, escape and are united. *The Italian* ends in the comic fashion, with wedding, banquet, and festive celebration. The end of Barker's novel is more subdued but equally evocative of the coming to the fore of a balance—both novels end in the outdoors and with tropes of space and freedom marking a tempered return to the normal world now seen as welcoming after a plunge into the morbidly abnormal. These examples situate a hybridization involving the comic and gothic forms, but even here, the gothic entails *relief* in the end rather than joyous affirmation.

One thing that radically separates horror action from comic is the enormity of the block confronting the vital spirit—the dreadfulness of the assault on life involved; in horror, the block is active and consuming and Eros loses at every turn, often, in fact, losing ultimately, as in the case of Ben and Sue in *'Salem's Lot,* wherein love and the lovers do not triumph. In horror, the life principle survives just barely or not at all. This dark side of the equation, which will be the object of the present investigation from here forward, may perhaps be suitably introduced through a passage from Thomas Ligotti's surreal horror collection *Noctuary* (1994). The chapter is the final one, "The Order of Illusion," in which a man founds a new sect, one of biological dead-endness and sterility, the comic-invertive markers of macabre literature. The man finds a place and structure in which he sets up what might be characterized as the altar of the gothic:

> . . . a place abandoned, old, isolated, decayed. . . . This numinous structure—bashed in roof and battered walls—he cluttered with fetishes of his new creed . . . anything he could find which had a divine aura of disuse, of unfulfillment, hopelessness, disintegration, of grotesque imbecility and senselessness. Dolls with broken faces he put on display in corners and upon crumbling pedestals. . . . Then he hung lamps of thick green glass by corroded chains from the ceiling, and the withered branches of the trees were bathed in hues of livid mold. As were the faces of the dolls and those of various mummified creatures, including two human abortions which were set floating in jars at opposite ends of an altar draped with rags. (192)

As we dread drought and famine against the appreciation of full harvest and largess, we find horror appalling in its lack of or distortion of what the comic celebrates—the waters of life, the fruits of the field, the exhilarating vitality pattern. Frye writes that "in the solar cycle of the day, the seasonal cycle of the year, and the organic cycle of human life, there is a single pattern of significance out of which myth constructs a central narrative." The fourth phase of the cycle, I would suggest, situates the roots of horror, it is "the darkness . . . and dissolution phase . . . the triumph of these powers; myths of floods and the return of chaos, of the defeat of the hero, and Gotterdammerung. . . . Subordinate characters: the ogre and the witch" (*Fables* 15–16). Whereas the comic mode, granted its sometimes grim moments, is pervaded by images of vitality and resurgence, horror is pervaded by a virtually unrelieved vision of dissipation, menace, and decline. If in comedy the livingness of the human world is abstracted and presented to us, in horror its "dyingness" is enacted and imaged forth. Creeping lethargy and sterility, biological failure—these are the horror mode's chief tropes. Horror literature represents a ritualized encounter with that which strikes us as most terrible, what somewhere Clive Barker, paraphrasing Emily Dickinson, calls "the soul at zero."

2

The Muse of Horror:
Traditions of Dreadful Imagining

He grabbed and mauled a man on his bench,
bit into his bone-lappings, bolted down his blood
and gorged on him in lumps. . . .

—*Beowulf*

A dreadful Plague in London was,
In the Year Sixty Five,
Which swept An Hundred Thousand Souls
Away; yet I alive.

—DANIEL DEFOE, *Journal of the Plague Years*

Everything monstrous happening in the world has an ancient
ancestry.

—FRANK CAWSON, *The Monsters in the Mind*

CRITICISM ADDRESSING THE LITERATURE OF HORROR IS
notoriously lacking in an established terminology. Efforts to elucidate its ty-
pological profile can become very nuanced and have tended to cause, as S. T.
Joshi notes, "an irremediable confusion of terms such as horror, terror, the supernatural, fantasy, the fantastic, ghost story, Gothic fiction, and others" (2).
Chris Baldick, in his introduction to *The Oxford Book of Gothic Tales,* having
noted that his anthology attempts to set forth "a relatively pure line of shorter
Gothic fiction," adds the following reservation: "I am aware, however, that a
broader definition of Gothic is possible and have at some points slackened the
line to accommodate this view" (xxii). Noel Carroll writes that in terms of the
theory propounded in *his* book, "most of Poe's work does not fit into the genre
of horror" (215n). Linda Badley calls *The Silence of the Lambs* a Gothic Romance
(144). And so on.[1] Of course, even the most rigorous literary taxonomies carry

a kind of implied "as a rule" caveat anyway, and even so brilliant a classifier as Northrop Frye notes in the introduction to his *Anatomy* that

> an objection of the "what about so and so?" type may be made by the
> reader without necessarily destroying statements based on collective
> observations, and there are many questions of the "where would you
> put so and so?" type that cannot be answered by the present writer. (29)

A broad distinction can be made, one would think, between macabre horror and the supernatural tale or ghost story, however. The latter's proximate source would seem to be the spiritualist enthusiasm mustered against eighteenth-century secular rationalism. The present descendants of these enthusiasms are arguably parapsychology, UFO lore, and science fiction, all of which combine with the macabre tradition in, for instance, *The X-Files*. The hybrid often works well, arguably due to the grounding contributed by the visceral, somatic element involved. On its own, however, the ghost story tends to be a comparatively airy, disembodied form reflecting perhaps the Olympian sky-god tradition rather than the older, chthonian spirit from which horror, arguably, and comedy, as well, stem. Linda Badley notes the important shift from supernatural terrorism "to horror body language," a shift she sees as "both a symptom of the repression of Thanatos and a vehicle for its expression" (22). The evolution she suggests might perhaps be drawn, for example, in terms of *The Twilight Zone* versus the later and much more visceral, clinical, and revulsion-provocative *X-Files*. There have been writers—Henry James, Edith Wharton, and Mary Wilkins Freeman are three American examples[2]—who possessed the skills to construct extraordinarily disturbing ghost tales, but in general, for deep horror effect, the supernatural tale needed to be wedded to the kind of fulsome, biomorphic imagination driving works such as those of Lewis, Maturin, Stoker, and others. In Lewis's *The Monk*, for instance, the supernatural Bleeding Nun episode constitutes a ghost story, but one set in the larger context of a luridly physical narrative, not to mention the biological anxiety implicit in the bleeding motif itself. The ghost of Allison Greening, in Peter Straub's *If You Could See Me Now*, like the Bleeding Nun, is eroticized and, after many inchoate expressions of itself, manifests in a distinctly physical form: She "was no shadow, no circling pattern in the grass, no tall outline of sticks . . . but a living person. . . . a perfect girl of bone and shin and blood" (317). Similarly, Stanley Kubrick's film version of *The Shining*, while it might technically be regarded as a ghost story, draws much of its terrifying power from the physical "sex and substance" provided, for example, by the young woman in the bathtub, "who withers into a crone before one's eyes and an elevator door that opens to release a torrent of blood" (Badley 44). Even in a visitation ghost story such as Edith Wharton's "The Eyes," we can trace the attempt to imbue a disembodied apparition with an element of repulsive physicalness. Culwin refers to "the physical effect" of the eyes that appear to him at night as an effect "equivalent to a bad smell: their look left a smear like a snail's" (Wharton 45).

Rudyard Kipling's "The Mark of the Beast" could have been one more Victorian supernatural tale in the "curse of the mummy" vein. In it, a foreigner, a British colonial in India, transgresses rudely upon a native holy place and thereby falls victim to a curse. But the story's terror is greatly deepened by its exploitation of revulsion, its triggering of disgust responses in the reader. The Brit, Fleete, becomes offensively drunk at a gathering and shortly after stumbles into the temple of the Monkey-god, where he puts out his cigar butt on the forehead of the god's stone image. If it were left that a week later he met with an uncanny accident, we would have the standard supernatural tale. Instead, Fleete is fallen upon almost immediately by a temple leper who emerges "out of the recess behind the image," a leper "whose disease was heavy upon him"; he has stumps for hands and feet, and his face is completely eroded. The leper, making a mewing sound, clutches Fleete to him and grinds his head into the offender's chest. Fleete's companions, one of whom is the story's narrator, pull the leper off him, but Fleete is later that night overwhelmed by violent chills and fever, his nostrils filled with the stench of slaughter houses—"Can't you smell the blood?" he cries to his companions (72). By the next day, he begins to call for undercooked meat; he hungers for chops— "bloody ones with gristle" (75). He is eventually in convulsions, foaming at the mouth, making "beast noises in the back of his throat." The narrator confesses the scene made him "actually and physically sick" (76). The leper later appears at Fleete's residence, where the narrator and another man tackle him and discover he is stunningly strong. The narrator puts his foot on the leper's neck: "and even through my riding boots I could feel that his flesh was not the flesh of a clean man" (78). The narrator's "affective reaction" here, to borrow phrasing from Noel Carroll, "is not merely a matter of fear, i.e., of being frightened by something that threatens danger. Rather threat is compounded with revulsion, nausea, and disgust" (Carroll 22).

Literary horror, on the other hand, does not need the supernatural; the febrile nightmares of the virulent flu siege recalled by Katherine Ann Porter in *Pale Horse, Pale Rider,* for example, require no conventional ghostly trappings: "A pallid white fog rose . . . insinuatingly and floated before Miranda's eyes, a fog in which was concealed all terror and all weariness, all the wrung faces and twisted backs and broken feet of abused, outraged living things." The fog might part at any moment, she writes, "and loose the horde of human torments" (192–93). In effective horror, the supernatural is not something added to the world of nature; it is the spiritual dynamism of that world (I paraphrase E. W. F. Tomlin from another context). Early high Gothic literature tended toward a realist or quasi-realist expression, toward the natural supernatural. The supernatural as such was played down or, ultimately, as in Radcliffe, turned out to have been only apparently extra-natural. The uncanny was likely to work up from the grass roots; Count Dracula, for instance, a demon emergent from the central European folk-mind, is living-dead, not dead and returning from a supernatural realm. The character of Satan itself suggests a chthonic derivation and lends itself readily enough to representations such as Stephen King's Randall Flagg, in *The Stand,* who is *a* devil if not *the* Devil manifested as a suave, or would-be suave, redneck. Frankenstein too is a natural phenomenon, a "creature made of clay," as it were. The ability of horror to function in the physical without resort to the *deus ex machina* possibilities of the supernatural is evident as well in films such as *The First Deadly Sin, Psycho,* and *Silence of the Lambs,* with their human monsters—Daniel Blank, Norman Bates, and Hannibal Lecter.

* * *

No attempt will be made here, however, to sort out more broadly the vexed problem of horror literature taxonomy. The present chapter seeks instead to reconnoiter the broad landscape of horror imagining that lies largely outside the traditional gothic literary box but which deeply informs all gotic literature. The point, as suggested earlier, is that there is a generic tradition of grotesque imagining, the essential spirit of which traces back as far as the comic does and to the same source—the cycles of biological life and the ritual-mythic inventions that express them. Such a biological line of thought has been readily accepted in theories of music and dance, of course, and even of poetry— "verse" referring to the turn in plowing or, some say, in ritual dance. Because we are organisms, Langer notes, "all our actions develop in organic fashion and our feelings as well as our physical acts have an essentially metabolic pattern" (*Feeling* 99). Camille Paglia refers to the body-rhythms and organic pulses that underlie poetry (*Sex, Art* 126–27). And E. W. F. Tomlin writes that "only an absurd prejudice, born of false notions of 'spirituality,' prevents us from re-

THE MUSE OF HORROR

alizing that our so-called cultural needs, such as the 'hunger' for music, art, and literature, are necessities first manifested by our organic nature" (144). This recognition of the physicalness underlying art should not be confined only to those modalities that are manifestly rhythmical. Sartre, as Marx had earlier, described the writer's voice, not just the poet's, as "a prolongation of the body" (*Literature* 7). The virtue of Langer's work is that it recognizes the biological element easily discernable in music as informing art generally.

The high gothic romance mode in this context represents a powerful and dramatic refinement and codification of a horror imagination rooted in fleshly peril; gothic artifices embody apprehensions reflective of the treacherous adventure biological life is involved in moment by moment. The present chapter, again, will interrogate some of the physiologically based elements of macabre imagination that constituted a generic horror tradition long before the novels of gothic romance—an imagination informed by catastrophic pestilences, martyrdom, religious terror, sadistic criminality, public torture, and execution—never mind witchcraft, werewolf legend, and so on. Oral legends, visual representations, and nonfiction accounts of horrors are *art* in that they allow for horror to be evoked—to be virtually experienced, regarded, contemplated as a verity of human life. The mind is interested in all aspects of reality, in everything that is part of the picture, and that interest did not begin with *The Castle of Otranto*. It is arguable, in fact, that the gothic literary nexus of the eighteenth and nineteenth centuries, for all its importance, has been emphasized to a degree that obscures some of the older, more varied roots of modern literary horror. "Witch, werewolf, vampire, and ghoul," writes Lovecraft, "brooded ominously on the lips of bard and grandam, and needed but little encouragement to take the final step across the boundary that divides the chanted tale or song from the formal literary composition" (*Supernatural* 18). Poe apparently reached back beyond the high gothic period in writing "Hop Frog," for instance, to the grotesque Bal des Ardents incident of the French fourteenth century. It might be argued that in doing so, he was plundering the medieval for horror material after the fashion of Radcliffe, Lewis, or Maturin, but the point is that he was going to real historical material, he was not confined to conventionalized gothic renderings of the medieval available in the work of his gothic antecedants. That King Charles's entourage, and nearly he himself, had been burned alive in an accidental fire at a masquerade ball was a piece of historical horror lore that Poe evidently transformed into a macabre tale. In the real event, as in Poe's fictional narrative, the King and his frivolous party, costumed—in highly flammable materials—as simian creatures, were ignited by a flambeau and incinerated, the King narrowly escaping in the actual case (Tuchman 504–5).

"The Fall of the House of Usher" too might be seen as reflecting influences other than just high gothic literary ones. In his *Horror Fiction in the Protestant Tradition,* Victor Sage describes the way in which, in the Pauline consolation tradition issuing from the seventeenth century, the aging house functioned as a metaphor for the body's inevitable decay and as a trope of decay and mortality in general. Sage quotes a seventeenth-century Huguenot text that, employing the house conceit, portrays the body assailed and ravaged by degenerative forces:

> Death labors to undermine this poor dwelling from the first moment that it is built, besieges it, and on all sides makes its approaches; in time it saps the foundation, it batters us with several diseases and unexpected accidents; every day it opens a breach, and pulls out of this building some stones. (1)

The text's author elaborates upon this metaphor before concluding with the house/body's final ruin, a conclusion that would bring the end of Poe's most famous story to mind and suggest perhaps a shared archetype: "[I]n this house defluxions fall down, vapours arise, the pillars and foundations tremble, the joints open, the windows are darkened, and the burning fevers, like violent fires, consume it" (Sage 1). Evident here as well is the horror genre's tendency to conceive of the physical body and its environment as a continuous organic fact.

A passage in Ann Radcliffe's *The Mysteries of Udolpho* evidences distinctive high gothic tropics:

> It may be remembered, that, in a chamber of Udolpho, hung a black veil, whose singular situation had excited Emily's curiosity, and which afterwards disclosed an object that had overwhelmed her with horror; for, on lifting it, there appeared, instead of the picture she had expected, within a recess of the wall, a human figure of ghastly paleness, stretched at its length, and dressed in the habiliments of the grave . . . the face appeared decayed and disfigured by worms . . . visible on the features and hands. (662)

But even here, after the conventional medievalistic dressing of "chilling curiosities" have been passed through—the chamber, the lifted veil, the recess of wall—Emily confronts, to borrow Julia Kristeva's phrase, "bottomless primacy": paleness and wormy decay, the putrefying fundament of the generic, existential macabre. Radcliffe and company did not invent such grotesque images; they are evident in the nonfictional epidemic literature of three centuries previous—in Thomas Dekker's plague account of 1603, for example, in which the same kind of appalled gaze as Emily's perceives hundreds of corpses upright in winding sheets and in decomposed coffins that "suddenly yawn wide open filling his nostrils with noisome stench and his eyes with the sight of nothing but crawling worms" (237). The death ship with the vampire in the hold drifting into Whitby Harbor in *Dracula* likewise is probably informed by collective Black Death memories of how in October 1347, for example, "Genoese trading ships put into the harbor of Messina in Sicily with dead and dying men at the oars" (Tuchman 92). Like Dekker, or Yossarian in the Snowden episode discussed in the last chapter, Radcliffe's Emily stands appalled in the face of pre-rational, unmediated organic dreadfulness, "at the boundary of what is assimilable, thinkable" (Kristeva 18). As suggested earlier, if the idea that primal wellsprings underlie horror literature, that its nightmare archetypes, its ventures into the realms of magic and taboo, are primordial, sacramental, and ultimately biological, seems at first blush far removed from *Night of the Living Dead,* say, it might be suggested that participants in the Greek Comus would not have thought that rite would lead to Laurel and Hardy either.

Speaking of film and atavism, one might note that the horror muse's modern predilections have often been cinematic and that the movie medium has provided an extraordinarily fertile situation for the atavistic gothic imagination. Linda Badley notes the primeval resonance of the atmosphere in the cinema theater: "[S]itting in the darkened theater, which recapitulates the [primitive] den or campfire, we re-encounter our earliest dreams" (8). She correctly observes that the literary work of Stephen King, Anne Rice, Clive Barker, and Thomas Ligotti, among others, derives in large part from the classic macabre films of the 1930s through the 1950s, which were viewed in a cave-like setting. Movies and the movie theater thus combined to enhance the primitivism the horror genre had always cultivated. Paglia notes that the gothic novel's caverns and tombs track the genre's attempt to withdraw "into chthonian darkness" (*Personae* 265). Stephen King too remarks horror's atavistic inclination, its search for something that "predates art" (*Danse* 4). Film continues the attempt evident in the late-eighteenth-century horror novel to revive pagan energies and atmospheres. The classic gothic novels marked not the appearance of weird literature ex nihilo but rather, as Lovecraft put it, "the advent

of the weird to formal literature" (*Supernatural* 3). Film blends in with the long
brewing process horror invention involves—"the progressive accumulation
in the racial memory of prodigious facts and innumerable crimes, so that the
necessary sublimations and schematizations can take place" (Lévy 16).

The comic modality would likewise seem to have undergone a variety of
historical collisions, sanctions, and refractions including the medieval appro-
priation of pre-Christian celebrations that redefined pagan festive days through
identification with Christian Saints—a *bricolage* mythic dynamic. The medieval Church, otherwise rigorous in its repression of departures from dogmatic
orthodoxy, was surprisingly complacent about pagan carryovers, even toler-
ating "the whole erotic conception and inspiration" of the *Roman de la Rose*
for instance (Huizinga 332–34). The process of Christianization was therefore
slow to take unmitigated hold on the peasantry of the continent and in rural
areas of England where folk tradition held on. Enid Welsford among others
has noted that as a rule, "the advent of new religions is apt to cause the destruction of the higher manifestations of the old beliefs and to leave the lower
aspects undisturbed" (112). James Joyce, describing the religious convictions
of Mrs. Kernan in the story "Grace"—in this case an early-twentieth-century
setting—notes that "if she was put to it, she could believe also in the ban-
shee and in the Holy Ghost" (158).[3] Such a pattern in turn provides fertile
ground for incursions of the grotesque, the buildup of that framework of
putatively retired beliefs Freud calls the "surmounted": "We have *surmounted*
such ways of thought: but we do not feel quiet sure of our new set of beliefs,
and the old ones still exist within us ready to seize upon any confirmation"
(*Studies* 54).

C. L. Barber quotes from a sixteenth-century sermon by Bishop Hugh
Latimer in which Latimer recounts an incident that occurred when he was
riding on horseback through a country area on his way to London, an incident
demonstrating the recalcitrant endurance of extra-Christian folk beliefs. He
sent word ahead to one village that he would preach there the next morning,
it being a holy day. When he arrived the morning of the next day, however,
no one was at the church, and when he finally found a local, he was told "we
cannot hear you . . . . The Parish has gone abroad for Robin Hood [festival]"
(16). The same kind of historical juncture is recalled in an eighteenth-century
verse Charles Maturin uses epigraphically to chapter 15 of *Melmoth the Wanderer,* wherein an inquiring traveler is bluntly made aware of the surviving and
prevailing vitality of the old festive ethos:

But tell me to what saint, I pray,
What martyr or what angel bright,
Is dedicate this day,
Which brings you here so gaily dight?

Doest thou not, simple Palmer, know
What every child can tell thee here?—
Nor saint nor angel claims this show,
But the bright season of the year.

(214)

This preservation of ancient seasonal homage among the common folk in the English countryside has its parallel, of course, in the more marginal folk preservation and no doubt reworking of darker superstitions—witchcraft, taboo, demon possession, and so forth. In Thrace, Dionysus, elsewhere a comic-fertility spirit, underwent a transformation, "haunting with terrible sounds, the high Thracian farms . . . linked on to one of the gloomiest creations of later romance, the werewolf" (Donoghue, *Pater* 166). The comic-festive retreat to the pastoral to celebrate "the bright season of the year" has its gothic parallel in the perception of the remote countryside as nurturing mean backwaters where less benign peasant beliefs hold sway. The flower gathering of the comic mythos translates in the gothic to the gathering of sinister herbs. Taking to the country is in fact a set piece of both the comic and horror modalities, but the latter is skeptical, indeed suspicious of the pastoral. The rural country in *An American Werewolf in London,* for example, is a place of malevolent, fog-bound moors and isolated, morose pubs where furtive country characters huddle. A young man from the city encounters an even more eerie country-side in Carl Dreyer's film *Vampyr* (1932). And in Le Fanu's "A Chapter in the History of a Tyrone Family," when a newly married young lady and her husband depart Dublin on a three-day carriage journey to the husband's remote rural family estate, gothic readers are not at all sanguine about her well-being (Baldick, *Oxford* 102–32). Nor is the film audience easy when in *Friday the 13th* a bright-eyed teenage girl arrives in a rural town bound for the sylvan retreat on Lake Crystal.

Dionysus in Thrace, shorn of his role as a fertility icon, and now a were-wolf, might be seen as defining the rise of a dark fertility antagonist perhaps out of the very material of comic ritual itself. As we will see in chapter 6, horror is so closely associated with the carnivalesque, for example, that it would seem implicit in it. Stallybrass and White observe that originally festive motifs out of the carnival tradition manifest as a grotesque mutation in Freud's patients: "It is striking how the broken fragments of carnival, terrifying and disconnected, glide through the discourse of the hysteric" (171). In his discussion of "Cask of Amontillado," Bakhtin remarks the festive-morbid conjunctions defining the tale and suggests that the contrasts structuring the story—festival joy versus murderous resentment; the gay costumes and bells versus murder; and so on—refer back to "a very ancient and time-honored matrix" in which these contrasts were not in opposition but in fact were resolved (*Dialogic* 199). This posits horror, originally an aspect of a fertility (comic) matrix, early on becoming a distinct species unto itself—"Cask," for example, presenting only fossilized traces, splinter images of the old ritual paradigm.

Even if much more remotely than at their point of origin, however, comedy and horror remain, it would seem, related forms, still involving elements of each other and sharing features of a common mythical-ritual project that presents a symbolic analog of "physical" life's metabolic adjustments, tropisms, and adversities, its opposed cadences of growth and destruction. "So, from hour to hour, we ripe and ripe, / And then, from hour to hour, we rot and rot" (*As You Like It* II.vii.26–27). The mystery of vitality and its antagonist is what engenders the two modes, comedy centralizing the "ripe" and horror the "rot"—a tale of two cities. Comedy's voices sing of the freeing of the waters as in the Rig-Veda hymns: "Thou hast set loose the seven rivers to flow. Thou causeth water to flow on every side" (qtd. in Weston 25). The social equivalent of this is the freeing of Eros, formerly socially impeded, to flow in young love as part of the mythos of Spring (Frye, *Anatomy* 163). Comic art abstracts the vital pattern of biological life, while horror in effect represents the devitalized, antagonistic pattern of drought, sterility, withering, and dread. Gothic voices speak of unlife; they are voices, to quote Eliot's "The Waste Land," singing "out of empty cisterns and exhausted wells."

* * *

A man had journeyed to his father-in-law's house in another city in Israel to make up with his wife, who, angry with him, had fled to her father's four months earlier. On the return journey, the man, with his wife and servant, avoided remote foreign villages and traveled until they came, as darkness gathered, to a town peopled with those who, while strangers, were of their own tribal identity. They rode their donkeys into the town and sat down in its dark open square, where they remained ignored, or so they thought, for some time before an old man invited them to spend the night in his house. There they washed, ate, drank, and were made comfortable, until shouting began to be heard out in the night, growing louder, and finally surrounding the house— shouts of a menacing and obscene nature.

The voices were those of the townsmen, who were calling for the traveler to be delivered to them that they might use him for homosexual gratification. The host pleaded with them, offering his concubine instead. They declined, but he threw her to them anyway, and they did finally accept her, molesting her wantonly all night long. And when first light came, she crawled back to the host's doorstep, where he found her dead later in the morning, her hands on the threshold. He dragged the body into the house, cut it up into pieces with a knife, and sent the body parts to all the tribal regions of the land.[4]

The events in this story, told in the Book of Judges 19–20, might occur in a Brian Lumley novel or a Cronenberg or Romero film; the people in a house encircled by a feral human pack in fact very much brings to mind the siege in Romero's *Night of the Living Dead*. Such parallels are what one has in mind in affirming an informal, generic horror tradition extant long prior to its being considered a literary species. The extensive body of grotesque material antedating the gothic novel—stories, records, legends of a weird tenor—apparently thrived outside formal literary channels. An analogous extraliterary comic corpus would be made up of stories, remarks, jokes, marketplace performances, and so forth. The macabre, as earlier remarked, has found different vehicles of expression in different cultures and historical periods, seeking out what material of a weird, carnal nature the historical context afforded. Bakhtin points out that the literary modalities of early Christianity continued preoccupations that had been characteristic of the pagan Menippea—"dream visions, insanity, obsessions of all sorts" (*Poetics* 135). And Lovecraft references "inverted theologies" that putatively long lurked in the European shadows:

Much of the power of Western horror-lore was undoubtedly due to the hidden but often suspected presence of a hideous cult of nocturnal worshipers whose strange customs were rooted in the most revolting fertility rites of immemorial antiquity. This secret religion, stealthily handed down among peasants for thousands of years despite the outward reign of Druidic, Greco-Roman, and Christian faiths in the regions involved, was marked by "Witches Sabbaths" . . . on Walpurgis-Night and Hallowe'en, the traditional breeding-seasons of the goats and sheep and cattle; and became the source of vast riches of sorcery legend. (*Supernatural* 18)

As noted, the Christian tradition of religious terror was another significant bearer of morbid motifs prefiguring later gothic ones: memento mori underscoring the ignoble end of our bodily careers, exotic postmortem punishment scenarios, and so forth. These horrors provided a rhetorical foil for Christian consolation arguments. Emphasizing bodily decomposition, corruption, and decay as the lot of physical life without benefit of the spirit, the consolation tradition sought to foreground the gruesome aspects of nature the better to confirm faith's indispensable role in existence. John Milton's "On the Death of a Fair Infant Dying of a Cough" (1628) is an example, as it accentuates morbid physical detail to underscore the insufficiency of unmediated biological life. The poem's fifth stanza performs the disconsolation trope, reciting the ultimate emptiness implicit in mere corporality:

Yet can I not persuade me thou art dead
Or that thy corse corrupts in earth's dark womb,
Or that thy beauties lie in wormy bed,
Hid from the world in a low delved tomb. . . .

(*Complete Poems* 35–37)

This of course sets the stage for a homiletic consolation to occur later in the poem. A similar species of Christian terror had found expression earlier in visual art; examples abound in medieval cautionary illustrations and in the sixteenth-century macabre art of artists such as Pieter Bruegel and Hieronymous Bosch that explored the ghastliest reaches of torture and nightmare torment in store for those enacting specific sins—Avarice, Gluttony, Vanity, and so forth. Nothing prevented the viewers of such art, of course, from appreciating it in a morbid, prurient, or sadomasochistic way as opposed to meditating upon its religious implications. Nor did this artistic mode and its preoccupation with exquisite refinements of punishment disappear with the coming of the Renaissance; it in fact flourished during the Reformation (Foote 41). And it flourishes still—in the recent movie *Seven,* for example, and Stephen King, in *Dance Macabre,* describes an early Ray Bradbury story involving an undertaker who performs hideous but curiously moral atrocities upon his 'clients'—for instance when three old biddies who loved to gossip maliciously are killed in an accident, the undertaker chops off their heads and buries these three heads together, mouth to ear, so they can enjoy a hideous *kaffeeklatsch* throughout eternity. (326)

The impulse in this tale, as in the original medieval forms, would appear to go well beyond theological legalism to an interest in visualizing the grotesque pre-mortem and postmortem punishment possibilities residing in the human body, the atrocities that might be worked upon the flesh. Another major step in the development of horror imagery had occurred in the thirteenth- to fifteenth-century development of a mortuary art "which emphasized the corporeal, tactile, and horrible presence of the cadaver," a development described lately by Jean-Claude Schmitt in his *Ghosts in the Middle Ages*: "Images of the living dead in the fifteenth century translated a greater attention to the . . . stages of [bodily] decomposition: sometimes the bones stick through the skin, which bursts and reveals the skeleton" (214–15). Idealistic, supernatural representation is abandoned in this "cult of death" expression as charnel house art waxes horrific and a cadaver is portrayed with clinical realism, in what would nowadays be a horror film manner. Death in this period, Barbara Tuchman notes, "exerted a ghoulish fascination. Emphasis was on worms and putrefaction and gruesome physical details. Where formerly the dominant idea of death was the spiritual journey of the soul, now the rotting of the body seemed more significant." Death is not represented as a conventional icon but instead in luridly individualized terms. In murals depicting the procession in the *danse macabre,* "the cadaverous figure who leads . . . is not Death but the Dead One" (506). In its rejection of the exalted idea of spiritual journey, this mortuary art exhibits, in Bakhtinian terms, the essential principle of grotesque realism—"degradation, . . . the lowering of all that is high, spiritual, ideal . . . a transfer to the material level, to the sphere of earth and body in their indissoluble unity" (*Rabelais* 19–20).

Evident in the tradition in question is a gathering of what would later be "gothic" literary elements, and it is probable that when first applied to horror literature the term *gothic* referenced not only things "medieval" but more specifically the morbid literature that appears, for example, as early as the thirteenth-century poem "Three Living and Three Dead." In the poem, "three rich young men out hunting . . . come suddenly upon three open coffins in which

lie corpses in progressive stages of decomposition. They draw back in horror
. . . an old hermit appears and tells them that the three bodies are—themselves!" (Boase 206). Here again are death and decay graphically presented in
their gruesome immediacy; the word *macabre* itself first appears in France
around 1376 (Tuchman 505). T. S. R. Boase notes "the appetite for repulsion"
during the period, "the cult of the charnel house" (241). In a tomb completed
around 1400, a sculpture of Francois de Sarra's body lies as toads attack his
face and "worms writhe over and into his limbs." Boase remarks of this sculpture that "physical horror can go no further" (206). In the fourteenth-century
tomb of a French aristocrat, the marble sculpture of the dead man "is the visible image of the corpse inside the coffin. The recumbent body is shown as it
was in death, naked, in extreme thinness of very old age with wrinkled skin
stretched over the bones, hands crossed over the genitals, no drapery or cov-
ering of any kind" (Tuchman 502). The fate of de Sarra's body in the medieval sculpture is paralleled four centuries later in the terrors undergone by
Agnes de Medina confined among moldering bodies in the crypt in *The Monk*:
"Sometimes I felt the bloated Toad, hideous and pampered with the poisonous vapours of the dungeon, dragging his loathsome length along my bosom.
. . . Often have I at waking found my fingers ringed with the long worms, which
bred in the corrupted flesh" (Lewis 415).

Nor is there a shortage of written texts contemporaneous to these visual
ones. *The Malleus Maleficarum* (The Witch Hammer), for example, written by
the inquisitors Heinrich Kramer and James Sprenger around 1484, assumed
all manner of witchcraft and demonology as a given and defined the appropriate punishments. The book appeared in fourteen editions from German,
French, and Italian presses between 1487 and 1520, and at least sixteen between
1574 and 1669 (vii–viii). And another proto-gothic literature influential upon
future horror imagining resided in the copious written accounts of the plagues
that struck Europe in the Middle Ages, ravaging its population—in Erfurt,
Saxony, twelve thousand corpses were thrown into open pits in 1350 (Boase
209). The final estimate from the papacy at Avignon was that 23,840,000 per-
ished from the pestilence that swept from China and India to Ireland roughly
from 1347 to 1350 (Tuchman 93).

It might well be argued that such epidemic horrors in medieval Europe
contributed as significantly to the stirring of later gothic literature, as they did,
according to Robert Gottfried, to the stirring of modern medicine (Gottfried
104–28). The influence is of course patent in the case of Poe's "Masque of the

Red Death" and "King Pest," for example. And there are ample examples of epidemic horror, fictional and nonfictional, in modern and contemporary literature from Camus's *The Plague*, Sinclair Lewis's *Arrowsmith*, Katherine Ann Porter's *Pale Horse, Pale Rider,* and Richard Preston's *The Hot Zone*, to recent films like *Outbreak* or Stephen King's *The Stand*, in both of which the body politic is poisoned first by an incompetent military biological warfare clique and then by inept military-governmental attempts at quarantine and surveillance. Plague has situated, in fact, a historical near approach to the end of the world—in the Black Death that apocalypse loomed before European peoples as an imminent likelihood (Tuchman 92–125). Pestilential contagions embody an atavistic shadow still brooding on the margins of normal life, especially, as earlier noted, given the all too imaginable scenarios in which deliberately induced plague may be visited upon modern cities by bio-terrorists.

As recently as 1918, Mary McCarthy's family boarded a train in Seattle on their way to Minneapolis, and on the journey, the ancient curse of pestilence descended:

> One after another we had been struck down as the train proceeded eastward. We children did not understand whether the chattering of our teeth and Mama's lying torpid in the berth were not somehow a part of the trip . . . and we began to be sure it was all an adventure when we saw our father draw a revolver on the conductor who was trying to put us off the train at a small station in the middle of the North Dakota prairie. (*Memories* 35)

Both her parents died. Brockden Brown used his own experiences of the 1793 Philadelphia yellow fever epidemic and the 1798 New York one in *Arthur Mervyn*. And Bram Stoker prevailed upon his mother to write for him an account of the cholera epidemic that struck County Sligo in 1832. Scenes in her narrative would suggest the return of the medieval past: "At night many tar barrels and other combustible matters used to be burned along the street to try to purify the air, and they had a weird, unearthly look, gleaming out in the darkness. The cholera carts . . . had bells, which added to the horror" (*Dracula*, appendix 502). And Catherine Ann Porter's earlier noted *Pale Horse, Pale Rider* issues from her experience of the same lethal pandemic that Mary McCarthy likewise barely survived.

Plagues and their accompanying quarantines are archetypal evokers of the social anxiety element of horror, as they situate the undermining of civilized institutions, the wasting away of social constraint, custom, and cohesion. "Most of the clergy of all denominations fled," wrote Mrs. Stoker of the Cholera contagion, "and few indeed were the instances in which the funeral service was read over the dead" (500). Even the quintessential horror scenario of burial alive has been associated with the desperate, makeshift medical-mortuary arrangements necessary during plagues. Close examination of infected victims is hazardous, and mistakes are made. Nor is there after a while much compassion for victims: "A poor traveler was taken ill on the roadside some miles from town. . . . They dug a pit and with long poles pushed him living into it, and covered him up quick, alive" (Dracula, appendix 499). Plague literature traces a grim continuum from the ravaged body and home, across the threshold and out into the public space, where citizens hear "God's terrible voice in the city"; the streets are vacant, papers blow idly, and the stricken walk as though possessed. The familiar commonplace is defamiliarized, polluted, and rendered terrible; the known has turned unheimlich—weird. Thucydides' record of people perishing "in wild disorder" in the ravaged public space at Athens during the 430–429 B.C. plague is vivid: "Bodies of dying men lay one upon another, and half-dead people rolled about the streets, and in their longing for water, near all the fountains. The temples, too . . . were full of the corpses of those who had died in them" (234). Plague tradition thus, among its other effects, broadens horror literature's focus by enabling the imagination of a greater than individual terror and dread striking on a community scale. Thomas Vincent describes victims in the grip of a London plague in the 1660s and the collapse of public-private spatial distinctions: "It would be endless to speak what we have heard and seen of some in their frensie, rising out of their beds, and leaping about their rooms; others crying and roaring at their windows, some coming forth almost naked, and running into the streets" (213).

Attempts to bring order in circumstances of public siege can create the second stage horror already alluded to—draconian, panoptic scenarios. Foucault describes the chilling public paralysis flowing from a seventeenth-century instance of a contagion emergency:

> The following . . . were the measures to be taken when the plague appeared in a town. First, a strict spatial partitioning; the closing of the town and its outlying districts, a prohibition to leave the town on the pain of death, the killing of all stray animals; the division of the town into distinct quarters, each governed by an intendant. Each street is

placed under the authority of a syndic, who keeps it under surveillance; if he leaves the street, he will be condemned to death. . . . Only the intendants, syndics and guards will move about the streets. . . . It is a segmented, immobile, frozen space. Each individual is fixed in his place. And, if he moves, he does so at the risk of his life. (*Discipline* 195)

King's *The Stand* would seem to owe more to the literature, lore, and racial memory of such events as this than it does to the *Castle of Otranto* line of traditional gothicism directly. An epidemic motif that registers especially eerily in the film version of King's book involves an extraordinarily tall and lank black man (Kareem Abdul Jabar), robed and apocalyptic, who strides through Times Square ringing a bell and intoning the grim medieval plague chant: "Bring out Your Dead!" Contagion literature, like medieval morbid art, privileges the "vile body" trope and additionally conflates it darkly with the trope of public siege and anarchy. David Cronenberg's film *Rabid* (1977), mentioned earlier, portrays a Montreal ravaged by an anomalous, incurable strain of rabies, the infected being shot in the streets by the police and military. Thucydides describes the way in which the Athenian pestilence

introduced into the city a greater lawlessness. For where men hitherto practiced concealment, that they were not acting purely after their pleasure, they now showed a more careless daring. . . . And those who before had nothing . . . in a moment were in possession of the property of others. (234)

The plague-besieged modern city situates such archaic, primordial horrors in a contemporary context such as the New York of *The Stand* or the Denver of *Pale Horse, Pale Rider*—"It seems to be a plague," Miranda remarks in the latter novella, "something out of the Middle Ages. Did you ever see so many funerals, ever?" (Porter 155). When she is herself taken ill, her boyfriend visits her room with news of what is going on outside in Denver: "It's as bad as anything can be . . . all the theaters and all the shops and restaurants are closed, and the streets have been full of funerals all day and ambulances all night" (181). There is no more room in the hospitals, and Miranda falls into a nightmarish semiconsciousness that endures for weeks.

Thomas Dekker's *The Wonderful Year*—a line of which I quoted earlier—describes a sixteenth-century epidemic in London and records the civic ravages of plague. The tenor of the rhetoric is strikingly "gothic":

What an unmatchable torment were it for a man to be barred up every night in a vast charnel-house hung, to make it more hideous, with lamps dimly and slowly burning in hollow and glimmering corners; where all the pavement should . . . be strewed with blasted rosemary . . . thickly mingled with heaps of dead men's bones—the bare ribs of a father that begat him lying there, here the chapless hollow skull of a mother that bore him; round about him a thousand corpses, some standing bolt upright in their winding-sheets, others half moldered in rotten coffins that should suddenly yawn wide open filling . . . his eyes with nothing but the sight of crawling worms. . . . Would not the strongest-hearted man beset with such a ghastly horror look wild? And run mad? (237)

Images of this kind have haunted the Western imagination; pestilence manifested in medieval Europe like an actual version of what medieval artists had set forth as the scourges of hell; the epidemics, as well as church and medical impotence and folly in the face of them, lodged in the darkest corners of the collective memory. Even when not directly addressed in classic Gothic novels, epidemic can be felt as a brooding background trope in, for instance, Le Fanu's *Carmilla* and Stoker's *Dracula*. In the former, when girls in the area around Laura's eastern European home begin taking ill and dying (in fact of vampire assailment), the sinister Carmilla and the heroine, Laura, out on the estate grounds, see a funeral pass: "[I]t was that of a pretty young girl I had often seen, the daughter of one of the rangers of the forest." "'I hope there is no plague . . . coming,'" Laura remarks, "'all this looks very like it. . . . The swineherd's young wife died only a week ago'" (Le Fanu, *Ghost Stories* 293–94). Vampirism, as it spreads beyond the localism of the house and into the countryside, thus takes on the broader horror implications of an epidemic. In *Dracula*, Lucy Westenra's mysterious illness leads Dr. Seward to summon Dr. Van Helsing from Amsterdam; the pattern is that of epidemiological emergency; the concern, at least at first, is indistinguishable from the anxiety triggered by the first signs of contagion. And vampirism enters England in Stoker's novel in the classic plague mode, via cargo from foreign places, moving from the docks into the port city and manifesting first in child victims.

There is an appropriateness, then, in editor Maurice Hindle's inclusion of Charlotte Stoker's earlier referred to account of the "Cholera Horror" as an appendix to the Penguin edition of Bram Stoker's vampire novel *Dracula*. Arguably appropriate as well, was F. W. Murnau's addition of a plague component to his silent *Dracula* film version *Nosferatu* (1922), winding plague horror in with Stoker's other gothic tropes. In Murnau's film, as referenced in my introduction, the Dracula figure, Count Orlock, is accompanied on his sea journey by an entourage of infested rats who then spread through the city, occasioning the "fall of the Great Death upon Wisborg" in 1843. Ten years later, Dreyer's *Vampyr* also conjoined plague and vampirism. David Gray, the film's protagonist, reads in an occult text on vampirism that "[t]wenty years ago in the village of Courtempierre a fiendish epidemic claimed eleven victims. In spite of the medical terms attached to the deaths, everyone knew that a Vampyr was at large." Werner Herzog retained Murnau's plague motif in his *Nosferatu* remake of 1979 and even extended the now traditional vampire text device to further the connection to epidemic. Cronenberg's 1977 film *Rabid* continued the tradition as well, conflating a vampiric motif with epidemic.

In Herzog's version, the bubonic plague is wedded to vampire lore in a scene in which the Jonathan Harker character comes upon an aged volume of vampire protocols that refers to "He who feedeth on the blood of mankind, who unredeemed taketh his refuge in caves, tombs, coffins filled with the . . . *unblessed soil of cemeteries wherein the Black Death hath reaped his horror*" (italics added). The soil in which the Count sleeps, that is, is infused with the putrefaction of plague victims. And in one of the most vivid examples of contagion horror in formal literature, Poe's "King Pest," a passage such as the following is almost indistinguishable from medieval documentary plague accounts:

> All England, but more especially the metropolis, resounded with the fearful cry of "Plague!" The city was in a great measure depopulated— and in those horrible regions, in the vicinity of the Thames, where, amid the dark, narrow, and filthy lanes and alleys, the demon of Disease was supposed to have had his nativity, Awe, Terror, and Superstition were alone to be found stalking abroad. (*Poetry and Tales* 242)

It might even be suggested, I think, that much of the particular imagery and detail in horror invention, especially as regards the zombie or living-dead figure, derives from racial memory of plague and infectious disease victims— things such as their vacant demeanor, lack of facial affect, paleness, and shambling walk. The Ebola victims Robert Preston describes in his *The Hot Zone* are hardly distinguishable from the traditional film representation of the zombie. Their facial muscles lose all tone because the virus dissolves the connective tissue; the face "appears to hang from the underlying bone, as if . . . detaching itself from the skull" (14). Similar effects have characterized many other historical epidemic diseases. Actual descriptions of plague victims walking disoriented through the streets particularly suggest a connection to later film renderings of the possessed and the zombie. The violent hemorrhaging characteristic of many exotic infectious diseases, along with his intimate acquaintance with tuberculosis, surely contributed to Poe's conceptualization of the Red Death. And the final description of Valdemar in Poe's "The Case of M. Valdemar" concludes: "Upon the bed there lay a nearly liquid mass of loathsome—of detestable putridity" (*Selected* 220). This probably owes far more to the clinical reality of human victimization by various pathogens than it does to the classical gothic literary corpus. Virulent viruses in fact do, and have since human life has been around, precisely and horrendously liquefy the human host's flesh, including the brain. Along with its glories, nature harbors loathsome outrages that almost defy imagining. Viruses, Richard Preston notes, have preyed upon living creatures since the beginning. "When a human being is fed upon and consumed by one of them . . . the event takes on the feeling of immense antiquity" (103). "A person falls into lethargy and the face becomes expressionless" (89). Depersonalization, mental derangement, and "zombie-like behavior" follow (74). An ancient virus strain such as Ebola will attack "every organ and tissue in the body except skeletal muscle and bone . . . it transforms every part of the body into a digested slime" (79). This situates the biological darkness out of which much macabre invention emerges.

* * *

Nonfiction annals other than plague ones have also constituted sources of grotesque lore. The literature of religious persecution and martyrdom offers many examples. John Foxe's *Acts and Monuments* (1563), for instance, a popular martyrology narrative in the Renaissance, contains graphic descriptions of sixteenth-century burnings at the stake, fire being perhaps the ultimate biological terror, the instant devourer of flesh. Foxe records, in awful detail, the burning of Nicholas Ridley and Hugh Latimer as Protestant heretics during the reign of Queen Mary, from the preparations the night before to the lighting of the faggots at a stake "in the ditch over against Bailliol College." Ridley, despite gunpowder being tied around his neck by friends to speed the process, is the victim of an incompetent stacking of the branches and a gruesome execution:

> The fire burned first beneath, being kept down by the wood; which
> when he felt, he desired them for Christ's sake to let the fire come

THE MUSE OF HORROR

unto him. Which when his brother-in-law heard but not well understood, intending to rid him of his pain . . . heaped faggots upon him
. . . which made the fire more vehement beneath, that it burned clean
all his nether parts before it once touched his upper. And that made
him to leap up and down under the faggots, and often desire them to
let the fire come unto him, saying I cannot burn. . . . In which pangs
he labored till one of the standersby with his bill [blade or weapon]
pulled off the faggots above, and where he [the victim] espied the fire
flame up, he wrested himself unto that side. And when the flame
touched the gunpowder he was seen stir no more. (R. McDonald
135–36)

"Execution" is a misnomer when applied to historically reported instances of
capital punishment such as this one, execution being precisely what the affairs
lacked, and the ghastly glitches involved made the killings even more the stuff
of horror.

Foucault begins *Discipline and Punish* by quoting contemporary accounts
of the ghastly execution of the regicide Damiens, carried out, likewise ineptly,
in Paris some two hundred years after Ridley's death. Damiens was judicially
ordered to be taken to the Place de Greve in a cart, where on a scaffold the
flesh would be torn from his breasts, arms, thighs, and calves with red-hot
pincers and on those places would be poured molten lead, boiling oil, and other
substances, after which he would be drawn and quartered by four horses.
Foucault quotes the *Gazette d'Amsterdam* account, which described the man's
agonies in detail, including his being pulled apart, which was not accomplished
without great trouble:

The horses tugged hard, each pulling straight on a limb, each horse
held by an executioner. . . . After several attempts, the direction of the
horses had to be changed, thus: those at the arms were made to pull
towards the head, those at the thighs towards the arms. . . . This was
repeated several times without success. . . . Two more horses were
added . . . which made six horses in all. Without success. The executioner finally had to employ a knife to butcher the man at the joints
of each leg and arm before the body gave way in four parts. (3–5)

There is ample documentation of regular, intensely interested attendance
at these theaters of torture by a particularly morbid element of the contem-

porary population. The Englishman George Augustus Selwyn was one of the many passionately drawn to such events and apparently could scarcely contain himself after he had traveled to Paris expressly to watch Damien's agonies; he pushed rudely forward through the crowd the better to see.

> He was at first repulsed by one of the executioners; but having informed the person, that he had made the journey from London . . . [t]he man immediately caused the people to make way, exclaiming . . . *"Faites place pour monsieur; c'est un Anglois, et un amateur."* (qtd. in Praz 416)

The point here is not only that *events,* morbid pageantry of this sort, provided material for the horror imagination but that the *texts* documenting the outrages already constituted a kind of nascent horror literature in the vernacular, often popular, and, for the Protestant taste, often replete with anti-Catholic elements to spice the other gothic makings. And worse ghouls than Selwyn existed in reality and blended later into folklore. The fifteenth century alone provides examples of monsters such as Vlad Tepes and Gilles de Rais. Vlad Tepes, sometimes viewed as the source of Dracula lore, was a fifteenth-century Romanian military hero who specialized in and relished impalements and exotic, intricately programmed and prolonged torture ordeals (Auerbach, *Vampires* 133–34). Gilles, a prominent French nobleman and the subject of Georges Bataille's book *Trial of Gilles De Rais,* would, along with his cohorts, fall upon country villages and seize youthful victims to be brought to his castle for his sadistic adventures in sexual torture and murder.

An example of a related literary shadow, one cast by the theological-macabre discourse of Catholic martyrology and hagiography, is Leonard Cohen's gothic poem-song "Joan of Arc," the second stanza of which is in the voice of the execution flames:

> "I'm glad to hear you talk this way
> I've watched you riding every day,
> and something in me yearns to win
> such a cold and very lonesome heroine"
> . . . .
>
> "Then fire make your body cold
> I'm going to give you mine to hold."

And saying this she climbed inside
To be his one, to be his only bride.

And deep into his fiery heart
he took the dust of Joan of Arc,
and high above the wedding guests
he hung the ashes of her wedding dress.

                                                                    (147–48)

Elements of a number of traditions converge ironically here. The French
martyr and saint is the heroine, and the tone of the discourse is that of courtly
love and chivalry; the fire aspires to "win" the heroine. The poem represents
if not *danse* then *romance macabre*. As in "Rime of the Ancient Mariner", the
comic-fertility associations of wooing and ultimately of wedding are subverted
by ones of dust, withering, and ashes.

The retreat section of James Joyce's *Portrait of the Artist* exemplifies another
representation of a quasi-gothic rhetorical practice surviving into modern
Catholicism. The retreat preacher's text is from Isaiah: "Hell has enlarged its
soul and opened its mouth without any limits" (117). The priest urges the
Belvedere College students to abandon all worldly thoughts and "think only
of the last things," to entertain in their imaginations a damnation vision that
extends over eighteen pages in Joyce's book. It constitutes a horror monologue
that would beggar the gothic talents of Poe or Lovecraft and that, as regards
morbid physicalness, might well be compared to the Clive Barker passage
quoted in my introduction as an example of the most repulsive reaches of
macabre rhetoric. In the infernal place of punishment, "all the filth of the
world, all the offal and scum . . . shall run as to a vast reeking sewer." The students are asked to imagine "some foul and putrid corpse . . . decomposing in
the grave, a jelly-like mass of liquid corruption" and "fetid carcasses massed
together in the reeking darkness, a huge and rotting human fungus" (120). And
so on. The retreat preaching has earlier brought forth in Stephen Dedalus's
own mind likewise grotesque imaginings:

> The faint glimmer of fear became a terror of spirit as the hoarse voice
> of the preacher blew death into his soul. . . . He felt the deathchill touch
> the extremities and creep onward towards the heart, the film of death
> veiling his eyes, the bright centres of the brain extinguished one by one
> like lamps, the last sweat oozing upon the skin, the powerlessness of

the dying limbs . . . the speech thickening and wandering and failing
. . . the poor breath, the poor helpless human spirit, sobbing and sigh-
ing, gurgling and rattling in the throat. . . . His body to which he had
yielded was dying. Into the grave with it! . . . Thrust it out of men's
sight into a long hole in the ground, into the grave, to rot, to feed the
mass of its creeping worms and to be devoured by scuttling plump-
bellied rats. (112)

Catholic influence is powerful, of course, within the classic gothic canon
as well, though the influence is at first negotiated largely by Protestant novelists. As already noted, Protestantism's reaction against what was viewed as too
liberal a reconcilement over time with pagan traditions functioned as a significant impetus toward the classic gothic novel. Protestant literalism's confrontation with the pagan mythic elements of the Roman tradition, its ritualism
and "superstition," is vividly evident in *The Monk, The Mysteries of Udolpho,
Melmoth the Wanderer,* and *Dracula,* for instance. The Inquisition and Jesuit
militancy provided primary themes for the exercise of anti-Catholic indignation; *Melmoth* is sprinkled with appalled exclamations at Catholic apostasy—
"Horrid Profanation!" (239). Another motivation for Protestant writers was
the chance to access the intriguing non-textual, oral, iconographic, and folk
energy of Catholicism, all of which Protestantism lacked, but to do so on
Protestant terms. The Protestant gothic novel exploited the lurid, carnal content of Roman practice. "The ancient chthonian mysteries have never disappeared from the Italian church," Camille Paglia writes:

Waxed saint's corpses under glass. Tattered armbones in gold reliquar-
ies. Half-nude St. Sebastian pierced by arrows. St. Lucy holding her
eyeballs out on a platter. Blood, torture, ecstasy, and tears. Its lurid
sensationalism makes Italian Catholicism emotionally the most complete cosmology in religious history. (*Personae 33*)

The St. Lucy tradition Paglia cites memorializes the saint's martyrdom, in
which, among other things, her eyes were removed. Matthew Lewis exploits
this tradition in *The Monk;* he describes the night procession in which monks
bearing torches are followed by the abbey's novices and then by "a young and
lovely girl" who represents St. Lucia:

She held a golden bason in which were two eyes: Her own were covered by a velvet bandage, and She was conducted by another Nun

habited as an Angel. She was followed by St. Catherine. . . . After her appeared St. Genevieve, surrounded by a number of Imps, who putting themselves into grotesque attitudes, drawing her by the robe, and sporting round her with antic gestures, endeavored to distract her from the Book, on which her eyes were constantly fixed. (347)

Such layers of weird pageantry and macabre physicalness were not to be found, of course, in the plain ecclesiastical modalities of reformed Christianity. The Catholic Mass in fact preserves the entire pre-Christian sacrificial practice in its symbolism and liturgy. The traditional Mass structure included the sacrificial banquet, the sacred victim, as well as obviously the altar of sacrifice, rites of cleansing, and the drinking of blood and eating of flesh in a rite affirmed to be *not* symbolic but actual. The corporeality of popular Catholic iconography is further evident in the church's graphically biological, indeed *pulmonary,* images of the sacred heart of Jesus in full, arterial realism.

The monastic tradition's cloistered secrecy also served to stir the darker imaginings of the European Protestant mind, as did the Inquisition's terrifying *auto de fe* ritual and sadomasochistic cast. Ann Radcliffe, for example, takes things such as cohabitation of monks and nuns in cloisters as a given, and Lewis, in *The Monk,* continues to imply much the same thing, noting the easy access to the convent of St. Clare from the monk's quarters: "The Abbey of Capuchins was only separated from the Convent by the Garden and Cemetery" (346). In conflating the Catholic Church with the medieval world and its bloody and perverse popular historical associations as well as with the range of occult superstition in general, Protestant literary invention created a practice that would bring the generic horror imagination into a contemporary novelistic focus.[5] Leslie Fiedler notes literary gothicism's suspicion of the traditional Catholic rubric and of what it might conceal:

By and large . . . the writers of gothic novels looked upon the "gothic" times with which they dealt . . . as corrupt and detestable. Their vision of the past was bitterly critical, and they evoked the olden days not to sentimentalize but to condemn them. Most gothicists were . . . anti-aristocratic, anti-Catholic, anti-nostalgic. They liked to think that if their work abounded in ghosts, omens, portents and signs, this was not because they themselves were superstitious, but because they were engaged in exposing "that superstition which debilitates the mind, that ignorance which propagates error." (137)

The further anxiety we are noting might be added here however: an anxiety issuing from Mediterranean Catholicism's organicism and incense—redolent sexuality.

The classic literary gothic's relationship to actual historical medievalism is thus largely an inverting, exploitative one—the medieval world provides certain eighteenth- and nineteenth-century writers a locus for dark grotesque imagining. The mode on one level is hostile to the historical gothic, even to the latter's energetic architectural expressions. Favoring images of decay and decline, gothic literature negates and sinisterizes the soaring, phallic energy of the art whose name it borrows and denies its putative grandeur. Claustrophobia, the physical dread of binding confinement and smothering, for example, finds as one of its favorite nineteenth-century gothic expressions the scenario of entrapment in the tyrannical, vaulted enclosures of a Mediterranean Catholic monastery. Even Poe's "The Fall of the House of Usher" has as one of its minor claustrophobic motifs an Inquisitional text among Usher's eccentric readings: the *Directorium Inquisitorium,* penned by a Dominican priest. Gothic novels in general presented the "romantic imprisonment" trope in a form frequently linked to the genre's anti-Catholic agenda.

Much of the intense gothic energy of *Melmoth the Wanderer,* for example, derives from its brooding anti-Catholicism and suspicious Protestant reading of the shadowy Catholic world and its monastic intrigues, added to which was the already noted element of graphic physicality in Catholic visual art and tradition, anathema to austere Protestant textualists. Even Maturin's choice of chapter epigraphs sometimes serves to insinuate, after the fashion of Radcliffe, sexual mischief amongst the Catholic clergy:

> Ye monks and nuns throughout the land,
> Who go to church at night in pairs,
> Never take bell-ropes in your hands
> To raise you up again from prayers.

(142)

"Prayers indeed!," is the implication. It is probably not coincidental that Maturin, Bram Stoker, Oscar Wilde, and Joseph Sheridan Le Fanu were all Irish Protestants who lived in close proximity to Catholic culture and ritual while at the same time being distanced from it by their Protestant backgrounds; the combination provides the ideal context for gothic literary invention in the "high" tradition. Le Fanu and Maturin especially, both of Huguenot extrac-

tion, came from a tradition highly sensitive to continental Catholic persecution of Protestants. Of Maturin, Chris Baldick writes that

> when he writes in *Melmoth* of the sinister power which Catholic priests
> have over the lives of Spanish families, we can guess that his "Spain"
> is partly a nightmarish extension of the anxieties he feels about the
> enduring priestly influence in Catholic Ireland, where the novel begins
> and ends. (*Melmoth* xiii)

The Protestant writers' rehearsal of Catholic times may be seen as a re-
visitation of the "surmounted," of that which as Protestants and, comparatively speaking, rationalists, they had supposedly gone beyond but which was
still there on a submerged level as the uncanny that threatens to return. Literary exploitation of such material is evident as well in the conventions of the
vampire genre, where Catholic icons and rites typically have occult power.
Dracula himself seems to have a taste for Catholic atmospherics; he tells
Jonathan Harker, his agent for the real-estate purchase in Britain, that he is
pleased there is "a chapel of old" on the grounds in question, a pre-reforma-
tional chapel presumably (B. Stoker 35). The vampires' approach-avoidance
impulse toward Catholicism in horror narratives is perhaps a projection of
Protestant authorial ambivalence; these writers seem to share with vampires
a begrudging sense of Catholicism's occult potency. Stoker, for example,
wavers in his anti-Catholic resolution. Harker, an Anglican, is discomfited
when, upon his arrival in Transylvania, a peasant woman insists on giving him
a crucifix by way of protection: "[A]s an English Churchman I have been taught
to regard such things as in some measure idolatrous" (12). But later, in his
terror in the Count's castle, he writes in his journal: "Bless that good, good
woman who hung the crucifix round my neck . . . it is a comfort and a strength
to me whenever I touch it" (41). He does not seek solace from something more
in the way of Protestant practice, the psalms for instance, against Dracula's
vampiric threat. It is as if Catholicism, having absorbed more paganism than
Protestantism would later be happy with, understands the pre-Christian idiom
and sacrificial vision, speaks paganism's language, and has a certain efficacy
against its dark spirits. Many gothic tropes stem from this liminal mythic area
Jessie Weston describes as "the mysterious border-land between Christianity
and paganism" (viii). The *Demeter,* the vampire commandeered ship that comes
unsteered into Whitby Harbor in *Dracula,* has a dead man, the ship's captain,
tied to the wheel, a rosary wound among and through the cords with which

he has bound his hands to the wheel. The ship's log reveals that the captain saw the rosary's crucifix, "that which He—It!—dare not touch," as a specific spiritual shield against vampiric power (114).

Thus despite the full measure of anti-Catholicism ingrained in classic gothic fiction, there are traces of the inevitable curiosity and hesitant respect the forbidden and comparatively exotic engender. And the literary dramatizing of Catholicism by Protestant gothic authors has ironically led to Catholicism's being established as the significant spiritual antagonist to uncanny evil in the horror mode. This assumption is apparent in contemporary American horror literature and film. Each week, American teenagers rent horror film videos such as *Stigmata* (1999), in which Catholic liturgy and dogma are taken very seriously and in which the church, for all its internecine plots and intrigues, is portrayed as the eminent source of weapons to neutralize occult powers. The Church, in many contemporary gothic films, is represented in the way Matt Burke comes to see it in Stephen King's *'Salem's Lot*—as viable, indeed as "a Force" (485). When, with the death of a second boy and the disappearance of yet another, Matt can no longer dismiss the evidence that vampire craft is abroad, he is terrified and realizes, as a faded Protestant, that he lacks "the old protections. . . . He had none of the holy things," that is, Catholic things. He phones his friend Ben Mears to come over and urges him to bring a crucifix. Mears, whose background is likewise Protestant, is able to borrow a crucifix on a chain from his landlady. Putting it around his neck—shades of Jonathan Harker—he feels "comforted" (258–59). Indeed the novel's author's note would suggest that King, in venturing upon a vampire novel, consulted not only a forensic medical specialist, but a priest, Father Renald Hallee of St. John's Catholic Church, located in Bangor, Maine.

Ann Radcliffe would presumably be appalled by what her anti-Catholic privileging of Catholicism in the gothic turns out to have begotten. "We'll have you all Hail Marying and Our Fathering yet," says Father Callahan in *'Salem's Lot,* to which Matt's irresolute Protestant reply is "That . . . is not so far-fetched" (442). In the same novel, Ben Mears and Mark Petrie, like medieval crusaders, bathe their heads in the holy water font at St. Andrew's, preparatory to doing final battle with the vampire Barlow (596). And in the end, in Mexico, where Ben and Mark are biding their time, each attending Mass on occasion, Mark announces to Ben that he plans to take instruction toward joining the Catholic Church. In no small part, it is the church's corporeality, its retention of lurid mystical praxis such as stigmata and exorcism, that continues to recommend it to gothic literature and film. And, symptomatic of the genre's general conservatism, it is clearly the *traditional* church, the more medieval the better, to which the contemporary macabre literary imagination is attached. The modernized, arguably Protestantized, church will not do at all. Father Callahan's lament on the revised liberal Catholicism in *'Salem's Lot* might be read as at the same time voicing the horror writer's rejection of a modern, liberal-positivist society antithetical to the gothic imagination: "He would pray . . . not to the new God, the God of ghettos and social conscience . . . but the old God who had proclaimed through Moses not to suffer a witch to live and who had given it unto his son to raise the dead" (534). A similar slant characterizes *The Exorcist,* in which the contemporary Jesuit community in Washington is spiritually lethargic, unable to muster itself against the occult forces at work in the region. Faltering priests look to psychiatry for their validation, to their clerical psychoanalyst Father Karras, who is himself floundering and without conviction. These are ironically the effete inheritors of the spiritual samurai tradition founded by Ignatius Loyola. It falls to the aged but intrepid Father Merrin, a throwback to the earlier dispensation, to show the way, to put on his stole and go forth to do battle with the demons.

The gothic surmise of an esoteric, antagonistic common ground shared by Catholicism and the satanic occult surfaces in contemporary films besides the already referred to *Seven* and *Stigmata.* In *Angel Heart,* a detective (Mickey Rourke) meets with the man who has hired him (Robert De Niro), and who is actually the Devil, in a New Orleans Catholic Church. The Devil, who chose the meeting place, is bothered in a fussy way by Rourke's language—his "f——ing" this and that—and, in deference to the ecclesiastical surroundings, scolds the detective, *"Please, we're in church."* This satanic-Catholic conjunction appears also in *Rosemary's Baby,* in which Rosemary's Catholicism and the Pope's visit to New York are a significant motif. The crucifix appears prominently as a sacred talisman even in a contemporary teen horror film such as *Nightmare on Main Street,* and the plot of Anne Rice's *Interview with the Vampire* significantly grows out of a Catholic Louisiana milieu, New Orleans being the perfect American gothic city in that it is historically a European Catholic enclave in the Protestant American South. And the iconography in Hannibal Lecter's cell in *Silence of the Lambs* reveals a predilection for Italian Catholic art. He has painted, on the one hand, the Pallazo Vecchio and the Duomo in Florence. A second painting is a crucifixion scene; Lecter is a connoisseur of the Cross and recommends the paintings of Duccio to Clarice Starling for their masterful crucifixional rendering (Harris 16). Brian DePalma even Catholi-cized, or at least quasi-Catholicized, the mother's religious mania in his film version of *Carrie,* providing himself with gothic visual imagery—candles and icons—not indicated, as Stephen King notes in *Danse Macabre,* in the book (171). In John Carpenter's recent film *Vampires,* finally, a Vatican hit squad does battle with vampirism. The old gothic assumption of an obscure linkage be-tween these spiritual contenders endures; a failed medieval exorcism gener-ated a fierce master vampire who now haunts the Spanish mission areas of the American Southwest and California in search of the crucifix used in the flawed rite that begot him.

Macabre Aesthetics

Every time we say nature is beautiful, we are saying a prayer, fingering our worry beads.

—CAMILLE PAGLIA, *Sexual Performance*

Nor is it a new thing for man to invent an existence that he imagines to be above the rest of life; this has been his most conscious intellectual exertion down the millennia.

—HENRI BERGSON, *Creative Evolution*

A man who will eat a dead chicken will do anything.

—GRAFFITI

THE 1983 FILM VERSION OF *INVASION OF THE BODY SNATCHERS* begins in media res—an apparent botanical-procreational process is occurring on a distant planet; an aqueous, determined sexual progression is traced in time-lapse. Spermy material glides on its way; offshoots and tendrils are generated as the planet Earth looms in the background. Spores of some kind rise to ride currents earthward and come down in rain. Drops of water carrying an alien vector tremble on leaves, glisten, fall to lower leaves, and trickle into the whorls and passages of plant interiors. Drowsy, colorful buds appear; the water drips to the ground, and an infection travels along rivulets out into the San Francisco morning to insinuate itself into the human life system, where—a thief of souls— it will proceed to stupefy and ultimately to obliterate human identities.

The biological drama enacted here and the apprehensions involved are those that typically characterize the literary horror species and are its animating principle; the organic world here provides material for the grotesque and macabre imagination. As Henri Bergson notes, "[T]he human intellect feels at home among inanimate objects;" it triumphs in geometry, he observes, but actual natural life it cannot grasp—"all the molds crack" (*Evolution* ix–x). The intellect deals in what it knows and finds the "absolute originality and unforeseeability" of natural forms disturbing (29). The rhetoric of horror is constructed toward summoning up and underscoring a readership's visceral sense of embodiment among these forms, of being situated in the treacherous landscape of physical life, in a dimension we are unable to comfortably rationalize. Living things, Langer observes, "strive to persist in a particular chemical balance, to maintain a particular temperature, to develop along particular lines" (*Feeling* 328). They do so, however, subject to antagonist forces; even the human cell, with its own metabolic agenda, its own precise regulation and respiration, must survive in an environment that includes a variety of aggressor agents. Robin Cook's *Mortal Fear* (1989), like *Body Snatchers,* enacts a horror scenario unfolding as a crisis on the cellular level:

> The individual cells of Cedric Harring's body knew exactly what disastrous consequences awaited them. The mysterious new proteins that swept into their midst and through their membranes were overwhelming, and the small amounts of enzymes capable of dealing with the newcomers were totally inadequate. Within Cedric's pituitary gland, the deadly new proteins were able to bind themselves to the repressors that covered the genes. . . . From that moment . . . the outcome was inevitable. The death hormone began to be synthesized in unprecedented amounts. Entering the bloodstream, the hormone coursed into Cedric's body. No cell was immune. The end was only a matter of time. (11)

Here the body undergoes an alien aggression as surely as do the people in *Body Snatchers,* a breaking and entering carried out by biological raiders. The recent horror film *Stigmata* begins, like *Invasion,* with the traveling of an "infection" from a remote distance to an American metropolis. In *Stigmata,* the infection is of a spiritual kind, but its expression is fiercely physical. A mother touring Brazil sends a rosary she has purchased from a street boy in a Brazilian village to her daughter, a beautician in New York. The rosary has belonged to a saintly priest recently diseased and is imbued with the spiritual torments that had miraculously afflicted him. The movie plumbs the bloodiest passional

depths of Catholic Christology as a very secular young woman, the beautician, finds her body recapitulating Christ's scourging, humiliation, crowning
with thorns, and crucifixion. As in narratives of contagion horror, lycanthropy,
or vampirism, her body is taken over by an uncanny force, and she has no idea
what is occurring or why. This is one representation of the chaos and disordering the horror aesthetic foregrounds in a wide variety of forms. If we can
refer, as Langer does, to "the comic rhythm," we might on the other hand refer
to the horror *arhythm*—a distortion of the pattern of wellness, something that
occurs all the time throughout the matrix of biological life. When Ellena, the
heroine of Radcliffe's *The Italian,* is waylaid by a clerical conspiracy and subjected to the suffocating regime of a cloister, her physical beauty, freshness,
grace, and intelligence are not beside the point. Incarceration in the cloister, the
bullying and diminishment involved, the domination by those who are small,
morbid, and mean, threatens the wellness of the world. Given Ellena's imprisonment, life becomes less vigorous, less healthy, less beautiful—the ugly and
horrible gain the upper hand. This arguably archetypal horror pattern is evident in a much earlier version in Beroul's twelfth-century telling of the Tristan
and Isolde story, in which the beautiful Isolde is handed over to a gang of one
hundred lepers. The gang's spokesman has convinced the king that Isolde's lot
with the lepers will be much more horrible and excruciating than if she is
burned alive:

> Look, here I have a hundred companions. Give Yseut [*sic*] to us and we
> will possess her in common. . . . There is such lust in us that no woman
> on earth could tolerate intercourse with us for a single day. The very
> clothes stick to our bodies. . . . She would rather have been burnt.
> (Beroul 74)

This is the foregrounding of physical corruption as antagonist to the extraordinary biological wellness that is implicit in beauty and that brightens the
world.

Anyone might assert discursively that physical life is shot through with
hazards, but that is an abstraction. Horror invention does not *document* the
flesh's perishableness and proneness to catastrophe any more than comedy
documents the delightful spirit of living things. Rather, horror dramatizes our
mortal vulnerability for a deeper emotional consumption and registration.
When Langer writes that the organism "tends to keep its equilibrium *amid the
bombardment of aimless forces that beset it*" (*Feeling* 328), I think the portion I have

italicized goes to the area of vital experience horror art addresses. Comedy, tragedy, and other modes may touch upon this darkness, but only the artistic invention characterizing the horror tradition centralizes it for our feeling and contemplation. It might be argued that horror's primary illusion is that of our being undercut—the plunge to the nadir, the fall into abjection, the experience of the center, our equilibrium, failing to hold. The governess in James's "The Turn of the Screw," for instance, refers to her "plunge into the hideous obscure" (122) and elsewhere to the "depths of consternation that . . . opened beneath my feet" (112).

Stephen King suggests a horror schematic reflective of this sense of menace and dark descent—an ongoing, atmospheric anxiety, he argues, can be as effective in horror as explicit goriness. A gnawing sense of things darkly unraveling in a gradual fashion, that is, may be as disturbing as a sudden shocking unravelment, or more so. The distinction might be put as one between a sustained atmosphere of *dread* versus the sudden eruption of *havoc,* both of which act and interact to create literary horror expression. In *The Italian,* Ellena's imprisonment and subjection to the evil whims of the abbess is an example of dread, of ongoing insidious threat, not one of spectacular and immediate violence. Fear and loathing, King maintains, "often arise from a pervasive sense of disestablishment; that things are in the unmaking" (*Danse* 9). In Ellena's case what is in the unmaking is her own vigorous health and freedom and that of her immediate society, which has been hijacked by tyrannical, malevolent forces. The fear and loathing level of horror, which, as King notes, is less spectacular that the "gross out" level, underpins sensational terrors as a pervasive, hovering anxiety. But whether set forth in terms of a sudden or subtle falling to pieces, "the melodies of the horror tale are simple and repetitive, and they are melodies of disestablishment and disintegration" (*Danse* 13).

"The House of Usher" emphasizes such disintegration by way of Usher's ·dis/ease, his "acute bodily illness." The infirm host, his own health and by extension that of his house, family, and lands, are on the threshold of extermination. Encountering him for the first time in years, the narrator cannot believe Usher's bodily decline: "Surely, man had never before so terribly altered, in so brief a period, as had Roderick Usher. It was with difficulty that I could bring myself to admit the identity of the wan being before me" (*Selected* 58). The weird tale's focus upon "terrible alteration," upon things coming apart or crumbling— bodies, minds, families, decorum, civic order—is clear here. Yeats's "The Second Coming" is analogously a horror *poem,* turning on a monster coming forth

from the desert heralding the awful disestablishment of sanity and order. Similarly, in one of the greatest gothic novels, as Edward Said notes, an obsessed
Captain steers his ship and crew into oblivion: "[T]he *Pequod,* named for an
exterminated Indian tribe, goes down like a coffin with its entire crew" (*Moby
Dick,* introduction xxvii).

In a more popular-cultural registration, *The Blair Witch Project* too exemplifies King's disestablishment paradigm. As is often the case in horror literature and film, the explosive, gross-out horror King references is postponed; in
fact, it never arrives in any really graphic form; dread and loss of bearings are
the film's primary terrors—events harkening *toward* catastrophe, and that
dread is extended over much of the movie's length. Its horror issues from a
kind of low-level but intensifying anxiety deriving precisely from a sense of
things profoundly unraveling: the coming apart of the "project" mentioned
in the title and, beyond that, the failure of all command and composure. The
witch project was to be unproblematic; the group would flirt with the witch
legend, but folklorically, under the protection afforded by camera objectivity
as well as by the detachment of art, science, anthropology, and educated
middle-classness. This illusory protective cultural cloaking, this assumed one-
upness on the spook legend, dissolves dreadfully in the haunted woods, leaving the threesome profoundly exposed. A paraphrase of Job 18:14 would ironically characterize the fate of the besieged campers: They are torn from the
tent in which they trusted and brought to the king of terrors.

The film begins on an energetic note, with, as mentioned, a "project" and
youthful optimism regarding its fulfillment. A documentary film, which will
interrogate a rural legend of witchcraft, is in the offing. Planning, that artifact of human rationality, is underway. Planning is projected safety; it is system. Heather has a *map,* the very symbol of secure bearings, which she has
studied and which will become a major trope in the film as faith in it and in
her reading of it weakens over time and her reassurances become enfeebled:
"Well, we have to go back a way that's . . . a little different because . . . because
we went in a—in a circle before and . . ." She and the two young men set out
on their venture with their upscale backpacks and all the anticipatory gear; they
are confident, quick witted, rugged and irreverent—even a little lusty and
bawdy; this is the image of vitality, youth on a pastoral sojourn that, as in *Friday the 13th,* will be cruelly undermined. This initially established energy expressed in design, foresight, and youthful spunk is preyed upon, cut through,
leeched, and scattered, until only the unfortified physicalness of the three re-

mains. The benign woodlands of romantic-ecological imagination turn into the grotesque forest of the nightmarish fairy tale in which children are lost. Camaraderie turns to anger, accusation, and suspicion. Cloying trepidation insinuates itself into the night camps and haunts the hikes by day. The hikers' dismay multiplies and feeds on itself, becoming an insistent hysteria, which the group tries desperately to dampen down, but the disintegration only gathers momentum. The recovered documentary footage records dwindling control, dwindling orientation, and increasing terror as the haunting presence asserts itself. The boys become irritated by Heather's camera, telling her to desist, that the film was to be about a witch, not about their getting lost. The dark irony is that the witch and their getting lost are not mutually exclusive and will come together in a final bloodletting. The threat waxes more and more frightening, and the group's defenses wane correspondingly. All this, as well as the hints about child murders in the area and so on, locates that subdued level of things in the unmaking that enables the gross-out events if there are to be any—in this case the final carnage at the abandoned house.

The fear response in this instance, that of being the material for some *other* to do with what it will, is one of primordial reach, one wherein we are violated from without and appropriated into the system and agenda of the predator. We find yet more awful, if possible, the idea that something might overwhelm us from *within* and redefine us in its own terms. As *Dracula* editor Maurice Hindle observes, "[T]he menace of the vampire is that . . . it works on us from the *inside,* taking over our bodies" (*Dracula* ix). This is as well the menace contagion horror privileges; in the throws of a hot virus's extreme amplification, "an eyedropper of the victim's blood may contain a hundred million particles of the virus. During this process, the body is partly transformed into virus particles. . . . The host is possessed by a life form that is attempting to convert the host into *itself*" (Preston 14). In vampirism, similarly, a distinct individual is "converted" by a malevolent visitant into a version of the visitant's life form, rendered as a depersonalized entity in the service of the vampire agenda. Caroline Bynum notes that "a fear of body swapping as destruction of person pervades recent films." She notes in the remake of *The Fly,* for example, "the eruption from within of an alien and uncontrollable 'something,' that, by replacing the material of the body, destroys the previous self" (9).[1] Some viruses, as remarked in the last chapter, in the course of pursuing their own ends, indeed transform the essential human body into themselves, leaving only so much undifferentiated liquefaction.[2] In *Invasion of the*

Body-Snatchers, a similar undifferentiation characterizes those infected with the foreign biological agent. The Chinese laundry owner says in horror to Donald Sutherland regarding his spouse: "Not my wife. . . . She not my wife!" His "wife" is now a depersonalized instrumentality functioning only in a dazed, mechanical way in the back of the store.

* * *

A paraphrase of what Elaine Scarry observes of John Donne's work would serve as a broad profile of horror literature: "Physical disease, plague, fever, accident . . . these loom large." Horror storytellers lead us through a world "where in every street / infections follow, overtake, and meete'" (72). We live subject to subtle and relentless wear and tear. A telling phrase in Anne Rice's work describes a dying person, the body refusing to surrender to "the vampire of time which has sucked on it for years on end" (*Vampire* 55). This personification is in the medieval tradition of figuring forth abstractions as personified spirits—Envy, Sloth, and so on. In Rice's characterization, entropy becomes Entropy, the relentless vampire. The consuming work of the horror spirit finds expression not in the tragic mask but in what may be the comic mask's true opposite, the repellent guises in molded rubber sold in Wal-Mart in October: faces deathly white, shading to green, wasted and hollow eyed, suggesting the inevitable spoilage and corruption that is the unavoidable fate of human flesh. These masks dramatize our physical precariousness and speak to our willingness, even eagerness, to confront in ritualized, pageant form the fact that we are subject to the patient, destructive progress of free radicals, the advance of virulent pathogens, or to the sudden, mangling chaos of deliberate or accidental violence. It is understandable that the shower scene in Hitchcock's *Psycho,* one wherein a naked body, the image of exposure to harm, is materialized, violated, and radically unmade, occupies such a predominant place in contemporary popular cultural memory.

The sense of threatening exposure that characterizes the horror aesthetic is evident in the following passage from John Cheever's dark tale "The Five-Forty-Eight." A businessman exits the elevator in his office building and finds he is being followed by a woman, a former employee, whose facial expression is one of "loathing and purpose." When he proceeds outside, it is raining, and after walking a ways, he stops and looks in a store window. Reflected in the window is the woman, standing behind him:

> She might be meaning to do him harm—she might be meaning to kill him. The suddenness with which he moved when he saw the reflec-

tion of her face tipped the water out of his hat brim in such a way that some of it ran down his neck. . . . The cold water falling into his face and onto his bare hands, the rancid smell of the wet gutters and pavings, the knowledge that his feet were beginning to get wet and that he might catch cold—all the common discomforts of walking in the rain—seemed to heighten the menace of his pursuer *and to give him a morbid sense of his own physicalness and of the ease with which he could be hurt.* (italics added, 237)

Literary horror seeks to put its readers in touch with this morbid sense of their own physicalness. A line in Edith Wharton's autobiography referred to in chapter 1 seems bio-psychologically analogous to the apprehensive effect Cheever notes here. Wharton, later to pen numerous chilling tales, remarks how the typhoid she contracted at age nine left her "prey to an internal and unreasoning *physical timidity*" (italics added, 301). The situation in Cheever's tale also parallels the one in Poe's "Cask of Amontillado," where the pattern of hunter following prey likewise occurs, and Wharton was for years haunted by the sense of a following menace "forever dogging my steps" (*Ghost Stories* 301–2). As the mad-woman determined upon revenge in Cheever's story follows the man through the wet, cavernous city streets, Montressor follows Fortunato through the wet, cavernous catacombs, calling the latter's attention to the moisture and nitre: "[S]ee . . . it hangs like moss upon the vaults. We are below the river's bed. The drops of moisture trickle among the bones." His aim is to heighten Fortunato's sense of his physicalness toward amplifying the ultimate terror effect of the revenge ritual he, Fortunato, is enacting. He later extends the strategy: "Pass your hand over the wall; you cannot help feeling the nitre. Indeed it is *very* damp" (*Selected* 224–25). The strategy is that of horror literature itself, which, by way of atmospherics, imagery, and so on, seeks to provoke and maintain a heightened sense of exposure to harm and subjection to being physically hurt. Nakedness or near nakedness in popular horror films such as *Psycho* is exploitative in a sense that goes deeper than its obvious lurid value; it exploits our fundamental sense of vulnerable exposure—one would rather be attacked by a knife-wielding assailant while fully dressed.

The water, wetness, and dankness in the Cheever example likewise serve to exacerbate menace, suggesting the physical vulnerability implicit, for instance, in the phrase "she died of exposure." Water functions as a primary trope in the literary macabre. The failing body of Emily in Faulkner's "A Rose for Emily" appears "bloated, like a body long submerged in motionless water" (*Collected* 121). In Clive Barker's story "Human Remains," a like image occurs: Gavin peers into a pond

> trying to work out the form at the bottom, his reflection floating amid the scum. He bent closer, unable to puzzle out the relation of shapes in the silt, until he recognized the crudely-formed fingers of a hand and he realized he was looking at a human form curled up into itself like a fetus, lying absolutely still in the filthy water. (*Books* 481)

In Cheever's story, the "rancid smell of the wet gutters" is remarked, in Poe's, the "foulness of the air." In the first, the victim's fear of catching cold is noted, whereas in the Poe story, the victim-to-be already suffers from a severe cold, coughing helplessly as moisture trickles down the walls. The same conjunction of dampness and wetness with illness and harm is notable in one of the Goyaesque interchapter pieces in Hemingway's *In Our Time.* There is as well the gothic *wall* motif of adamant finality, here reinforced by the nailed-shut shutters of the hospital:

> They shot the six cabinet ministers at half-past six in the morning against the wall of a hospital. There were pools of water in the court-yard. There were wet dead leaves on the paving of the courtyard. It rained hard. All the shutters of the hospital were nailed shut. One of the ministers was sick with typhoid. Two soldiers carried him down-stairs and out into the rain. They tried to hold him up against the wall but he sat down in a puddle of water. . . . Finally the officer told the soldiers it was no good trying to make him stand up. When they fired the first volley *he was sitting down in the water with his head on his knees.* (italics added, 51)

The man has collapsed into abject, mortal indignity ironized by his lame position title (no country designation is given to contextualize the now meaningless governmental rank); sick, helpless, suffering, he is infantilized, recapitulating the infant's inability to get up or to help itself, its subjection to lying soiled and in wetness.

The importance of Fortunato's cough—note the cabinet minister's typhoid—is underscored by Poe's extraordinarily extended representation of it: "Ugh! ugh! ugh!—ugh! ugh! ugh!—ugh! ugh! ugh!—ugh! ugh! ugh!—ugh! ugh!

ugh!" (*Selected* 223). Significantly enough, the terms *cold* and *chill* can function semantically between usages having to do with illness and, on the other hand, ones having to do with terror—"a chilling tale," and so on. In *The Blair Witch Project,* a small incident, Heather's slip from a log and her boots becoming soaked, marks a dark turn in the narrative. For the first time, she becomes seriously angry when her companions laugh, and she refers to the uncomfortable prospect of hiking all day with wet feet. If the pronouns are altered, John Cheever's observation quoted above would fit Heather's situation and *The Blair Witch Project* with considerable exactness: "The knowledge that her feet were beginning to get wet . . . seemed to heighten the menace of their pursuer and to give her a morbid sense of her own physicalness and the ease with which she might be hurt." The same centralizing of physical vulnerability in terms of what might seem a small matter shows up in Werner Herzog's 1979 film *Nosferatu.* The crewless ship bearing the count and many dozens of plague rats in its hold comes up the river to dock—the city will thus imminently be ravaged by epidemic. The camera isolates, very briefly but tellingly, a baby girl sitting on the wharf by her parents, and the child *sneezes.* The baby's sneeze— cognate to Fortunato's cough, the minister's typhoid, and Heather's wet shoes—situates the delicacy of human wellness and foreshadows the contagion about to overcome the city.

Foreboding coughs and sniffles function similarly in the film version of Stephen King's *The Stand,* where they are the first signal that the lethal disease has found a mark. And a passage in Stoker's *Dracula* tracks other senses of "chill" and their common origins in nature's ecological workings, noting the confluence of human biological rhythms and tidal and diurnal ones:

> I could not help experiencing that chill which comes over one at the coming of the dawn, which is like, in its way, the turn of the tide. They say that people who are near death die generally at the change to the dawn or at the turn of the tide; anyone who has when tired, and tied as it were to his post, experienced this change in the atmosphere can well believe it. (37)

"The Turn of the Screw" likewise uses cold as a trope of heightened exposure, employing the elemental image of fading flame and growing chill: "On the removal of the tea-things I had blown out the candles and drawn my chair closer; I was conscious of a mortal coldness and felt as if I would never again be warm" (112). And a humbled Lear on the heath is brought by exposure to the wintry elements to this simple, humane address to his fool: "[H]ow dost, my boy? Art cold? I am cold myself" (III.ii.68–69).

★ ★ ★

Cheever and Poe use other devices besides cold and wetness to amplify and ironize the horror in their tales; Poe uses costumes, for instance—Fortunato grotesquely arrayed in harlequin clothes—but the deep menace in each story flows from bodily apprehensions and aversions, marking the "phobic pressure-points" that macabre literature seeks out (King, *Danse* 4). The gothic imagination uncovers aspects of the organic environment we find repulsive or unsettling, conjuring "the repugnance, the retching that thrusts me to the side and turns me away from defilement, sewage, and muck" (Kristeva 2). Defilement and degradation, as earlier noted, have an entirely different resonance within the carnival-festive configuration Bakhtin analyzes wherein the downward and earthward biases have ultimately rejuvenating implications (*Rabelais* 21). Though carnival degradation included vulgarities such as beatings, the gauntlet, and other chastisements, the rite was "linked with fertility, with procreative force," in that what was pressed to earth would rise again.[3] Darker versions of degradation ritual are manifested prominently in horror, even in the more refined kind associated with Henry James. The governess in "The Turn of the Screw," after her frightening encounter with Flora and Miss Jessel by the lake, in which she has experienced her "situation horribly crumble," falls prone upon the rank earth and experiences "an odorous dampness and roughness" (111). In Poe's "King Pest," Legs and Tarpaulin are commanded by the "president" to submit to a standard formality of ritual humiliation: the swallowing, while on bended knee, of a loathsome brew in a single draught (*Poetry and Tales* 249–50). Cheever's "The Five-Forty-Eight" culminates in a similar defilement bearing the marks of the carnival pageant and ritual initiation. The mentally ill Miss Dent, armed with a pistol, has ridden the train to the suburbs with her former boss—himself as psychopathological as she, but in an uncertifiable way. They have detrained:

> When the train had passed beyond the bridge . . . he heard her screaming at him, *"Kneel down!* Kneel down!"
> He got to his knees. He bent his head. . . . "Put your face in the dirt! *Put your face in the dirt!* Do what I say. Put your face in the dirt."
> He fell forward in the filth. The coal skinned his face. (394–95)

This scene enacts the humiliation trope, the fall toward filth that manifests in carnival and in all manner of fraternal initiatory rites such as those revealed in the following description of an Odd Fellowship initiation. The ritual parallels what occurs in Cheever's story and in Poe's "Cask" as well:

> Suddenly [he] was pushed to the floor. "Now, presumptuous mortal," someone declaimed, "where is your greatness? Low, level with the earth. . . . For thou art dust."
>
> "Prepare the emblematic chains at once!" The clerk was jostled and he felt chains being wound around his body, arms behind. Then there were shouts.
>
> "Now, bind him to the stake!" (Carnes 19)

Montressor's ritualized chastisement of Fortunato in "Cask" manifests the same degradation archetype—a figure brought down and reduced to his or her oneness with dirt and wetness, the condition of infancy. But in horror, as earlier mentioned, this degradation is not part of a larger schema of revival and renewal.[4] As Blake's face is brought into scathing contact with coal, an ancient fossil material of the earth, Fortunato is led into tunnels of degraded organic material, including human remains. As noted, Montressor pointedly invites him to touch the wet catacomb walls and to regard the drops of moisture trickling among the skeletons.[5] This is not water associated with the origin and preservation of life; it is the stagnant water that is the signature of death and disease, which is why Montressor wants Fortunato to note it. Water here, as so often in Poe, is vitiated and unholy, divested of water's traditional fertility associations as well as of its symbolic baptismal-renewal ones. The horror mode's imaginative disposition, not just Poe's, favors this kind negative water image. Early in the film *Jacob's Ladder,* the protagonist finds himself in an underground, an offshoot cavern in the New York City subway system where the walls ooze and the ceiling drips. He slips and steps into a deep puddle of water, leaping out and stamping his wet feet not unlike Heather in *The Blair Witch* scene. An anti-baptismal event has been enacted, and he moves from here into an increasingly frenzied and macabre journey. This is the phlegmatic, tarn water the genre privileges; to come in contact with it is befouling rather than invigorating. In *Pale Horse, Pale Rider,* which takes place at the height of First World War anti-German hysteria in the United States, Miranda, in her critically ill, hallucinatory state, dreams of her doctor, who has a notably German name, in a Prussian helmet, approaching across a field carrying a "huge stone pot marked Poison in Gothic letters" and bearing a child on the point of a bayonet. "He stopped before the well that Miranda remembered in a pasture on her father's farm, a well . . . bubbling with living water, and into its pure depths he threw the child and the poison, and the violated water sank back soundlessly into the earth" (Porter 193).

Nor in Poe, for instance, is gothic *light*—along with water and air, the essence of organic vitality—living light. Living light, like living water, belongs to a healthy, energetic biology and is at the center of photosynthetic life-nurture. The light in Poe, what there is of it, is artificial; it is not the light that begets and nourishes the green world; indeed it evokes a sense of natural light's significant absence. The lack of clear light, water, and fresh air inverts the entire system of the biologically wholesome and vital. Almost at random in, for example, *The Oxford Book of Gothic Tales,* one finds such passages privileging devitalization, ones wherein the body, the threatened organism, serves as a stage for macabre theater. In Patrick McGrath's story "Blood Disease," for instance, an anthropologist in an equatorial rain forest is bitten by a malarial mosquito:

> From the thorny tip of her mouthparts she unsheathed a slender stylus, and having sliced through Bill's skin tissue, pierced a tiny blood vessel. Bill noticed nothing. Two powerful pumps of the insect's head began to draw off blood while simultaneously hundreds of tiny parasites were discharged into his bloodstream. Within half-an-hour, when the mosquito had long since returned to the water, the parasites were safely established in his liver. For six days they multiplied, asexually, and then on the morning of the seventh they burst out and invaded the red blood cells.

When this formerly "vigorous young man" returns to England: "He was haggard and thin now, and forced to walk with a stick. His flesh was discolored, and his fingers trembled constantly. He looked . . . like a man who was dying" (502). This concern with assaults upon the flesh and the sickening of the body consistently underlies and contextualizes the literary conventions and rhetorical strategies of the gothic narrative—a preoccupation with vitality depleted, the bloodstream inhabited by things pathological, and so on. It is notable in McGrath's story that the *fact* that the man was bitten and contracted malaria is far from sufficient; the fine details of the biological event, whereby the skin surface is breached, parasites introduced, and so on, are closely followed in order to evoke a sense of physical trepidation, peril, and awful dissolution; again, the idea is to get under the reader's skin. The same kind of preoccupation is evident in what the narrator of Poe's "The Case of M. Valdemar" notes upon arrival in Valdemar's chamber; the negative physical detail is clinically, obsessively observed: "His expectoration was excessive. . . . His left lung had been for eighteen months in a . . . cartilaginous state, and was . . . entirely useless for purposes of vitality. . . . the right merely a mass of purulent tubercles, running one into another" (*Selected* 213). As Carroll Smith-Rosenburg observes, "[T]he body's physical integrity constitutes as significant a material vehicle for symbolic representation as the body's evocative sensuality" (161). For macabre symbolic representation, the body's physical integrity breached and compromised is the vital image. The malevolent horror creature is often an analog to disease itself. We often don't feel that the arch villains in macabre narratives are culpable in the ordinary sense (nor are they any less dreadful for that), any more than bubonic plague was culpable in the fourteenth century or AIDS in the twentieth. Dracula and other vampires, for instance, are driven in the way disease agents are toward their hosts. Like viruses, which Robert Preston describes as "molecular sharks," the werewolf, the vampire, the succubus is essentially "a motive without a mind" (65). There is something simply parasitic and ultimately pathetic about Dracula wasting away in the morning light because he is helpless to detach himself from feeding on his beautiful prey. When Mina Murray is troubled by Lucy's mystifying decline owing, unbeknownst to Mina, to the count's nightly ministrations, she speaks in the idiom of disease: "I do not understand Lucy's fading away . . . the roses in her cheeks are fading, and she gets weaker and more languid day by day" (127).

In these terms, as noted earlier, many lesser ghost stories merely exercise a set of customary contrivances of the sort E. F. Bleiler has described in some Victorian literature; their authors "felt they had done enough if they declared a house haunted; from this there followed automatically ghosts dragging chains, shrieking phantoms." There is a lack of visceral registration. Bleiler contrasts such conventional practice with the body-horror aesthetic prevalent in the work of Le Fanu, the sense of "the nightside of nature," the "perverse eroticism of 'Carmilla'" (*Ghost Stories,* introduction xii–viii). In effective macabre horror, it is not enough for a person to have returned from the grave; there must be at least the implication that the revenant trails the grave with him or her—the clay must cling, suggesting mire, slime, and corruption. The reader's biological aversion responses are assaulted by the true macabre literary work. As John E. Mack, M.D., notes in *Nightmares and Human Conflict,*

"[T]he potentiality for . . . fear responses is innately present in the organism and requires only the appropriate releasing stimulus" (42). The rhetorical strategies of horror try to find a way to these deep-seated organic responses. A recent television documentary pointed out obvious aversion response to the sight of snakes in the behavior of some monkey communities—shivering, clutching one another, and so on. An Emily Dickinson poem registers much the same body-horror response in humans. Walking, she sees the tall grass divide, "as with a comb," and the "spotted shaft" of a snake:

> Several of nature's people
> I know, and they know me—
> I feel for them a transport
> Of cordiality—
>
> But never met this Fellow
> Attended or alone
> Without a tighter breathing
> And Zero at the Bone.

(459–60)

Fear responses, it is true, may be differently articulated in different cultures and are no doubt significantly culturally configured. But while Mary Douglas, for instance, has pointed out the culturally varied readings of abomination, defilement, and so on, I don't think her thesis is fully satisfactory. She argues that

> in chasing dirt, in papering, decorating, tidying, we are not governed by anxiety to escape disease, but are positively reordering our environment, making it conform to an idea. There is nothing fearful or unreasoning in our dirt avoidance: it is a creative movement. (2)

But isn't the categorical "nothing" too strong here? Clearly not all purification efforts, ritual or domestic, are consciously fear driven, and dirt avoidance and all it implies is indeed a creative movement, a matter of deep-seated and essential aesthetics, but the absence of this aesthetic sense, as horror literature "argues," is abhorrent; it tracks toward abjection.[6] A gothic rendering of the matter would note that to come home to a defiled apartment, the wallpaper stained and flaking off, pet droppings here and there, weeks of unwashed dishes and garbage in the sink, would indeed speak to us not of something uncreative only but of something *fearful*—what Georges Bataille describes as

"the inability to assume with sufficient strength the imperative act of excluding abject things"—the intrusion of that lethargy whose signature is the rat
and the roach (qtd. in Kristeva 56). Regarding order, Anne Rivers Siddons
would seem to be closer to the mark than Douglas when she notes that "a
house askew is one of the most not-right things in the world" (qtd. in King,
Danse 272).

Such a response arguably represents one expression of the aversions exploited by horror literature—the dread occasioned by images of enervation,
malaise, and retrogression, whether in a single victim or writ larger in terms
of a crumbling human environment. Coleridge's narrative of a languishing
ship and its thirst-ravaged crew marooned on a listless sea, "nor breath nor
motion," is thus one of the defining expressions of dissolution in English literature. The same abjection figures significantly in Poe's "The House of
Usher," where the Usher bloodline has become enfeebled and, like the tarn,
stagnant, "dull," and "sluggish." In the early-nineteenth-century gothic classic *Melmoth the Wanderer,* Stanton, Melmoth's first victim, is locked in an asylum and trying unsuccessfully to maintain his physical and mental integrity.
Unlike in the comic pattern, here the organism is overwhelmed by the assaults
upon it; rather than an image of resilience and reestablished balance, here there
is, to use Baldick's phrase again, a "sickening descent into disintegration" (*Oxford* xix). Stanton is determined to remain up and functioning and not to let
the influence of the asylum destroy him, "but the utmost efforts of his resolution began to sink under the continued horrors of the place."

> He had at first risen early . . . and availed himself of every opportu-
> nity of being in the open air. He took the strictest care of his person
> in point of cleanliness . . . and all these efforts were even pleasant . . .
> but now he began to relax them all. He passed half the day in his
> wretched bed . . . declined shaving or changing his linen, and, when
> the sun shone into his cell, turned from it. (40–41)

The metaphors of Baldick here and of Maturin go to descent, disintegration,
sinking, and decline, as against the tenor of "resolution," "sun," and "risen."

The same nature/antinature, confinement/outdoors motif appears in Victor Frankenstein's description of *his* possessed, unhealthy state. In effect he,
like Stanton, turns away from the sun: "It was a most beautiful season; never
did the fields bestow a more plentiful harvest, or the vines yield a more luxu-
riant vintage: but my eyes were insensible to the charms of nature" (32–33).

Both in Stanton's and Frankenstein's cases, Thanatos is overruling Eros, achieving ascendancy. Stanton languishes—"squalid, listless, torpid, and disgusting in his appearance." He cannot summon the necessary will-to-art that wards off abjection, art here being shaving, maintaining himself and his immediate surroundings. A powerful literary expression of this enervation-in-captivity trope is available in Frederick Douglass's nonfiction *Narrative of the Life of an American Slave,* confirming Lovecraft's observation mentioned earlier that some of the most compelling horror writing occurs outside what some might take to be the strict confines of the genre, "scattered through material whose massed effect may be of a very different cast" (*Supernatural* 16). While the massed effect of Douglass's narrative is indeed of a different cast—concluding in liberation—the book delves into a nightmare world of sadism, malice, and horror. African slaves experienced a historical and literal invasion of the body snatchers, and Toni Morrison would later venture into the gothic horror implications of slavery as well in her novel *Beloved* (1998).

Douglass possessed a gothic rhetorical sense, something the American South seems to generate, and his account in parts recalls the stark horror of Harker's journal, written in Dracula's castle. One thinks too of the gothic entrapment motifs in Maturin's and Radcliffe's novels. Douglass writes, for instance, of Mr. Covey, the harshest of his slave overseers, whose sinister observational capabilities are uncanny:

> He had the faculty of making us feel he was always present. . . . He would creep and crawl in ditches and gullies, hide behind stumps and bushes. . . . We fancied that in his eyes and his gait we could see a snakish resemblance. . . . We were never secure. He could see or hear us nearly all the time. He was, to us, behind every stump, tree, bush, and fence. (570)

Douglass here is subject to the humiliation Foucault refers to, with reference to Bentham's prison model, as "panopticism"—the practice of intense and virulent hierarchical observation. Covey has perfected the practice wickedly, and his surveillant presence has been interiorized by the slaves, imprinted so that his gaze is felt even when he is absent because he has conditioned them to the point that he is in effect never absent, never not watching. Covey has gotten under Douglass's skin in the most awful sense of that idiom. There is the sense in Douglass's account, one familiar in horror literature, of being ridden, possessed as though something fiendish had appropriated one's existence.

A similar trope, which might be designated as *malevolent hovering,* occurs in Melville's "Benito Cereno," wherein the minimal space requirements of Cereno's body are transgressed by the oppressive Babo, like Covey a genius of control psychology, who monitors the Spaniard's every breath and gesture.[7] A frequent marker of victimization and abjection in horror narration is this element of insinuation into personal space and subjection to exhaustive monitoring.

The trope, already noted in Cheever's "The Five-Forty-Eight," appears in narratives as remote from one another as Clint Eastwood's 1971 film *Play Misty for Me* and J. S. Le Fanu's 1899 gothic novel *Uncle Silas,* in both of which the hero and heroine, respectively, are, like Douglass, plagued by hovering, depraved *watchers.* In each case, the horror aversion is elicited by the invasion of the heartland of a person's life by a grotesque, overwhelming stalker, one who presumes to dictate the intimate terms of one's existence. Glenn Close's Loathly Lady portrayal in *Fatal Attraction* is of course a classic instance of the malevolent hoverer profile, as is Annie Wilkes's in Stephen King's *Misery.* Like Covey, both, over and above their obsessive actual surveillance, possess an ability to seem uncannily omniscient. Like Covey, they have the faculty of making their victim feel they are always, preternaturally, present. Madame de la Rougiere in *Uncle Silas,* in order to control and intimidate Maude, seeks to suggest she has uncanny powers of presence and gaze. When Maude thinks she is finally alone in the "picturesque solitude" of her father's estate, she is under the misimpression that her scheming governess has departed on her travels. Having let her guard down, she suddenly hears Madame's voice in her ear, feels her hand on her shoulder, and realizes she has been overtaken by an antagonist possessed of "an awful instinct." "You did not expect to see me here," says the menacing governess, "I will perhaps appear as suddenly another time. . . . And although I shall not always be near, yet I shall know everything about my charming little Maude. . . . I shall indeed, *everything*" (Le Fanu 100–101).[8] This pathological drive to control, possess, and manipulate arguably mimics the drive of infectious biological organisms toward their hosts.

Douglass's narrative and "Benito Cereno" have in common this visceral horror and diminishment involved in being kept an eye on, in falling under the treacherous power of unremitting examination. Access to withdrawal, retreat, invisibility is an animal requirement; it is the abject lot of the caged creature or the institutionalized insane to have no such retreat. On the other hand, to be in the position Covey relishes, that of the empowered observer, is the dream of a particular species of sadist. Foucault argues that panopticism—this ability to examine without permission—goes to the heart of power and tyranny. And Edmund Burke, in his *A Philosophical Enquiry,* remarks the other side of the surveillance equation: "Those despotic governments, which are founded . . . principally upon the passion of fear, keep their chief as much as may be from the public eye" (54).

Douglass has come under Covey's power after a period of comparatively benign slave existence in Baltimore, where he has taught himself to read and where his spirit has been energized and enlivened. At Covey's slave-breaking plantation, however, Douglass comes perilously close to spiritual annihilation, to the death-in-life that is the horror, rather than the tragic, fate:

> We were worked in all weathers. It was never too hot or too cold; it could never rain, blow, snow, or hail too hard for us to work in the field. Work, work, work was scarcely more the order of the day than of the night.
> . . . I was somewhat unmanageable at the first, but a few months of this discipline tamed me. Mr. Covey succeeded in *breaking* me—in body, soul, and spirit. My natural elasticity was crushed; my intellect languished. (58)

Like Stanton in the asylum in *Melmoth the Wanderer,* Douglass loses his belief in life, his will to art—"the disposition to read departed, the cheerful spark that lingered about my eye died out; the dark night of slavery closed in upon me, and behold a man transformed into a brute!" The other half of the horror-comic dialectic is evident in a later passage in which Douglass is emboldened and revived. From "broken in body, soul and spirit" he finds the vein of life again when he gets into a physical brawl with "the snake," Covey, and prevails: "It rekindled the few expiring embers of freedom, and revived within me a sense of my own manhood. I felt as I never felt before. It was a glorious resurrection . . . from the tomb of slavery" (65).

This is the death and resurrection motif, life rebounding from degradation—the comic rhythm. Taken in terms of the full narrative cycle, the descent into torpor, it turns out, plays its part as a negative complement in the resurrection motif celebrating the return of the vital spirit from "the tomb." Taken by itself, however, the earlier passage is the essence of gothic horror as Douglass is reduced to sluggish desolation. Horror and comedy both thus situate us in physicalness, tracking adventures in the mysterious, contingent, organic scheme. Rather than on fertility, however, horror centers upon withering; rather than on renewal, it focuses on degeneration; rather than on an intrepid human vitality, it centers upon the eminently assailable human body and the deep-rooted anxieties it situates. In the gothic, even murder serves as a decadent and faded thing, a failure, tracing energetic decline—as in "Cask of Amontillado," where the homicide is no sooner accomplished than the project goes flat and its perpetrator sickens. Emily Dickinson's poem 1509 almost seems to speak directly to Montressor's spent anger and the emptiness when his victim no longer stirs, and the "palace of hate" is no longer keen. If one wants revenge, she notes:

> Let him be quick—the Viand flits—
> It is a faded Meat—
> Anger as soon as fed is dead—
> 'Tis starving makes it fat—

(634)

The primitive concern with infertility and vital failure we have been discussing suggests macabre literature's debt to rites of propitiation, which attempted to ward off drought and famine. The counter-fertility bias of the horror modality is evident in the rhetorical conceits of a gothic poem such as Philip Freneau's "House of Night" (c. 1777), where all vegetational images are constructed negatively:

> Its lately pleasing flower *all drooping stood*
> Amidst *high weeds that in rank plenty* grew.
> The primrose there, the violet darkly blue,
> Daisies and fair narcissus *ceased to rise.*
> *No* pleasant fruit or blossom gaily smiled
> Nought but *unhappy plants or trees were seen.*

(italics added, 268–69)

Nature and vegetation are centered here in order to convey vitality's absence, much as Eliot would later do in "The Waste Land": "And the dead tree gives no shelter, the cricket no relief, / And the dry stone no sound of water" (38). The same entanglement of "comic" and horror imagery is apparent in Hawthorne's "Rappaccini's Daughter." Giovanni, coming to Padua to study, takes lodgings in an edifice over the entrance of which are the armorial artifacts of an *extinct* family line. Hell is summoned in the story's first paragraph by the intelligence that Giovanni is "not unstudied" in Dante, and he recalls that an ancestor of the lapsed family had been pictured "as a partaker of the immortal agonies of his Inferno" (*Complete* 257). The concierge, Lisabetta, the crone-who-warns, urges the young man to put his head out the window and partake of the bright sunshine, which establishes a healthy, fertile opposition to the indoor, decadent, exhausted imagery heretofore. Taking her advice, Giovanni discovers that his window overlooks a lush garden. This would suggest a vegetational thematic emerging, but the garden, it turns out, with its gigantic leaves and purple blossoms, is *preternaturally* lush. The garden's master comes into view, a man "emaciated, sallow, and sickly-looking," avoiding the flowers' touch. His demeanor is "that of one walking among malignant influences" (258). The vegetational references are invariably laced with hints of the sinister—this is not your Father's nature. Among his plants, the gardener, Dr. Rappaccini, wears a mask over his mouth and nostrils "as if all this beauty" concealed "a deadlier malice" (259). Indeed his scientific overreach has created an "Eden of poisonous flowers." Nature, garden, flowers, plants—all their normal associations with biological life and health have been inverted. Nature provides the basis for antinatural themes, for tropes going to violation and transgression, perversions of the purity of physical life.

★ ★ ★

To return in conclusion to the sacrificial ritualization evident in Poe's "Cask" and widely perceivable in the gothic genre, an aspect of their antinatural and antifertility valences might be further remarked. Ritual functions negatively in horror, as do tropes of nature. Perverted ritual behavior occurs, for example, in the pig slaughter in Stephen King's *Carrie,* a part of the larger distorted ritualism that is the prom. Even Kenny, who witnessed the pig's sledge hammer execution while dumbly munching potato chips, when carrying pails of blood back to the car, is not so dense but that he vaguely senses sacrificial overtones to the killing: "[H]is mind made a dim, symbolic connection" (114). This is horror sacrifice, pointless and simply evil. Ritualization has been remarked also in the "Mad Trist" episode of "The House of Usher," notably by Barton Levi St. Armand, in his essay "The 'Mysteries' of Edgar Allan Poe: The Quest for a Monomyth in Gothic Literature." The essay analyzes the abundant ritual and romance themes running through Poe's work, the brief "Trist" narrative read by the "Usher" narrator serving to impart a quest-romance frame for the story's denouement and, St. Armand argues, underscoring the narrative's identity with vegetation legend:

> What is important about the "Mad Trist" in the context of the original Egyptian Mysteries is that it functions as a pageant or dumb show

of the trials and torments that the questing aspirant has to endure. The ordeals of entering the City of the Sun, the "palace of gold, with a floor of silver," include the struggle with the monster of doubt and will, the Dragon "of pesty breath," and the successful confrontation with the obstinate hermit . . . who holds the keys to the gates of full initiation. At the same time, Madeline is enduring the trial of earth, the ordeals of the labyrinth, and the premature burial which shadows forth the death of the old self and the rebirth of a new untrammeled soul. . . . Since both Madeline and Roderick have attained the status of gods, . . . their union is a sublime, awe-inspiring one. . . . The veil of Isis has been lifted, then, with sublime consequences for Madeline and Roderick, whose earthly tenement is superseded by the radiant glories of Heliopolis. (89)

There is a misreading here though, I think. Taking Poe's story to in fact *be* a traditional quest tale rather than a fractured gothic-arabesque version of one, St. Armand sees the narrator as essentially the fool of the piece, unable to recognize the sublime rite that is performed before him to the glory of the Ushers. This would seem too systematic an application of ritualism to Poe's story. "The House of Usher" is no more an authentic initiation legend than is the pseudo-Grail "Mad Trist" that occurs within it, or indeed than is any given Masonic or Odd Fellow exercise. If St. Armand's interpretation were credited, Poe's tale would be "comic" in nature, dealing with rebirth and the refreshment of the spirit of life, a proper fulfillment of the fertility paradigm. It is clearly not that. "The House of Usher" is, however, like gothic literature generically, fertility preoccupied and fertility referential, but for anti-mythic purposes—so that *non*-completion, collapse, a *broken,* ironic version of fertility rite can be disturbingly manifested and contribute to a sense of radical destabilization and disconnection, underscoring a failure of the ritual project that seeks to achieve accord with natural-supernatural forces. Ritual *fragments* are deeply significant to the horror aesthetic—ordeal, labyrinth, the journey underground, and so forth, but the sublime resolution of the ritual conflict is a comic resolution. True horror such as "Usher" privileges unremitting, irremediable decline. The House of Usher and all who dwell within it are doomed, as D. H. Lawrence said Poe himself was, "to seethe down . . . in a great continuous convulsion of disintegration" (*Studies* 70). Poe is working with decadent ritual elements in "Usher," one might even say with ritual junk, such decadent material being the stuff of gothic bricolage. What I quoted in the introduction from Maggie Kilgour regarding gothic literature is relevant here, that it "feeds upon and mixes the wide range of literary sources out of which it emerges and from which it never fully disentangles itself. . . .The form is thus . . . assembled out of bits and pieces of the past" (4). Gothic literature exploits what mythic possibilities are at hand, be they Egyptian forms, medieval Christian ones, folkloric ones, or others.

That the organic focus of fertility ritual held forth grim as well as comic possibilities for later literary development is evident in the perhaps darkest of modern poems whose debt to Jessie Weston's elucidation of the Grail legend— particularly the "Fisher King" motif—Eliot's footnotes to "The Waste Land" acknowledged. The poem is through and through absorbed with matters of fertility, as much so as any festive comedy might be. But the comic rhythm would in contrast have privileged, as in Chaucer, the "dull roots" of line four having survived winter and becoming mysteriously enlivened again. C. L. Barber notes that inherent in May holiday was "a realization of a power of life larger than the individual, crescent in both men and their green surroundings" (24). Horror, conversely, jams or catches at one point in the fertility cycle and stalls, falls back, stagnates. In a dark context like that of Eliot's poem, the preoccupation remains with the dull roots, the river that "sweats with oil and tar," the "unreal city," crude pharmaceutical abortions, the Fisher King *un*resurrected.

4 The Anxiety of Organism

The unholy, mute flesh . . .

—LINDA BADLEY, *Film, Horror, and the Body Fantastic*

The great slime kings were gathered for vengeance.

—SEAMUS HEANEY, "Death of a Naturalist"

A little chill touched him as he looked down at the bright plastic grass, wondering why it had to be a part of every funeral. It looked like exactly what it was: a cheap imitation of life discreetly masking the heavy brown clods of the final earth.

STEPHEN KING, *'Salem's Lot*

A GARY LARSON "FAR SIDE" CARTOON PICTURES AN INSECT cinema in which a gathering of appalled bugs watches a horror film titled "Attack of the Killer Windshield." On the screen, insects are smeared on a car windshield; bug matter and hemorrhage spatter across the implacable glass. The insects are watching a graphic, virtual demonstration of what they basically are: fluids perilously contained within a rather fragile shell. "Tis so appalling it exhilarates"—to quote Emily Dickinson—"So over Horror, it half captivates . . ." (129). The bugs are oddly excited by what they are watching.

The film enacts an arthropod version of a significant spectacle—the gothic body, "that which is put on excessive display, and whose violent, vulnerable immediacy gives . . . Gothic fiction [its] beautiful barbarity, [its] troublesome power" (Bruhm xvii). The anxiety that flows from their physical nature begets the imagination the bugs are exercising here, but it is art horror they are consuming, not horror per se. In this virtual form, horror may be viewed as at a distance, a framed and aesthetic version of the "real thing."[1] During the time in which the present book was being written, on the other hand, in the 1999 baseball season, a major league player got his foot entangled in running across first base, and the torque was violent enough that a bone broke and exited through the skin. The player went into shock and collapsed, which he presumably would not have done in the case of an ordinary fracture. This experience was *not* a matter of art horror; it was the anxiety of organism in its raw form. We are unnerved when our "flesh" appears to us as meat, as we may be when "meat" appears to us as dead animal—the vegetarian epiphany. The ballplayer's shock expresses an anxiety in the face of the horror within: "The body's inside . . . shows up. . . . It is as if the skin, a fragile container, no longer guaranteed the integrity of one's 'own and clean self' but . . . gave way before the dejection of its contents" (Kristeva 53). In accidents such as this, the familiar body thus becomes the uncanny. A similar anxiety—in literary form—at not being able to maintain one's bodily integrity, at the body's insides showing up as a biological miasma, shapes the following exsanguination scene in Robin Cook's *Mortal Fear*. The novel's main character, a doctor, is meeting with a colleague, a wealthy foundation's experimental biochemist, at the latter's urgent request, in a crowded North Boston restaurant.

> Hayes stopped in mid-sentence. He stared at Jason with an expression that started out as confusion but rapidly changed to fear. "What's the matter?" Jason asked. Hayes didn't reply. His right hand again pressed against his chest, a moan escaped from his lips, then both hands shot out and gripped the tablecloth, clawing it toward him. The wine glasses fell over. He started to get to his feet but he never made it. With a violent chocking cough he sprayed a stream of blood across the table. . . . The blood didn't stop. It came in successive waves, splattering everything as nearby diners began to scream. . . . The blood was bright red and was literally being pumped out of Hayes's mouth. (53)

Horror invention exposes such taboo aspects of the fleshly reality we inhabit. In Judeo-Christian mythology, our flesh itself became in effect taboo as part of the Fall. And Lewis's *The Monk* famously concludes with Ambrosio's seven-day bodily torment including his burning in the sun, having his eyeballs eaten by birds, and having his wounds ravaged by insects. Horror is the most physiological of genres, Linda Badley observes, "with the possible exception of pornography" (11). A major myth within the larger mythology of horror is the Faustian one based on vain denial of the organic endgame, a myth manifesting in wide-ranging expressions from Goethe's and Marlowe's Fausts through *Melmoth the Wanderer* and *The Picture of Dorian Gray* to a film such as *Angel Heart.* The myth has contemporary American resonance as the media feature articles and "experts" assuring us that death is being made daily a more and more remote likelihood, that aging, decrepitness, and sexual diminishment are in fact not biological but merely mental and attitudinal—this despite the glaring evidence to the contrary that we see in horses, dogs, cats, everything from cows to canaries. The Faustian character seeks some form of redress from the contingency and constraints of organic reality, from vital process. "Our reasoning, so sure of itself among things inert," writes Bergson, "feels ill at ease on this new ground. It would be difficult to cite a biological discovery due to pure reasoning" (*Creative Evolution* x). As earlier noted, much recent gothic literary criticism, in a period of cultural-historical relativism, has tended to underacknowledge the physicality of the genre. Such an evasion might be implicit in Mary Chapman's introduction to the Broadview edition (1999) of Brockden Brown's *Ormond,* for instance, wherein she cites favorably contemporary critics such as Jane Tompkins who view biomorphic tropes in early American texts as a matter of *metaphorical* reference to cultural situations, reading "recurring tropes of incest, rape, seduction, murder, suicide, pestilence, and other threats to the physical body as a metaphorization of the more political threats to the national body" (Chapman 12). This would conceive physicality as symbolically registering a social-political anxiety, as if physicality were an unlikely medium of significance in and of itself. It is arguable that, quite the contrary, the recurrent bodily tropes in question are expressions of the gothic literary character at its deepest level, the gothic genre's interrogation of "the condition of being flesh and blood" (Clive Barker, qtd. in Booe 8).

By Thompkins's measure, one would have to seek for a political psychology driving, for example, *The Monk* (1796), that prototype of the salacious dark novel. And since the immediate influences upon the novel's author lie in German *Sturm und Drang,* and since the Bleeding Nun episode is drawn from a German folk tradition, a shared political matrix between London and Weimar would probably have to be supposed; the matter becomes complicated. All meaning of course resonates with other meanings, and flesh is potentially a symbolic element, but threat to the physical body is surely a primary enough concern that the immediate presumption that something more remote is being referenced is unjustified. In *The Monk,* as in Poe's "House of Usher," it is not only threats *to* the flesh but threats *of* the flesh on which the narrative turns. The novel situates an anxiety regarding the power of organic drives to overthrow the social-ecclesiastical constraints designed to thwart them. The fleshly energies the comic perspective sees as positively shaking up stodgy institutions are portrayed in horror works such as Matthew's novel as *fearsomely* powerful forces of social, familial, and personal psychic upheaval. Indeed Lewis's narrative sees institutionalized religious structures as shot through with the fleshly and erotic energies they were intended to counterbalance. The summons of throngs to prayer and preaching at the Capuchian Abbey in Madrid, for instance, is on the folk level a call to secular carnival, superstition being the closest the affair comes to spirituality:

> Do not encourage the idea that the Crowd was assembled either from motives of piety or thirst for information. . . . The audience now assembled was collected by various causes. . . . The women came to show themselves, the men to see the women: some were attracted by curiosity to hear an Orator so celebrated; Some came because they had no better means of employing their time till the play began. (7)

The anti-Catholicism here might be viewed as locating an ideological subtext in the novel similar to that found in Radcliffe's *Udolpho* or *The Italian,* but if Lewis's agenda deep down had to do with censuring the superstitious matrix of Mediterranean Catholicism, he would hardly have written scenes such as the one in which the gypsy fortune-teller turns out to in fact *have* clairvoyant powers and the individual articulating the rationalist and arguably Protestant, anti-superstitious, anti-folkloric point of view is Antonia's foolish and obnoxious aunt (36–38). And when Raymond and Agnes, at the Castle of Lindenburg, take lightly the legend of the Bleeding Nun, they live to regret their skepticism. Already in Lewis's work the Protestant gothic writer's intriguement with the literary horror potential of Mediterranean Catholic physicality is evident.

The Monk foregrounds the prurient sexual curiosity and anxiety created by prohibition, celibacy, and cloister. Lorenzo and Cristoval hang around the Abbey-Chapel when the nuns from the St. Clare Priory arrive for confession because the nuns' faces are then unveiled. The intended modesty of veiling in inverted by the men's imaginations into a sexual tease. This mild and even puerile cultivation of the mystery of flesh is extrapolated in the novel to the dimension of overwhelming and murderous psychopathology centering in the character of the monk Ambrosio, at first a model of celibacy, devoutness, and religious erudition. But this ideal product of monastic instruction crumbles pathetically at the accidental sighting of Matilda's exposed breast—the whole religious ordering falls away:

> His eye dwelt with insatiable avidity upon the beauteous Orb. A sensation till then unknown filled his heart with a mixture of *anxiety* and delight: a raging fire shot through every limb; the blood boiled in his veins, and a thousand wild wishes bewildered his imagination. (italics added, 65)

Clerical celibacy supposes a surmounted eroticism, but the more hedged about bodiliness is, the more dangerously provocative and ultimately demonic it may become. The Catholic Spain of Lewis's novel is a heartland of erotic intrigue and eroticized religion. But, as I will be arguing particularly in the next chapter, the rejection or marginalization of the flesh was not confined to monasticism but prevailed and continues to prevail in Western cosmology and philosophy—the Spanish and Italian cloister provided gothic novelists like Lewis, Radcliffe, and Maturin with a convenient and dramatic special case of the deepseated anxiety of organism prevalent in the modern European psyche.

This anxiety haunts Poe's "The House of Usher," wherein a disembodied intellectualism is under siege and an inescapable physicality intrudes upon it in the form of the dead-alive Madeline. As the narrator approaches the House of Usher, and during his first experiences within, it becomes disturbingly evident to him—and this recapitulates Usher's plight—that all the mental capacity he commands is proving inadequate to rationalize the grotesque intuitions that occur to him. He becomes ever more disoriented and ever closer to the condition of his host, for whom things refuse to fit into the patterns of his private intellectual ordering, and for whom the fear and loathing of the grave will not be kept at bay. As noted early on, in King's *'Salem's Lot,* fear is traced along distinctly biological paths as Sue Norton, attempting to keep the realization at bay, is finally forced to recognize that vampire intrigues are at work in the town. Her physical brain and nervous system are manifested as fear wells up "from a part of her brain that was usually silent and probably as obsolete as her appendix." Her rational brain forces her to investigate the mystery at hand, however, "in spite of the warnings of that instinctive part, which is so similar in physical construction to the brain of the alligator" (388). The brain is flesh subject to dissolution, as the rest of the body is; it cannot, and Usher learns this dreadfully, count on a separate peace apart from the body, however much it might like to. Humans, perhaps particularly those in the tradition of Athens and the Enlightenment, are inordinately proud of and dependent upon the rational powers and rational independence that horror subverts—"I struggled to reason off the nervousness which had dominion over me," writes the "Usher" narrator (*Selected* 67). David R. Saliba, referring to Poe's typical narrator, notes this "incessant rationalizing" (67). Our symbolic, intellectual powers themselves, in fact, are as likely to intensify nightmarish illusions as they are to neutralize them. We may begin to suspect, as the "Usher" visitor does, that an overwrought imagination, our own thought, is implicated in the very fear we would wish to overcome, and we are then lost in a cognitive hall of mirrors. Thought thus becomes self-referential, feeding on itself and giving vitality to its terrors. The "Usher" narrator proclaims this dynamic the "paradoxical law of all sentiments having terror as a basis"—that is, that awareness of the presence of fear is fearful, and accelerates fear, which is all the more fearful (*Selected* 56). Indeed because humans are so dependent upon their synthetic/symbolic world, they are easily victimized by it, and, as Langer points out in a remark particularly applicable to horror literature: "Even the dead may still play into [their lives]" (*Feeling* 330).

A further expression of the distrust of intellectuality evident in the gothic appears in the "obtrusive and eager enquiries" the doctors make concerning Madeline's corpse, which trouble Usher, who suspects that the physicians may, stumped by his sister's malady, violate her grave and her body postmortem in order to satisfy their scientific curiosity. This body sacrilege trope, common in horror fiction, is one more expression of the mode's physiological inspiration and its recognition of the rent in the fabric of life—the intellect imagining itself divorced from the physical body and consequently dishonoring it. Gothic literature consistently portrays science, the intellect's militant wing, in its most Faustian, alchemical guise. Science's intellectual prying into the seamless organic mystery and presumptuous attempts to gain control over it— cloning being perhaps the height of that aspiration—are viewed as an errant violation of the natural order. In the gothic, Science exacerbates the hideous obscure rather than alleviating it. Rappaccini's daughter's body ends up so poisoned that what should be a healthful restorative kills her; her body can no longer tolerate things natural. Captain Obed's cross-species adventuring in Lovecraft's *The Shadow over Innsmouth* generates a loathsome, defective breed. And it is noteworthy that it is the unnatural *gait* of these creatures, a sign of their physical incongruities, that particularly horrifies the narrator—the discrepancy between their bodily movements and those of healthy human beings: "Their crouching, shambling gait was abominably repellent." He describes their flopping march in the moonlight as a "malignant saraband," that is, a freakish similitude of courtly dance (94). Their physical aberrations reflect the biological transgression involved in their begetting. In a likewise macabre scene in the 1995 film version of *Frankenstein,* the science-besotted Victor Frankenstein joins in a dance with the experimentally devastated body of his beloved. Their waltz is a ghastly anti-dance, a pathetic semblance of natural dance's celebration of the body's graceful potentials.[2] This Frankenstein interpretation extended the one established in the earlier Boris Karloff version—that of the Frankenstein monster as physically distorted and awkward, which, in Mary Shelley's novel, he was not.[3] Like most all monstrosities, Yeats's "rough beast" (i.e., sketchily defined), lacking natural physical integrity, *slouches* toward Bethlehem; things misbegotten bear marks; the beast is dis/graceful and distorted.

Linda Badley refers to "the threat to the body that is memorable in Poe" (9). The controlling motif in "Usher" is that of physical dissolution—a single, organic decline taking in family line, the contemporary consanguinal Ushers, the whole estate. Vitality is flow, dynamic movement, constant revitalization and refreshment; thus we are repulsed by what, on the contrary, suggests the stagnant, stale, desiccated, musty—we recognize all the latter as anti-life. Poe uses image upon image throughout "The House of Usher" to evoke an atmosphere of pervasive enervation stemming from a pathologically in-turned orientation. The Ushers have been biologically reclusive. D. H. Lawrence, in his Poe chapter of *Studies in Classical American Literature,* refers to the primary organic imperative—that each organism, "intrinsically isolate and single in itself," tend to its private preservation, the needs requisite to its distinctness and differentiation. He points out that there is a secondary law of organic life, however, that goes to refreshment—"each organism only lives through contact with other matter, assimilation of new vibrations. . . . Each individual organism is vivified by intimate contact with other organisms" (71). The Ushers have not successfully negotiated between these organic essentials. It is notably the second imperative that the House of Usher has neglected to its ruin, leaving it unrefreshed, listless, and stifling.

The atmosphere surrounding the Usher mansion, devoid of natural air and light, has "no affinity" to fresh air but rather has "reeked up from the decayed

trees . . . and the silent tarn—a pestilent vapor, dull, sluggish . . . leaden hued"
(*Selected* 56). There is reference to woodwork "rotted for long years in some
neglected vault, with no disturbance from the breath of the external air" (57).
Usher himself, like Faulkner's Emily and so many other characters in gothic
literature, has not left the house for years—everything, including the family
tree, is biologically static and spent. Madeline lingers in "a settled apathy, a
gradual wasting away" (60). The narrator remarks that even the books and
musical instruments in Usher's quarters, for example, "failed to give any vitality to the scene" (57–58). The remark points to the element of biological
inversion in the gothic framework—the negation of all that is vigorous and
life-beneficial. "The Fall of the House of Usher" is one extended trope turning on enfeeblement and deterioration—the absence of Eros.

Usher's entire perspective reflects an infirm, jaundiced version of the comic
festive perception C. L. Barber describes as "an experience of the relationship
between vitality in people and nature" (19). Usher sees the ancestral estate,
its grounds and "natural" environs, as radically continuous with his own de-
crepit organism, which is itself the contemporary embodiment of the Usher
family line. He is convinced of the "sentience of all vegetable things," and so
on. What in the comic-festive tradition is a robust and exhilarating perception—the recognition of "all living things stirring together" (Barber 21)—is perceived by the helplessly intellectualizing Usher as a sickening undifferentiation,
a collapse of the border between objective reality and the uncanny. He feels
himself infringing "upon the kingdom of inorganization." In his sister's final
clutch, the Ushers become undifferentiated mire. He cannot sustain the demarcation between himself and corpseness, on which level he is identical with
Madeline, one in putrefaction. A plank in reason has broken; he is himself slipping into corpseness, "cadaverously wan"; only the finality is lacking. As
Kristeva observes:

> The corpse (or cadaver: cadere, to fall), that which has irremediably
> come a cropper, is cesspool, and death. . . . Without makeup or masks,
> refuse and corpses *show me* what I permanently thrust aside in order
> to live. These body fluids, this defilement . . . are what life withstands,
> hardly and with difficulty. There, I am at the border of my condition
> as a living being. (2)

Usher the rationalist has an appointment with the unmediated flesh that finds
its way up from the grave. He is caught in "a vortex of summons and repul-

sion [that] places the one haunted by it literally beside himself" (Kristeva 1). When she falls upon him, Usher and sister are one in corpseness, one in defilement. He must acknowledge the her that is *it,* which acknowledged, all meaning collapses. The narrator recalls: "I saw the mighty walls rushing asunder."

★ ★ ★

To return to the issue raised by Jane Tompkins—physicality serving as metaphor for cultural concerns—John Cheever's well-known short story "The Swimmer" provides a fairly recent model of a work arguably grounded in a sense of embodiment running deeper than its surface social critique. While the story undeniably reflects a satirical concern with the nature of wealthy American suburban life in the 1950s and early 1960s, its gothic force, not unlike that of "Bartleby the Scrivener," issues from its concern with life in jeopardy in a biological sense. The anti-life spirit and bewildering social environment of the upper-middle-class suburbs define a distinctly physical threat not distinguishable from the spiritual one involved. Neddy Merrill's neighbors are well-to-do grotesques inhabiting an upscale wasteland. He is himself mentally and physically far gone and conceives a rite of atonement—a swim home, to where he believes his wife and three daughters are, by way of a chain of outdoor suburban pools. The obvious salmon allusion evokes the sacramental-fertility symbolism of the fish as well as the salmon's particular association with the journey-agon of return to the fertile origin. Merrill dives into the first pool: "Being embraced and sustained by the light-green water seemed . . . the resumption of a natural condition, and he would have liked to swim without trunks. . . . That he lived in a world so generously supplied with water seemed like a clemency, a beneficence" (604). It is the "natural condition" that is under assault. A reverse fertility undercurrent enters in as the swimmer's "river" is broken up; the continuity he seeks is not there—the Welch's pool, for example, is dry. "This breach in his chain of water disappointed him absurdly, and he felt like an explorer who is seeking a torrential headwater and finds a dead stream" (606). He must cross a highway in his swim trunks; a driver throws a beer can at him. He must use a crowded public pool reeking of chlorine and suntan oil, where he is yelled at by the lifeguards for not having an identification tag.

The swimmer's faltering organism situates his decline and growing desolation; the narrative scans his body: "The swim was too much for his strength. . . . His arms were lame. His legs felt rubbery and ached in the joints. The worst of it was the cold in his bones and the feeling that he might never be warm again" (609). In need of a drink to go on, he stops at the Sachs's pool, but no drink is to be had. Mr. Sachs no longer drinks, having had a major operation, evident as he stands by the pool in his trunks. "Ned's eyes slipped from Eric's face to his abdomen, where he saw three pale, sutured scars. . . . Gone was his navel, and what, Neddy thought, would the roving hand, bed-checking one's gifts at 3 a.m., make of a belly with no navel, *no link to birth*" (italics added, 610). This extended biomorphic allegory—concluding with Ned, like a crippled salmon, swimming a "hobbled sidestroke"—is one of a failed attempt to return to the vital source. His home turns out to be vacant, fallen into disrepair. The allegory is surely not put together just as part of a project in social irony or bourgeois satirization; more deeply it renders the archetype of separation from life's sacramental, that is, life-giving, waters.

Contrary to the tendency to de-emphasize the physical, Ellen Moers's earlier referred to analysis of *Frankenstein* sees the biological in Shelley's novel metaphorically related to childbirth: "the motif of revulsion against newborn life, and the drama of guilt, dread, and flight surrounding birth and its consequences" (218). This interpretation recognizes the anxiety that can afflict the intellect in confronting elemental biological reality; the astonishing, determined drive of organic things to feed and duplicate, for instance, can be oppressive in its defiance of rational understanding. There is that remote, uncanny, and characterless level of dumbly impelled organicism typified in Whitman's reference to "the sacs merely floating with open mouth for food to slip in" (*Collected* 105). In a waking nightmare, the narrator of "The Yellow Wallpaper" finds that the disturbing forms in the wallpaper suggest a fungus, "a toadstool in joints, an interminable string of toadstools, budding and sprouting in endless convolutions" (Gilman 96). A related kind of revulsion is evident in chapter 59 of *Moby Dick,* which relates the encounter with the great squid. The pulpy mass "lazily rose" and, "furlongs in length," lay on the water, revealed briefly to mankind by "the secret seas. . . . No perceptible face or front did it have; no conceivable token of either sensation or instinct; but undulated there on the billows, an unearthly, formless, chance-like apparition of life." When the thing disappears, it is with "a low sucking sound" (Melville 318–19). Melville frequently noted the kind of intellectual vertigo and anxiety aroused by unrationalized organicism, by the uncanny energy abounding entirely outside humanistic considerations and intellectual grasp. His poem "The Maldive Shark" captures the sluggish, vacant efficiency of the shark's marauding, enabled by the scouting skills of the pilot fish, which function in the shark's service as "Eyes and brains to the dotard lethargic and dull, / Pale ravener of horrible meat" (*Collected* 200). The shark's single-minded predatory purpose is foreign to the profile of mammals, which invariably are possessed of other more complex dimensions and of richer character. The dim, mechanical livingness of the squid and shark are uncanny to humans, as is that of a slug or a leech. Freud, in his essay titled "The Uncanny," references a study by E. Jentsch in which the author remarks the "uncanny" effect of epileptic seizures for example "because these excite in the spectator the feeling that automatic, mechanical processes are at work, concealed beneath the ordinary appearance of animation" (Freud 31). Humans are chilled by encounters with unhumanized, characterless aspects of life. The experience arguably involves another version of the Freudian encounter with the "surmounted"—the anxiety involved in reencountering shades of evolutionarily surmounted material.

Similarly uncomplex and charmless are the creatures in the fishy, hopping parade watched from hiding by the narrator of *The Shadow over Innsmouth* as they come along the Rowley road. He thinks not only of his own safety but also, more to the point here, of the "irredeemable pollution of that space they occupy" (Lovecraft 92). Horror monstrosities typically carry primarily the threat to pollute and infect, or they epitomize a repugnant and nauseating organicism, a fleshy stupidity. When Jonathan Harker finds the satiated Dracula lying indolently in a castle chamber, his reaction is one of abhorrence: On the Count's lips "were gouts of fresh blood. . . . It seemed as if the whole awful creature were simply gorged with blood; he lay like a filthy leech" (Stoker 71).

In H. P. Lovecraft, horror more often than not is connected with the threat of repulsive contact with anomalous, proliferating biological *stuff* that falls short even of thingness, or repulsive organic matter—molds, slime, markers of "decay's effacing fingers."[4] Horror literature broaches the question of what in fact we are to make of the organic, how we are to reconcile the inner and outer biological, to negotiate the evident continuity. What if the fierce procreational drive of living things is meaningless, a pointless cosmic jag? What if, as Celine wrote, "a man . . . is nothing but arrested putrescence" (qtd. in Kristeva 143)? None of the major Western cosmologies has been able to account for organicism to the mind's satisfaction, least of all perhaps the scientific Enlightenment view roughly coinciding with gothic literature's "high" period. Lovecraft was an ardent scientific materialist for whom the organic suggested the unclean, a harbor of vileness. This phobia contributed positively to his tales of terror, but it unfortunately extended to his virtually psychopathic social philosophy and politics, wherein he projected his loathing upon selected racial groups. In a 1924 letter to Frank Belnap Long, recounting his visit to New York's Chinatown two years earlier—"a nightmare of perverse infection"—Lovecraft reveals a depraved biomorphic imagination in a rant that is beyond Hitlerian:

> The organic things—Italo-Semitico-Mongoloid—inhabiting that awful cesspool could not by any stretch of the imagination be call'd human. They were monstrous and nebulous adumbrations of the pithecanthropoid and amoebal; vaguely moulded from some stinking viscous slime of earth's corruption, and slithering and oozing in and on the filthy streets. . . . They—or the gelatinous fermentation of which they were composed—seemed to ooze, seep and trickle thro' the gaping cracks in the horrible houses . . . and I thought of . . . unwholesome vats, crammed to the vomiting point with gangrenous vileness. (qtd. in Lévy 28–29)

Celine was, as Lovecraft arguably was as well, a Fascist; works like *L'Ecole des Cadavres* are driven by a morbid xenophobia, a revulsion at "the Jews, Afro-Asiatic hybrids, quadroons, half-negroes, and Near Easterners, unbridled fornicators" (qtd. in Kristeva 183). What Kristeva observes of Celine's anti-Semitic pamphleteering would seem relevant to Lovecraft's similar racism, that it is "a *delirium* that literally prevents one from going mad, for it postpones the senseless abyss that threatens" (137). I take her to mean that such writers must project and objectify their suffocating biological anxiety in order to survive, however marginally, mentally; it is not an *abstract* abyss that threatens. They must rationalize, though it be irrationalization, the annihilating horror that confronts them as inexplicable, burgeoning, bio-formations. Celine's and Lovecraft's political imaginations were arguably employed in the same deflecting project as their literary works were. For example, a line from the Lovecraft letter quoted above: "They—or the gelatinous fermentation of which they were composed—seemed to ooze, seep and trickle thro' the gaping cracks in the horrible houses" represents his ordinary literary idiom, his fictional horror rhetoric, and might have been taken from any of a number of his weird tales.

    The projected anxieties evident in these two writers raise again the question referred to earlier regarding why certain notes and images within our biological context are repulsive—among these, it would seem, are things going to our sense of the primordial ooze, the fertile, swampy, sexual river system that brings us into the world. Physical processes appear to have disturbing, unhuman overtones—they are out of our control and possessed of a determination, a fierce, uncanny resolution that seems to know only an impulse to drive forward. Melville's Maldive shark represents only one of his many imaginative encounters with the urgent biological impetus in nature. In "The Encantadas," he recounts lying in his hammock aboard ship in the night and listening to the giant land tortoises some of the crew had brought aboard:

> I heard the slow, weary draggings of three ponderous strangers along
> the encumbered deck. Their stupidity or their resolution was so great,
> that they never went aside from any impediment. One ceased his
> movements all together just before mid-watch. At sunrise I found him
> butted like a battering-ram against the immovable foot of the foremast
> and still striving . . . to force the impossible passage. (*Short Works* 105).

The tortoises seem possessed by a "diabolical enchanter" in their "strange infatuation with hopeless toil." Their curse, he observes, is their "drudging impulse to straightforwardness." The monsters of literary horror reflect the same thing in their awful straight-ahead vector and their absence of personality. "Their stupidity or their resolution was so great, that they never went aside from any impediment" would characterize the possessed people in *Night of the Living Dead* as well. Godzilla, like Nosferatu, or the Encantadas tortoises, likewise lumbers stupidly ahead into Tokyo regardless of high-tension wires, heavy artillery fire, or bridges—driven by some mindless, reptilian must-do. The possibility of human devolution to some such version of dumb drivenness is a chilling horror image. Even a scene far removed from Melville's islands and those preoccupations can elicit the aversion reaction in question. This from Eliot's "The Waste Land," for example:

> Unreal city,
> Under the brown fog of winter dawn,
> A crowd flowed over London Bridge, so many,
> I had not thought death had undone so many.
> Sighs, short and infrequent were exhaled,
> And each man fixed his eyes before his feet.
> Flowed up the hill and down King William Street. . . .

(39)

The lack of individual will evident here, the mindlessness of "flow," suggests so much organic matter, and the indolence of the "sighs," the eyes fixed before the feet, suggest a collective, zombie-like vacantness.

The blind impulse of the tortoise and the feeding drive of the Maldive shark arguably surface in human pathology, in the submission of human monsters to analogously voracious, pre-rational drives. The very title *Fatal Attraction* is suggestive of a devolution to the level of comparatively uncomplex life-forms driven by tropisms, persons who know only a vivid *want,* like the vampire whose world is confined to thirsting "always for a scorned elixir, / the salt quotidian blood." Richard Wilbur, from whose poem "The Undead" these lines are taken, captures the terribly narrow drive of the vampire:

> Secret, unfriendly, pale, possessed
> Of the one wish, the thirst for mere survival
> . . . .
> Now to their Balkan battlements
> Above the vulgar town of their first lives,
> They rise at the moon's rising.
>
> (196–97)

The poem elsewhere remarks the vampire's "utter self-concern," and suggests the pattern of human monstrosity—serial killers, for example, who are similarly estranged from "the vulgar town of their first lives." In the town of his first life, John Wayne Gacey was engaged in many civic activities and was once Jaycees "Man of the Year"; he owned a construction business, and so on. The sexual predator is a psychological analog to the vampire—empty save for the unquenchable need. Alex in *Fatal Vision* and Annie Wilkes in *Misery* are one dimensional—devoid of charm, humor, flair, élan. There is a scene in *Fatal Attraction,* following upon the killing of the little girl's rabbit, when Dan Gallagher (Michael Douglas) goes to the stalker Alex's apartment and nearly chokes her (Glenn Close). He stops, however, and falters, retreating slowly backward out of the apartment. The action could be misread as reflecting his shock at almost having killed someone, but in fact I think it reflects a sudden, horrified repulsion, his recognition that the woman is a monster, preternaturally ravenous and insatiable, that his physical fighting with her and having nearly killed her is, for her, intimacy, as her demented grin indicates; he has fed her obsession; to her this has been a lover's spat.[5] Her demands are of an atavistic absoluteness, uncomplicated by considerations of his being married and so forth; Dan's wife is a meaningless obstacle in the path of Alex's narcissism, which seems to command the eradication of all boundaries that would define Gallagher as separate from her. It is as if her impulses recapitulate microorganismic drives; germ-like, she wishes to *inhabit* him. (A similarly repulsive presumption of intimacy occurs in *Play Misty for Me* when Evelyn, based on one sexual encounter, walks into the Clint Eastwood character's house the next day and begins stocking and arranging his refrigerator.) Alex's noting that "part of you is growing inside me" does not carry the phrase's normal and familiar sentimental value; rather it marks a victory in her attempt to envelope and *incorporate* him. "I feel you," she says in her taped message, "I taste you. I think you." Her motivation seems to approach that of viruses, which, to quote Preston again, are "molecular sharks . . . motive without a mind . . . hard, logical, totally selfish" (64–65). The virus's impulse, as previously noted, is to possess the host, to translate the host into itself (14). People exist only with reference to Alex's consuming *lack;* and there is no *she* but her drive. Freud refers to the "eternal suckling" type "who hold fast all their lives to their claim to be nourished by someone else" (124). Gallagher's repulsion derives from his recognition that he is dealing with something inexorable, to which there is no rational appeal, any more than there would to a school of piranha. Alex, Evelyn in *Play Misty for Me,* Annie Wilkes in *Misery,* and many real-life stalkers suggest this pathological slide to a rudimentary, less than human order of complexity, one below the level where they are even candidates for moral judgment. They must simply be stopped.

The conception of monstrosity and horror resonating in the inexplicable scheme of biological life and its elemental drives is extraordinarily drawn by E. L. Grant Watson in his *The Mystery of Physical Life.* This passage, in which he describes deep ocean species at a natural history museum, is the equal of anything in Melville and plumbs the *unheimlich* depths of the organic imperative:

> Despite complete darkness, monotonous cold and enormous weight of waters some small fishes have become adapted to the great deeps; creatures of horrific appearance, seeming to the human glance as though made of ill-fitting parts, joined together by hazard. . . . One, *Platocorynus spinicarpa,* carries a nose-lamp like the headlight of a motor car; another has a luminous lure on a flexible rod . . . as enticement to smaller fishes, which are thus attracted into the jagged-toothed mouth: the gaping cavern of hell as depicted by Hieronymous Bosch.

In this world, a male fish finds it difficult to locate his mate, since few exist under such conditions. Once found he does not loose her, uniting with her substance, sucking her juices for substance—an adhesion finding a counterpart in no few human associations—a mere parasite, losing all functional activities save that of sperm-making. . . .

At the Natural History Museum of South Kensington there are dried specimens of such fish . . . food for imaginations: enormous, gaping mouths, unwinking eyes of unflinching purpose—original myths of creation . . . the deep dreams of the mentally deranged, frightful visages, endowed with powerful and irrational determination, fixed ideas incarnate in deep waters. . . . The weight of oceans has precipitated their startled, indignant and suffering faces. In sex alone, a dim luminosity in the darkness. (122–23)

Here again we witness the return of the evolutionarily surmounted. And arguably the idiom and expression of the fixated stalker characters of contemporary film, their parasitic nature, their "powerful and irrational determination," are disturbingly discernable.

★ ★ ★

Another aspect of distressing organicism may be found in Seamus Heaney's poem "Death of a Naturalist." The gaze is that of the poet as a young boy, who, venturing out to an area he is familiar with, comes upon, this time, nature in unromantic guise:

Then one hot day when fields were rank
With cowdung in the grass the angry frogs
Invaded the flax-dam; I ducked through hedges
To a coarse croaking that I had not heard
Before. . . .
Right down the dam the gross-bellied frogs were cocked
On sods; their loose necks pulsed like sails. Some hopped:
The slap and plop were obscene threats. . . .
. . . .
I sickened, turned and ran. The great slime kings
Were gathered for vengeance and I knew
That if I dipped my hand the spawn would clutch it.

(15–16)

Here, to quote Bakhtin, "something frightening is revealed in that which was habitual and secure" (*Rabelais* 37): The slimy frog motif might recall Lovecraft's evil Innsmouth. Located on a fish-smelling mudflat, the town of Innsmouth is dominated by a family called the *Marshes*—suggesting the spawning, amphibious monsters that dwell there. "The swamp world of the Great Mother precedes the world of Christ and is ready at any moment to engulf it," writes Camille Paglia (*Personae* 324). She rejects the romantic image of primal nature as benign and affirms the gothic's pagan privileging of earth spirits as opposed to the neat Judeo-Christian sky-god cosmogony wherein "[c]reation is rational and systematic. The evolution of forms proceeds majestically, without carnage or cataclysm. God presides with workmanlike detachment" (*Personae* 40). Paglia notes that Coleridge spoke of the "Sands and Swamps of Evil" and elsewhere of lust as "the reek of the Marsh " (*Personae* 324). This identifies an element of gothic biomorphism mentioned earlier in connection with "The House of Usher"—the horror of undifferentiation, of fading into the swamps of the Great Mother, the plenum of organic generation where thought can gain no purchase. Nietzsche in fact aptly characterized Poe and like writers as "idealists from the vicinity of swamps" (qtd. in Poe, *Selected* xi). Paglia's analysis of the pagan dynamic in the Christian Pietà, Christ devolving to Adonis, the dying god, is compelling in its liquifying imagery:

> Early Christian and Byzantine Christs were virile, but once the church settled in Rome, Italy's vestigial paganism took over. Christ relapsed into Adonis. . . . Jesus is remarkably epicene, with aristocratic hands and feet of morbid delicacy. Grieving in her oppressive robes, Mary admires the sensual beauty of the son she has made. His glassy nude limbs *slipping down her lap,* Adonis *sinks back to earth,* his strength drained by and returned to his immortal mother. (italics added, *Personae* 53)

Her neo-pagan sensibility leads Paglia to perceive the lacuna in the major Western cosmologies—their asexuality, their marginalization of the body and organicism in general. "Philosophies of Mind or Spirit or the Psyche, however elaborate and ingenious," writes E. W. F. Tomlin, "are rendered futile unless they succeed in throwing light upon *incarnate being*" (14). The stainless steel Newtonian model current in the eighteenth-century context out of which the high gothic romantic emerged was perhaps the most rigorous of all in its evasion of the organic. In a period when science was virtually synonymous with physics, biological life was "simply located," to use Whitehead's term, just *there,* absent any reference to a more encompassing, meaningful scheme. Biological matter was a mucky, unaccountable superfluousness in which, worst case, humankind or mind was stuck like the ancient mariner in a slimy sea. And this was not a temporary fix in which Western philosophy and religion found itself. Biology has tended to be the ugly stepsister among the sciences and has been marginalized in philosophy.[6] It is still exceptional to find in philosophical works the kind of chapters we do in Bergson, ones with headings such as "The Plant and the Animal," "Animal Life," "The Nature of Instinct," and so on. On the contrary, as Whitehead notes, the hegemony of physics-based science and philosophy has been the norm from the seventeenth century to the twentieth, and its concepts are ill fitted to biology, which creates for it

> an insoluble problem of matter and life and organism, with which biologists are now wrestling. . . . One unsolved problem of thought, so far as it derives from this period [seventeenth century] is to be formulated thus: Given configurations of matter with locomotion in space as assigned by physical laws, [how] to account for living organisms. (41)[7]

The same problem is noted in another way by Stuart Kauffman in 1995:

> If the swarm of stars in a spiral galaxy, clustered swirling in the high blackness of space, astonishes us with the wonder of the order generated by mutually gravitating masses, think with equal wonder of the order of our own ontogeny. How in the world can a single cell, merely some tens of thousands of kinds of molecules locked in one another's embrace, know how to create the intricacies of a human infant? No one knows.

The present information age, as earlier noted, exhibits its own particular repression of biological livingness, perhaps in fact the most Faustian denial of embodied reality yet. The whole period might be grimly summed up in this regard by N. Katherine Hayles's characterization of Alan Turing's 1950 paper "Computer Machinery and Intelligence": "Here at the inaugural moment of the computer age, the erasure of embodiment is performed so the 'intelligence' becomes a property of the formal manipulation of symbols rather than an enaction in the human life-world" (xi). Hayles argues that the traditional constructions of humanness are currently giving way to posthuman ones in which

> embodiment in a biological substrate is seen as an accident of history rather than an inevitability of life. . . . The posthuman view thinks of the body as the original prosthesis we all learn to manipulate, so that extending or replacing the body with other prostheses becomes a continuation of a process that began before we were born. (2–3)

The contempt for embodied life implicit in such constructions is, as we have seen, only epiphenomenally new however, manifesting a bent that extends back in time to earlier historical versions of the same evasion. The anxiety of organism in medieval morbid art arguably reflected an earlier distress regarding incarnation—the question then being what had flesh and bone to do with end things and the heavenly realm? Was the body merely a meaty vehicle bearing the spirit for a while? Stephen Greenblatt quotes an account of a fourteenth-century monk's self-mutilation that arguably bespeaks desperation to negotiate the mind-body dichotomy and to spiritualize the flesh: "Then stabbing the stylus backwards and forwards, in and out of the flesh, he engraved the name of Jesus . . . over his heart. Blood gushed out of the jagged wounds and saturated his clothing" (224). Such scourging testifies to the flesh's primal mystery and power. For modern and postmodern people, the anxiety persists at least in the form of trying to reconcile the organic with a scientific cosmology informed by physics and mathematics, neither of which have any more real need for the organic than did the medieval Christian cosmology. Hence the modern gothic continues the foregrounding and interrogation of denied primitive organicness. Contemporary horror films, as Paglia argues, "unleash the forces repressed by Christianity . . . the barbarism of nature. Horror films are rituals of pagan worship" (*Personae* 268).

Folk-inspired carnival culture, Bakhtin asserts throughout *Rabelais and His World,* was negatively capable in this regard; it let the biological in all its manifestations be and laughed, in effect, with it. His formulation would seem to suppose a different spirit among the peasantry than what was already prevailing among contemporary aristocracy and intellectuals whose anxiety medieval macabre art reflected. Medieval *folk* culture's "grotesque realism," Bakhtin maintains, was comparatively at ease with the biological, the latter in fact being the energizing vitality informing the period's frequent holiday fairs and folk spectacles.[8] But that hardy carnal spirit drained away, he suggests, in the Dark

Romantic grotesque, one expression of which was the gothic novel. The positive sense of fertility, the pagan-peasant comfort with the body and things earthy, waned:

> The differences appear most distinctly in relation to terror. The world of Romantic grotesque is to a certain extent a terrifying world, alien to man. All that is ordinary, commonplace, belonging to everyday life . . . suddenly becomes meaningless, dubious and hostile. . . . Something frightening is revealed in that which was habitual and secure. . . . On the other hand, the medieval and Renaissance folk culture was familiar with the element of terror only as represented by comic monsters, who were defeated by laughter. . . . Folk culture brought the world close to man, gave it a bodily form in contrast to the abstract and spiritual mastery sought by Romanticism [in which] images of bodily life, such as eating, drinking, copulation, defecation, almost entirely lost their regenerating power and were turned into "vulgarities." (*Rabelais* 37)

In gothic literature, raw biological reality returns as taboo to haunt a too neatly rationalized world—as Usher's sister's fleshly physicality with all its mortal implications returns and falls horribly upon him. The organic *unheimlich,* that with which our reason is uncomfortable, is not a mere philosophical blank or an absence in nature; it is a plenum of proliferating matter; it is animate. What Whitman called "the procreant urge of the world" can be perceived as overwhelming. The sense of biological associations becoming increasingly insidious and alien arguably reached a modern literary culmination in Sartre's novel *Nausea* (1959), the narrator of which, Roquetin, is sickened (one thinks of Lovecraft) by the world's fulsome, organic presence: "I have seen enough of living things, of dogs, of men, of all flabby masses which move spontaneously" (24). This disassociation plagues the narrator to the extent that he experiences his own body and his face in the mirror through what he describes as "a dumb, organic sense." The mirror presents "redundant flesh blossoming and palpitating with abandon." He describes what he sees as "on the fringe of the vegetable world, at the level of jellyfish" (17). In what has become a rather famous scene, viewing a chestnut tree, Roquetin recoils at the gratuitous excess *(de trop)* of life forms:

> [E]verywhere blossomings, hatchings out, . . . my very flesh throbbed and opened, abandoned itself to the universal burgeoning. It was re-

pugnant. . . . What good are so many duplicates of trees? . . . That abundance did not give the effect of generosity, just the opposite. It was dismal, ailing, embarrassed at itself. Those trees, those great clumsy bodies. . . . (133)

That the romantic too, despite its protestations to the contrary, was, as Bakhtin argues, assailed by an alienation from the organic is evident, for example, in Walt Whitman's remarkable poem "This Compost," which, though it attempts to evade the alienation, by its own testimony, falls short. Whitman famously celebrates the body and the biological in his poetry; *Song of Myself* is the great American glorification of physicalness:

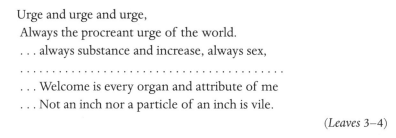

Urge and urge and urge,
  Always the procreant urge of the world.
  . . . always substance and increase, always sex,
. . . .
  . . . Welcome is every organ and attribute of me
  . . . Not an inch nor a particle of an inch is vile.

(*Leaves* 3–4)

But there are notes of unease in his work at nature's inexplicable "exuding"—"[s]omething I cannot see puts upward libidinous prongs," and so forth (*Collected* 84). In "This Compost," contemplating the earth's power of absorption and renewal, even Whitman's romantic sense of an essentially benign natural scheme falters at, in Kristeva's phraseology, "the boundary of what is assimilable," the relentless element of decay and organic turnover:

Something startles me where I thought I was safest
I withdraw from the still woods I loved,
I will not now go on the pastures to walk,
. . . .
Is not every continent work'd over and over with sour dead?

Where have you disposed of their carcasses?
. . . .
I will run a furrow with my plow, I will press my spade through the sod and turn it up underneath,
I am sure I will expose some foul meat.

(*Leaves* 211)

It's true that in the second section of the poem there is a tribute to the world's mysterious chemistry, but like Heaney in the poem quoted above, Whitman refuses to yield to easy romantic platitude; "I am terrified at the earth," he writes at one point. The encounter for both poets, using Kristeva's phrasing again, is with "a massive and sudden emergence of uncanniness, which . . . harries me as radically . . . loathsome" (2). Sebastian's garden in Tennessee William's *Suddenly Last Summer* is likewise possessed of this uncanniness tracing to forgotten evolutionary life; it contains "some of the oldest plants on earth" and is of a sinister, stifling lushness. The burgeoning feminine garden, continuous with Sebastian's smothering mother, is described at the start of act 1:

> . . . a mansion of Victorian Gothic style in the Garden District of New Orleans. . . . The interior is blended with a fantastic garden, which is more like a tropical jungle, or forest, in the prehistoric age of giant fern-forests when living creatures had flippers turning to limbs and scales to skin. The colors are violent, especially since it is steaming with heat after . . . rain. There are massive tree-flowers which suggest organs of a body, torn out, still glistening with undried blood; there are harsh cries and sibilant hissings and thrashing sounds in the garden as if it were inhabited by beasts, serpents and birds, all of savage nature. (*Four Plays* 9)

This again belies the benign nature of Romanticism, suggesting repulsive amphibious forms and fierce biological drives entangled in a sweltering rain forest. This is the delta of Venus, and—in the film version—Mrs. Venable, the Great Mother, rises from and descends into the garden by way of a gilded, birdcage-like elevator.

The organic enters into modern American literature in yet another way in the work of Flannery O'Connor. Her use of the Joycean epiphany is widely remarked, but her Catholic sense of incarnation, of the "incarnate Word" is not. Her stories begin as quasi-cartoons, her characters as flat, vain, inane caricatures who interact in mean and even hateful ways, mouthing moral platitudes all the while. Readers enjoy O'Connor's distanced, ironic, and often hilarious characterizations and her narrators' notorious lack of affect, until, without warning, those characters in effect commence to bleed literally or figuratively. In "A Good Man Is Hard to Find," the moment of incarnation is arguably when, the car having rolled over, Bailey's wife, heretofore a virtual nonentity, is described as "only" having a cut on her face and *a broken shoulder,* as she sits in a ditch holding the baby (126). "Broken shoulder" brings readers up short: There is an unexpected intrusion of real physicalness—as there is in the mother's heart attack in "Everything that Rises Must Converge"—causing readers to have to suddenly reconfigure their reading. The danger the "Good Man" car accident might have caused to the *baby* now crosses one's mind. It is as if the reader has become disoriented in the rollover, and from this point on, the story is recast—these are flesh and blood people. The nerdy Bailey calls out of the story frame to us: "Listen, . . . we're in a terrible predicament! Nobody realizes what this is." The guns become real, the anguish is real, these people have taken on physicalness like Christ, and they will suffer. When John Wesley takes his father's hand and the two are led into the woods by the shooter, the joke has ceased, and ironic distance has disappeared: "They went off toward the woods and just as they reached the dark edge, Bailey turned and supporting himself against a gray naked pine trunk, he shouted, 'I'll be back, Mamma, wait on me'" (128). This is unmitigated desolation—"zero at the bone." O'Connor's people become real in becoming physical.

It is hard to imagine, incidentally, the film *Fargo* coming about without an awareness on the part of the Coen brothers of O'Connor's work, though it may have.[9] The same transition from a cartoonish framing to a horrific living-ness occurs in the film. The wife whose kidnapping is central to the *Fargo* plot is the typical O'Connor blank, a characterless cliché about whom the viewer cares nothing. Then, in a critical scene, an incarnation occurs; the reptilian thug guarding her in a remote cabin, when the television reception fails, turns and appears to begin focusing pruriently on her body. Her head is hooded, and the material moves in and out with her frightened breathing—she is no longer a cliché. Viewers have the disturbing need to radically revise their sense of this woman's unimportance and to suddenly encounter the enormity of what is to befall her. Embodiment, our breathing flesh, situates our mysterious, vulnerable actuality.

5 Acquaintance with the Night: America and the Muse of Horror

Let others draw from smiling skies their theme,
And tell of climes that boast unfading light,
I draw a darker scene replete with gloom,
I sing the horrors of the House of Night.

—PHILIP FRENEAU, "The House of Night"

Poe is not a "fault of nature." . . . It is to save our faces that we've given him a crazy reputation, a writer from whose classic accuracies we have not known how else to escape.

—WILLIAM CARLOS WILLIAMS, *In the American Grain*

There are terrible spirits, ghosts, in the air of America.

—D. H. LAWRENCE, *Studies in American Literature*

THE UNITED STATES PROVIDES A SPECIAL GOTHIC STUDY and merits a chapter of its own in that American literature traces the journeying of the horror mode into a new region, a migration that tends to call into question attempts to strictly historicize the gothic genre or to confine its genius geographically. As America emerged increasingly more distinct from European culture and politics, its literature became no less "gothic." The immigration of the horror muse was so successful, in fact, that Leslie Fiedler could write by the late 1950s that "images of alienation, flight, and abysmal fear possess our fiction. Until the gothic had been discovered, the serious American novel could not begin . . ." (143). Even that gothic-modernist icon "The Waste Land" issued from an American poet, however Anglicized; or some would say from *two* American poets. This despite the fact that "American gothic" had at first been regarded as so unlikely as to be oxymoronic; the historical American landscape was considered inhospitable to literature in general and especially so to the dark romantic need for decadent tradition and antiquarian setting. Similarly antagonistic to gothic superstition and morbidity was the Enlightenment reason and optimism out of which the United States' cultural identity in large part emerged. But a mere few years after the nation's founding, in the rationalist ambiance of promising America, "screams were heard from the distempered ground" (Freneau 284). Near "the wide extended Chesapeake," Philip Freneau saw the gothic "black ship traveling" and raised horror's skull and crossbones banner as it were on behalf of his American literary descendants, issuing a terse manifesto: "Let others draw from smiling skies their themes / . . . I sing the horror of the House of Night" (267–68).

The view that prevailed for a long time—that the new continent would not be a seed ground for dark literary expression—ignored the fact that the body, the organism, is the gothic's a priori landscape, its essential *place*. The reactionary European opinion regarding the unfeasibility of an American gothic literature was abroad, however, even as late as the 1970s, in remarks like the following by Maurice Lévy:

> The American fantastic tradition lacks unity and depth. The reason for this is that it is not rooted in a homogeneous . . . culture. . . . To create an adequate atmosphere for a fantastic tale, we must have old houses and medieval castles that materialize in space the hallucinatory presence of the past, the houses we can find *authentically* only on the old continent. (36)

Only in the comparatively recent work of Lovecraft does Lévy see the requisite "surfacing of the primordial in the contemporary." Lévy's Eurocentrism creates weaknesses in his generally sound analysis of Lovecraft's work. In discussing the latter's predilection for seaports, for instance, "whence anything could come," Lévy refers to these ports as "oriented toward the old continent" (36). Lovecraft's work, on the contrary, is Pacific and Antarctic oriented, privileging the China trade and the South Sea Islands, where Captain Obed of Innsmouth, Zadock reports, found out more than was good for him (*Innsmouth* 60). In general, for that matter, the uncanny is likely to make its entry into the New England imagination from Pacific, South Atlantic, Caribbean, or Arctic/Antarctic locales, as it does in Poe's *The Narrative of Arthur Gordon Pym,* Sarah Orne Jewett's "The Foreigner" and "Captain Littlepage," and Lovecraft's "At the Mountains of Madness," or earlier on in the actual, or alleged, incursion of voodoo lore into Puritan Salem from the Barbados via the domestic servant Tituba. And a recent article by Andrew Fieldsend refers to "the grotesque Pacific in Moby Dick" (1). Both *Benito Cereno* and *Moby Dick* received inspiration from real events on the seas off the western coast of South America, the first from the seizure by slaves of a Spanish merchant ship, and the second from the sinking of the Nantucket whaler *Essex* by an angered Pacific sperm whale—a consequence of which was a notorious occurrence of cannibalism aboard the only surviving boat. The geographical coordinates in *Arthur Gordon Pym*, a book also influenced by the *Essex* horror, are set forth on Poe's extended title page and are far from Europe; they go from Nantucket south to "the eighty-forth parallel of Southern latitude" and ominously "still farther south" (*Selected* 239).

Poe's sea novel is atypical among his works, however, which largely reflect an introverted literary aesthetic that ignores American location and arguably does not contribute significantly to the development of a particularly *American* gothic literature as such in any obvious way. Brockden Brown and Freneau, by contrast, had been cognizant of writing within a developing American macabre tradition, discovering native gothic materials, and breaking ground in literary horror. Fiedler sees Brown as in fact having himself overcome most of the supposed blocks in the way of Americanizing horror: "[H]e single-handed and almost unsustained, solved the key problems of adaptation" (145). Some six years prior to Poe's birth, Brown writes in a preface to *Edgar Huntly* (1803):

> One more merit the writer may at least claim; that of calling forth the passions and engaging the sympathy of the reader, by means . . . unemployed by preceding authors. Puerile superstition . . . Gothic castles and chimeras, are the materials usually employed to this end. The incidents of Indian Hostility, and the perils of the western wilderness, are [far] more suitable; and, for a native America to overlook these, would admit of no apology. (*Three Novels* 641)

Forty-three years later, the "perils of the western wilderness" would be starkly dramatized in another American cannibalism horror at Donner Pass in the Sierra Nevadas. Lévy probably has the more traditional work of Poe in mind, however, when he refers to the European bent of American macabre literature. "The Fall of The House of Usher" seems set in a British landscape, "Cask of Amontillado" is set in Italy, and so on. Diane Johnson sees Poe as more an English Romantic writer than an American one, arguing that he "wrote in a particular English literary tradition, in the Gothic mode popular in his day . . .

using the predominant motifs and genres of Romantic literature" (Poe, *Selected* xii).

But Lévy's argument would erroneously cast the whole American horror tradition in accord with the Poe model, or at least the Poe model Johnson, for one, advances. Lévy's view that actual European atmosphere was essential for true horror reflects the misperception Ernst Cassirer, for one, argued against—the idea that real objects and events, European castles, and so on, in this case, generate myth—as opposed to accommodating, reinforcing, and enabling myth. It is normally the case that *myth* generates myth, and myth is ubiquitous in all manner of discourse. The 1957 Wisconsin serial murder case involving Ed Gein, who gutted, dismembered, and skinned his victims, apparently influenced Thomas Harris in conceiving *The Silence of the Lambs*. But Harris was not a witness to the events in Plainfield, Wisconsin, that winter—the Ed Gein case became a part of American horror legend, and it was that, as much as the historical actuality, that played into Harris's novel.

And mythic leaps are relatively easy. Stephen King recalls, for instance, that it required no more than a casual "what if" remark on his wife's part—what if Dracula came to rural Maine—to trigger the beginnings of his vampire novel *'Salem's Lot*.

> That was really all it took. My mind lit up with possibilities, some hilarious, some horrible. I saw how such a man—such a *thing*—could operate with lethal ease in a small town; the locals would be similar to the peasants he had known and ruled back home, and with the help of a couple of greedy Kiwanis types . . . he would soon become what he always was: the *boyar,* the master. (introduction, xix–xx)

The absorbing process King describes occurred early in the history of the American novel; Kathy N. Davidson notes that the early novels

> fed upon and devoured . . . literary forms such as travel, captivity, and military narratives; political and religious tracts; advise books, chapbooks, penny histories and almanacs. It appropriated . . . non-literary forms such as letters . . . oral forms such as local gossip, rumor, hearsay. (12–13)

A surfacing of the basic gothic mythology occurred in the United States, as mentioned above, as early as a couple of years after independence, in "The House Night" (1778). Even a Christian, as well as rationalist, milieu did not prevent Freneau's eerie gothic exercise. The poem is justified by an introductory apologia, an "Advertisement," in which the author notes that the work is "founded upon the authority of Scripture" and that it references the text from Corinthians "the last enemy that shall be conquered is Death" (266). The poem's conceit is the visionary dream—"when Reason holds no sway." The theme is the death of Death who lies suffering upon his own death bed: "Death on the couch, / With fleshless limbs, at rueful length, was laid." Herein Death is a shadow of the figure-in-languishment of the quest romance, and the lands around are incorporated into his illness; the trees are fruitless as he is fleshless—only the deceptive blossoms of the poppy flourish (268–69). A compassionate young man sees to Death's dying needs as best he can. Though it is May, the month of fertility and vitality in nature, "No wild pinks blessed the meads, no green the fields, / And naked seemed to stand each lifeless tree." These sterile images mark the reign of Thanatos and the denial of the vitality associated with Eros-Spring. Death is suffering, as death's victims normally do, not a split-second end to existence but a protracted and humiliating agony "midst grief, in ecstasy of woe run mad" (270). He dies in terror that the Devil, not content with his soul, will find his body too, his "moldering mass of bones." The *physical* terror of death's coming breaks through the poem's theological surface; beneath the poem's nods to Christian interests and its concluding perfunctory piety, lie the biological-vegetational tropes of decay, wasting, and unlife. The poem's real or at least horror conclusion is the dreaded approach of "woeful forms," hell having heard of the imminent death, as Death dreaded would happen:

> At distance far approaching to the tomb,
> By lamps and lanterns guided through the shade,
> A coal-black chariot hurried through the gloom,
> Specters attending, in black weeds arrayed.

(286)

In effect, American literature had only to let the traditional, archetypal imagination in play here find its place in the field of the new continent and its realities for gothic thematics to find their niches as they had begun to do in Freneau's poem and would significantly do in the work of Brockden Brown by around 1796. Puritan theology and its preaching of infernal punishment had of course still earlier provided a rich native vein of macabre invention. Joyce Carol Oates notes

how uncanny, how mysterious, how unknowable and infinitely beyond
their control must have seemed the vast wilderness of the New World
to the seventeenth-century Puritan settlers! The inscrutable silence of
Nature . . . that not heralding God, must be a dominion of Satan's.

So would the Pacific later seem to Ahab. Oates remarks the dark anxiety suggested by the titles of early American religious texts such as *Day of Doom,
Thirsty Sinner, Groans of the Damned, Memorable Providences Relating to Witchcraft and Possessions*—"these might be the titles of lurid works of gothic fiction" (1–2).

Despite the Colonial Puritan projection of a new American moral dispensation radically free of the Romish-pagan past, and the American Enlightenment vision of a likewise non-nostalgic and unsuperstitious clear day dawn-
ing, the country early on had had its own lapse into "medieval," inquisitional
hysteria in the Salem trials. And earlier still William Bradford in his history of
Plymouth Plantation had had to acknowledge by 1642 that "things fearful to
name . . . have broke forth in this land"—fornication, sodomy, and bestiality
among them (351). One case of the latter, involving a boy named Thomas
Granger, provided the material for a documentary poem of Charles Olson's
that appeared in a posthumous 1971 collection *Archeologist of Morning*. Using
mostly Bradford's own words, the poem gothically concludes with the boy's
death—the animals he had molested gathered in the execution pit with him.

> It being demanded of him
> the youth confessed he had it [bestiality] of another
> who had long used it in old England
> and they kept catle togeather.
>
> And after executed about ye 8. Of Septr, 1642
> A very sad spectacle it was; for first the mare,
> and then ye cowe, and ye rest of ye lesser catle,
> were killed before his face, according to ye law
> Levit: 20:15
>
> and then he him selfe
> And no use made of any part of them.

(n.p.)

The antiquated diction and spelling, the theocratic cultural setting, and the backdrop of taboo biological impulse heighten the terrible darkness of the execution scene, creating the kind of hallucinatory materialization of the past that Lévy, as noted above, would suggest America necessarily lacks.

Traces of this sort of dark imagination were notable too in colonial reading habits, which were notoriously drawn to the dark and sensational. The maiden's-virtue-in-jeopardy theme, dear to the sentimental novel and the gothic both, was popular. "The new American nation," Carroll Smith-Rosenburg observes, "and the new middle class were formed at least in part by these lurid tales" (Scarry 160). As early as the 1680s, a Boston book merchant sold a record sixty-six copies of the *History of the Damnable Life and Deserved Death of Dr. John Faustus*. Fiedler notes the proximity of the American myth itself to this Faustian one: "[T]hey held in common the hope of breaking through all limits and restraints, of reaching a place of total freedom where one could with impunity deny the Fall" (143).

The records of circulating libraries of the day indicate that the eighteenth-century gothic novels of Radcliffe, Lewis, and many others published by Minerva Press (Brockden Brown's British publisher) terrified the New England region at the time, and in a preface to "The Algerine Captives" (1797), an American writer "speaks of a dairymaid, Dolly, and a laborer, Jonathan, who 'amused themselves into so agreeable a terrour with the haunted houses . . . of Mrs. Radcliffe that they were both afraid to sleep alone'" (Lévy 13 n12). America thus feasted on the European literature in the genre before establishing its own gothic voice, but when it did, the voice was formidable and the material, as earlier mentioned, in time became less identifiably European in influence. Fiedler argues that the novels perhaps most often cited as the greatest American achievements—*The Scarlet Letter, Moby Dick,* and *Huckleberry Finn*—are at root gothic and that "it is not merely a question of certain trappings of terror" (137). In *Huckleberry Finn,* he notes "the delirious visions of Huck's father, the body dragged at midnight from the grave, the signs and portents of impending disaster discovered in howling dogs and slaughtered snakes, the ghostly visions through the fog" (142). That Fiedler feels the need to spell out the gothicism of these novels, something he would not do in the case of *The Monk* or *The Mysteries of Udolpho,* also indicates one of the things that differentiates American gothic from the European examples of the genre—a less obvious paying of respects to the familiar gothic conventions, a disguised gothicism that often puts itself forward as something else such as boyhood adventure or the South Sea tale.

American "True Crime" novels following upon Capote's *In Cold Blood* (1965) likewise have tended to have a decided gothic undercurrent. Thomas Thompson's *Blood and Money,* for instance, narrates the macabre true story of a pretty young woman from the wealthiest of Texas social circles who is slowly and hideously poisoned by her physician husband who daily brings home pastries he has contaminated with putrid matter gleaned from hospital lab specimens. And *In Cold Blood* itself, while a "nonfiction novel," occupies a place among the darkest of American narratives. A wholesome American family on River Valley Farm on the high plains of western Kansas, far from the corruption of old Europe or even the U.S. big-city versions of that, are being approached along Interstate 70 from the east by a pair of wanton killers. The town of Holcomb, the Jeffersonian agrarian ideal with its amber waves of grain, is to be visited and savaged. A black Chevrolet proceeds inexorably toward the Clutter family home, the feral pair stopping to purchase rope and to approach a convent, seeking nun's stockings to wear over their faces during the planned atrocity. (As a child, one of the pair, a bed wetter, was beaten by nuns in the dark of night at an orphanage.) The killers are physically grotesque; one has stunted, childish legs poorly supporting an overdeveloped weight lifter's upper body. The other has a face the two sides of which clash in a disturbing mismatch.

Odd notes of foreboding occur in the Clutter home—the teenage daughter smells cigarette smoke when no one in the family smokes. The mother, who has for some time suffered overwhelming, unaccountable anxiety, confines herself to her bedroom. A neighbor recounts a visit to the Clutters during which she heard sobbing from Mrs. Clutter's room and, gothically enough, went upstairs and pushed open the door: "When she opened it, the heat gathered inside the room was like a sudden, awful hand over her mouth" (29). The Clutter daughter, Nancy, is sixteen and pretty, "the town darling." She bakes cherry pies and plays Becky Thatcher in a school play; it is mid-November, and she is looking forward to the upcoming Thanksgiving family gathering. The drifter with the mismatched face meanwhile drives ever nearer, looking forward to raping her before proceeding with the robbery in the earliest hours of that next Sunday. In the morning dark that terrible day, "certain foreign sounds" impinge on the normal western night ones—"on the keening hysteria of coyotes, the dry scrape of scuttling tumbleweed, the racing, receding wail of locomotive whistles"—American gothic motifs (5). The power of fact-

based horror narrative is such, and the transgression involved here is so heinous, that it feels improper to cast the fate of Nancy Clutter in terms of the
monster's pursuit-of-the-maiden horror trope, though mythically that
tradition's literary presence is undeniable, as is the horror backdrop of wailing and keening—coyotes in Kansas provide the weird chorusing wolves would
in a Transylvanian context.

There is no literary need of castle-keeps and medieval dungeons; the Clutter family cellar is dungeon enough when Mr. Clutter is suspended from its
pipes and the cellar echoes with his frantic inhalations as the intruders cut his
throat. Human physicality, again, marks the gothic's fundamental space—and
most any landscape will offer to the imagination biomorphic analogues to the
conventional high gothic ones. New England and Southern antiquarianism
have mostly replaced the European variety in modern American works of
horror, as after Poe the short story form replaced the novel as the genre's primary vehicle, and no doubt other conventions will in time replace them—Anne
Rice, Peter Straub, Stephen King, and Clive Barker would seem even now to
be returning gothic literature to its novelistic tradition, for instance. What is
necessary is some version of decadence or disintegration—the shambling, degenerate pair of losers in *In Cold Blood* are in effect deteriorating human constructions themselves. The waning of the Middle Ages offered two cultural
landscapes, one of new usages, styles, and energies set against the decaying,
cumbersome cultural matrix of feudalism. Any historical change that produces
a similarly disintegrating mise-en-scène presents an analogue of human organic decline that horror can make good use of. An abandoned mansion, "old"
by American standards, serves as well for a horror context as would a many
centuries older European one.

The American Southern Gothic has thus thrived on surviving vestiges of
the antebellum South. A two-landscape framework is evident in the second
paragraph of Faulkner's "A Rose for Emily":

> It was a big, squarish frame house that once had been white, decorated
> with cupolas and spires and scrolled balconies in the heavily lightsome
> style of the seventies, set on what had once been our most select street.
> But garages and cotton gins has encroached and obliterated even the
> august names of that neighborhood; only Miss Emily's house was left,
> lifting its stubborn and coquettish decay above the cotton wagons and
> the gas pumps—an eyesore among eyesores. (*Collected* 119)

Modern and contemporary gothic perception seems to find this kind of properly faded setting in which to express itself, even if, as in the film *Rosemary's Baby,* the setting is merely a formerly fashionable hotel now slightly gone to seed, a little off the beaten track, and just old enough to allow for unsavory rumors about its past to have accrued. And living in California, the youngest of American locations, did not prevent John Steinbeck from writing a superior American gothic story, "Johnny Bear," in which two sisters, not unlike Faulkner's Emily Gierson, are the remaining social exemplars in Loma, a Salinas Valley village in decline. The narrator is a foreman on a reclamation project involving the dredging of a swamp—from which a "heavy pestilential mist . . . sneaked out . . . every night and slid near to the ground" (145). The story is in fact enveloped in fog: "I saw the rags of fog creeping around the hill from the swamp side and climbing like slow snakes on the top of Loma" (159). One of the sisters, again not unlike Faulkner's Emily, commits a dark sexual transgression, becoming pregnant by a Chinese laborer on the place and shattering what dim sense of decorum and old nobility the shabby village had retained. Moving through the narrative is Johnny, a grotesque, bear-like figure, possessed of an idiot-savant ability to duplicate voices and overheard dialogues with tape recorder fidelity. These narrative ingredients come together to produce a full-fledged American dark tale. Indeed the point might be carried even further to note that American literature does not even depend on its *own* macabre historical heritage, never mind Europe's. As Dickinson writes, we don't need historical witchcraft, we find "all the Witchcraft that we need / Around us, every Day" (656).

Not that the United States does not have its especially horror-friendly times and places, however—the South, as just mentioned, being one. H. P. Lovecraft had the good fortune, given his gothic disposition, to be born in what was a decadent milieu by American standards—a traditional New England in decline and thus conducive to a nocturnal imagination—the circumstance that Van Wyck Brooks described as follows:

> The Yankee sun had shone over the world. It was time for the moon to have its say. . . . There were colonies of savages near Lenox, queer, degenerate clans that lived "on the mountain," the descendants of prosperous farmers. There were old poisoners in lonely houses. There were Lizzie Bordens of the village, heroines in reverse who served the devil. There were Draculas in the northern hills and witch-women who lived in sheds, lunatics in attics. (463)

Lovecraft editors Joshi and Schultz in fact note how the faded-Georgian Newburyport, Massachusetts, visited by Lovecraft in 1923, with its mansions hearkening back to the China trade, its run-down center, and its moribund nineteenth-century commercial buildings, inspired the author's exaggerated fictionalized version of it in the form of Innsmouth. Lovecraft himself wrote of his visit to Newburyport: "[T]here is to me something evilly fascinating in the decadent types which evolve in ancient and neglected backwaters" (*Innsmouth* 17). The biological nature of this image is striking—throwback organic forms evolving in backwaters. The marshes of the Parker River area and of the Cape Ann area in general resonate in the metaphor. But Lovecraft's native Rhode Island offered gothic possibilities too, ones that had been tapped as early as 1833 in an American true crime classic antedating *In Cold Blood* by well over a century. Catherine Williams's *Fall River: An Authentic Narrative* was published in Providence in 1833. In her account, the outcropping of archaic horrors in an American landscape is evident as surely as in the earlier fiction of Brockden Brown. Williams frames her nonfiction story of a contemporary Massachusetts murder in idioms and usages borrowed from the gothic literary tradition and is clearly aware of the emergence in an American context— if there had been any doubt they *would* emerge—of exotic horrors of the gothic kind.

Williams's book involves Sarah Cornell, a woman in her twenties, who was found hanged from a barn roof on the Rhode Island-Massachusetts border in December of 1832, her body evidencing someone's frantic attempt to work an abortion before she died. Sarah had been an enthusiastic attendant at evangelical revival meetings in and around Fall River. "[T]here was at the time a great reformation, as it is termed, in the neighborhood . . . a great stir about religion, and much going to meeting, and many professing" (68). Camp-meeting Methodism provided a new religious excitement in the New England area, especially among working class people not affiliated with the older, more staid, Congregational churches and most particularly among young female mill workers who could now venture out at night with religious justification and cultivate an energizing emotional experience in their otherwise monotonous lives. Problematically, however, these girls would often develop crushes on the younger, more charismatic itinerant preachers. Williams censures "that idolatrous regard for ministers, for preachers of the gospel, which at the present day is a scandal to the cause of Christianity" (4). The old dread of the *Catholic* cleric expressed in gothic literature here takes on an American evangelical form. In Lewis's *The Monk,* Lorenzo is indignant at the hypocrisy of Spanish Catholic clergy "who chaunted the praises of their God so sweetly" but "cloaked with devotion the foulest sins" (345). Now, in the youthful United States, it is the rogue Methodist preacher who infatuates audiences of working girls and then takes advantage of them. An investigation traced Sarah Cornell's path over the previous few years and found it recurrently corresponding to and crossing that of Reverend Ephraim Kingsbury Avery, a married preacher. "She was not only three years at Lowell, the greater part of which time she sat under his daily and nightly ministrations, but she heard him at Great Falls and at other places in the neighborhood of Boston" (77). The Reverend Avery turned out to have been Sarah's "pastoral advisor" as well as that of many other young women with whom he was daily shut up in his study, "which stood at the head of the stairs and contained a bed; and was rather remote from the sitting room and lodging room of his wife" (78–79).

One aspect of the doubts that once prevailed regarding the viability of an American literary gothicism, Fiedler notes, was that

> the gothic . . . had been invented to deal with the past and with history from a . . . Protestant and enlightened point of view. But what could one do with the form in a country which, however Protestant and enlightened, had (certainly at the end of the eighteenth century!) neither a proper past nor a history? (144)

But in Williams's book an irony works off just this alleged American shortcoming. The clerical iniquity the Protestant gothic had imagined as a scandalous idiosyncrasy of the Catholic European centuries, the dirty secret of shadowy Spanish and Italian cloisters, ironically manifests in the New World, and in of all things a reformist Protestant context. The buried past has gotten up and walks in new clothes. Here is the perverted religiosity of *The Monk* and *The Italian,* but with one of Protestantism's own in the role of the hypocritical clergyman-lecher. Here as well is the anima and animus convergence Fiedler cites as a primary gothic trope, "the haunted victim and the haunted persecutor . . . each the other's obsession" (131). Williams chronicles, too, institutional Protestant church intrigues—shades of Vatican conspiracies—mustered to protect the clerical perpetrator. She is convinced there has been collusion among Methodist leaders to cover up the minister's guilt. The illusion Fiedler refers to, "that the true source of moral infection is to be found only in the decaying institutions of Europe," is darkly undermined (401). There is a neo-gothic recognition here that, deeply, there is no reformation; the erring past has not been given the slip but instead reemerges, overthrowing the myth of the United States as a renewed world. Physicality, the unpredictable, dangerous force of sexuality, will have its say, enabling—to return to Lévy's phrase—the "surfacing of the primordial in the contemporary."

The New England setting in towns such as Fall River was being dramatically altered at this time—virtually swept by an economic revolution that was creating squalid industrial towns housing a drifting factory-worker population. Williams notes that there were at least forty thousand spindles in operation in Fall River at the time, "and it is only twenty-one years since the erection of the first manufactory" (8). Sarah, the innocent in danger of violation, negotiates this ambiguous and altering landscape in the evening shadows—red brick mills standing amid faded, once-wealthy houses, empty traditional churches suggesting a faltering ecclesiastical structure, everywhere signs of a fading *gemeinschaft* culture. This provides an American matrix analogous to the ancient Catholic cultural one, with its moldering feudal infrastructure that had fed the earlier gothic imagination. The essential horror idiom of this narrative, the gothic overcast pervading Sarah Cornell's evening excursions through Fall River, was not lost on Williams, and she anticipates the irony of Fiedler's much later observation that in the United States "certain special guilts awaited projection in gothic form. A dream of innocence had sent Europeans across the ocean to build a new society immune to the compounded evil of the past" (143). Williams writes:

> In the countries of Europe . . . scarce a village or hamlet is past [*sic*], where attention of the traveler is not called to some circumstance of notoriety connected with the history of the place. . . . [H]ere once stood the monastery of some religious fanatics. Here was the cell of an anchorite, and here the home of . . . unbridled licentiousness. . . . [T]his was the scene of a black and midnight murder. Here dwelt the witches of yore, and here the sorcerers. (14)

She contrasts this European environment with that of the new world, in which it was first thought that the old world's "unenvied distinctions conferred by the monuments of former greatness and vengeful crimes" had been set aside. But in the narrative of Sarah Cornell's terrible fate, things turn menacing:

The primeval curse which spreads over the whole earth, has not left
our plains and vallies without some demonstrations of its universal-
ity . . . and the cry of murder, borne on the midnight blast, has sometimes been heard, even in some of the most secluded parts of happy
America. The traveller in the future ages . . . shall point to the lowly
grave on the side of yonder hill, and say "even here has the curse been
felt . . . has murder stalked abroad . . . here executed a scheme of cruelty which the savages of the western woods might have shrunk from."
Here at this lonely grave whose . . . stone just tells the *name and age of
a female*, . . . shall the young and beautiful read the warning against the
wiles of man. (14–15)

There are no feudal ruins on those New England hills, but the classic horror materials—the convergence of old and new landscapes; the merging of sex,
religion, and treachery; the villainous cleric in pursuit of the maiden—are all
near at hand. There is even, it might be noted, a presumptive transgression of
a gynecological nature in the attempted abortion—something looking forward
to Popeye's perverted abuse of Temple in Faulkner's *Sanctuary.* Patricia Caldwell, editor of a 1993 edition of Williams's book, remarks that the author,
"wishing to shield her subject—and specifically her subject's body—from 'indelicate exposure,' passed quickly over much of the medical testimony offered at
the trial." That testimony included, Caldwell notes, autopsy reports detailing
things like the precise measurements of the fetus and "a detailed exploration
of Cornell's recent menstrual history, including testimony about her bedding
and underclothing as proof of her menses just prior to the camp meeting" (xix).

Williams's apostrophe quoted above acknowledges her narrative's conscious gothicism in her reference to "the primeval curse" and at the same time
exploits the historical gothic graveyard setting and the genre's phraseology in
"the cry of murder, borne on the midnight blast." Her account calls into question Protestant reformational optimism, New England Puritan optimism, and
eighteenth-century Enlightenment optimism, about the possibility of escaping or transcending the past—as Poe's "Gothic emtombments," Camille Paglia
notes, would later "shut down the American frontier and repeal the idea of
progress" (*Personae* 572).

* * *

Williams's book, as an early instance of gothicized American crime literature,
or of American literature examining crime of gothic proportions and impli-

cations, anticipates later American film, as well as literature, in which crime would take on gothic implications. A set of films from the 1980s particularly exemplify the melding of American crime and horror—movies such as *The First Deadly Sin* (1980), *Blowout* (1981), *True Confessions* (1981), *Tightrope* (1984), *Angel Heart* (1987), and *Fatal Attraction* (1987). The significance of these hybrid works in the twentieth-century development of the horror modality has yet to be critically clarified or creatively exploited, though *The X-Files, Silence of the Lambs, Seven,* and *Stigmata,* to mention a few examples, suggest their influence. Not that the 1980s films lacked for precursors; detective literature and horror had been edging toward each other for a long time—Poe of course comes to mind, and Radcliffe's *The Italian,* for example, is structured like a detective novel, its complex, mysterious elements explained and accounted for at the end. Conversely, a detective work such as Conan Doyle's *Hound of the Baskervilles* used gothic trappings extensively. Two or three of Hitchcock's works as well as Eastwood's *Play Misty for Me,* Alan Pakula's *Klute,* and Roman Polanski's *Chinatown,* the latter three of a decade earlier, might be seen as more immediately anticipating the five I have identified—certainly *Play Misty* anticipated *Fatal Attraction.*

Both Eastwood's film and *Fatal Attraction,* it should be noted, can be regarded more as heirs to the James M. Cain line of noir than to the Dashiell Hammett–Raymond Chandler one. Like *Play Misty* and *Fatal Attraction,* Cain's work, while almost always mentioned in discussions of the hard-boiled detective genre, did not include a detective element. Whatever detection went on in Cain's novels—Keyes's sleuthing in *Double Indemnity,* for example—was distinct from the narrator (Huff in *Indemnity*) and even directed against him, and detection is marginal in *The Postman Always Rings Twice* and *Mildred Pierce,* if it is there at all. Cain's influential work in fact calls for the employment of the term *hard-boiled crime* literature rather than *hard-boiled detective.* Lawrence Kasdan's neo-noir *Body Heat* (1981) is another film more specifically in the Cain line than in that of Chandler and Hammett. It turns on the kind of gothic, Faustian element that typically informed Cain's work—the making of a mortally evil decision or pact and the fateful coming around of consequence.

By now it is something of a commonplace, in fact, that the tough crime tradition in America rejected high-IQ deduction and sleuthing as its driving force and emerged as a distinct literary species having next to nothing to do with the whodunit model. The film noir paradigm arguably always provided an open invitation to gothic influences and has easily accommodated narratives in which realism undergoes incursions of the uncanny, enchanted, pathological, or hallucinatory—*Chinatown* or *Wolfen,* for instance. Alan Parker's *Angel Heart* begins by rigorously establishing the hard realism of Dashiell Hammett—the rather seedy office of the seen-it-all, acerbic private investigator, the well-to-do client who offers a caper off the track of the detective's usual divorce-insurance rounds, and so forth. But in this case the gumshoe, it turns out, has by no means seen it all yet. The film's tough-noir profile, its realistic dimension, belies its uncanny possibilities, the entertainment of "surmounted beliefs" like that of, here, the unconscious, murderous, Satan-indebted alter-ego. Contemporary American gothic, conversely, shows signs of fertilization by the noir detective mode—in the narrative voice in Stephen King's work, for example, where bleak, Chandleresque similes often occur: "His face looked sad and old, like the glasses of water they bring you in cheap diners" (*'Salem's Lot* 592). Noir and horror share an interest in rejected, dejected locale and mood. *The X-Files,* too, suggest a surreal rendering of the American noir crime tradition, but much earlier, the novels of Raymond Chandler and James M. Cain were tending toward a hallucinatory aesthetic themselves, as were Ross MacDonald's a little later and as James Ellroy's presently are.

The medium of film, structured along the lines of dream, drew out the nightmare qualities already implicit in the dark crime texts of Cain, Chandler, and Hammett. "Cinema is 'like' dream in its mode of presentation: it creates a virtual present, an order of direct apparition. That is the mode of dream. . . . The dreamer is always 'there,' his relation is . . . equidistant from all events" (Langer, *Feeling* 412–13). The original noir films, pre-video, were of course viewed in the dreamscape darkness of the public cinema, and dark pulp fiction gained a yet greater darkness in translation, the later introduction of a gothic dimension to the genre completing the hybridization, as noted, in the 1980s. Brian DePalma has been arguably the contemporary director most sensitive to noir's horror dynamics as he returns, in a surreal mode, to classic film noir images—the first of the serial murders in *Blowout,* for instance, reprises the night murder of Archer in John Huston's *The Maltese Falcon,* the victim crashing backward through a construction area fence and downhill into a dark urban excavation. Films such as *True Confession, Blowout, Tightrope, Wolfen, The First Deadly Sin,* and *Silence of the Lambs* are a notable few among many to similarly conflate noir and gothic traditions to create a crossbred form—*Angel Heart,* perhaps the most powerful rendering of the hybrid so far, did so with astonishing power and a kind of gothic perfect pitch. The film interweaves Ameri-

can horror thematics with an elegant and terrible surrealism. The bleak landscape of upstate New York situates a sinister institutionalism that harkens back
to the church institutions of classic dark romantic imprisonment. Caribbean-
African-American occultism parades weirdly along New York back streets and
ties in later with a Creole Louisiana version of the same thing. Santeria altars
situate a glut of Catholic and Voodoo objects eclectically assembled, including the eyes-in-a-dish icon tracing back to the hagiography of St. Lucy discussed in chapter 2. The chicken-blood rituals of these sects blend uncannily
with motifs of necromancy and incest, with the wealthy occultism of Margaret "the witch of Wellesley" and her father, as well as with the carnival fortune-teller world of Coney Island, and the lust for 1940s crooner fame that
leads to a Faustian bargain with Lucifer. The film is a tour-de-force of American gothic-noir, and we will be discussing other 1980s detective-horror hybrid
films in future chapters. This mode closes the traditional investigator's distance
from the material being investigated and collapses the cerebral, detached investigative model. *Chinatown* ends with Jack Nicholson vanquished and overwhelmed, and the fate of Mickey Rourke, the gumshoe in *Angel Heart,* is worse
yet. The detective in this film genre becomes eminently vulnerable, descending into the dark night of the soul usually associated with horror invention—
witness Clarice Starling in *Hannibal,* Scully and Mulder in many *X-Files* episodes, and so on. In *Wolfen,* the tough and streetwise detective (Albert Finney)
disintegrates in the face of a preternatural challenge. In *Tightrope,* the Clint
Eastwood character, likewise tough and experienced, becomes lost in the por-
nographic labyrinth an investigation takes him into. The investigator (John
Travolta) in *Blowout* is emotionally mangled despite his efforts to technicalize
the investigation and distance himself through his electronic expertise. In these
films, contrary to the cerebral detective story tradition in which, as Linda
Badley describes it, "the rational subject separates itself from the body of evidence," there is no such remove; rather the protagonist "descends into primal
fear and desire. It is a loss of ego in cellular chaos" (Badley 10).

Unlike the prior, analytic detective model, the American tough-detective
genre often veers close to literary gothicism's extravagant transgressions
wrapped, as in *Chinatown,* in intricate layers of plot. This was so even before
noir fiction became translated into a major film genre. Chandler's works provide numerous examples of grotesque, quasi-gothic characters such as the
hissing, childish-murderous Carmen Sternwood of *The Big Sleep.* And Phyllis,
in James M. Cain's novella *Double Indemnity,* as opposed to the parallel charac-

ter in Billy Wilder's film, was a literal witch, a monster and serial murderer numbering children among her victims—a precursor of Annie Wilkes in *Misery,* who is likewise a nurse-murderer. Cain's book concluded with a full measure of horror tropics and atmospherics. Phyllis and Huff, having fled California, are aboard a ship in the Gulf of Mexico but are aware their options have run out. Phyllis tells Huff that "the time has come," and when he asks what she means, she replies, "For me to meet my bridegroom. The only one I ever loved. One night I'll drop off the stern of the ship. Then, little by little I'll feel his icy fingers creeping into my heart." A shark is following the ship; Huff as narrator notes, "I saw a flash of dirty white down in the green." As Phyllis grooms for her fatal leap, Huff describes her ritual preparations in their stateroom:

> She's made her face chalk white, with black circles under her eyes and red on her lips and cheeks. She's got that red thing on. It's awful looking. It's just one big square of red silk that wraps around her, but it's got no arm-holes, and her hands look like stumps underneath it. . . . She looks like what came aboard the ship to shoot dice for souls in the *Rime of the Ancient Mariner.* (465)

Here "realistic" crime literature is able to accommodate gothic preternaturalism, extraordinary psychopathology replacing the literal Satanic evil of the kind found in *The Monk* or, much more recently, in *Angel Heart* or *The Exorcist.* Unlike in *Angel Heart,* Satan does not manifest in Cain's *Double Indemnity,* but events approach that; the extremity of Phyllis's evil reaches at least the threshold of the supernatural, as does the evil of Alex in *Fatal Attraction.* The same is true of the evil in films such as *Tightrope, The First Deadly Sin,* and *Seven.* Film noir shared a complimentary framing with the gothic species all along—bleak, stylized landscapes and interior decor, investigation moving into uncharted territory, convoluted plot, aberrant psychology, claustrophobic spaces, disintegration, a sinister world viewed in nocturnal shadow, and so on. The American noir film tradition, spun off from the hard-boiled crime novel— itself born out of pulp fiction—now provides horror with a new and energizing frame, one as amenable to it as decadent aristocratic estates once were. Film noir offered it own version of the superannuated mise-en-scène anyway; the city in noir is largely a retro-reality. James Ellroy's current crime fiction, *L.A. Confidential,* and so on, is set in the Los Angeles of the 1950s, and the New York and New Orleans cityscapes of *Angel Heart* are those of an urban America from decades before the rise of suburbia. This city of classic crime fiction and

ACQUAINTANCE WITH THE NIGHT

film noir is by now a receding memory but endures as a crime-horror trope. It provides an apt setting for American psychopathological crime as well as for the whole range of traditional horror artifice. Part of a reconfigured and urbanized rendering of gothic archetypes, the noir cityscape suggests one recent signature of the horror muse's continuing work in the American grain.

Dark Carnival:
The Esoterics of Celebration

And terror's free—
Gay, Ghastly, Holiday!

—EMILY DICKINSON

Eros, like Dionysus, is a great and dangerous god.

—CAMILLE PAGLIA, *Sexual Personae*

None of these restrictions apply to
the Joker of course; the Joker is wild.

—*Westly's Rules of the Games*

THE DIALECTICAL TRANSACTIONS BETWEEN COMEDY
and horror are manifested graphically in carnival, the surface of which is festive, but which, given a slight shift in imagination, tracks off into the treacherous and transgressive. While Bakhtin takes up the comic spirit at the point
of its medieval carnival manifestations, his view regarding the wellsprings of
the comic imagination, not unlike Langer's theory, is grounded a priori with
reference to the body and physical life.[1] The "material bodily principle" informing the work of Rabelais and the carnival-informed works of the early Renaissance, he argues, is an inheritance from folk culture, and its leading images
address biological vitality—"fertility, growth, and a brimming over abundance"
(*Rabelais* 18–19).

I think Denis Donoghue is correct in noting that such concerns in Bakhtin's
work are not far removed from those evident in C. L. Barber's already refer-

enced study of Shakespeare's festive comedy (127–28). Bakhtin's analysis of carnival, Barber's of Elizabethan holiday, and more recently Terry Castle's of masquerade's "radical festivity" are of interest in terms of horror in that all deal with the suspension of prosaic time and the establishment of a temporal frame in which ordinary social assumptions are in abeyance. This condition was originally part of an act of utopian imagination; Castle's characterization of original masquerade would apply to carnival as a whole—"the giddy, estranging visual play, the exquisite 'comedies of the body' informing the occasion . . . its dream of a perfected human community free of the ravages of difference and alienation" (107–8). But carnival images informed by the material bodily principle often occurred as well in what we would regard as macabre forms of social expressions, dark homages to mortality. The cemetery of the Innocents at Paris, serving twenty of the city's parishes, was a popular medieval gathering place and, it would seem, one expression of carnival's ghastlier folk elements and degradation impulse. This mortuarial comedy of the body situated a pageant of gruesome inspiration:

> The old dead had to be continually disinterred . . . to make room. . . . Skulls and bones piled up . . . were an attraction for the curious. . . . Shops of all kinds found room in and around the cloister; prostitutes solicited there, gallants made it a rendezvous, dogs wandered in and out. Parisians [who] came to tour the charnel houses [and] watch burials and disinterments . . . shuddered as the Dead One blowing his horn entered from the Rue St. Denis leading his procession of awful dancers. (Tuchman 506–7)

The darker possibilities of masquerade are explored as well in Poe—in "Hop Frog," "Masque of the Red Death," "King Pest," and "Cask of Amontillado." Castle, as mentioned earlier, identifies "an aura of excitement and moral danger" surrounding masquerade, an atmosphere that is notably amenable to horror. "Carnival," "revel," "romp," and so forth—like the contemporary usage "to party"—carry both festive and illicit connotations, the latter stemming from an implied liberty, which can enable aberrant impulses and lead to a carnival of the perverse.[2] The Woodstock versus Altamont, flower children versus Manson family, oppositions of the 1960s, for example, played out very different scenarios of suspended social restriction and festive liberation. "Altamont was our Waterloo," writes Paglia, "there the Dionysian forces released by the Sixties showed their ugly face" (*Sex, Art* 212).

Comic and gothic sensibilities both gravitate toward the various genres of carnival—masque, parade, fair, festival. In the Disney Company's *Fantasia 2000* segment, based on Hans Christian Andersen's toy soldier story, it is the leering jack-in-the-box character, the harlequin in cap and bells out of masquerade tradition, who looms menacingly and has unsavory designs upon the little ballerina. It is likewise a nefarious jester figure who haunts Gotham in *Batman*. The narrator of Ligotti's "Last Feast of Harlequin" remarks that "clowns have often had ambiguous and somewhat contradictory roles to play." He has earlier observed that "the jolly, well-loved joker familiar to most people is actually but one aspect of this protean creature" (*Nightmare* 209). In his novel *It*, site of the demon clown Pennywise, Stephen King describes carnival tracking into horror territory as the evil clown exploits the circus's enticement to lure a five-year-old boy:

> "Can you smell the circus, Georgie?" George leaned forward. Suddenly he could smell peanuts! . . . He could smell cotton candy and frying doughboys. . . . He could smell the cheery aroma of midway sawdust. And yet . . . under it all was the smell of flood and decomposing leaves and dark storm drain shadows. That smell was wet and rotten. (13)

What Castle notes in her Bakhtinian study of masquerade characterizes carnival broadly and gestures toward revel's horror-comic synergy. As "promiscuous gathering," she argues, masquerade draws comedy and danger together, since, at least in its excessive forms, it embodies both potentials by licensing misrule, the subversion of routine, established reality (2). The gothic often situates precisely this transgressive, excessive carnival dynamic, the darker ramifications of carnival looseness. In a video rental store, I recently noted in passing a legend on one of the sleazier and more lurid horror-flick boxes, one which would tend to confirm Castle's observations: "EVIL LOVES TO PARTY." This suggests the carnivalesque regarded as a walk on the wild side and dark carnival's ancestry in "the circus side show, the phantasmagoria show, the wax museum, the Theatre du Grand Guignol . . . and the Theatre of Cruelty" (Badley 9). Crime and abomination blend in with and disguise themselves readily in the whirl of festive holidays. In *Angel Heart,* the macabre occult designs of Johnny Favorite and his Satanist cohorts are carried out in the midst of New York's 1943 New Years Eve celebration. A lone GI, Harold Angel, is lured from the Times Square holiday reveling to an apartment where he is ritually gutted, his heart eaten by Favorite while still beating. Montressor, in

"Cask of Amontillado," similarly takes advantage of "the supreme madness of the carnival season" to waylay his victim. And the psychopathic killer in DePalma's *Blowout* (John Lithgow) is also drawn to the highest pitch of festival to carry out his murder of Sally, whose screams are drowned out by the sounds of celebration and fireworks. John Travolta must desperately navigate through this incongruous hilarity and celebration in a vain attempt to prevent the murder of the young woman. It is not surprising that the hallucinatory atmosphere of carnival, its anarchic and destabilizing elements, make it anathema to the hysterical personality for whom stability and predictability are at a premium. Stallybrass and White note that in Freud's *Studies on Hysteria,* "many of the images and symbols which were once the focus of various pleasures in European carnival have become transformed into the morbid symptoms of private terror" (174). In Freud's study, they note, "carnival debris spills out of the mouths" of hysterical patients. "Don't you hear the horses stamping in the circus?" one woman desperately implores Freud (171).

Festival's primary association, of course, places it in a more benign and comic context. Comedy, according to Langer, "is an art form that arises naturally wherever people are gathered to celebrate life; in spring festivals, triumphs, birthdays, weddings, or initiations" (*Feelings* 331). Bakhtin's description of the original carnival matrix has been referred to previously—carnival's disestablishment of official social norms, its suspension of the allegiance normally afforded workaday reality, its revivalist function. This Dionysian disestablishment is evident right away in Isak Dinesen's story "Carnival," for example, which opens with a party related to the Copenhagen Opera Carnival of 1925. Four pretty young ladies are present, one of whom is Soren Kierkegaard. Reality teeters like this in the atmosphere of revel, and gender identities in this tale fluctuate wantonly. Such carnivalesque looseness, though mild enough here, can open the way to licentious misrule, generating what might be called festive *horror,* a genre in which carnival's "material bodily principle," its base of promiscuous carnality, blasphemy, scatology, and ritual degradation, is translated from a comic social discourse into a pathological one. Then the joyous, however crude, bio-erotic thematic pattern of normal carnival is antithetically rendered, and its weirder prospects aired. Referring to its "deadly siren song," Stephen King characterizes this sinister version of carnival as "the taboo land made magically portable, traveling from place to place and even from time to time with its freight of freaks and its glamorous attractions" (*Danse* 330). And Clive Barker, retrospectively regarding his work in the horror short story, remarks that after fourteen years "it's odd to revisit the carnival." He uses carnival metaphors to describe his macabre tales; they are "little journeys; little *parades*, . . . which wind away from familiar streets into darker and darker territory" (*Books* xiii).

The carnival or fair, often on the edge of town, locates phantasmic events in cases ranging from films such as *The Cabinet of Dr. Caligari, Black Orpheus,* or *Something Wicked This Way Comes* to literature such as Poe's "Masque of the Red Death," Hawthorne's "My Kinsman Major Molineaux," or Ligotti's "Harlequin." *Black Orpheus* (1959) may in fact present the quintessential film evocation of festival laced with menace as the malevolent figure stalking Eurydice transforms the masquerade, the jubilant rhythms and images of Carnival in Rio, into something ominous and hallucinatory—a spectacle of, to borrow Terry Castle's phrasing, "seething, grotesque, and paranormal forms" (53). The narrator in "The Last Feast of Harlequin" notes the wavering, unpredictable potentials of celebration in remarking Christmas holiday suicides in the town where the tale is set—suicides by individuals "who are somehow cut off from the vitalizing activities of the festival" (*Nightmare* 218). The story also references the abusive aspect of carnival tradition when the narrator observes the holiday reveler's shoving a victim in clown's dress from one to another. Harassment and humiliation of this kind and worse were part of the darker side of the historic carnival profile. At the Flemish *kermesse* of the sixteenth century

> rat poison salesmen swung strings of their victims in the air. Showmen exhibited madwomen gibbering in their chains. Young folk joined hands to skate . . . on ripe garbage. Organized fights pitted blind men with clubs against each other. . . . [B]eneath the frantic surface jollity lay somber violence. (Foote 118)

Even the villainous themselves can become ensnared in dark carnival's swirling surreality, as does Schedoni in Radcliff's *The Italian.* He travels back toward Naples with a guide and Ellena, whom he has recently attempted to murder, only to learn—erroneously as it turns out in the long run—that she is his daughter. The three come upon a carnival in a rural marketplace where "peasants in their holiday cloaths, and parties of masks crowded every avenue. Here was a band of musicians, and there a group of dancers; on one spot the outre' humor of a zanni provoked the . . . laugh of the Italian rabble" (273). The party of three become wedged by the crowd against a stage on which an amateurish vignette is being badly enacted. But like the "Trist" in "The House of Usher," this skit begins to converge uncannily with Schedoni's own situation and to seemingly proclaim his depravity. He looks away, but his guide, though unaware of the attempt on Ellena's life, "seized his arm, and pointing to the stage, called out, 'Look Signor, see! Signor, what a scoundrel! What a villain! . . . he has murdered his own daughter!'" (274).

Even when not sinister in and of itself, carnival can create an incongruously festive context for horror, as it does, for example, in the merry-go-round climax of Alfred Hitchcock's *Strangers on a Train*. In a similarly bizarre scene, the Ringling Brothers Circus rolls up to the contagious, quarantined town in Stewart O'Nan's *A Prayer for the Dying*, creating a weirdly incongruous tableau (131). These ironies define carnival's ambiguous potentials, an esoterics of celebration wherein cheerful and sinister elements may share the stage at revel, fair, masque, and so forth. Among the ancient protocols of the fair tradition, for example, a central one was "the peace of the fair," which enjoined a moratorium on grievances and disputes for the duration of the event. This etiquette was essential if the fairs/markets were to work as secure mercantile gatherings. On the other hand, in time—perhaps another evidence of the way in which carnival vitality degenerated postmedievally—the fair represented as much this protocol's very opposite, becoming associated with the revisiting of old disputes. In Ireland, the yearly Donnybrook Fair near Dublin became synonymous with brawling and the settling of scores. This carnival association with retaliation and thus the breach of the festive peace tradition is exploited by Poe in "Cask of Amontillado." Another example of the fair's wayward, transgressive possibilities appears in Thomas Hardy's *The Mayor of Casterbridge*, where the portrayal of a rural English fair would tend to bear out Terry Eagleton's negative characterization of carnival as "by no means as attractive a world as it sounds . . . full of aggression, male bravado, and coarse buffoonery" (207).

In the promiscuous atmosphere of the fair, and after some drinking, Michael Henchard falls in with a few of the more disreputable representative's of the fair subculture and ultimately sells his wife to one of them. Carnival becomes increasingly decadent, Bakhtin argues, as it is more and more separated in time from its vital folk origins. As happened in the special case of masquerade, carnival comes to speak to us "from the realm of temps perdu" (Castle 107). It turns into a lingering myth to which actual instances fail to measure up. American "carnivals" tend to be bland church affairs or at the other extreme shabby events like the "Gas Station Carnivals" in Thomas

Ligotti's tale of that name: "[O]nce a visitor had gained admittance to the actual grounds of the carnival, there came a moment of let down at the thing itself—that spare assemblage of equipment that appeared to have been left behind by a traveling amusement park in the distant past" (*Nightmare* 502). Festive elements thus frequently function ironically in dark literature—situating decadence and festive failure.

Coleridge's "Rime of the Ancient Mariner," for instance, commences with a wedding feast—that primary celebrational event with its associations of spring, fertility, and renewal. But it does so to set in motion a dialectical opposition. We encounter the classic makings of comedy at the outset of a narrative that is to be for the most part about anything *but* that. The poem's second stanza evokes a scene that is lilting and Elizabethan, the epitome of festive expectation:

The bridegroom's doors are opened wide
And I am next of kin;
The guests are met, the feast is set:
May'st hear the merry din.

Feasting, kinship, the merry din of celebration—these the wedding guest would bring to bear against the spectral figure, the "ancient" man who has accosted him and holds him with his "skinny hand." The mariner hinders the guest on his way to the fertility rite, the renewal ceremony, and brings a dark obsession, a spell to freeze the guest in his tracks. The guest is waylaid by this phantom figure and drawn away from celebration, much as Fortunato, in "Cask of Amontillado," is drawn away from the carnival by Montressor. The comic-horror polarity obtains: wedding, fertility, and abundance versus the skinny hand of lack, desiccation, and deterioration. The poles define each other; wedding feast in the "Ancient Mariner" functions as an ironic foil to the hellish journey to follow and a subversion of wedding's folk-festive potency.

In "Cask," masquerade costume lends a bizarre, operatic quality to the terror. This tale too occurs at the juncture of the comic and horror modes, beginning in the dreamlike ambivalence of the masquerade—the carnival being the traditional vehicle carrying the folk-aesthetic, body principle Bakhtin calls "grotesque realism." In all its vulgar energy, traditional carnival was a comic exercise. "During carnival time life is subject only to its laws, that is, the laws of its own freedom . . . it is a special condition of the entire world, of the world's revival and renewal" (*Rabelais* 7). But Montressor is psychologically immune to the revival spirit; he is not a participant in the main festival, which he, in the vein of Freud's hysteric patients, perceives as "madness." Stranded in his own resentments, and in violation of the "peace of the fair" folk tradition, he is driven by his revenge agenda toward the private execution ritual he has meticulously planned. He is analogous in type to the butts in the festive plays who "consistently exhibit their unnaturalness by being kill-joys. On an occasion 'full of warm blood, of mirth,' they are too preoccupied with perverse satisfactions like pride . . . to 'let the world slip' and join the dance" (Barber 8).

Turning away from the communal swirl of the carnival, Poe's tale moves underground, to the dank realm of the Romantic grotesque and to a cynical parody of the festive. The givens of carnival tradition are all in place, even the inverted world device, the Saturnalian reversal: "Do" is "don't" and vice versa. Montressor warns his servants not to go out while he is away in order to in-sure that they *will* indeed be gone on his return with his victim. Fortunato is appealed to repeatedly *not* to proceed into the underground as part of Montressor's plot that, on the contrary, he will proceed.

To the point here as well is the issue of laughter—the extensive laughter of Fortunato toward the conclusion of the tale. Bakhtin remarks the "disap-pearance of laughter's regenerating power" in the Romantic grotesque of which the gothic was an extension. In the new-grotesque, he observes, laugh-ter "was cut down to cold humor, irony, and sarcasm . . . there is no hint of its power of regeneration" (*Rabelais* 38). The revival laughter of the old medieval configuration is a far cry from that which Montressor hears issuing out of the crypt and is chilled by: "a low laugh that erected the hairs upon my head." And the closest he himself gets to laughter is mockery. Laughter is worked by the horror imagination for its own antithetical purposes. Part of the inverted, dark carnival project Poe's tale carries out is the supplanting of genuine laughter with bitter irony, in effect, a stunted laughter at laughter's expense. Fortunato's hysterical laughter has no rejuvenating energy and is powerless to overcome the morbid situation in which he finds himself. He appeals pathetically to the spirit of carnival thriving in the streets above, the exuberant festivity, but his own counterfeit exuberance is in vain. "Ha! Ha! Ha!—he! He!—a very good joke indeed. . . . We will have a rich laugh . . . over wine—he! he! he!" The gesture is toward wine and good fellowship, but the laughter merely echoes in the catacombs and the victim's appeals are answered with Montressor's satiric scorn—like a cruel child, he merely parrots Fortunato's pleas (*Selected* 227).

While macabre elements would seem always to have been involved in the comic pattern, Bakhtin suggests that in the folk-cultural, Rabelaisian days of carnival everything fell together finally in comic resolution—Paglia also suggests that in the pagan pattern, in Greek tragedy for example, "comedy always had the last word" (*Personae* 6). That paradigm survived into Rabelais's time, when folk-festive protocols and ritual based on laughter "built a second world and a second life outside officialdom, a world in which all medieval people participated . . . in which they lived during a given time of the year" (*Rabelais* 5–6). We may have difficulty conceiving of Rabelais's Middle Ages retaining a pagan vitality and informed by robust peasant laughter, but Paglia for one would ascribe that difficulty to modern criticism's retrospective projection of "Protestant high seriousness" upon pagan cultures whose "savage realities" led "not to gloom but to humor" (*Personae* 8). At any rate, a survival of the folk cultural attitude Bakhtin describes is arguably evident, for example, at the conclusion of Dinesen's "Carnival," expressed, appropriately, in a debate trope.[3] Signor Lothario quotes an old Danish saying that "everything has got an end, and foolery as well." Arlecchino's reply gives voice to the sensibility that Bakhtin argues informed the vigorous grotesque realism of carnival: No, she replies, "everything is infinite, and foolery as well" (121).

Bakhtin sees the emergence of Romanticism as marking a pseudo-revival of the traditional grotesque genre with in fact "a radically transformed meaning." The transition arguably enabled what we are calling "festive horror," a form adapting the old, essentially affirmative conventions of celebration to the service of a dark travesty of the carnival spirit—"Cask" being an obvious and cogent example. While elements of authentic carnival were retained, the carnivalistic genre, Bakhtin argues, acquired an individualistic outlook, taking on a "private chamber character. It became, as it were, an individual carnival, marked by a vivid sense of isolation" (*Rabelais* 36–37). Barber identifies another aspect of essentially the same historical watershed in the weakening of the folk dynamic in Elizabethan drama, the latter's professionalization:

> Shakespeare's theater was taking on a professional and everyday basis functions which until his time had largely been performed by amateurs on holiday. And he wrote at a moment when the educated part of society was modifying a ceremonial, ritualistic conception of human life to create a historical, psychological conception.

Hal's rejection of Falstaff in *2 Henry IV* marks the sea-change. Shakespeare here, Barber notes, "confronts the anarchic potentialities of misrule when it seeks to become not a holiday extravagance but an everyday racket" (14–15). Hal perceives Falstaff now not as an admirably carefree spirit but as a besotted old fat man who has misled him. Hal regrets his own former naivete and now affirms a disciplined, Apollonian attitude:

> But being awak'd, I do despise my dream.
> Make less thy body, hence, and more thy grace;
> Leave gormandizing. Know the grave doth gape
> For thee thrice wider than for other men.
>
> (5.5.55–58)

Insistent holiday revel is "gormandizing," a dangerous Dionysian indulgence. And "the grave doth gape" references one's appointment with mortality.

In *The Dialogic Imagination*, Bakhtin cites multiple other ways, besides those already noted, in which "Cask of Amontillado" makes use of carnival materials, transforming them into horror instrumentalities. The carnival matrix of food, laughter, death, drink, and sex, originally part of a robust assertion of life, is altered in Poe's tale. "The wholeness of a triumphant life, a whole that embraces death, is lost. Life and death are perceived solely within the limits of the sealed-off individual life" ("sealed off" being especially interesting here given Fortunato's fate and in general the gothic's radical, stifling enclosures). "Cask", Bakhtin argues, exemplifies the reconstituted Romantic grotesque version of carnival wherein the festive elements represent only twisted traces of the originally comic configuration:

> The entire . . . story is structured on sharp and completely static contrasts: the gay and brightly lit carnival / the gloomy catacombs; the merry clown's costume of the rival / the terrible death awaiting him; the cask of Amontillado and the gay ringing of the clown's bells / the horror at *impending death* felt by the man being immured alive; the terrifying and treacherous murder / the calm, matter-of-fact and dry tone of the protagonist-narrator. At the heart of the story lies a very ancient and time honored complex. . . . But the golden key to this complex has been lost: there is no all-encompassing whole of triumphant life, there remain only the denuded, sterile and, therefore, oppressive contrasts. (*Dialogic* 199–200)

The festive masquerade motifs in "Cask" and those in films such as *Blowout, Carnival of Souls,* and *Tightrope,* for example, are laced with such oppressive elements. The murderers in films such as *Psycho* and *Dressed to Kill* are, in effect, masquerade figures. Masquerade license—its "world upside-down" climate—provides a context for dark literary invention in Ligotti's already referred to "The Last Feast of Harlequin" as well. The story's narrator is an anthropologist and amateur clown drawn to a small Midwestern town's annual festival when he hears that clowns are included "among its other elements of pageantry." Like Lovecraft's "The Shadow over Innsmouth," or the movie *Angel Heart,* this tale involves a central character who believes his investigative drive is professional, antiquarian, or hobbyist when in reality it is an inexorable, preternatural tropism, a biological pull toward an appalling self-realization. His line "I had no idea where my disguise would take me that night" (Oates 434) resonates with masquerade's treacherous allure. Terry Castle notes that masque accommodates atavistic behavior and erotic taboos creating "a symbolic space wherein 'whirl is king'. . . a world of dizzying transformation." She quotes Roger Caillois's observation that in its extreme forms, masquerade involved surrender "'to that spasm, seizure, or shock which destroys reality with sovereign brusqueness.'" "Caillois has argued that shamanistic rites and other so-called primitive forms of festive mania derive their power from the *deeply gratifying bodily sensation* the participants experience" (italics added, Castle 53). A biological element in fervent festival is suggested here, a kind of collective ritual dance in which whirling there is a "labial and convulsive power."

Noting such masquerade eroticism brings to mind the amateur clowning element in the serial murder career of John Wayne Gacey. One wonders if Gacey, like Ligotti's character, at least at first thought that his interest in clowning was unproblematic and incidental when in fact it appears to have been an expression of a depraved imagination relishing masquerade's uncanny "free familiar contact" wherein perverted erotic-homicidal possibilities might be realized through the unusual possibilities for fraternization and anonymity the clown context offered. Evil and monstrosity look for a complementary setting in which to work; vampires don't operate at any old time but materialize in a specific situation and ritual context: "Into the pallid night emerging, / Wrapped in their flapping capes, routinely maddened / By a wolf's cry" (Wilbur 196).

In its suspension of established order, the carnivalesque situates such a complementary frame for the psychopath who himself perpetrates, to quote Philip

Simpson, "a violent penetration of boundaries that upsets epistemological, ontological, and teleological conceptions" (12). (This derangement perhaps comes through to those children who are disturbed by live clowns and their antics—a not uncommon reaction that would seem to stem from the child's inability to grasp the publicly sanctioned nature of behavior that appears to be hysterical.) Carnival mayhem, it's world-out-of-kilter character, speaks to the psychopath's wanton desire to violate and affront "notions of propriety and civilized conduct." It can also, in actual and in literary terms, facilitate entry into an uncanny landscape, what Simpson characterizes as "the mythic territory reserved for the most extreme taboo. . . ." Gacey, like Montressor, executed his macabre projects with single-minded and systematic perfection. Carnival-masquerade provides a useful *messiness*—Simpson's term—a social derangement in which the psychopath's narrow, obsessive agenda can be carried out (11–12). Holiday departure from social high seriousness is presumably healthy, but careless tinkering with elements of social order—and this situates the conservative conviction of horror—can be catastrophic. "Go read *King Lear*," Paglia suggests, "to see the anarchy and wolfishness, the primitive regression that results from a sentimental deconstruction of social institutions. Stormy nature in our hearts and beyond the gates is ready to consume us all" (*Sex, Art* 31).

Murderous psychopathology in real life, Simpson notes, is characterized by the "aesthetic decentering of meaning common to horror narrative strategy." The shifting terms of festival darken easily into the evil phantasmagoria, and the identity-play of masque suits the promiscuous murderer well since, as Simpson notes, "the murderer's identity is not solidly cast" (11).[4] In the film *Tightrope,* the serial murderer aggressively and eerily mixes and merges his identity with that of the detective (Clint Eastwood); slipping out of the role of the pursued, he takes on that of the pursuer—a classic carnival-Saturnalian inversion. The investigator becomes the object of investigation, the bearer of guilt; the police detective finds himself the subject of panoptic surveillance, caught in the psychic crosshairs of the criminal's gaze. Asked by his girlfriend if he is getting any closer to the killer, Eastwood replies: *"He's* getting closer to *me."* Carnival themes inform the movie—Eastwood tracks the killer through a warehouse in which carnival (Mardi Gras) paraphernalia is stored. Mardi Gras street celebration provides a context in which Eastwood's two young daughters interact unwittingly with the serial killer, who is in clown dress, handing out balloons. He releases one balloon, the upward traveling of which the camera follows in a probable allusion to the pedophile pickup scene in Fritz Lang's classic *M.*

Letting the world slip, the freedom of festival, seems to the so inclined, ones like the maniac in *Tightrope,* to suggest and sanction transgression, and among demonic things nothing is more bizarrely so than the demonic parade, fair, carnival, or masque. Bakhtin notes the vulgar physicality that once grounded popular-festive celebration, that "in the atmosphere of Mardi Gras, reveling, dancing, music were all closely combined with slaughter, dismemberment, bowels, excrement . . ." (*Rabelais* 223–24). In gothic presentation, the latter elements, without the ameliorating framework of festive renewal, darkly revise the carnivalesque model. This is the case in "Masque of the Red Death," where again festive motifs incongruously contextualize gruesome action and a weird bio-horror prevails:

> The "Red Death" had long devastated the country. No pestilence had ever been so fatal, or so hideous. Blood was its Avatar and its seal—the redness and the horror of blood. There were sharp pains and sudden dizziness, and then profuse bleeding from the pores, with dissolution. The scarlet stains upon the body and especially upon the face of the victim, were the pest ban which shut him out from the sympathy of his fellow men. And the whole seizure, progress and termination of the disease, were the incidents of half an hour. (*Selected* 156)

The material bodily principle, carnival's bent toward physicality, is here expressed in a morbid idiom. Against the threat of this devastation, Prospero would muster the force of festival tradition—Eros in the face of Thanatos. Religious asceticism on the one hand and—Prospero's choice—carpe diem abandon on the other were the typical responses to the terrors of plague. Prospero's response suggests, as Bakhtin notes, a Boccaccian configuration: "the *plague* (death, the grave)—a *holiday* (gaiety, laughter, wine, eroticism)." But "Masque" situates a disfigured Boccaccian theme in that "in Poe these contrasts are static and the thrust of the entire image is, therefore, oriented toward death" (*Dialogic* 200).

A similar use of a deviant carnival pattern is evident in Poe's "Hop Frog," a story discussed earlier, set in a historical time when, to use the narrator's description in Ligotti's "Harlequin," "madmen, hunchbacks, amputees, and other abnormals . . . were considered natural clowns . . . which could allow others to see them as ludicrous rather than as terrible reminders of the forces of disorder in the world" (*Nightmare* 209). Poe employs the kind of paired, opposed images that are characteristic of carnival thinking. "Hop Frog" transposes power and powerlessness, high and low, strong and weak. The story bears all the elements of carnival's Menippean reversals: The fool, a crippled, powerless dwarf who can only move in a distorted way and with great pain, gains ascendancy while the King and his privy-councilors, in monkey suits, are burned to death *en masse* in a masquerade ruse—a radical rendering of a carnival set piece, the decrowning of the carnival king (Bakhtin, *Poetics* 124–25). The high/low inversion is carried out to the extent that the dwarf, his revenge accomplished, ascends to the roof of the palace hall and away through the skylight in a victorious resurrection from the purging bonfire. The story has even included the carnivalesque irony that the ill-fated king of the piece, we are told, had a "Rabelaisian" sense of humor (Poe, *Selected* 228).

The incineration of the king and company fulfills not only the carnival-festive convention of decrowning but also that of consummation in fire; the king and his men become the "carnival trash" for bonfire: "In European car-nivals there was almost always a special structure (usually a vehicle adorned with all possible sorts of carnival trash) called 'hell,' and at the close of carni-val this 'hell' was triumphantly set on fire" (Bakhtin, *Poetics* 126). A flameless version of this tradition occurs in the Ligotti story mentioned earlier, when the "clowns," the trash of the Mirocaw winter carnival and masquerade, are hauled away from the town in a pickup truck to be deposited in the under-ground site where they will ritually dissolve into worms—tribute to the Con-queror Worm and a macabre, gothic enactment of the carnival degradation theme (Oates 450–51).

Castle notes that such dark employment of the masquerade topos was typical of nineteenth-century American literature, where it "was revived al-most exclusively in dreamlike, exotic, or morbid settings" (335). In Poe and Hawthorne, the masque is detached from its historical connection to real fes-tive occasion and from its role in realistic fiction. It becomes co-opted into what Castle characterizes as the era's "intensified subjectivity and increasingly pri-vate phantasmagoria" (332). In Poe, masquerade is "sinister and otherworldly"; in Hawthorne, it is "perverse—a fantastic omen of estrangement and death":

> Near the end of *Blithedale Romance* (1852), for instance, the hero, Coverdale, returning to the failing utopian community of Blithedale, stumbles upon an al fresco masquerade put on by the residents. . . . It strikes him as a hallucination or waking dream. This confused scene of Arcadian shepherds, Kentucky woodsmen, necromancers, "gay

Cavaliers" and "grim Puritans" mingling. . . . The disillusioned Cover-
dale flees from the "Fantastic rabble" like "a mad poet hunted by chi-
meras." The scene itself gives way to the macabre: The marvelous
Xenobia, the masquerade's organizer and "Queen" (also the woman
behind Blithedale itself), is soon after found drowned. (Castle 337)

Among nineteenth-century American writers, Hawthorne was perhaps the
most keenly aware of the decadent carnivalesque, of once naturally occurring
holiday merriment being untranslatable to American terms. He was also conflicted, well aware of the killjoy role of Puritanism—its determination to eradi-
cate every vestige of the European festive inheritance—an imaginative legacy
invaluable to writers and artists like himself. On the other hand, he distrusted
efforts to market a counterfeit Arcadian myth. The issue arises most explicitly in "The Maypole of Merry Mount," where the action turns on the question of whose vision of the "New World" will prevail, that of the Puritans or
that of the revelers who would carry over a romanticized version of the European carnival paradigm to the colonies: "Jollity and gloom were contend-
ing for an empire" (*Complete* 40).

"Maypole," which evokes much of the carnival system parodically, is of
course a fictionalized version of the actual confrontation that occurred in the
1620s between the Puritan Plymouth Plantation authorities and a settlement
of unaffiliated, libertine Englishmen over the issue of a maypole the latter had
erected in Mount Wollaston, Massachusetts. "All the hereditary pastimes of
Old England were transplanted hither"—flowers, banners, Morris dancers,
scapegoats, the Lord of Misrule, masqueraders in various guises including the
sexually suggestive garb of a he-goat (*Complete* 43). It might be expected that
the narrator would side with the revelers against the sanctimonious, stiff-
necked authorities. As the tale progresses, however, it becomes clear that the
revel is deeply flawed. The celebration is characterized as "fantastic foolery,"
the celebrants as "Gothic monsters"; some of them wear masks of faces which,
like that of the Joker in *Batman,* are "stretched from ear to ear in an eternal fit
of laughter." The overdrawn "spontaneity" of these party-goers "rioting in the
flow of tipsy jollity" turns suspect and disturbing; this is the devitalized carnival Bakhtin claims replaced the genuine medieval-Renaissance article:

Having followed the line of court masquerade combined with other
traditions, the style of popular festive forms began . . . to degenerate.
It acquired alien elements. . . . The ambivalent improprieties related

to the material bodily lower stratum, were turned into erotic frivolity. The popular utopian spirit began to fade. (*Rabelais* 103)

The new grotesque in effect brought whores to Elysium, to borrow a phrase from Ezra Pound. Absent its original folk energy, the carnival becomes artificial, a choreographed exercise in desperate mirth and frivolous eroticism as the decadent masquerade becomes "connected with exoticism, morbidity, and death" (Castle 336). The maypole erected by the colonial celebrants, abstracted from its folk roots, has lost its phallic potency and fertility resonance; the Puritans use the pole as a whipping post, its sexual implications turn Sadean. Masks, in terms of this dynamic, also lose their folk-ritual authenticity:

> [N]ow the mask hides something, keeps a secret, deceives. Such a meaning would not be possible as long as the mask functioned within folk culture's organic whole. The Romantic mask loses almost entirely its regenerating and renewing element . . . a nothingness lurks behind it. (Bakhtin, *Rabelais* 40)

The decline of carnival/masque from "revelatory and life enhancing" sensual delight (Castle 108) to something forced and cynical is deeply inscribed in "Maypole." Hawthorne's description of the "silken colonists, sporting round their Maypole" tracks an effete expression of carnival in which "erring Thought and perverted Wisdom were made to put on masques and play the fool. The men of whom we speak, after losing the heart's fresh gaiety, imagined a wild philosophy of pleasure and came hither to act out their latest daydream" (*Complete* 42–43). Whether historically there ever was wholly authentic carnival embodying "the heart's fresh gaiety" may be questioned, of course, but even in a relative context, decadent carnivalesque like the affair at Merry Mount as Hawthorne portrayed it revealed a disguised anxiety, a desperation decked out in anachronistic regalia, and its sinister overtones afforded American gothic writers and filmmakers some of the critical material they would put to use in later horror invention.

Hawthorne further explores the theme of decadent revel in "My Kinsman Major Molineaux." When the naif Robin arrives from the country, the atmosphere in the darkening town hints at some festivity underway. "[S]urely some prodigious merry-making is going on," Robin reasons. But the setting waxes increasingly sinister, and the streets become a nightmare labyrinth for the innocent seeker. Fresh from his pastoral home, the novice is at first easy and confident, but his venture increasingly becomes a trial; his simple search for his successful uncle, who has promised to help him get started in the world, takes on a distorted, threatening character. The disintegrative gothic course prevails—from certainty into the delusional, from energy to fatigue, from confidence to trepidation, from order to turmoil. Drifting figures, barely discernable semblances, move in the shadows. The anxiety of masquerade is captured in the costumes described as marching as if on their own, disembodied: "Embroidered garments, of showy colors, enormous periwigs, gold-laced hats, and silver hilted swords, glided past him and dazzled his optics" (*Complete* 521). Robin wanders "desperately and at random" (523). An Every-Young-Man in this initiation narrative, he becomes decentered and superfluous, encountering his mutability and his uncle's as well, blundering into a landscape of phantasms. He hears "the shrill voices of mirth or terror" in which phrase carnival ambiguity, the proximity of festive and nightmare elements, is evident. Unbeknownst to Robin, the masquerade is part of a tar and feather party for his uncle, Major Molineaux, a Crown appointee who has run afoul of shifting popular sentiment in the American colonial town. But Robin is aware only of some unfolding dark ritual, an "uproar," "tuneless bray," "discord," something broken forth from a "feverish brain." The march culminates in hallucinatory havoc:

> A dense multitude of torches shone along the street. . . . When Robin had freed his eyes from those fiery ones, the musicians were passing before him, and the torches were close at hand; but the unsteady brightness of the latter formed a veil which he could not penetrate . . . confused traces of a human form appeared at intervals, and then melted into the vivid light. A moment more and the leader thundered a command to halt; the trumpets vomited a horrid breath, and held their peace. (527–28)

There is a provocation to nausea in festival-masquerade's vertigo, in its paranormal inversions and its overwhelming, dissociative laughter. Robin senses "tremendous ridicule" in this affair of the night, uncanny laughter at his own expense. "In all periods of the past there was the marketplace with its laughing people," Bakhtin observes. But he then quotes from a scene in Pushkin's *Boris Godunov,* wherein Dimitry, the pretender to the ancient Russian Crown, experiences laughter, like Robin, in its nightmare form: "The people swarmed on the public square / And pointed laughingly at me, / And I was filled with shame and fear" (*Rabelais* 474).

Robin's quandary is that he cannot determine if he is caught in a public carnival, a private hallucination, or some sickening conflation of the two—whether he is in the house of mirth or the house of terror. Stallybrass and White, as noted earlier, point out that carnival in excess tends toward the idioms of a hysterical, schizophrenic discourse. They remark that

> it is striking how the thematics of carnival pleasure—eating, inversion, mess, dirt, sex and stylized body movements—find their neurasthenic, unstable, and mimicked counterparts in the discourse of hysteria. It is as if the hysteric has no mechanism for coping with the mediation of the grotesque body in everyday life. (182)

The torchlight march in "Molineaux" locates another element of the carnival-festive thematic—parade. Parade in its ordinary expression suggests order and discipline. Loose, joyous marching characterizes Mardi Gras, Brazilian Carnival, and the like—but there, too, the celebration goes on within an overarching design. But this carnival feature too may offer a vehicle for sinister expression in the form of the *fiendish* parade, a demented affair that presents a disturbing caricature of order. In "The Shadow over Innsmouth," the horridness of the noisome, flopping, patrol—"a legion of croaking, baying entities"—is heightened by the group's obvious aspiration to some kind of orderly progression. Their regalia too, gesturing as it does toward a disfigured idea of formality—including tiaras no less—reinforces still more the sense of fumbling lunacy on display. An image of such an aberrant, deranged parade appears as well in Tennessee Williams's gothic *Suddenly Last Summer* when Catherine describes the march of beggar children, some of them his former sexual prey, who pursue the ill Sebastian through the streets of Cabeza de Lobo. He and Catherine are in a "fish place" along the harbor.

> There were naked children along the beach . . . that looked like a flock of plucked birds, and they would come darting up to the barbed wire fence as if blown there by the wind . . . , and they were making gobbling noises with their little black mouths. . . . [They] began to serenade us. . . . Make music!—if you could call it music. . . . the instruments were tin cans strung together. . . . other bits of metal . . . flattened out, made into . . . *Cymbals.* . . . And others had paper bags . . . to make a sort of a . . . Oompa, oompa, oompa. (83–87)

The "music" tends to make of the urchins a single, concerted organism and suggests a macabre festivity. Sebastian panics and runs off in the burning sun through the streets near the harbor, but is overtaken by the band and fallen upon. When Catherine finds him, "they had *devoured* parts of him."

> Torn or cut parts of him away with their hands . . . or maybe those jagged tin cans . . . they had torn bits of him away and stuffed them into those gobbling fierce little empty black mouths of theirs. . . . there was nothing to see but Sebastian . . . that looked like a big white-pa-per-wrapped bunch of red roses had been *torn, thrown, crushed!*— against the blazing white wall. (92)

This is the height of that horror that appropriates festive elements—here the oompa-pa of carnival—to create a bizarre, celebrative accompaniment to havoc.

★ ★ ★

Festive horror is not without its contemporary popular cultural manifestations. Ritual analogies, Northrop Frye observes, "are most easily seen, not in the drama of the educated audience and the settled theater, but in naive or spec-tacular drama" (*Anatomy* 107). The classic teen horror films, spectacular indeed, were gory melodramas frequently marked by festive themes and fertility in-version. John Carpenter's *Halloween* (1978) and Sean Cunningham's *Friday the 13th* (1980) are seminal movies in what has become a thriving genre, but I will be considering them separately from the self-parodying "slasher" sequel indus-try that exploited their success and that arguably developed a distinct, campy dynamic of its own. Both these films involve carnivalesque, holiday motifs. Carpenter's occurs on two Halloweens, fifteen years apart, in the masquerade atmosphere of the autumn harvest celebration. Pumpkins are everywhere in the small Illinois town—bright, fertile gourds reflecting the feast's earthward inclinations, its drive to bring things down "to the reproductive lower stratum, the zone in which conception and new birth take place" (Bakhtin, *Rabelais* 21). In one scene, Jamie Lee Curtis, on her way to baby-sit, carries a pumpkin be-fore her in such a way that in profile she appears pregnant.

Likewise carnivalesque in the two films is the earthy bawdiness and physi-cality, the erotic atmosphere. The latter is expressed in the endless sexual pre-occupation of the teens and, in a pathological form, in the sex-associative murders carried out by Michael Myers in *Halloween,* the first of them when he is wearing a harlequin outfit. Even notes of vaguely surviving folk or mar-ketplace ribaldry are evident—in one scene, as the three girls walk together Linda remarks to Annie that the only reason to baby-sit is to have a place to—

"Shit," Laurie says, apropos of something else entirely. "I *have* a place for *that,* Laurie," Annie says, quick on the uptake.

Friday the 13th involves spring and vivid traces of festive holiday ritual. A group of youths have gone a-Maying—it is June in fact—to the remote Crystal Lake. The setting is sylvan and frequently beautifully filmed—the lake does seem crystal, and choirs of crickets and frogs sing in the forest night. The pattern one associates with pastoral comedy is suggested—escape from society and the affirmation of the Arcadian mythos. The assembled youths in merry spirits have frolic and sexual gambols in mind. The camp director, Steve Cristy, is determined to renew the youth camp that formerly stood on the lakeshore, which reinforces the comic topos of rejuvenation. He is attempting this revival in the face of unanimous local opposition from town folk who are convinced the pastoral site is cursed and evil. Cristy is perhaps a shadow of what Frye describes as the Aristophanian "central figure who constructs his . . . own society in the face of strong opposition, driving off all the people who would prevent him, and eventually achieving a heroic triumph" (*Anatomy* 43). The comic paradigm is established—quite aside from the fact that "slasher" expectations of course prevail on the surface. The comic mythos would predict that the camp, energized by its vigorous young crew, will, in festive-comic tradition, rise from its long winter; the tired old naysayers in the town will be proved wrong, the lie put to their trepidations; the pastoral playground will be restored; Steve will get Alice, the pretty counselor he has his eye on. Erotic summer will thus triumph over withering winter, life over death, in a carnival of dance and song. But viewers are aware, as the young people at the lake are not, that one of their party has already been butchered in the spring forest.

Older than his teen employees, Steve is the no-nonsense man in charge who puts the newly arrived counselors to work immediately readying the camp for the arrival of their young charges in two weeks. With some reluctance, the teenagers begin their assigned tasks, but Steve has obligations in town and will be gone until the following day. Once he drives off in his jeep, the Apollonian work ethic dwindles, and left to their own devices, the youths soon lighten up, and the spirit of revel begins to take over. A cop making it his business to intrude on the campers serves as the killjoy figure familiar in festive drama. He is an ass, a conflation of Barney Fife and Sergeant Friday, policing, he tells the counselors, for "pot, Colombian gold, grass, hash, the weed—dig it?"

But as in "The Maypole of Merry Mount," where a reader's expectation is that the dour, unsympathetic Puritans are going to be the laughing stock and the young revelers the heroes, as this movie proceeds, things begin to darken, and its mythos-of-spring expectations are squelched. The film in fact brutally inverts traditional pastoral-romantic assumptions, exploiting festive-comic conventions for the purposes of horror. The *Friday the 13th* teen audience laughs at the film's melodramatic excesses, perhaps, but presumably fails to notice, at least consciously, its crypto-conservative underplot indicting *them*. The consumers of this kind of film—teenagers in an American culture that, at least on the surface, glorifies them—have a stake in the festive-comic glorification of youth over age but are watching a film in which ultimately their *parent's* values are peculiarly credited, affirming Stephen King's observation that the moral stance of most horror films "is firmly reactionary" (*Danse* 261). Parental warnings that if their daughter goes off to the woods with other teens who think they are free spirits, she will become involved in drugs and sex, and probably be murdered, turn out to be justified. The youth versus age opposition in the film thus plays out against the vast majority of its viewers. The Archie Bunkerish truck driver who gives a pretty camp hiree a lift and in reaction to whose advice she is sweetly patronizing—calling him "an American icon"—turns out to have been *right* in warning her to turn around immediately and go home. The movie's makers recognize the horror imperative of suggesting, beyond mere episodes of gore, the collapse of the *viewer's* world and assumptions, so an adult ideology holds uncanny sway in this and other films in the genre. Camille Paglia notes a critically important principle of horror art: "Gothic horror must be moderated by Apollonian discipline, or it turns into gross buffoonery" (*Personae* 268). Few film critics, however, have taken the conservatism of these original slasher films seriously or credited their moral concerns. Stephen King, on the contrary, does so regarding horror in general, remarking the importance of the Apollonian element, the sensibility *opposed to* "partying and physical gratification; the get-down-and-boogie side of human nature" (italics added, *Danse* 75).

Thus Alice, the only camp staff member alive in the end, is also the only girl who is sexually abstemious or at least reserved. When Steve, who is fond of her, touches her hair familiarly, she visibly stiffens at the presumption. She never appears unclothed, and in a scene in which she is party to a strip monopoly game—another girl's idea—at the moment when she would have to remove her blouse and is reaching for the top button, the game is interrupted by a storm blast flinging open the barrack door as if by supernatural intervention. Alice is also the serious and responsible one among the campers, seen working while the others frolic.

In contrast to her, Neddy is the camp's Lord of Misrule, to whom everything is a joke; he is forever affecting an inauthentic, impish jollity and devil-may-care irresponsibility. When a girl is setting up an archery target on the camp range—doing her job—he shoots an arrow into the target, coming close to hitting her, and dances in a strained glee in response to her horrified reaction. He fakes drowning as an elaborate practical joke, carrying the hoax all the way to where the other campers are frantically attempting resuscitation on the dock. When the lights go out and one of the boys speculates that it might be the generator, Ned is quick with flippant contempt and sarcasm: "'Probably the generator,'" he mocks. "'Don't you love that macho talk?'" This bogus festive spirit wears thin; a black snake appears ominously in one of the barracks. Marcie becomes pensive, like Edith in Hawthorne's "Maypole," and remarks to her boyfriend that Neddy "is acting like a jerk." She is melancholy; the midsummer romp and pervasive frivolity are losing their charm, and she recounts a recurrent dream of rain—it has just begun to rain—turning to blood. The spring spirit is waning and horror taking command.

Ned is the first murdered in the camp itself. His earlier faked drowning had recapitulated the drowning of Jason years earlier—one which occurred when two indifferent counselors, whose task it was to watch the children swimming, instead took to the woods to make love. Jason's insane mother has watched Neddy's pretended drowning from the cover of the tree line and has presumably viewed it as a mocking pageant within the general camp frolic, one cruelly rehearsing her son's calamity. The mother, Mrs. Voorhees, is the film's conservative avenging angel, the magician-witch and Jungian "terrible mother," here an instrument of righteous rage wreaking havoc on the languid American airheads in their forest festival. Only the relatively ascetic Alice is possessed of the dignity and moral right stuff to survive the bloodbath of retribution. This moral theme is frequently simplistically represented, as in Wes Craven's glib parody *Scream,* as merely avowing *virginity* and admonishing sexual profligacy, but in fact it situates much more complex issues of personal discipline and self-respect and a more serious concern—"there is no liberal dignity of the person in the Dionysian" (Paglia, *Personae* 98). The turning of the original slasher films into a smug-hip genre may well in fact represent an attempt to evade the dark revelations of the originals—indeed this film species appears to have petered out in a series of lame, self-mocking movies. The original slashers might be viewed as norm-affirming in the sense that *Frankenstein* and numerous other gothic classics are and in the sense *2 Henry IV* is—concerned with the repercussions of excess, triviality, laxity, and disengagement. An ancient Apollonian imperative is arguably being avowed, and it may be erroneous or only partially accurate to describe horror as a reactionary "cultural apparatus for keeping the sexually active woman in her place" (Badley 102). Horror is conservative, and the conservative element in a dialectic is almost always regarded as less interesting, less sexy, than the liberal one. For a long time, for instance, in the realm of pop-modern linguistics, the truism that language in constantly changing was harangued; the even more important if less dramatic truth that language is constantly and necessarily remaining the same went unremarked. It would seem that a conservatism running deeper than Democratic-Republican politics finds an articulate popular form in horror—a spectacular, visceral, sensational expression—and has its say through the various expressions of the gothic mode.

Friday the 13th sustains ironic traces of the festive modality even to the film's conclusion, when, Mrs. Voorhees having been decapitated, Alice goes down to the lake and pushes off in a canoe that drifts through the quiet water as dawn comes on gently—the music is a calming tone poem. Alice falls into a sleep, her hand trailing in the cool water; the scene is almost Pre-Raphaelite. The violence is over, and a pastoral peace finally reigns. This romantic pattern is carried out so patiently and to such an elaborate extent that its sudden violation—the undead, partly decomposed Jason rising to the surface and pulling Alice overboard—can only be read as a final mockery of the Arcadian romantic tradition. The young world does not prevail; a refreshed social order has not come about; the adults, the dour skeptics in the town, were correct in their paranoia.[5]

The affirmation of discipline and dignity characterizing *Friday the 13th* had occurred as well in the earlier *Halloween,* where likewise only the restrained, more sexually and generally responsible girl survived the murderous rampage. Laurie (Jamie Lee Curtis), the surviving heroine, is likewise the nonsexually active girl, the serious student in an otherwise frivolous crowd. One of the girls, Annie, who is supposed to be baby-sitting, takes advantage of Laurie, leaving the child in Laurie's hands in order to run off for a tryst with her boyfriend—immediately after which she and the boy are—in keeping with the genre formula—murdered. Neglected baby-sitting or some form of neglected child care is thus a motif shared by *Friday the 13th* and *Halloween*—casual sex is not the only

transgression the films address. The inability of the teenagers in these movies to function responsibly even in terms of care of the young is itself a disturbing marker of social degeneration, a sign of the decline of even critical mammalian instincts. When Linda in *Halloween* notes that baby-sitting is about having
a place to have sex with one's boyfriend, her observation reinforces the film's
opening murder scene wherein the boy, preparatory to the couple's taking to
her upstairs bedroom, asks Judith Myers if they are indeed alone, to which she
replies listlessly that "Michael is around somewhere." Michael, her little brother,
for whom she is supposed to be caring, has in fact been watching the necking
couple through a window from outside. *Friday* recapitulated this event in that a
series of murders is set off when, as mentioned earlier, two promiscuous camp
councilors in charge of children swimming, having gone off for sex in the
woods—more languid carelessness—occasion Jason's accidental drowning.

Rather than of vipers, the *Halloween, Friday the 13th* teens are on the whole
a generation of vapids—generally idle, insubstantial, and characterless. They
represent the dangers of indolence and Dionysian incontinence; it is not a
coincidence surely that both these movies appeared when the 1960s zeitgeist
was still prevalent. The high-school principal's rage in *Scream* would tend to
sum the teens up: "You make me so sick! You and your entire . . . feeding,
whoring generation disgusts me. . . . heartless, desensitized little shits." An
updated twenty-first-century version of this social phenomenon might present
as something like what Lucia Perillo, a professor of creative writing, describes
turning up in some contemporary student writing that seems to have "no
moral core": The typical writer of this cast in her experience "seemed to feel
that he was entitled to be any way he wanted to be in the world. He did not
seem to feel responsible for the repercussions of the person that he was, nor
did he feel that he had the ability, or the obligation, to shape that person in
any way." A recent *Spin* magazine article, she notes, "referred to this demo-
graphic as 'mook' culture: a product of pornography, hip-hop, and pro wres-
tling" (Perillo B24).

Halloween's horror is not confined to its manifest bloodletting—Michael's
precocious homicidal feats—but is also infused throughout by a disquieting
sense of social, generational lapse. And, as in *Friday*, parental warnings are
validated; when Judith Myers indulges in casual sex with her boyfriend of the
moment, he is keen to split immediately afterward, and when she asks if he
will telephone the next day, his insincere "yeah . . . sure" tellingly confirms the
old-fashioned moral ethos. These are youths who, raised in a culture of nar-

cissism, have never been exposed to serious moral discourse, for whom such discourse has always been mocked and caricatured, and to whom it is now as taboo as once sexual discourse was. Caught in the void left by "the fading presence of religion and tribal authority" (Arlen 279), bereft of tradition and custom, "the pure products of America go crazy," as William Carlos Williams put it (53). Arguably, this is the grave recognition that teenagers saw in the first slashers and that the later imitations sought to refract and diminish.

In *Halloween,* Laurie serves as the kind of moral gauge Alice would later be in *Friday,* providing the Apollonian, ascetic counterbalance to the behavior of the other teens, whose only motivation seems to be that they are mindlessly drawn toward their sugar fix—"fun." Her seriousness, politeness, bookishness, and sense of focus leave her without a boyfriend, cut off from much of her peer's idle frolics. She takes her baby-sitting seriously—planning the evening's games, prepared with a pumpkin on Halloween night that she will carve with Tommy, her charge. Her personality contrasts with that of Linda particularly, one of whose wisdoms emerges when Laurie, as the girls walk home from school, is shocked to discover that she has forgotten her chemistry book, a shock Linda cannot understand: "So who cares? I always forget my chemistry book . . . my math book . . . my English book, let's see. . . my French book. Who needs books anyway? I don't need books. I always forget all my books. You don't need books."

The film distinguishes Laurie from this teenoid sensibility. As against their peers, Alice and Laurie are austere, disciplined and dignified, and this seems to imbue each with a potency, a chivalric charisma none of their fellows possess; indeed each is able, with a power none of the prior victims have had, to physically resist the film's homicidal monster in the final confrontation. Laurie defeats a killer who has heretofore dispatched his victims, male and female, effortlessly. Nor, in the confrontation, are her clothes ripped in any revealing way—continuing the uniqueness of her never having been viewed in the slightest undress previously in the film.

A similar general ethos is evident in *Carrie,* wherein the high-school teen community is made up in good part of feral sadists who are finally incinerated in the context of that ritual most sacred among American teen festivals: the Prom. Carrie's basic decency sets her apart, as Alice is set apart in *Friday the 13th* and Laurie in *Halloween.* The moral character of the three is particularly critical in the films in its implications regarding the tone, the organic health of the respective communities. These horror melodramas arguably could not function without their affirmation of discipline and morality—which confirms the fact that horror cannot be purely wanton. The conservative strain in these works, validating a sense of proper proportion, is arguably primitive and mythic in character, indeed biological—it is not a matter of specific-case moral instruction in the sense of recommending attention to one's baby-sitting duties, not letting lovemaking get in the way, and so on. Rather the injunction is the Apollonian one implicit in the line from *2 Henry IV* quoted earlier: "Make less thy body . . . and more thy grace." Frank Cawson concludes his book *The Monsters in the Mind* on an interrogatory note that would seem relevant here. "Could it be that the problem of evil and of our future is basically biological . . . ?" he asks. "Could it be that . . . the nurture of the young and the proper stewardship of our imaginative inheritance are the crucial issues of survival?" (162).

7 Languishment: The Wounded Hero

The Community of the life principle . . .

—JESSIE WESTON, *Ritual to Romance*

In Eanna, high and low, there is weeping. . . .
The wailing is for the plants; the first lament is they grow not.
The wailing is for the barley; the ears grow not . . .
The wailing is for the great river; it brings the flood no more.

—Lament of Tammuz

The first was with base dunghill clads yclad . . .
Of morbid hue his features, sunk and sad
His hollow eyen shook forth a sickly light;
And oe'r his lank jawbone, in piteous plight,
His black rough beard was matted rank and vile . . .
Meantime foul scurf and blotches him defile. . . .

—JAMES THOMPSON, "The Castle of Indolence"

NORTHROP FRYE OBSERVES THAT "IT IS PART OF THE critic's business to show how all literary genres are derived from the quest-myth" (*Fables* 17). That may put the matter more strongly than some would be comfortable with, but the mythic signature referred to, especially in terms of the Waste Land motif, is indeed evident in the literature of horror and related literary expressions. Chrétien's "The Story of the Grail" begins on notes of vegetational health, with bounteous metaphors of sowing, harvest, reaping, plant, and seed. It is spring and "trees bud, bushes leaf, and meadows turn green . . . everything is aflame with joy" (Chrétien 340). Evoked is that vitality Barber refers to in which all living things stir together (20). But in the course of the tale, notes opposed to these original energetic ones occur. Early in his travels, Perceval comes upon a settlement dissipated and under siege; the bridge approaching the town's gate is "so feeble that he thought it could

scarcely support him" (Chrétien 361). What he finds within are further markers of enfeeblement and destabilization, of things amiss: "Everywhere he went
he found the streets empty and the houses old and fallen down." There are
two former abbeys, "one of frightened nuns, the other of helpless monks. . . .
Throughout the town there was no mill grinding or oven baking. . . . The town
was so desolate . . . that there was no bread, pastry, wine, cider, or ale." The
settlement is a study in exhaustion; there is no art, no creative endeavor, no
affirmation. There are "no fine decorations or tapestries . . . only split and
cracked walls and roofless towers" (361–62). The mythic polemic of vitality
versus depletion, in effect of illness and wellness, is thus established.

The besieged town here situates the Bad Place of the horror mythos—that
trope, complementary to that of the besieged body, represents the spirits of
torpor, dissolution, and flagging volition through the landscape of human
artifice—soulless streets, buildings, and so on. Even in *The Exorcist,* the diabolical inroads are not confined to the girl's physical body but extend out into
cultural *place*—into the Georgetown community in the form of mysterious
desecrations of churches and dwindled religious conviction among the Jesuit
community—as mentioned before, traditionally the vigorous, militant arm of
the Church. The same body-place, organism-environment continuum, "the
community of the life principle" (Weston 35), marks the grail story in which
Perceval is burdened with an esoteric obligation to affect the cure of the Fisher
King's malady and thereby restore the faltering kingdom. Shades of this fertility archetype, one with roots no doubt far more ancient than Chrétien's tale,
figure commonly in gothic literature, wherein an uncanny continuity from
wounded protagonist to wasted place and torn social fabric is assumed. James
Thompson's Spenserian verse narrative "The Castle of Indolence" (c. 1738)
situated the theme in an allegorical tale of a wizard's castle and its landscape
dedicated to repose and a listless, drifting existence. A traveler, lured by the
appeal of apparent ease, once caught in the Wizard's thrall, deteriorates, becomes pallid, wan, and wasted. "The plant and the tree subsist in a kind of
hypnotic sleep," E. W. F. Tomlin notes. And the pull toward indolent drift—
the attraction of opium, for example—manifests a kind of insidious organic
nostalgia for the "virginity of the primary condition" (135).

The quest pattern informs "The Fall of the House of Usher," in which a
traveler not unlike Perceval comes on horseback to the estate of a waning figure, one whose dissolution is at the same time the dissolution of house, lin-
eage, and land. The Waste Land curse hangs over the estate: "I looked upon

the scene before me—upon . . . the bleak walls—upon the vacant, eye-like windows—upon a few rank sedges—and upon a few white trunks of decayed trees—with an utter depression of soul" (Poe, *Selected* 54). Archetypally enough, it falls to the visitor to determine the nature of his host's malady and to restore him to wellness. In Henry James's "The Turn of the Screw," it is two children who are unwell and whose estate is beleaguered; the arriving governess attempts heroically to get to the bottom of the malevolent influence, the occult siege that embraces the Bly property, and to rescue the children.

The pattern in question appears as well in Herman Melville's "Bartleby the Scrivener," in which, as in James's story, an undercurrent of anxiety and an insistent sense of some malevolence abroad, rather than a bloody surface calamity, characterizes the horror. The dread is situated in failing physicality; "Bartleby" is an extended metaphor of organic deterioration, of mortally jeopardized personal and communal vitality. The setting, an eccentric stock lawyer's deathly dull New York office, portrays a kind of white collar Waste Land. The story narrates a catalog of assaults on the human body; insults to the eyes, the back, the digestive and nervous systems; assaults on life and nature by modern civilization epitomized in The Office, whose occupants are "walled up" as surely as Fortunato in Poe's "Cask," though here the claustrophobic element is expressed as a sustained quotidian reality.

Of the lawyer's employees, Turkey, like Roderick Usher and Benito Cereno, is manic, hyperactive, and unpredictable: "There was a strange inflamed, flurried, flighty recklessness of activity about him" (*Short Works* 41). Nippers, on the other hand, is sallow, plagued with indigestion and nagging back trouble: "If, for the sake of his back, he brought the table at a sharp angle up to his chin . . . then he declared that it stopped the circulation in his arms." All the copyists suffer from the punishing effects of paperwork on their eyes, and of junk food—ginger cookies—on their stomachs. They have become grotesques, commercial artifacts; the analogy these days might be to those artificially raised chickens whose feet never touch real ground. The scriveners carry out their disabling work in a setting gothically lacking natural light and devoid in fact of virtually any intercourse with the outside, natural world. The lawyer/narrator's chambers look out upon a shaft at one end and at the other command "an unobstructed view of a lofty brick wall, black by age and everlasting shade." Indeed the very concept "life" is understood only as the jargon of the art world. The narrator concedes that the view from his office might be considered deficient—he does not say in *life*, but rather—in what *landscape painters* call life, and the word *life* is in quotes, as if it were of questionable or dubious meaning (41–42). Bartleby himself, in his unspeakable dejection, is a dead man walking, embodied entropy; he is quintessentially rundown.

The horror tale's ancestry in fertility ritual and story surfaces here. Bartleby is the figure fallen into indolence; his infirmity is representative; it has implicit in it a broader social infirmity, a languishment of the commonweal and of threatened life overall. While Bartleby is the title character, the subtitle foregrounds the business heart of New York: "A Tale of Wall St." The scrivener's work is "a dull, wearisome, and lethargic affair" carried on in an environment of paper—that epitome of dryness—from which the scriveners send out for ginger cookies, but there is no mention of accompanying drink, of water. To quote Frye again regarding quest romance, it turns on "the victory of fertility over the waste land" (*Anatomy* 193). Horror's inverted version of the quest configuration narrates instead the victory of the wasteland, as here in "Bartleby," over fertility. Jessie Weston refers to the part played by the healer figure in many surviving fertility ceremonies: "[E]ven where an active share is no longer assigned to the character, he still appears among the *dramatis personae* of . . . folk plays and processions" (101). He appears as well in gothic horror narratives as the visitor/would-be healer who seeks to solve the mystery of the host's torpor. The pattern is that of the descent into indolence and languishment found, according to Weston, in the Adonis cults, the European Spring Festivals, and the Mumming plays of the British Isles, in all of which the salient point is that "the representative of the Spirit of Vegetation is considered dead, and the object . . . is to restore him to life" (119). If the restoration agon is fulfilled, the implications are comic-erotic; if it fails, they are horrific. In the original film version of *The Invasion of the Body Snatchers,* for example, when a small-town doctor returns from a journey to find the townspeople possessed by a strange apathy, a creepy indifference, it falls to him to function as healer and to figure out the preternatural contagion. When he cannot, no more spectacular horror device is called for; the film's effect is chilling. The would-be healer in "Bartleby" is the narrator, who earnestly attempts, within his limited powers, to rescue the devitalized Bartleby from the mysterious possession that has overcome him. While Bartleby is initially the visitor, himself the guest in that the office is the lawyer's, their roles significantly enough are later reversed, Bartleby becoming the quasi-proprietor, thereby bringing things into accord with the archetypal pattern. The lawyer goes to his office one Sunday morning only to discover that his key will not open the door:

When to my consternation the key was turned from within . . . and
holding the door ajar, the apparition of Bartleby appeared, in his shirt
sleeves . . . saying quietly that he was sorry, but he was deeply engaged
just then . . . and preferred not admitting me at present. (*Short Works*
53–54)

"Bartleby" rehearses the grail-waste land pattern in its darkest implications;
there is to be no ultimate healing—the lawyer does his best, but the wounded
character is a study in dwindling vitality and increasing demoralization unto
death.

It is a narrative wherein the life impulse struggles with the death impulse
and oddly—though not unlikely in so eccentric an artist as Melville—this
struggle goes on in a context that frequently verges on screwball comic, even
in terms of Bartleby's behavior. The lawyer, driven by a sense of spiritual,
chivalric obligation, goes to the most heroic lengths in hopes that his broken
scrivener's spirit might be revived. The lawyer is good hearted, for all his peculiarity—much of which, it is important to note, is self-acknowledged. He
has a warm eye for human oddities, cherishes anecdotes about his employees'
personal quirks, and is extraordinarily patient and forbearing in the knowledge
that the world is deeply flawed. He sees his copyists not as functionaries but
as "an interesting and somewhat singular set of men" whose stories, if he recounted them, might, he says, "make the good-natured smile and the sentimental weep" (39). Innocent of scorn, derision, or boredom, he manifests the
comic spirit in the tale, adapting and adjusting to a difficult environment, keeping his humor and sense of the absurd all the while.[1] The organism, Langer
observes, against what besets it, and within a wide range of conditions,
"struggles to retrieve its original dynamic form by overcoming and removing
the obstacle, or if this proves impossible, it develops a slight variation of its
typical form and activity and carries on life with a new balance of functions;
it adapts to the situation (*Feeling* 328).

The lawyer is a master of adaptation—which does not, however, diminish the horror of his narrative. He knows his limitations and is, by his own
testimony, "an eminently *safe* man." His characterization of himself is emphatically antiheroic; he makes his way as best he can in his given environment
and circumstances. Uninterested in doing battle in the arena of courtroom law,
he cultivates the "cool tranquility of a snug retreat, [doing] a snug business

among rich men's bonds and mortgages" (40). Living thus within the constraints and compromises of a contingent social reality, he manages a kind of peculiar survival. In the context of his Wall Street existence, he is in fact a thriving comic character, not taking himself seriously, making his way in the world as he finds it. For all his adaptability and willingness to compromise, however, as well as his self-affirmed antiheroism, he is willing to go to the most astonishing lengths in the struggle against Bartleby's affliction, the insistent darkness.

The revival imperative and the failed-healing motif evident in "Bartleby," in *Catch*-22, and, to be discussed later, in "The Fall of the House of Usher" and "Benito Cereno" mark one of many apparent traces of fertility ritual surviving in horror literature. In both "Bartleby" and "Benito Cereno," the would-be restorative meal Weston identifies as a theme in grail narrative is arranged by the visiting agent to be given to the languishing figure. In "Bartleby," the lawyer pays the grub-man at the prison to bring Bartleby "the best dinner you can get" (Melville, *Short Works* 71). In an analogous scene in "Benito Cereno," Captain Delano brings baskets of fish, bread, water, and cider to the ailing Spanish Captain. The connection of these narrative patterns to the mystic meal, and especially the sacramental fish meal (Weston 146–48), are notable.[2] The broader languishment theme appears interestingly in a horror-crime movie earlier referred to, *The First Deadly Sin* (1980), in which a heroine (Faye Dunaway) rather than a male hero is the wounded, failing figure. The writer held captive in the film *Misery* is another example, though in that case, as is not uncommon, the element of the hero's languishment equating sympathetically with the failing condition of the outside world in not significantly a part of the construction.

The sympathetic motif is conspicuous in *The First Deadly Sin,* however. The film begins in a nocturnal urban landscape, one feature of which the camera emphasizes—the large lighted cross of a Christian street mission. Parallel editing indicates simultaneous events occurring, in one of which a woman is being wheeled into emergency surgery and in the other of which a shadowy figure, well dressed, is prowling a dark New York street. The scene switches abruptly back and forth between the co-occurring actions. The surgeon's scalpel parts the woman's abdomen, cutting through the layers of flesh, and a crucifix is flashed full screen. On the street where the lighted cross has been shown, the shadowy figure passes a man, spins around, and slams a glinting metal instrument down into the passerby's head. Again the crucifix is shown, as is the scalpel cutting deep into the woman's flesh, blood pouring out and down into the operating room drain. The suggestion is not of simultaneity merely but of convergent realities, the esoteric oneness of the events. For the rest of the film, the narratives continue to run in parallel at critical, violent points as the woman becomes more and more ill. The film's crosscutting makes clear that she is in crisis sympathetically with the city and that, arguably reflecting the community of the life principle, her body and the city are affected by the same morbid influence. She is Mrs. Delaney, the wife of Detective-Sergeant Delaney (Frank Sinatra), who is investigating murders, which turn out to be a uniform series of arbitrary slayings involving the use of an unidentified metal implement. Delaney rushes from the scene of one slaying to the hospital when he hears of his wife's emergency surgery and is stunned to find her grievously ill. The distressingly evasive surgeon informs the detective that his wife's kidney had to be removed, that they had found it to be "diseased . . . rotting." It is a Catholic hospital, and wall crucifixes are a constant symbolic accompaniment as Delaney talks to his wife or desperately interviews the doctor in an attempt to understand what is happening to her.

Returning to the investigation, the detective visits the morgue, the gruesome abattoir possibilities of which are fully exploited—cadavers are being laid open, and the camera follows the blood running on white tile into the drain beneath the table, a repetition of the same motif that occurred earlier in the operating theater scene. A little later, Delaney is walking through—gothically enough—a medieval hall with armored knights on horseback and weapons under display glass. He is talking to the curator—an eccentric antiquarian who, like Delaney, is on the verge of retirement. The detective believes the murder weapon may be a medieval artifact of some sort.

As the film follows Delaney's investigative work, the dissolution of the city becomes a prominent theme; its sickness is presented as uncannily connected with that of his wife—not in Delaney's *mind* but in fact. Delaney is forced to address the pathology devastating his wife, which, as the film's viewers are presented it, is on a continuum with the pathology of the city. The city is a wasteland, the fate of which is somehow spiritually bound up with that of the languishing heroine in the hospital. Like her, the metropolis is essentially poisoned. The commonweal, the public square, is under an influence manifested in cynicism, dishonesty, crime, and meanness; it is fractured along ethnic and linguistic lines. Mrs. Delaney's doctor turns out to be an ambitious careerist not unlike the precinct captain around whom Delaney, in his quest ordeal, must steer if he is to get anything done in terms of the serial-murder investigation. When one of the detectives is told the street on which one of the murders has occurred, he comments, "That used to be a safe area." "Nowhere is safe," Delaney replies. The systemic breakdown takes in the legal network—the killer "Mr. Blank" has connections that, it is made clear, would more than suffice to keep him on the loose even if he were caught and arrested.

Gothic's traditional Catholic and medieval motifs are abundantly exercised in the film, and biological images return consistently in quick but lurid views of the operating table, the autopsy table, and the psychopathic butchery enacted on the city streets. Blank, the killer, at one point babbles incoherently about his origins in "the cellar." And when in the end Delaney's wife is beyond hope of recovery, he is reduced to ineffectually reading to her from *Honey Bunch,* a child's book, as she dies, and the reading at one point—echoing the dual incongruous narratives concluding "The House of Usher"—serves as an over-voice as the stalker reconnoiters his Manhattan hunting grounds, moving toward another homicidal assault. All of which testifies to the remarkable survival of the gothic's body of themes in contemporary film as well as written literature and to the fact that the themes are endlessly renewable, an indication of their mythic potency.

This brief summary can only suggest the quest, Waste Land conception informing *The First Deadly Sin.* The Fisher King figure, a woman in this case, is visited by a concerned ally who attempts to free her of her illness— he brings gifts, encouragement, and prayer. But, as in "Bartleby," the affected character declines inexorably, recapitulating, em-*body*-ing, the larger communal dissolution.

If this mythic element in the film is missed, the significance of the gothic-crime dynamic explored in the 1980s films referenced earlier will likewise be passed over, and the Faye Dunaway character's place in the film will seem gratuitous, the cutting to the hospital an arbitrary departure from the crime investigation, a sentimental, tacked-on love interest. Thus the *Variety* review of the film reductively observed that "paralleling the crime-and-detection yarn, and slowing down the entire proceedings, are Sinatra's visits to wife Faye Dunaway, who is not recovering well from a kidney operation" (*Variety Portable* 421).

The languishment motif manifests, to take another example, in Ernest Hemingway's "A Pursuit Race," but before considering that story, we might remark the gothic traces, or lack thereof, elsewhere in Hemingway's oeuvre. Even Leslie Fiedler, a critic keen to demonstrate the ubiquitous gothicism of American literature, fails to note its presence in Hemingway's work. Gothic literary conventions of the familiar sort are indeed almost entirely absent in Hemingway's minimalist fiction, but a gothic concern with primitive fertility motifs are by no means absent. Hemingway's gothicism is in fact of the kind evident in, for example, Ambrose Bierce's "What I Saw at Shiloh," which, for all its striking nonfictional exactness, is as macabre as any piece in the American canon. Carlos Baker notes in Hemingway's case that his narratives are "dressed in the sharp vocabulary of the naturalistic writer. We are given (almost coldly) the place, the facts, the scene, out of which grows, however, an awful climate of hopelessness and despair" (123).

This awful climate is readily discernable in Hemingway's dark carnivalesque themes, however un-Poesque their rendering—in *The Sun Also Rises* and in a number of stories. Bakhtin himself observed that Hemingway's work on the whole "is deeply carnivalized . . . influenced by contemporary forms and festivals of a carnival type. . . . He had a very keen ear for everything carnivalistic in contemporary life" (*Poetics* 179n). The fiesta in *The Sun Also Rises* provides a public square where the energies of the ancient quasi-antagonists, Catholicism and paganism, mingle in pageant and celebration. Jake Barnes, as narrator, notes the dual character of the San Fermin fiesta, in effect its at once Bacchic and Catholic elements: The peasants "had been in the wine-shops . . . since early morning. . . . I heard them singing through the open doors of the shops. They were warming up. There were many people at the eleven o'clock mass. San Fermin is also a religious festival" (Hemingway 156). A counter-fertility motif enters in, however, in the form of Barnes's experience of war and his wound and consequent impotence, which cut him off from the fertile-erotic dynamic of the celebration.

Carlos Baker notes the pagan-Christian opposition in the festival as "the *riau-riau* dancers unabashedly follow the patron saint through the streets of Pamplona" (88–89). But if it is an opposition, it is one Jake brings to the event; it would not seem an opposition to the Mediterranean folk sensibility of the native celebrants, a consciousness long since grown comfortable with the conflation of Christian and pre-Christian pageantry. Bakhtin, too, would see the two religious configurations positively united in carnival, carnival knowing no absolute dissociations. The fiesta, however, as part of the carnival rubric, affirms the comic fertile glory of the earth abiding forever, bitterly ironizing Jake's war-torn soul and sexual wounding. He must move through the lusty Spanish fair as a Jamesian American, less than a full participant in its vitality. Thus while not a gothic novel—Harold Bloom calls it "elegy"—*The Sun Also Rises* is involved with the gothic mode's ritualism and underlying physicality. It is at least a dark novel whose epigraph references "a lost generation," a novel whose story Hemingway himself described as being about "how people go to hell" (qtd. in Baker 81). Bloom correctly compares Jake Barnes to "the wounded Fisher King of *The Waste Land,* impotent and yearning for spiritual salvation" (*Reviews* 5).

To return to one of Hemingway's lesser known but most intriguing tales, "A Pursuit Race" represents an even clearer evidence of Hemingway's gothic sensibility, in many ways inviting comparison to Poe stories or to "Bartleby the Scrivener" and, like the latter, tracing a character's wasting and decline. Baker relates "A Pursuit Race" to the also at least quasi-gothic Hemingway story "A Clean Well-Lighted Place" and quotes Malcolm Cowley's observation describing Hemingway as one "'of the haunted and nocturnal writers akin, in his deeper reaches, to Melville and Hawthorne" (132). "A Pursuit Race" involves, though, the "problem" Leslie Fiedler identifies in Melville—the merging of the naturalistic and the symbolic—what Fiedler terms the analytic and the projective—so that readers are not always sure which rhetorical mode is engaged; Baker calls the story "half-symbolic" (123). It perhaps bears comparison to "Big Two-Hearted River," another Hemingway story in which the attempted restoration of wellness is an issue. Of that story, Fiedler observes: "[I]t is impossible to tell whether the hero . . . is moving through reality or phantasy" (356). Such a disorienting narrative further suggests Hemingway's deep-seated nocturnalism. In "A Pursuit Race," even the narrator's seemingly careful explanation, set forth at the start, of what a bicycle pursuit race *is* becomes strangely blurred as to the rules, and the symbolic nature of the race is far too obviously drawn not to be deliberate—making the story already irrealistic.

The first two paragraphs, traditionally devoted to orienting the reader to the story's world, are in this case reader-*disorienting,* not unlike something in Poe. Campbell's role as a racer—having to avoid being caught up with by the other competitors—and his role as an advance man for the traveling carnival, are confused in the narration as, we come to realize, they are confused in Campbell's mind. The following two sentences, for example, are oddly run together: "In most pursuit races, if there are only two riders, one of the riders is caught inside of six miles. The *burlesque show* caught William Campbell in Kansas

City" (italics added, 350). The narrative voice here is not objective-reportorial but rather is laced disturbingly with the "voice" or thinking of Campbell, an example of the coinciding rhetorics Bakhtin calls "double-voiced discourse" (*Poetics* 185–99). The psychic field of the third person, "spoken about," Billy Campbell, intrudes into the field of the speaker-narrator, creating—by the standards of realism—an anomalous text. Campbell's muddling of his bike-racing role and his promo-advance man role creates a blurring of the senses in which he has been "caught up with" or, more darkly, "caught." The confusion is compounded by the fact that the race and its rules as existential metaphor have oddly surfaced in the "narrator's" voice. The third person narrative appears to be at times under the uncanny influence of, and to reflect, Campbell's distorted thought processes. The consequence is a psycho-narration in which, as mentioned, "authorial," informative writing sometimes is invaded by character thought and idiom (Bakhtin, *Dialogic* 306–7). As early as the story's opening sentence, there is an unsettling ambiguity: "William Campbell had been in a pursuit race with a burlesque show." Does this mean he was in a race *against* the show or *as part of* it?

Apparently William Campbell has been working as a bicycle racer in a traveling carnival of some sort. Presently, however, he is an advance man for that carnival, going ahead of it to various cities on its itinerary. He has thus been preceding the show and has been employed to do so all the way to the west coast. But he can't go on, and the carnival overtakes him in Kansas City. He has been "caught up with" and so is out of the race, must leave the track. But this last detail has to do with the rules of pursuit racing, which have here become confused with his obligation to stay in advance of the traveling show; reality has turned into allegory. As long as he remained ahead of the show, we are told, Campbell was being paid, but when the show overtook him, the burlesque manager, Mr. Turner, found him in bed. Turner has come and gone, and Campbell is still in bed. From this point, the story flashes back to the manager's visit, which "had been a little strange" (Hemingway, *Short Stories* 351). When Turner enters Campbell's room, he sees clothes on a chair, an open suitcase, and the ex–bike-racer's form hidden beneath the covers on the bed. From under the covers, Campbell says that Mr. Turner cannot fire him because he got down off his bicycle—here again it is clear that Campbell has his advance man job, his bicycle racing job, and the rules of the latter, merged in a confused allegory of his situation. He is "caught"—by the other racers, by the carnival, and by Bartleby-like abjection.

The carnival spirit that so often moves in the margins of the gothic tale, bearing its vestigial associations with the festive and fertile, resides here in the fact that Campbell was first a performer in, and then an advance man for, a festive enterprise, the traveling burlesque. He rode a bicycle, with its ironic sporting suggestions of health, play, balance, élan. The word *burlesque* is used no less than five times in the second paragraph of the story, a sign, in Hemingway's rhetorical practice, that an effect is being wrought. Horror's negotiations with the comic are in play here; the incongruously festive implications of carnival are established contrapuntally to Campbell's mental collapse.

Campbell converses with the carnival manager through the sheet he has over him and becomes, as the conversation progresses, increasingly preoccupied with the virtues of the sheet itself—its texture, the pleasure of talking through it, breathing through it. It is evident that Mr. Turner, a bald, middle-aged man, is, like Bartleby's boss, a decent person, and that Campbell, like Bartleby, has come to a helpless standstill. Like Usher or Bartleby, Campbell is the afflicted host visited by the sympathetic figure whose mission in the fertility narrative is to minister to the languishing individual. "You ought to stop off here, Billy, and take a cure," Turner tells Campbell. "I'll fix it up if you want to do it" (351). And as in "The House of Usher," "Benito Cereno," "Bartleby the Scrivener," and other tales in this tradition, the would-be healer's entry into the infirm host's domain, the crossing of the threshold, is not assumed but is carefully noted. A writer of Hemingway's skill and minimalist aesthetic would never ordinarily tell his readers, as he does here—after the fashion of Goldilocks—that Mr. Turner "had knocked on the door" and that Campbell had said, "Come in!" (351). There is arguably an archetypal, ritual imperative being attended to. Once he is in the room, Turner's benevolent concern for Campbell is made clear; at one point we are told—and again, it is difficult not to think of "Bartleby"—that Mr. Turner "was very fond of William Campbell; he did not wish to leave him. He was very sorry for him and felt a cure might help" (353).

Turner is under the impression that Campbell is drunk, which he has apparently been frequently before. Stray details of what has gone on begin to suggest themselves—it appears that Campbell, originally a competitive rider, had to be relieved of that role and that Turner gave him a promotional job instead—shades of "Bartleby"—and that now he has become incapable even of that. Campbell, in a confession interspersed with affirmations of his love for the shroud-like bedsheet under which he remains, reveals that, contrary to what Mr. Turner thinks, he is not drunk but in fact "hopped to the eyes." Like the narrator of Poe's "Ligeia," Campbell is in effect "a bounden slave in the trammels of opium" (*Selected* 46). He pushes his exposed forearm out from beneath the sheet, revealing blue needle marks running up to his elbow and almost touching one another. Turner's response is the one he offered when the subject was alcohol—that they have cures for drugs. Campbell's reply is a quintessentially abject and Bartleby-like one: "No," he says with dark finality, "They haven't got a cure for anything" (353). The mythic restoration task cannot be accomplished; the healing venture has failed—*Thanatos,* the death force, not Eros, reigns. As Carlos Baker comments regarding Hemingway's collected story oeuvre: "[T]his besieging horror of the limitless, the hallucinatory, the heartland of darkness, bulks like a Jungian Shadow. . . . Outside the circle which Hemingway has drawn by the special magic of his geometry, man's relations to the shadow stop nowhere" (132).

Analogously to *his* employer's attempts to reason with Bartleby, Turner's efforts to reason with Billy Campbell define the divide between everyday life and the figure fallen into despair beyond remedy. Like Bartleby as well, Campbell's speech tends to the non sequitur. To Turner's assertion that Billy can't just quit, that he must fight it out, the enthralled Billy replies, "Dear sheet, I can kiss this sheet and see through it at the same time." Faced with the emptiness that haunts the old man in "A Clean Well-Lighted Place" as well as Bartleby, Campbell is reduced to a drugged infantilism and is regressing further toward the womb-realm of indolent, sensuous drift. His end figures to be something along the lines of Bartleby's: "Strangely huddled at the base of the wall, his knees drawn up and lying on his side, his head touching the cold stones . . ." (*Short Works* 73).

A particularly interesting part of the dialogue between Campbell and Turner occurs toward the story's conclusion; here the haunting word *caught* returns. Mr. Turner has concluded his arguments about the possibility of cure, when Campbell begins to offer a bleak metaphor for his condition, a trope that defines the story's oppositions: movement/stopping, energy/exhaustion, agon/surrender, carnival/despair. It further defines the critical opposition in the tale's mythology—the comic-horror poles: "Listen Billy," William Campbell said,

> I want to tell you something. You're called "Sliding Billy." That's because you can slide. I'm called just Billy. That's because I never could

slide at all. I can't slide, Billy. . . . It just catches. Every time I try it, it catches. . . . It's awful when you can't slide. (353–54)

Compounding the horror implications in this "awful," the word *caught* has returned in "it catches." The two men, significantly both named Billy, figure forth comic and horrific possibilities. "Sliding Billy," like the lawyer in "Bartleby," gets by; he is flexible; he has retained a certain optimism, survived whatever stresses and threats he has had to undergo. He is described as "having many things to do," but he is willing nevertheless to arrange medical care for Campbell—"I'll fix it up if you want to do it." He represents the human figure able to maintain its balance in an often treacherous world, a figure of the energetic, and one appropriately associated with the carnivalesque. Campbell has in mind the comic sense of life, an organism able to regain its balance, to adapt, when he calls Turner "Sliding Billy." But, as pointed out previously, this inspiring sense of life ongoing implies its opposite. It is grimly ironic when Turner says to Campbell: "Don't try to be funny. You aren't funny" (351). Campbell is a creature of the other side of the organic equation, of life overwhelmed, "caught" and unable to "slide" or recover. As Baker observes, quoting a phrase from Carlyle, Hemingway's work tracks into "the vast circumambient realm of nothingness and night" (132).

As noted previously, not all modern and contemporary literature reflecting the grail, Fisher King pattern reflects the full community of life principle, extending out into social ramifications. "A Pursuit Race" does not reflect the full Waste Land motif in that the world outside the languishing figure is not overtly presented as imaging the figure's condition. This is perhaps a reflection of the overall tendency Bakhtin sees as characteristic of the Romantic grotesque, its focus narrowing into terms of individual isolation (*Rabelais* 39). Such a modified version of the archetype occurs as well in the 1990 film *Misery,* referenced earlier, the screen version of Stephen King's novel, starring James Caan and Kathy Bates. Paul Sheldon (Caan) is a writer who has written a series of shallow romance novels featuring a heroine named Misery Chastain. The popular success of the series has brought him wealth and fame, but he has been sidetracked creatively thereby and feels he has compromised himself as a writer. Never having intended to devote himself to trivial literature, he now seeks escape from his successful series and an opportunity to attempt more significant literary work. The implications are spiritual; he tells his New York agent he wants to accomplish something he might be proud to have

mentioned on his tombstone. The theme of the freeing of the waters, the liberation of stymied creative energy, is evident. In hopes of rescuing his integrity, Sheldon resolves to sacrifice his heroine; he concludes the current book
in the series with Misery's death in childbirth. The sacrificial death is thus associated with new life, fertility, and the liberation of Sheldon's deeper vitality.
His quest is chivalric and ascetic; not unlike Cheever's swimmer, he seeks return to the source, to the spiritual wellsprings of which he has lost track.

But his quest for that kind of salvation turns agonizing when he falls victim to Annie Wilkes, the classic fertility antagonist, the way-layer lurking on
the path of the chivalric journey, the hag, the loathly maid, the hideous dam-
sel, the pig women. Camille Paglia's description of the primitive "Venus of
Willendorf"—30,000 B.C.—would fit the gruesome Wilkes rather precisely:
"She is mired in the miasmic swamp . . . slumping, slovenly, sluttish, in a rut"
(*Personae* 57). Wilkes embodies the harpy, that "aspect of femaleness that
clutches and kills in order to feed itself" (*Personae* 51).[3] Kathy Bates is shockingly able to convey this whole mythic-demonic rubric in her now famous
portrayal as she captures Sheldon and keeps him in sickened captivity through
deception, painkillers, and physical disablement—a morbid inversion, though
she is a nurse, of the healer's role. Her rebreaking his legs starkly inverts the
recovery theme in the Fisher King paradigm. But it is notable that in her own
psychotic reasoning, she in fact *is* healer, is ministering to Sheldon's physi-
cal-spiritual needs, and is devoting herself to his recovery. Perhaps the true
would-be healer figure is a minor one in the film—the Colorado sheriff who
will not give up the search for Sheldon and enters the monster's lair looking
for him, only to find him in the underground (cellar), where he, the sheriff, is
killed by Wilkes.

The faltered state of all the figures so far discussed in this chapter might
also be conceptualized in terms of some manner of possession, the fall into
abjection—a life of self-inflicted, or other-inflicted, acquiescence. In James's
"The Turn of the Screw," the characters under possession are a nine-year-old
boy, a "dark prodigy," and his younger sister. As noted earlier, the visitor, the
ministering figure whose task is to save them, is the governess. There is a great
deal of Jamesian evasion and verbal roundaboutness as regards the evil and
defilement that prevail at the Bly estate; it is talked around, hinted at, suggested—creating a hovering sense of anxiety. The occult evil is conversation-
ally approached but repeatedly veered off from: The governess refers to "the
poison of an influence that I dared but half-phrase" (97). Things left thus half-

articulated open the way for reader speculation as to what is going unsaid.[4] Evil in the abstract cannot be the unmentionable thing since "evil" is mentioned frequently in the governess's narration. The specific acting out of evil by the precocious children is what a fine point is not being put on. Is the evaded thing some aspect of physicality; does their evil precocity include a sexual dimension? Mrs. Grose tells the governess that the sinister Peter Quint "was a hound." That "he did what he wished." The governess asks, regarding that statement, "With *her?*"—meaning with Miss Jessel. "With them all," Mrs. Grose answers, meaning the children, Flora and Miles, as well as Jessel (48). Certainly sexual implications are more than allowed for by the phrasing employed here and in a similar earlier scene: "'Quint was much too free,'" observes Mrs. Grose, and the governess interrogates the implication with "a sudden sickness of disgust": "'Too free with *my* boy?'" she asks. "'Too free with everyone,'" is the reply (39). The dialogue bobs and weaves and teases—perhaps violation of class distinction is being referred to. And obviously it is not; the choice of "sickness" and "disgust" indicates visceral repulsion, as when she later describes the truth she wishes to close her eyes to as "revoltingly, against nature" (122). And what is the unnamed offence Miles has been expelled from the boy's school for? What transgressions other than sexual ones would merit the extraordinary verbal avoidance? If it were theft, for instance, as is later implied by way of diversion, the hushed horror surrounding the matter would be excessive. And the story's deliberate hints that the transgressions involved might be merely class-based ones are obviously further obscurantism subverting the reader's perception of what is occurring and creating thereby a kind of heightened sense of anxiety and impatience. The vagueness becomes irritating, and it is as if the governess speaks for the reader when she finally, in exasperation at Miles's evasive rhetoric concerning the actions that occasioned his expulsion from school interjects: "'Stuff and nonsense! . . . What were these things?'" (133). The story in fact is characterized by, in Kenneth Burke's phrase, "a sexuality surrounded at every point by *mystification*" (qtd. in Paglia, *Personae* 612).

Miles's possible ability to "contaminate" and "corrupt" is entertained in one discussion between the same two women. These organic metaphors, which are set next to "naughty" in the discussion, are far too extreme for the comparison. *Corruption* might, on the other hand, be the word Victorians would apply to initiating other boys into homosexuality at a public school, arguably the implied offence that merited Miles's expulsion. If the worst implications of all this, including revenant pedophilia, are brought out from behind the veil of upper-class British decorum and Jamesian phraseology, an exotic brand of horror invention lies beneath the story's surface and a possession scenario rivaling the ghastly physicality of *The Exorcist* informs the work. Camille Paglia's profile of the narrative suggests this; she says of Quint and Jessel: "[T]heir lust is for homosexual capture. . . . [They are] malign *genii loci*, guardians of a territory one may enter but never leave. By cohabitation rather than blood, they construct an unholy family, a house outside the law" (612). Repressing the luridness in the tale, James still needs the implication of tangible, physical transgression and depravity in order effectively to achieve a real horror resonance and a paradoxically frigid eroticism.

Arguably referencing her role as would-be healer and exorcist, the governess frequently remarks her amazement at herself—the boldness and capability she finds, as though miraculously, at her disposal in her attempt to rescue the children from their demons. She writes proudly of her composure upon encountering the specter of Quint, that "no woman so overwhelmed ever in so short a time recovered her command of the *act*" (129). The story seems in fact built upon a romance or fairy-tale template: The "daughter of a poor country parson" is set a task by a Master, sent on a mission that will turn out to involve overwhelming, supernatural dangers. And she is oath-bound; the kind of arbitrary, cryptic constriction often put upon heroes in folktales is put upon the girl: In no case whatsoever may she appeal to the remote, handsome master of Bly or in any way seek his assistance. (As a girl-knight figure, a horror heroine, she anticipates the likes of the Jamie Lee Curtis character in *Halloween*.) She embraces her heroic role with a knightly spirit of daring-do, relishing the opportunity to serve her liege as it were: "I now saw that I had been asked for a service admirable and difficult; and there would be greatness in letting it be seen—oh! in the right quarter!—that I could succeed where many another girl might have failed. . . . It was . . . a magnificent chance" (41–42). She remarks her own "fierce rigor of confidence"; and at one point she says, apparently amazed at her competence and speaking out of an adrenalin rush: "[O]h, I was grand!" (123). She sees her inspiration as transcendant and herself as champion of a moral cause, remarkably able to confront, if it comes to that, the "white face of damnation," and notes her quickened courage when she momentarily has Quint stunned and wavering, "a baffled beast." She takes her mission to be a quest romance one: "fighting with a demon for a human soul" (129–30). Bartleby's employer has the same exalted task; his own conception of it is simply more modestly drawn. The mission of Father Karras in

The Exorcist is likewise cognate to that of the governess, and like her, he must undergo a trial of self-doubt and torment along the way, overcoming his modernist spiritual doubt and indolence. One event in "The Turn of the Screw" that particularly parallels the possession in *The Exorcist* is Flora's precocious physical ability, analogous to Regan's, evident in the scene in which the governess and Mrs. Gross find Flora on the far side of the lake having easily handled the formidable oars and having rowed the flat bottom boat across the choppy waters. The governess remarks "the prodigious character of the feat" (106). Another parallel between the two possessed girls is each's darkly inspired and precocious verbal obscenity; Mrs. Grose describes Flora's obscene observations regarding her governess as "beyond everything," and this is a girl many years younger than Regan and inhabiting a far more conservative culture. Flora and her brother are, like Regan, depraved, indeed "mad"—the governess so characterizes them (74). Like Regan too they are captured channels for diabolical expression; the siblings differ from Regan not in that they are less in the possession of the demonic but in that they are more in possession of themselves socially and therefore more able to hide their affliction. When the governess ventures into the territory of the possessing spirit, however, the demon response is the same as what Father Karras encounters in his exorcist efforts in Georgetown: "[I]t came in the form of an extraordinary blast and chill, a gust of frozen air and a shake of the room as great as if, in the wild wind, the casement had crashed in. The boy gave a loud, high shriek" (99). Beneath its rhetorically cultivated surface, the story is the potboiler horror piece James himself said it was.

The lethargy motif in gothic invention might be remarked, finally, in another form, as it surfaces in the guise of unsympathetic possession or in depraved characters or monsters who become merely empty, soulless physicality whose fate no healer is attempting to recover. The possessed in *Night of the Living Dead,* for example, are not sympathetic; they have been translated irrevocably into an undifferentiated *It.* Often vagueness is situated as frightening in and of itself—the zombie is vague, as are the pod people in *Invasion of the Body Snatchers,* or those film characters drained by vampiric molestation. Stephen King notes this in *Danse Macabre,* that no outstanding grotesqueness marks the pod people, only that they are a little out of it—indifferent and characterless. Their illness is manifested in an attenuated cognitive energy and social focus, a bland inattention, a diminished discernment, and narrowed functioning. In *The Howling,* the cult initiates at the California camp seem at first sociable in the normal sense, but in short order, their cultish sensibility, the way their minds are really set exclusively on werewolf matters, shows through their inauthentic, treacherous gregariousness. Karen White's husband, once bitten, evidences the distant, preoccupied manner of the possessed; he becomes increasingly far away though physically present. A scene in Thomas Ligotti's "Last Feast of Harlequin" situates the same motif of envelopment-fear that informs both these films, the dread of being appropriated into some enervated and diluted homogenization (the psychic terror politically exploited by anticommunist literature and films of the 1950s). The story's main character has entered a gathering place for the zombified townspeople of Mirocaw, upsetting their assembly, and some go mindlessly toward him with their worm-like affect and physical movement:

> They said nothing. Out of the backroom others began to emerge. . . . In a few moments the room was crowded . . . all of them gazing emptily in the dimness. . . . Actually, I felt as if it was quite within my power to pummel them easily into submission, their mousy faces almost inviting a succession of firm blows. But there were so many of them.
>
>   They slid toward me. . . . Their eyes seemed empty and unfocused, and I wondered a moment if they were even aware of my presence. Nevertheless, I was the center upon which their lethargic shuffling converged, their shoes scuffing softly along the bare floor. I began to deliver a number of hasty inanities as . . . their weak . . . bodies [nudged] against mine. . . . I could not focus my attention strongly enough to act. . . . In a sudden surge of panic, I pushed through their soft ranks and was outside. (*Nightmare* 211–12)

This ghastly scene turns on the horror of a final victory of pathology and contamination, of physical/psychic diminishment, the threatened ascendancy of an unlife that is sluggish, dumb, and soulless. The statement "I could not focus my attention strongly enough to act" situates the ultimate horror imagining—that of being unable to ward off that which is disgusting and heinous, being subject to its embrace.

In Mary Wilkins Freeman's nineteenth-century "Luella Miller," the vampiric Luella, like Siegle's pod people, is simply a little vague, and like them she is lax, neglectful of everyday chores, which instead fall to her spellbound, acquiescent victims. Luella leeches energy, apparently without the vampire's bloodsucking, from her housekeepers and anyone else who falls within her domestic sway. While concerned with a seemingly psychic-energetic vampir-ism, in comparison to what occurs, for example, in Le Fanu's "Carmilla," wherein Carmilla's passion for her unfortunate girlfriend's lifeblood is at the same time a sensual, lesbian obsession, "Luella Miller" still manages to be a frightening tale, owing in large part to its evocation of morbid *indolence*. Free-man employs an understated narration describing how one resident after an-other, healthy heretofore, degenerates in Luella's house, has his or her vital-ity mysteriously drained away, and dies, all the while maintaining a kind of numb, mesmerized devotion to the beautiful and thriving mistress. But it is not only Luella's enthralled victims who are bland and unaware; for all her outstanding physical health, she is herself vague and flat in affect. When Luella's Aunt Abbey is too far gone to get up from bed, Luella's feisty neigh-bor, Miss Anderson, suggests that Luella make her own coffee: "'I never made the coffee in all my life,' says she, dreadful astonished." When another victim, Maria, is failing, Miss Anderson again scolds Luella and asks why she doesn't do her own housework: "Then Luella looked at me like a baby who has a rattle shook at it. She sort of laughed as innocent as you please. 'Oh, I can't do the work myself, Miss Anderson,' says she. 'I never did. Maria *has* to do it'" (88). This listless vacancy and characterlessness, registered in small matters, be-comes disturbing as the reader realizes that the beautiful Luella is a devour-ing force, apparently no more morally aware than is a parasitic plant.

The disgust that such lack of normal affect and presence triggers is so powerfully evident in the Ligotti story recently noted that I would return to it here in conclusion. The weird residents of Mirocaw are repulsive in their slackness and insubstantiality, their seeming aimlessness and "inhumanly limp expressions" (*Nightmare* 218). The narrator remarks the way the inhabitants "leaned lethargically" as they walked, their "nauseating passivity and languor." A group of townspeople are described as occupying a *vacant* diner.

> "Vacant" is the appropriate word here. . . . The congregation of that half-lit room formed less a presence than an absence, even consider-ing the oppressive number of them. Those eyes that did not or could not focus on anything, the pining lassitude of their faces, the lazy march of their feet. I was spiritually drained when I ran out of there. (217–18)

Later, as yet unaware he is one of them, he remarks that he "would simply wander around in that lackadaisical manner I had learned from them" (445).

The horror here is of that which is sound and healthy backsliding into devitalized, deathly mire, the swamp of unlife—the body as squalor. This theme will be taken up in the next chapter in terms of its bearing upon squalid, soulless places, the gothic sinister loci.

Sinister Loci:
The Properties of Terror

And cold madness wandered aimlessly about the house.

—CZESLAW MILOSZ

Babylon . . . is fallen and become a dwelling place of demons and a lurking place of every unclean exhalation, and a lurking place of every unclean and hated bird.

—Revelation 18:2

. . . but there was something about the atmosphere of this place that took the heart out of you and made you no good.

—STEPHEN KING, *'Salem's Lot*

CHARLOTTE PERKINS GILMAN'S CLASSIC "THE YELLOW Wallpaper" begins by recounting a couple's renting of a rural estate, one that was available at a remarkably appealing price. In the gothic context, there tends to be much ado about such real-estate matters, a reflection of the genre's notorious spatialization of fear. In his autobiographical *Something of Myself*, Rudyard Kipling describes an encounter he and his wife had with an actual malevolent house they rented in 1896 upon their return to England from the United States, a rental that "seemed almost too good to be true." And indeed a dark revelation ensued upon their renting the property

> in the shape of a growing depression which enveloped us both—a gathering of blackness of mind and sorrow of heart. . . . It was the Feng-shui—the Spirit of the house itself—that darkened the sunshine and fell upon us every time we entered. . . .

[Finally] we paid forfeit and fled. More than thirty years later on a motor trip we ventured down the steep little road to that house, and met . . . quite unchanged, the same brooding Spirit of deep, deep Despondency within the open, lit rooms. (78–79)

The realtor in horror fiction holds the keys to the anomalous house of gothic imagining and is often the unwitting enabler of horror events wherein taking possession of a property is more deeply a matter of being taken possession of *by* a property. The realtor thus accommodates a preternatural negotiation—the protagonists' move from the light of day world of the business transaction across a threshold and into regions of Amityville horrors. The significance of thresholds has been discussed in previous chapters here, and not for nothing is "Knock" the name of the grotesque property agent at the service of the vampire count in Murnau's film *Nosferatu*. The gothic realtor is involved in ritual admission or entry; Janus, the gatekeeper in Roman mythology, guarded a threshold of rebirth, a significant verge, but the gothic gatekeeper opens the way to grimmer realities. Jack Nicholson, in *The Shining*, sees promise of new creativity and spiritual reinvigoration in the mountain hotel he and his family are to occupy for the winter, but the keys he is given open gates verging instead upon things sinister. The couple in *Rosemary's Baby* similarly associates their new abode with a new beginning and initiation into the world of happy parenthood.

Roman Polanski's *The Tenant* (1976) begins, as did *Rosemary's Baby*, with issues pursuant to a party's occupation of a new apartment. A timorous office worker seeks a flat and unfortunately rents a haunted one from which the former tenant finally leaped to her death. A piece of real estate in Portland, Maine, a projected Portland Mall and Shopping Center, figures in the coming of vampires to 'Salem's Lot in Stephen King's novel of that name. In a deal involving this valuable site, Lawrence Crockett, a mercenary local realtor, facilitates the vampire Barlow's acquisition of the evil-ridden Marsten house and his entry into the 'Salem's Lot community. This echoes of course Stoker's *Dracula*, in which a real-estate deal occasions Jonathan Harker's protracted and fateful journey to eastern Europe and in which Dracula's purchase of a British property, along with events involved in occupying it, take up an extended early portion of the novel.

Dracula's aristocratic status and wealth are not beside the point here either in that, in Transylvania and in England, they afford access to properties

remote and private—the ideal gothic setting—estates wherein one may in-
dulge in dark practices. The familiar gothic pattern situates an aristocratic
dwelling high above the vulgar village, radically exclusive, cut off from scru-
tiny and normal moral conventions, and immune to the ordinary reach of law.
The Marsten house is a modern equivalent, a structure off from and above the
working world of the Maine town, but the model is medieval and not without real historical precedents. The predator Gilles de Rais in fifteenth-century
France ruled over a castle of horrors wherein children kidnapped from surrounding villages were subjected to abominations and dismembered in the
chambers of his privileged property.

> This anguish is that of the feudal world, over which are cast the shad-
> ows of massive fortresses. Today, tourists are attracted to these fortresses;
> then they were monstrous prisons, and their walls evoked only occasion-
> ally muffled cries. In the presence of Gilles de Rais' fairy-tale castles
> . . . we ought to recall these butcheries of children presided over not
> by wicked fairies, but by a man drunk with blood. (Bataille, *Trial* 14)

Dark fairy-tale and historic reality converge here, and such settings would
become part of classic horror mythology. More modest malevolent habitations
of course characterize more current literary horror, but even the space of the
modern apartment, as in the case of the Polanski films just mentioned, has been
sinisterized. The more traditionally gothic house in Shirley Jackson's "The
Lovely House" is not a medieval fortress, but it retains the gothic remoteness,
elaborateness, and seclusion that lend themselves to grotesque occurrences.
Such houses, as earlier alluded to, are often to be purchased or rented at un-
commonly agreeable prices. The father of the family in Mary Wilkins Freeman's
"The Vacant Lot," who purchases an apparently very desirable Boston house
in a nice neighborhood for one-fifth its obvious value, lives to regret it. The
married couple in Edith Wharton's "Afterward," like the couple in Gilman's
"The Yellow Wallpaper," also unwisely rent peculiarly inexpensive estates.
Gilman's narrator wonders, regarding the house she and her husband have
taken: "[W]hy should it be let so cheaply? And have stood so long untenanted"
(Oates 87). The Marsten house and the house in *The Haunting of Hill House* have
also stood long untenanted, cultivating their nightmares.

It is significant, returning to the threshold and gatekeeper thematic, that
no less than five pages of Jackson's novel are devoted to Eleanor's detainment
at the gate of the Hill House property. She is delayed by a shabby realtor's

hireling, who guards the grounds, a delay that underscores the occult importance of her admission. In *The First Deadly Sin,* Frank Sinatra is denied entry
to the evil apartment of Daniel Blank by another sleazy functionary, the
building doorman and key-keeper. And though no gatekeeper as such detains
him, some three pages opening "The Fall of the House of Usher" mark the
narrator-visitor's threshold—and arguably ritual—*pause* before proceeding
over the causeway into the Usher mansion (Poe, *Selected* 54–57). The private
space in "The House of Usher," and in many other gothic examples, is the
uncanny one entered from the comparative sanity of the public realm. But
often, conversely, the private space, the household, is the benign place threatened by madness from without. The body, analogously, may be invaded from
outside, its threshold transgressed by a pathogen; or the body may enter a
malefic area, crossing into unsound regions—in either case a verge is crossed.
Mary Chapman has described thresholds and doorways as sites that "buttress
the divisions between the private household and the public sphere at the same
time they acknowledge their permeability." The landscape of Brockden
Brown's *Ormond,* she observes, "is rendered monstrous where the distinctions
between private and public collapse and the vulnerability of the private space—
the body, the household . . . is exposed" (23–24). That dynamic, the transition
from threatening public space to the secure household suggests the nature of
Edith Wharton's threshold terror cited previously as well as the poignant reaching out for the threshold by the gang-raped concubine in the Book of Judges.

Occupying what was formerly another's private space is problematical in
horror literature and in fact in reality. Advisors to those putting their houses
on the market these days emphasize the advantage of depersonalizing the
premises, removing one's stuff so that the place appears neutral and not suggestive of someone's lingering presence—to which buyers tend to have an aversion. A house that retains the personality of its former owners remains in their
spiritual possession; it is *possessed.* The scrubbing, painting, retiling of floors,
and refurnishing of a purchased house enact a rite of exorcism ridding the
place of the carryover from the former inhabitants. Furnished rental properties are especially worrying for this reason since the tenant is often constrained
from performing a full exorcism. Gothic houses, with their abundant secluded
spaces, nurture psychopathic carryover, projecting a "lived in" character in the
most distressing sense, a karma, and realtors in gothic fiction and film are frequently puzzled and dubious when intellectuals and artists, for example, given
to indulging antiquarian tastes, express interest in such properties. Count

Dracula, in fact, is a confirmed antiquarian who declares to his real-estate agent that to live in a *new* house would kill him (35).

★ ★ ★

The world we construct has us implicit in it; we anthropomorphize our space. Much of the immediate *res extensa* we encounter publicly is a product of human artifice and design. Architecture—buildings, houses, interiors—constitute a text configured in terms of human physicality. A house in its layout speaks of human comings and goings, of people's ways—their size, reach, behavior, and interactions; their work, their recreation, their eating and sleeping. Stuart Kauffman suggests, further still, that the crafting of artifacts by humans recapitulates in some ways at least the crafting of organisms by natural, biological energies. "Might the same general laws," he asks, "govern major aspects of biological and technological evolution?" (192). The radical intimacy of house and householder in gothic tales marks an extreme expression of this kind of intuition. Anne Rivers Siddons writes of any house that "it is an extension of ourselves; it tolls in answer to one of the most basic chords mankind will ever hear. My shelter. My earth. My second skin" (qtd. in King, *Danse* 272). Our house defines our safe, familiar space; it is *heimlich.* Freud, in his essay "The Uncanny," makes much of this German word, which I have used previously and for which there is no good English equivalent. The word's literal meaning, he notes, is "belonging to the house" (23), and its opposite is *unheimlich,* that which is "unhomely." *Unheimlich* has been translated as "uncanny," that is, disturbing, somehow wrong, freakish, and anomalous. The *unheimlich* falls outside the categories we are at home with, familiar with. In this etymology, the house is the defining symbol of what is right and normal, the violation and defilement of which situates primitive anxieties. In *Huckleberry Finn,* a whole two-story house drifts down the predawn river emerging as a disturbing image of the domestic site subverted, become *unheimlich.* Within the uncanny house lies a naked dead man, shot in the back, whose face Jim warns Huck not to look at; "it's too gashly." The drifting house's interior is a deranged, surrealized human space—women's underclothes, a milk bottle with a rag in it for a baby to suck, a fiddle bow, a wooden leg lie around (Twain 47).

In *In Cold Blood* an orderly family house is entered by killers out of the feral American night. And the same fear pattern is found in *Beowulf.* Heorot Hall situates a domestic place wherein familiar communal protocols obtain; its violation by something issuing out of the wild darkness touches upon a primordial terror. If the boundaries of the house, the sleeping place, can be transgressed, it

is near to the fundamental defensive line, the skin, being crossed. The tropics
of threatened household are one more expression of the gothic mode's essential preoccupation with decline, wasting, abject exposure, and disintegration; it
is fearful when the guards cannot protect the communal place and its integrity
is lost: "My household-guard / are on the wane, fate sweeps them away / into
Grendel's clutches" (*Beowulf* 33). Grendel's coming to the hall, like the coming of Smith and Hickock to the Clutter homestead, marks the encroachment
upon civilized space by something bred in terrifying nocturnal reaches:

> But when the dawn broke and day crept in
> over each blood-spattered bench
> the floor of the mead-hall where they had feasted
> would be slick with slaughter.
>
> (*Beowulf* 33)

Much macabre literature and film centers upon the violation of home sanctuary, the terrible image, as in *In Cold Blood,* of the house become radically
unhomelike, a place of carnage, the terrors of the public streets barging in.

Langer argues, referencing in effect the same "community of the Life principle" Jessie Weston notes (*Feeling* 35), that indeed all human expression reflects
our physiological nature; the human environment is throughout informed by
our organic idioms. "Therefore any building that can create the illusion of . .
. a 'place' articulated by the imprint of human life, must seem organic, like a
living form" (99). To the peasantry in the vicinity of the Usher estate, the
house-building is identical with the house-genetic material (Poe, *Selected* 56).
In the gothic framework, deteriorating place speaks emphatically of organic
deterioration in general. In literary horror, places often enable the trope of
languishment and lethargy discussed, mainly in terms of people, in the preceding chapter. Images expressive of the dissolution of architecture, infrastructure, and spatial ordering, resonate in our psycho-physical imaginations, eliciting a sense of a generally dissolving integrity, an objectified schizophrenia.
"Things fall apart; the center cannot hold" is by now an over-referenced line
of Yeats's, but it is so arguably because it touches so precisely on a fundamental element of horror—degeneration, a critical unraveling.

The properties of terror, houses or other sites, are ones that, should we
imagine horrible things unfolding, we would imagine them unfolding *there*—
in "evilly shadowed seaport[s] of death and blasphemy" (Lovecraft, *Innsmouth*
31). These are places marginal, degenerated, and soulless—providing openings

for terror. "There are . . . some freakish occurrences to be recounted," Clive
Barker writes in one of his horror novels, ". . . most of them take place in backwaters, in ill-lit corridors, in shunned wastelands among rain-sodden mat-
tresses and ashes of old bonfires" (*Damnation* 277). In *Beowulf,* the encounters
with demonic threat occur in "three archetypal sites of fear: the barricaded
night-house, the infested underwater current, and the reptile haunted rocks
of a wilderness" (Heaney, *Beowulf* xii). Nor is the temporal map evenly secure;
horror has its favored places in time as well as in space. There are comparatively uninhabited, unsavory areas of time in which atrocities are most imaginable and likely, derelict hours, as it were, in the twenty-four-hour cycle. That
dread may situate in time is implicit, for instance, in Scott Fitzgerald's remark
in *The Crack-Up* that in a really dark night of the soul it is always three o'clock
in the morning (75).

Deteriorated places, neglected buildings, discarded streets and facilities
may reveal uninspired and perhaps repressed sectors of cultural life, a lack of
common renewal, a failure of the fertile, creative spirit. Such corrupted places
are outcroppings of a social system's underground, unadorned areas of the
communal psyche. They represent lapsed zones where the city, for example,
the polis, is not managing to put up a civilized front—where its fly is open and
its nose running. Thomas Ligotti describes a malefic town set in rural Illinois:
"Mirocaw has another coldness within its cold, another set of buildings and
streets that exists behind the visible town's facade like a world of disgraceful
back alleys" (*Nightmare* 209–10). "Disgraceful" is apt here. And there is no reference to the town's *people,* but on the other hand, there of course is in that
they are implicit in the place; the alleys are the lanes of the communal psyche,
the communal body.

Invasion of the Body Snatchers (1956), though its central horror turns on alien
possession of the body, leans on sinister place, as many horror films do, to
register objectively the effects and ramifications of demonic contamination.
Stephen King writes of Don Siegle's book on which *Body Snatchers* was based:
"The roads leading to Santa Mira . . . are so full of potholes and washouts that
pretty soon the salesmen who service the town—who aerate its municipal
lungs with the life-giving atmosphere of capitalism—will no longer bother to
come." The growing squalor reflects the inability of Santa Mira's possessed
residents to any longer act upon their surroundings properly; they cannot act
to stave off this dissolution, to accomplish that fundamental gesture, that *art.*
The residents "don't mow their lawns or replace the garage glass that got bro-

ken. They don't repaint their houses when they get flaky" (King, *Danse* 5–6). Similarly, the overwhelmed ship in "Benito Cereno" suffers from "long unacquaintance with the scraper, tar, and the brush" (Melville, *Short Works* 241). The narrator of Ligotti's "Last Feast of Harlequin," walking around a town dominated by a grotesque pathology, notes the "formidable shoddiness" of the buildings (*Nightmare* 211). Eleanor Vance describes Mrs. Dudley, the keeper at Hill House, as projecting "an indefinable air of dirtiness" (Jackson *Hill House* 36). And the vampiric inroads in King's 'Salem's Lot, Maine, are devastating in their implications for the safety of the citizenry, and part and parcel of that horror, as with any pestilence, is a degeneration of community order—family, government, infrastructure.

Gothicism is often equated with its most garish expressions, as typified perhaps by Poe—Madeline Usher falling upon her petrified brother; the immolation in "Hop-Frog" when "the eight corpses swung in their chains, a fetid, blackened, hideous, and indistinguishable mass" (*Selected* 237); the ultra-lurid morbidity of the conclusion to "The Case of M. Valdemar": "[H]is whole frame . . . crumbled—absolutely *rotted* away beneath my hands. . . . Upon the bed . . . there lay a nearly liquid mass of loathsome . . . detestable putridity" (*Selected* 237). The squalid places of horror imagining are of a piece with the squalid physiology Poe presents here. Stephen King remarks that in *Invasion of the Body Snatchers* the pod people are not monstrosities; their bodies appear physically normal. What is disturbing about them is that they are "a little vague, a little messy." Their soullessness, that is, is to be read in the gradual disintegration of their houses, streets, and so forth—"messy" has dire psychic implications. The terrible thing about the pod people "is that they lack even the most common and easily attainable sense of aesthetics" (*Danse* 5–6). When Wittgenstein observes that "bad housekeeping within the state fosters bad housekeeping in families" (63), he is not merely affirming a bourgeois social ethos respecting prim neighborhoods; something more significant is being referenced. Housekeeping, in its deepest implications, is a primal imperative, part of our warding off of abjection—of decay, rot, squalidness. Healthy, civilized communities and individuals evidence an aesthetic interest and care, an engagement with themselves and their environment, that goes beyond the bare minimum to the dimension of a critical practice, an art. Places that evidence the lack of this critical endeavor bespeak incursions of morbidity into the communal body.

Newspapers gathered on a house's front porch unretrieved may suggest an atrocity within. A neglected, disheveled place, as surely as a neglected and disheveled body, may trigger the fear and loathing that arises, to quote King's phrase again, "from a pervasive sense of disestablishment; that things are in the unmaking" (*Danse* 9). It is a horrid discovery, however anticipated by the reader, when Susan peers through the shutters of the Marsten house in *'Salem's Lot* and finds that the repairs and refurbishing the townspeople had assumed Straker and his partner were undertaking over recent months are not evident: "Why they haven't done a thing to it," she says. "It's a mess" (419). This disrepair evokes the entire complex of evil and desolation of which it is a part; in this defiled *place,* Sue sees the defiling hands of vampirism. Even small, subtle lapses in domestic upkeep can suggest a deeper dimension of things-not-right. As mentioned in the last chapter, Luella Miller's absentness and disregard is analogous to the syndrome presented by the pod people in *Body Snatchers;* in Freeman's story, the presence of vampirism is registered in an environmental unconcern and neglect. When Mrs. Anderson visits the house and remarks "I don't believe Luella had swept since Maria died," it is not a banal observation; rather it is a quiet version of the sinister loci motif, a signature of horror in a socially coded form. The dehumanized lose their sense of the elemental positive gesture, the endeavor toward beauty and grace. This is implicit in E. W. F. Tomlin's observation that probably no great human culture has existed that "did not place emphasis upon the skilled preparation of food" (139).

Cobwebs, a standard gothic signifier, suggest stagnation in terms of time and place, inactivity, abandonment of the area involved, the absence of effective human presence and concern. This trope is extended eerily in Dickinson's "How Many Times Have These Low Feet Staggered," quoted in part previously, wherein the dereliction of household duties—flies not swatted, windows begrimed, cobwebs not swept—reflect someone's absence and a prevailing listlessness, a silence that amplifies the buzz of flies and the atmosphere of death. All normal movement is extinguished; everything is frozen in the "soldered," "adamantine" finality of the housekeeper's grave. The house is now *unheimlich:*

Buzz the dull flies—on the chamber window—
Brave—shines the sun through the freckled pane—
Fearless—the cobweb swings from the ceiling—
Indolent Housewife—in daisies—lain!

(88)

Essential warding off is no longer being undertaken. Indolence and death are near things to one another; lack of upkeep points toward the grave.

Areas shut off and not kept up are as well locales where things twisted and repulsive may take place. A smell emanates from Emily Grierson's house—a marker of her growing peculiarity and unsoundness. Mark Edmundson describes the *Nightmare on Elm Street* boiler room as "the place where the school pervert, be he janitor or teacher, goes to ply his vice" (54). The standard gothic real estate is remote too, cut off, like Lovecraft's Innsmouth, which is "badly cut off from the rest of the country by marshes and creeks" (35), or the Bates Motel in *Psycho,* which is left behind by the interstate highway system. In Lovecraft's work, Maurice Lévy maintains, "[the bizarre] is a type of gangrene that gnaws, wears away, and finally rots the familiar world through and through" (38). Significantly, he adds that "the strain obviously spreads to architecture." The biological metaphor is notable here—a "gangrene" that "rots" and "gnaws." The body is the primary, elemental household. When Tom Jarndyce's nephew recalls his uncle's suicide in Dickens's *Bleak House,* he tells Esther, with a shudder: "When I brought what remained of him home here, the brains seemed to me to have been blown out of the house too." The siege of mortal contagion described in Poe's "King Pest" represents a social, structural contamination correlative to the contamination befalling individuals. The plague brings about districts of "dismal solitude" set off behind barriers from the rest of the city, wretched no-man's-lands of pollution and criminality.

Jarndyce describes another family property likewise desolated by the gangrene of a Kafkaesque inheritance litigation, and here again the architectural object, the house, is part of an organic continuum with its human inhabitants and shares their fate:

> It is a street of perishing blind houses, with their eyes stoned out; without a pane of glass . . . with the bare blank shutters tumbling from their hinges and falling asunder . . . the stone steps to every door turned stagnant green; the very crutches on which the ruins are propped, decaying. (89)

Bad places in other instances map not only the despair but the corruption and depravity of their inhabitants. Though the "fine furnishings" establishment co-owned by Straker and Barlow in *'Salem's Lot* is only recently opened, when Mark, Jimmy, and Ben break in through the back, the air is "noxious and stale, the air of a room shut up for centuries rather than days" (564). The bad place testifies to the gothic's biological slant in that "bad" conflates the moral sense "evil" and the organic sense "rotten."

★ ★ ★

"It is reasonable to say," Gaston Bachelard writes, "that we 'read' a house, or 'read' a room, since both room and house are psychological diagrams" (38). Spatial realities and forms trace back primordially; the gothic's corridors and staircases are dreamscapes resurrecting the "meandering or labyrinthine paths, spirals, mazes, actually followed in ritual . . . the archetypal endeavors of the divine ancestor . . . to be born" (Brown 38). The horror mode's landscapes are hallucinatory; and things lose their ordinary character, as they do in this excerpt from a Robert Bly poem:

> Come with me into those things that have felt this
>   despair for so long—
> Those removed Chevrolet wheels that howl with a terrible
>   loneliness,
> Lying on their backs in the cindery dirt, like men drunk, and
>   naked,
> Staggering off down a hill at night to drown at last in the pond.
> Those shredded inner tubes abandoned on the shoulders of thru-
>   ways
> . . . .
> And those roads in South Dakota that feel around in the
>   darkness . . .
>
> (13)

Because horror literature is disposed to this kind of surreality, things "outside" tend to shed their positivist framing and may take on an animistic character—affect, intention, agency. The gothic "outside" familiar world provides no relief from an inner haunting; instead, "inner" terrors flicker in structures, objects, and landscape. The outside is normally that against which we check our subjective impressions as to their validity—our empirical touchstone. But rather than putting fears to rest, the sinister loci of the gothic disturbingly confirm a character's unsettling suspicions and exceed them. Sue in *'Salem's Lot* is engaged in a kind of reconnoitering of, or dialogue with, location: "As she passed the turnoff which led to the dump, a ripple of unease went through her. On this gloomy stretch of road, nebulous possibilities seemed more real" (386). In "The House of Usher," the narrator finds the objective insinuating a detestable reality that he hopes the *inside,* in the form of an unaffected ratio-nalism, will dispel. The genre exploits the fact that in human perception, es-pecially under stress, objective and subjective can become slippery categories. What Eleanor Vance is "thinking" within Hill House is often presented as perhaps being thought *to* her by some *genus loci:* "She shivered and thought, *the words coming freely into her mind,* Hill House is vile, it is diseased; get away from here at once" (italics added, Jackson, *Hill House* 33).

This destabilized perception of "objective" and "subjective" reality in fact manifests often in dark romantic literature outside the strictest confines of "Gothicism," for example, in Thomas Hardy's *Return of the Native.* The men and boys of the countryside are lighting the customary winter bonfires of Guy Fawkes Day, and the pageant flames impart a chthonian imagination of the surroundings. Hardy captures the alchemy of firelight and shadow that col-lapses ordinary reality, creating a pagan phantasmagoria wherein the putatively surmounted returns:

> Black chaos comes, and the fettered gods of the earth say, Let there be light. Yet the permanent moral expression of each face it was im-possible to discover, for as the nimble flames towered, nodded, and swooped through the surrounding air the blots of shade and flakes of light upon the countenances of the group changed shape and position endlessly. All was unstable, quivering as leaves, evanescent as lightning. Shadowy eye-sockets deep as those of a death's head suddenly turned into pits of lustre; a lantern jaw was cavernous, then it was shining; wrinkles were emphasized to ravines, or obliterated entirely by a changed ray. Nostrils were dark wells; sinews in old necks were gilt mouldings; things with no particular polish on them were glazed; bright objects, such as the tip of a furze-hook one of the old men car-ried, were as glass; eyeballs glowed like little lanterns. Those whom nature had depicted as merely quaint became grotesque, the grotesque became preternatural. (15)

"All was unstable" defines the gothic-romantic ideal in which landscape-dreamscape-mythscape intermingle polymorphically.

Roderick Usher and the Usher mansion thus intermingle and decompose together. In *The Shining,* the Overlook Hotel and Jack Torrence are in a simi-lar occult sympathy. In *The Silence of the Lambs,* as Clarice Starling flies in a twin-engine Beechcraft out of the Quantico marine base, she studies the case file photos on Buffalo Bill's psychopathic homicides. She is led to contemplate the significance of the *locations* the photos reveal, the sites contextualizing the skinned bodies, and then to be aware—a morbid loop—of her *present* context mingling with the pictured one and influencing her gruesome perceptions:

> Here they had not even their skins as they lay on littered riverbanks amid the outboard-oil bottles and sandwich bags that are our common squalor. . . . Starling reminded herself that their teeth were not bared in pain, that turtles and fish in the course of feeding had created that expression.
>
> They wouldn't have been so hard to look at, Starling thought, if this airplane cabin wasn't so warm and if the damned plane didn't have this crawly yaw as one prop caught the air better than the other, and if the God damned sun didn't splinter so on the scratched windows and jab like a headache. (Harris 99)

In the projective realm of horror fiction, things run together like this in a unified terribleness. The photos present atrocities that befouled riverbanks, an unstable aircraft, fish and turtles, sun and scratched glass—all weirdly contextualize and exacerbate.

Even cyberspace by now has its sinister, *unheimlich* regions, its corridors down which children are cautioned not to go, its beasts baiting traps and lying in wait—and the places are not clearly marked. Horror exploits such ambiguities. The coastal retreat in *The Howling* would appear to be terrible only owing to its werewolf inhabitants, but the hideous Dance Academy in Dario Argento's film *Suspiria,* a Bad Place tour-de-force, seems organically penetrated by the wickedness of the witch coven that owns the building. The Usher mansion, like Hill House, bears down upon the spirit of its inhabitants; the visitor remarks "an effect which the *physique* of the gray walls and turrets, and of the dim tarn into which they looked down, had, at length, brought about upon the *morale* of [Usher's] existence" (*Selected* 60). But even here the narrator's independence from Usher's paranoia is subject to question. Nor in *The Haunting* are we sure where to locate Hill House in the place-person continuum:

> To what extent may the "derangement of Hill House" be blamed on the derangement of the people who were, are, and probably will be in it? . . . Is there something wrong with that spiral staircase in the library or just with the clumsy people who try to climb it? The only safe

bet is that something is wrong. . . . Our poor quartet . . . Dr. Markay, Theo, Luke, and Eleanor . . . are not only helpless to untie themselves from entangling puppet strings; they can't even find the knots. (Ligotti, *Nightmare* xiv)

Houses and other human structures in the gothic framework are thus not givens but rather potentials, altering weirdly in relation to the observer. Like Hardy's heath, they can be imaginatively reconstructed by storms, darkness, firelight, and so on. But *site* is all important—"the truly fantastic exists only where the impossible can make an irruption, through time and space, into an objectively familiar *locale*" (italics added, Lévy 36–37).

A house, like a ship or, for that matter, a gothic tale itself, is biogenic. Our cars are bilaterally symmetrical like the human organism, two eyed as we are and as were the horses that preceded them, and their power capabilities are expressed in terms of horses as well. Langer refers to the obvious, rationalized examples of this organic principal in the works of Louis Sullivan and Frank Lloyd Wright. That even houses in the insistently ungothic tradition of Wright may function gothically is evident in Anne Rivers Siddons's *The House Next Door,* however, in which the domicile in question perfectly realizes the Wright ideal of organicism but turns out to have a freakishness of its own evident in the sketches in that the house is an organism rather than the structural realization of a theoretical organic ideal:

> I do not as a rule care for contemporary architecture, [but] this house was different. It commanded you, somehow, yet soothed you. It grew out of the penciled earth like an elemental spirit that had lain, locked and yearning for the light, through endless deeps of time. . . . I could hardly imagine the hands and machinery that would form it. I thought of something that had started with a seed, put down deep roots, grown in the suns and rains of many years into the upper air. In the sketches, at least, the woods touched unpressed around it like companions. The creek unfolded its mass and seemed to nourish its roots. It looked— inevitable. (24)

When literary conventions such as the bleak, antiquated mansion become deeply familiar, they are often dropped of course or become narrative blanks; a readership, that is, brings these conventions to a reading, and they need not be overtly presented. The Jamesian "terror in sunlight" turns on the very absence of conventional gothic darkness. Siddons cites *Rosemary's Baby* as the quintessential employment of this device that depends on "the juxtaposition of the unimaginably terrible with the utterly ordinary" (qtd. in King, *Danse* 275). The menacing place is understated in *Rosemary's Baby* in such a way that the very understatement becomes disturbing—Hitchcock the obvious influence here. Rosemary's new apartment, which is to be the place in which her child will be nurtured and protected, is occupied by Satanists who are decidedly ordinary and even charming and thoughtful in their way—when they bind and secure Rosemary for Satan's insemination, for instance, one of the women is maternally concerned that the binding not be uncomfortable on Rosemary's wrists and ankles. But here again the conflation of house-apartment violation and body violation, their situation as a continuum, is evident.

Le Fanu exploited the power of this identification between house and body in his novel *Uncle Silas* and novella *Carmilla,* in both of which an intruder insinuates herself into an erstwhile sane, established household. The aversion response in the heroine is of the sort Siddons describes; the "desecration" of the house/body, the "corruption, as it were, by something alien takes on a peculiar and bone-deep horror and disgust" (qtd. in King, *Danse* 272). These transgressions of a deep-seated ethos of household sanctity create a sense of things out of control, a distorted social frame underscoring the main horror plot involving, in *Carmilla,* the fiendish girl. The casket as house is also a traditional somber image, as in William Cullen Bryant's reference to the "breathless darkness and the narrow house" in his "Thanatopsis," for example (56). And Dickinson links house and grave in her "Because I Could not Stop for Death": "We paused before a House that seemed / A Swelling of the Ground— The Roof was scarcely visible—The Cornice—in the Ground" (350). The ground, like a python, patiently envelops the human artifact in time.

Raymond Chandler was a past master at capturing the dark expressionist values of buildings in writing. The following, for example, registers the sinister character of a California business complex of the 1930s gone to seed:

> A single drop light burned far back, beyond an open, once gilt elevator. There was a tarnished and well-missed spittoon on a gnawed rubber mat. I . . . looked at the building directory. . . . Numbers with names and numbers without names. Plenty of vacancies or . . . tenants who wished to remain anonymous. Painless dentists, shyster detective agencies, small sick businesses that had crawled there to die, mail order

schools that would teach you how to become a railroad clerk or a radio technician or a screen writer—if the postal inspectors didn't catch
up with them first. A nasty building. A building in which the smell of
stale cigar butts would be the cleanest smell. (170)

This presents, very much as in the gothic tradition, the environment as
counterpart to human life, what Langer defines as place "articulated by the
imprint of human life" (*Feeling* 99)—imprinted in this case by human deceit,
evil, despair, corruption, and demoralization. Such places speak minimally to,
or directly subvert, human vitality, aesthetic sense, or civic-cultural order.

Structures themselves, in their very geometry, may disturbingly violate aesthetic rightness, provoking another species of anxiety. The effect of the incoher-
ent wallpaper designs in "The Yellow Wallpaper" is an obvious example. Stephen
King noting that Lovecraft "was struck by the horror of wrong geometry" observes that "when you tamper with a man or woman's perspective on their
physical world, you tamper with what may actually be the fulcrum of the
human mind" (*Danse* 289). Eleanor's room in *The Haunting of Hill House* is

of an unbelievably faulty design, which left it chillingly wrong in all
its dimensions, so that the walls seemed always in one direction a frac-
tion less than the barest tolerable length; this is where they want me
to sleep, Eleanor thought incredulously; what nightmares are waiting,
shadowed, in those high corners—what breath of mindless fear will
drift across my mouth. (Jackson 289)

The house on the estate at Bly in "The Turn of the Screw" is characterized by
such uncanny mismatching too; like so many gothic houses, it involves tense
shifts—some parts are older than others: "It was a big ugly antique . . . embodying a few features of a building still older, half-displaced and half-utilized"
(James 14). In Ligotti's "The Last Feast of Harlequin," the buildings in Mirocaw

did not look as if they adhered very well to one another. . . . [T]hey
conveyed the illusion of being either precariously suspended in air,
threatening to topple down, or else constructed with unnatural lofti-
ness in relation to their width and mass. This . . . created a weird distortion of perspective. (*Nightmare* 196–97)

Many places accidentally occurring in the urban landscape situate a similar disturbing wrongness. Two planned buildings, for example, may generate
an unplanned, *unheimlich* juncture between them; bridges and overpasses be-

get discarded, soulless areas beneath them. In J. G. Ballard's novel *Concrete Is-land,* a man driving home from work in his Jaguar spins out from a high-speed exit lane in London due to a blown tire. The car crashes through a temporary construction barrier and down an embankment into a gully. He finds himself in a no-man's-land of intersecting routes, tunnels, and junctions, and though within sight of London office buildings, he discovers in the course of his at-tempts to get help that he is marooned on a concrete island within the high-way traffic system. Trapped in this crevice in the megalopolis, he is in a non-place that has fallen between the cracks of ongoing London life and business. One night: "[T]he whole city was now asleep, part of an immense, unconscious Europe, while he himself crawled about on a forgotten traffic island like the nightmare of this slumbering continent" (25).

Such forsaken areas are, as just mentioned, oddly and unintentionally gen-erated by the construction of refined ones, as if the squalid will not be denied. Construction disrupts and defamiliarizes established places, making them queer and enigmatic. These dispirited sites haunt the rationalized social land-scape, hinting at deeper nether regions. Dismissed from the ordinary traffic of life, they are privileged in the horror context because they are open to evil occupation. Alleys are typically not places in their own right but rather voided areas readily associated with murder and rape; they provide imaginative open-ings where terror can enter the normal, constructed landscape. Construction itself often implies its opposite—destruction and detritus. Improvements such as elevators can render stairways marginal, as air travel rendered bus stations seedy, the hangouts of "losers." An anomalous area is exploited in *Rosemary's Baby* when the young couple shows up to view an apartment in a charming old Manhattan building, a formerly exclusive hotel. They enter a warm, pol-ished-wood elevator, but as the conveyance ascends, the camera reveals that the car is open in front to the shaft—bare, oily, and ominous, hinting at ugly things lurking behind the building's quaint facade. A similar trope is exercised in *Fatal Attraction,* in which the flirtation of the vixen Alex and the lawyer Dan Gallagher is at first cast in idyllic, charming terms. They retreat to a snug bar to escape a city downpour; their dalliance seems lighthearted eroticism. Mark-ing the transition from this note of Eros, to the vilest obsession and menace, however, is a liminal, expressionist scene. Alex's neat, loft apartment is accessed through a grimy, damp, *unheimlich* service zone. The couple has sex there in an open, cage-type delivery elevator rising toward her apartment along tomb-like, dank, unfinished walls. The scene has a film noir texture and suggests murky, uncivilized zones—uncanny outcroppings analogous to the deranged psyche of Alex. Gallagher appears confused and edgy; she is the sexual aggressor, and this is her cave; it is a version of the female demonic such as is encountered in Melville's "The Tartarus of Maids." This damp, brick-walled shaft is the nether part of her lair, lying below the facade that is her neat loft (lofty) apartment. On the landing, wires snake up the bare wall from a fuse box. Later, the tomb-cave motif is repeated, this time in a dark urban parking garage where again a cage elevator rises through a building's ugly, muggy levels past smutty walls, wires, fuse boxes, fire extinguishers. Dan carries a rabbit in its cage, so there is a cage within a cage, Dan being the rabbit in the larger cage, watched by the menacing Alex, the predator, from the garage shadows.

In *Rosemary's Baby,* Rosemary converses with a young girl whom the "nice old couple" resident in the building have befriended. The conversation occurs in the building's laundry room—a cultural icon associated with remoteness, drabness, and social ambivalence—an *unheimlich* place that—the urban suspicion is—attracts dangerous and peculiar tenants. The laundry room in *Halloween* is similar, one wherein a half-clothed girl is *not* murdered, but there is every expectation she *will* be, given the setting and its malevolent implications. In his *Society, Evolution and Revelation,* the Irish Freudian psychiatrist Jonathan Hanagan notes the semiotic significance of rejected physical spaces that belie the secure, civilized message of our arranged fronts:

> European man declares his deceit and snobbery in his houses, their arrangements and decorations. Their fronts are often artistically decorated whilst the backs are barbaric. Take a walk down your back lanes and look at your houses from the rear and you will be looking into the European soul. (qtd. in Rukeyser 101)

Evident here is the recognition, as in the work of Bachelard, that areas of landscape, objects, and buildings are extensions of body-psyche. Horror exploits this character of structures in space—that they are "supposed" to be perceived in their quotidian, practical, context but, deconstructed, readily yield cryptic, delusional values. In *The Poetics of Space,* Bachelard points out regarding the cellar that while we may rationalize it in terms of practical convenience and function, "it is first and foremost the dark entity of the house, the one that partakes of subterranean forces. When we dream there, we are in harmony with the irrationality of the depths" (18). Breer, the loathsome agent of Mamoulian in Clive Barker's *The Damnation Game,* hates the house he has rented while in search of Mr. Toy but cherishes the cellar that speaks to his monstrosity—"there was something about the darkness and the sense of being underground, that answered an unarticulated need in him" (169). The murderer took Jon Benet Ramsey's body to the basement and left it in this place *off stage*—which is the literal meaning of "obscene." Theodore Roethke's poem "Root Cellar" enters the irrational depths of a greenhouse root cellar and demonstrates how ostensibly practical areas can become defamiliarized, in this case situating a phantasmagorical organicism:

> Nothing would sleep in that cellar, dank as a ditch,
> Bulbs broke out of their boxes hunting for chinks in the dark
> Shoots dangled and drooped,
> Lolling obscenely from mildewed crates,
> Hung down long yellow evil necks, like tropical snakes.
> And what a congress of stinks!—
> Roots ripe as old bait,
> . . . .
> Nothing would give up life:
> Even the dirt kept breathing a small breath.
>
> (*Collected* 36)

"Ditch" in line one identifies a liminal point in landscape, a kind of anti-space whose associations are nihilistic—as are those of "gutter." A ditch is off the road, a nowhere, outside the energetic tracks of life. "Nothing would give up life," referencing the biological proliferation going on in the dark recesses, situates the anxiety of organism theme discussed earlier. It is in a root cellar that the vampire Barlow in Stephen King's *'Salem's Lot* takes final refuge, one "small and cell-like, empty except for a few dusty bottles, some crates, and a dusty bushel basket of very old potatoes with sprouting eyes" (604). And the terror of being pulled down into the realm of subterranean forces noted by Bachelard, into the demonic cellar, resonates in Stephen King's *It*:

> He did not even like opening the door to flick on the light because he always had the idea . . . that while he was feeling for the light switch, some horrible clawed paw would settle lightly over his wrist . . . and jerk him down into the darkness that smelled of dirt and wet and dim rotted vegetables. (6)

The boy stands in a civilized space confronting the *unheimlich* darkness below.

Not only such mildewed sites and unintended, intersectional regions of cityscape suggest the sinister; so do intended but hardly energized ones that are brutally functional and uninhabited except for a narrow frame of human purposes and times. The film camera seems skilled in defining these vicinities, moribund areas behind, within, and among modern urban buildings—interstices where no one is meant to live or linger. Film has, in fact, modernized and expanded upon the gothic mode's stock of dread-provocative spaces, going well beyond the overworked ones related to faded feudal estates. The gothic sense of disintegration is broadened in *Road Warrior,* for instance, to take in the demoralization of the entire cultural and civic infrastructure—the proliferating potholes of *Body Snatchers* writ large. The still and movie cameras over time have discovered a widened range of soulless, disturbing places at which the flesh recoils. To the camera lens, loading docks at night lit by a single yellow bulb are grim stages for scurrying rat theater, dumpsters are ominous, parking garages foreboding. Suburban industrial parks are nihilistic blanks. Business offices, uncomfortable sites even in their workaday reality, at night, their function suspended, can suggest the abstract mindscapes of *The Cabinet of Dr. Caligari.* Walter Neff as he confesses into an office dictaphone in the early hours of the morning is at the soul's dead end. The lights-out, after-hours office figures grimly in other classic noir films that explore the eerie visual possibilities of nocturnal office interiors when they become a maze of shadowy cubicles, an expressionistic geometry. In such a setting, Canino, in *The Big Sleep,* forces Harry Jones to drink cyanide, and in a like office environment setting, in the film *Klute,* Jane Fonda's character encounters the sadistic ghoul. A Quonset hut on a construction site situates dismemberment murders of young women in *True Confessions,* one of the set of 1980s crime-horror movies discussed previously. The film foregrounds the traditional gothic theme of Roman Catholic political intrigues as well, but the scene in which the Quonset hut interior is revealed to have been used as a human slaughterhouse owes much of its gruesomeness to the *unheimlich* character of the setting—the sadistic sexual murder having been enacted in this incongruous commercial building.

The boiler room in *Nightmare on Elm Street,* as mentioned earlier, is another powerful example of sinister loci, the kind of place that, like the Quonset hut, has a defined practical function but is more off the social-business map. Here the building's unenhanced innards are evident; wiring, pipes, valves, and meters are undisguised, there being no aesthetic imperative. It is perhaps poetically correct that until recent laws were enacted, such areas were often rife with hazardous asbestos dust from pipes wrapped in the material. In Freddy Krueger's boiler room, Nancy is in the belly of the beast, a place that oozes and steams as does Freddy's vile body. In *Coma,* too, the hospital's boiler room and internal plumbing create a dank labyrinth where the pipes sweat like the walls in Poe's "Cask" underground and where pressurized steam seems to represent some madness seeking vent. Analogous places in the outside landscape are found in gothic literature by way of the lostness motif—highway turns, for example, leading to greater and greater uncanniness, farther and farther from where one had one's bearings. The narrator of "The Last Feast of Harlequin" leaves a main highway in search of a town seven miles away. But the seven miles mark a divide between ordinary and demonic place. Detours mark diversions from traveled ways; one is being rerouted to older, uncertain roads that may well lead into horror's grim backwaters. This version of sinister place engages another gothic motif—that of bewilderment, the next chapter's concern.

Apotropaion and the Hideous Obscure

And then a plank in Reason broke . . .

—EMILY DICKINSON

He is torn from the tent in which he trusted
and is brought to the King of terrors.

—Job 18:14

. . . its only news is nightmare.

—THOMAS LIGOTTI, *The Nightmare Factory*

EDMUND BURKE, IN HIS *A PHILOSOPHICAL ENQUIRY*, NOTED
the role obscurity plays in horror:

> To make anything very terrible, obscurity seems in general to be nec-
> essary. *When we know the full extent of any danger . . . a great deal of the
> apprehension vanishes.* Everyone will be sensible of this, who considers
> how greatly night adds to our dread, in all cases of danger. (italics
> added, 54)

A blurred or obfuscated sense of danger and iniquity is characteristic of film
and literary gothic—confusion is elementally dreadful and physically situated.
The human animal is not naturally adept at night navigation, for example, and
we tend to become still less so as, due to electric light, we are increasingly

estranged from the experience of deep darkness. We are not among those species visually equipped in such a way that night suggests predatory possibilities to most of us; rather we are among those species disadvantaged by darkness and more suited to be nocturnal prey. Night to us is a wild region, a frontier that we have only gradually made inroads into and, with our artificial light, civilized.[1]

Diurnal darkness is only one of the many factors that may limit our functioning and critically obscure our environment. The rhetoric of horror itself reflects and exploits the anxiety we feel when we lose our bearings. *Melmoth the Wanderer* is an almost unnegotiable rhetorical labyrinth of reports within reports within reports. In the werewolf film *The Howling* (1981), as early as the opening credits, a jumbled background of distorted electronic information—jittery off-track visual confusion, static, intruding radio transmissions—creates a sense of general shakiness and unreliability. There are frightening disconnects; later in the film, for example, newscaster Karen White wears a wire as part of a plan to entrap a serial killer, and at the crucial moment, the transmissions to the police surveillance unit become garbled and are lost. The horror film itself tends to stumble uncertainly, and the gritty cheapness of some of the cinematic classics has even come to be regarded as part of their horror aesthetic. The technical awkwardness of *Night of the Living Dead* seems integral to its grammar of dread—the evident lack of quality control contributing to the overall sense of impotence against the threat. A viewer is uncertain as to the source of his or her discomfort in the opening scenes—is it in part due to the sense that the movie itself, as a production, is tremulous and uncertain—*unheimlich*—robbing us of the usual reassurance that these images and this project are backed by the substantial reality of corporate Hollywood? Horror literary practice strives for such a sense of pervasive unsettledness. Norbert Wiener, who coined the term *cybernetics*—from the Greek for steering or navigation—notes that "to live effectively is to live with adequate information" (18). "The westerner knows by seeing," Paglia observes. "[P]erceptual relations are at the heart of our culture . . . this recognition is our apotropaion, . . . our warding off of fear" (*Personae* 5). Clear, stable seeing is our primary charm against evil and horror. But in gothic literature, the reader's conception of a situation is by design insufficient; he or she may gather intelligence only through a glass darkly, negating that charm, that apotropaion. In the dark, we tend to walk into trees or fall into ditches. The putting out of the eyes and the consequent flooding in of darkness thus represents an especially fearful horror, a fear Freud views as nearly on a par with the fear of castration—"no bodily injury is so much dreaded as an injury to the eye" (36).

The opening chapter of *The Italian* establishes obscurities that run throughout the novel. A figure not fully discernable moves among obscuring pillars in the church; to the extent he can be perceived at all in the shadows of the portico, his face is cloaked, and he disappears into a confessional that is covered with a black canopy and located below a painted window "the colors of which throw, instead of light, a shade over that part of the church" (Radcliffe 3). This is a layering of obscurity over obscurity, shadow over shadow, and the blurring of course will be exacerbated in due time by layers of ecclesiastical intrigues and subterfuges wrought by the full complement of hooded monks and veiled nuns—the clandestine clerical cabal dear to the high gothic imagination. And it is not only an inadequacy of physical light that prevails in horror works but an inadequacy of rational light as well. The theme of rationalistic insufficiency is a staple of the modality—medical science, for example, typically falls short in the face of the uncanny; medical experts are at a loss to deal with the preternatural events in Freneau's "The House of Night" and in Poe's "The Fall of the House of Usher." The motif becomes psychiatric later on; in "The Yellow Wallpaper" and in films such as *The Exorcist* and *Stigmata*, wherein psychiatry proves a feeble force and, in the two films, has to withdraw from the field, yielding to older ritual nostrums.

As remarked in chapter 3, the governess in "The Turn of the Screw" refers to her "plunge into the hideous obscure" (James 122), a metaphor strikingly resonant of *physical* vertigo, as is her reference elsewhere to the "depths of consternation that had opened beneath my feet" (112). These phrases evidence the physicality intrinsic to the metaphoric patterns of our thinking—something that, as earlier noted, the theories of Lakoff and Johnson sustain. In these phrases, the governess encounters the embodied registration of her psychic dislocation, and her characterization of her distress would seem to underscore the inadequacy of merely psychologistic analyses of horror. She is not merely puzzled; she feels herself *falling*.

The Blair Witch Project exemplifies a fairly deft employment of obscurity, distortion, and bewilderment as it exploits the unsteadiness characteristic of the handheld camera or camcorder to disestablish the viewer's sense of physical stability and confidence. Whatever manifestations there are of the wrathful revenant who threatens from the Maryland woods—crude symbolic markings and so forth—are seen by way of the jerky, uncertain, tunnel vision of the amateur documentary camera; the audience is prevented from adequately getting hold of what is "going down." Indeed, "apprehension" etymologically refers precisely to this inability to get hold of something—a metaphor again reflecting the embodied, biomorphic dimension of "thought." Horror speaks to our fear of losing our grasp on things; it is not only what happens in a gothic tale that is significant but, as earlier noted, the rhetoric of the event's transmission as well—the way in which the reader or motion picture viewer is allowed to access what is occurring. The lurching unreliability of the *Blair Witch* camera constitutes a broken perceptual syntax. Nor is obscurity merely an *absence* to human perception; we actively people and structure darkness, making the best we can of it, trying to read and rationalize the shadows. Horror often indeed involves—as in *The Blair Witch Project*—an ambiguous, nervous negotiation between what we see and what we think we see.

Henry James's rhetorical practice, as mentioned before, his characters seeming to endlessly talk around the subject, lends itself to a similar kind of horror effect in "The Turn of the Screw." If, as Burke noted, knowing the full extent of danger diminishes fear, the rhetoric in James's story works in the contrary direction; the nature and extent of the danger is clouded by maddeningly evasive dialogue, and apprehension consequently increases. The salacious core of the tale is hedged about by so much circumlocution and avoidance of the indelicate facts that readers are uncomfortably aware that the narration is providing them only a very imperfect handle on things. Victorian propriety comes to function as a kind of obscuring and disturbing fog. Human perception needs a valid basic stuff to work with, a reliable input lacking which the brain experiences the dread that it may be working with flawed or inaccurate material. In the case of "The Turn of the Screw," the governess and the reader share just this disadvantageous position, and readers have to glean what they can from the frigid fastidious and repressive conversation James sets forth. All the while evil inroads are presumably being made and secured at the estate, readers must be satisfied with what emerges from conversation such as this between Miles and his governess:

> "Well—so we're alone!"
> "Oh more or less. . . . Not absolutely. We shouldn't like that! . . ."
> "No—I suppose we shouldn't. Of course we've the others."
> "We've the others—we've indeed the others. . . ."

"Yet even though we have them . . . they don't much count, do they?"

". . . It depends on what you call 'much'!"

"Yes . . . everything depends!" (123–24)

Such conversation is as much obscurity as revelation; it is informed by a dreadful urgency, and at the same time it progresses, if at all, in an eerily stylized vain, out of keeping with the degree of peril. The pattern would recall the nightmare scene, also discussed previously, in *Catch-22,* wherein Yossarian's earnest first-aid efforts are grotesquely frail in the face of the prevailing havoc. Likewise in dreams, one is unable to run at a speed one's plight requires. Fritz Lang's *M* turns on the outrageous incongruity between the single-minded savvy of the pedophile killer in realizing his purposes versus the confused and stumbling police investigative efforts. Employing this discrepancy devise, the investigation in "Turn of the Screw" is insistently restrained and rhetorical while the evil is insistently physical and immediate. The endangered parties go round and round in dialogue while the sinister parties, Quint and Jessel, say nothing, act, and prevail.

In horror literature and film, anything that creates a veil between a sympathetic threatened party and the threatening danger adds enormously to the reader/viewer's sense of anxiety. The exploitation of this device in *The Howling* has been noted, and Brian DePalma among current filmmakers seems especially alive to the technological possibilities of this principle, which he uses in *Scarface, Body Double,* and *Blowout.* In *Blowout,* the John Travolta character, a sound technologist, is haunted by the death of an undercover cop whom he had wired and on whom the wire failed, leading to the man's death at the hands of mobsters, Travolta surreally unable to reach the victim as his connection fades into interference. The scene is flashed back to—the anxiety of knowing the agent is in trouble and the garbled electronic lifeline fading. The film's climax involves a kind of gothic doubling trope—the remembered horror pattern being helplessly repeated as in a nightmare: Travolta attempting to rescue a girl he has wired, a girl of whom he has become fond.

"The Fall of the House of Usher" and numerous other Poe stories are obscure and dreamlike in other ways as well since they are, as earlier remarked, generic—indefinite or uncertain as to the time and place of the setting, lacking which coordinates the reader is already a little disadvantaged and unsettled. A horror communication model, unlike a normal one, would stress the strategic *encouragement* of static, interruption, deception, and flawed transmission. In this way, the *Blair Witch* audience, like its characters, is on edge, but in the audience's case, the jittery camera earlier referred to is significantly implicated. In watching critical scenes in the film, a viewer's nervous system in effect begs for clearer input while the camera pitches and yaws in distressing discoordination. Darkness, the form of interference that virtually defines the horror mode, exacerbates the consternation when the agitated camera attempts to track an equally lurching flashlight beam over irregular forest terrain. At the end, Heather's camera reels about hysterically in the abandoned house in a final dreadful vertigo.

★ ★ ★

Melville's "Benito Cereno" (1855) obviously owes much to "The Fall of the House of Usher" and employs similar disorientational rhetorical strategies. In some ways, Melville's story might have been appropriately titled "The House of Usher Goes to Sea." Like "Usher," "Benito Cereno" centers upon the pivotal horror element of deterioration, things falling apart—a trope that itself blurs demarcation. Usher's hereditary line has dissolved; the whole aristocratic rationale that would contextualize and sustain it is gone. Benito Cereno's dissolution is more sudden: Anarchy (from the European perspective) has robbed him of all that defines *him*—the likewise aristocratic order of the nineteenth-century merchant ship backed by the whole institutionalized colonial structure of the period. Here again a plank in the larger order of things has broken, and only a shadow—the frightened, decontextualized "self" of Cereno—remains, easy prey, like Usher's collapsed self, to the intrusions of nightmare material.

The derelict, unmaintained ship is a recurrent image of failing apotropaion in gothic tales and a vivid reflection of a faltering system providing openings for dreadful incursions. Besides in "Benito Cereno," the image occurs in *Dracula,* in Poe's "The Narrative of Arthur Gordon Pym," in Coleridge's "Rime of the Ancient Mariner," and it is hauntingly visualized in Murnau's original *Nosferatu* and in Werner Herzog's revival of that film. The sailing ship in its ordered elegance, able to gracefully ply the most treacherous seas, epitomized optimum design achievement for centuries—the most finely coordinated and precisely applied methodology and technology deftly addressing the exigencies of sea, sky, weather—an analog to the "clean and proper body." The sailing ship was high art, and the gothic floundering ship iconography inverts that ideal. The ship serves at the same time to situate a microcosm, a structure of human culture, society, and even politics.

"Benito Cereno," as earlier noted, is a strange blending of Poe and documentary material. As in Poe's earlier story, in "Benito Cereno" a visitor approaches a crumbling house (here ship), that is enveloped in a shrouding haze. The narrator specifically stresses the house-ship analogy, noting the particular "enchantment" effect of a ship upon a stranger coming aboard. The boarding experience is queer, *unheimlich,* like "entering a strange house with strange inmates in a strange land. . . . The ship seems unreal; these strange costumes, gestures, and faces, but a shadowy tableau just emerged from the deep, which directly must receive back what it gave" (*Short Works* 242). Further recalling "Usher," the imperfectly informed visitor, here Delano, senses something wrong and tries to right it through a determined rationalizing effort. Like the "Usher" narrator, he tells himself his forebodings are mere manifestations of his own over-active imagination: "Trying to break one charm," he discovers later aboard the peculiar ship, "he was but becharmed anew. Though upon the wide sea, he seemed in some far inland country; prisoner in some deserted chateau" (269). The wide sea and the ship are being gothicized. The visitor encounters a distraught "host" in Cereno, the nature of whose enigmatic malady he tries unsuccessfully to figure out, and, again as in "Usher," the dismayed narrator seems disturbingly obtuse, a quality that further exacerbates the readers' sense of unease in that they are perceiving matters through a flawed reportorial intermediary.

Captain Amassa Delano's 1817 nonfiction *Voyages and Travels,* the documentary basis for "Benito Cereno," has been available since its republication in *PMLA* in 1928. In his account, the actual Delano tells of how the American merchant ship of which he was captain encountered a hobbled Spanish ship in the bay of an uninhabited island off the southern coast of Chile in 1805. Investigating, Delano found the faltered ship inhabited by a devastated, inadequate Spanish crew and by surprisingly free-ranging African slaves who, it ultimately turned out, had commandeered the vessel and were now, unbeknownst to Delano, in control. Only after being taken in by a long charade prepared by the slaves did the American captain discover the truth and understand what had up to then seemed bizarrely melancholic behavior on the part of the overwhelmed Spanish captain. Comparing Amassa Delano's text with "Benito Cereno" demonstrates how Melville recognized and drew out the inherent gothic possibilities in Delano's narrative as well as overlaying his own gothic elements upon the captain's original account. Grey birds cast dark shadows over the water in Melville's version, "foreshadowing deeper shadows to come" (239). One might expect *space* from a sea tale—fresh breezes, light, color, and bracing salt air; but, as in "House of Usher," refreshment there is none here, quite the contrary. The initial atmospheric note struck in the story is static; Melville's effort from the beginning is to render the scene claustrophobic despite its outdoor character—this is Melville's grotesque Pacific. There is essentially no outdoors in the gothic tale, *contra naturam* is its bent—even the sea itself in this tale is rendered in the devitalized, lethargic mode of "Rime of the Ancient Mariner." The ocean seems fixed, "like waved lead that has cooled and set"; the mysterious ship is caught in doldrums and mantled in vapors (239). What Paglia points out in Coleridge's influential "Rime" would apply as well to "Benito Cereno": "[It] transports its Gothic tale out of the historical world of castles and abbeys into the sublime theater of a desolate nature. But expansion of space is just another cul-de-sac . . . the demonic womb of Gothic" (*Personae* 325). Benito Cereno's vessel is in fact caught in a literal cul-de-sac, having run into an enclosed bay. But Melville brings as much of the gothic castle and abbey motifs as he can to this circumstance. Rocking in the gray swells, the slave ship looks to Delano like "a whitewashed monastery after a thunder-storm seen perched upon some dun cliff among the Pyrenees." The landscapes and idioms of Radcliffe, Lewis, and Maturin are summoned up. Gothic-medieval simulacre intrude upon the American captain's perceptions— "fitfully revealed through the open portholes . . . dark moving figures were dimly descried, as of Black Friars pacing the cloisters" (240).

In discussing Poe's sea-gothic *Narrative of Arthur Gordon Pym,* Harold Beaver makes a point much the same as Paglia's—that even here, "where Poe seems his most boyish exuberant . . . turning to the open sea, he is still trapped . . . in the holds of ships . . . the runaway is also the stowaway . . . inevitably on the edge of nightmare" (9). The cabin lights on Cereno's ship, "for all the mild weather, [are] hermetically sealed and caulked" (Melville, *Short Works* 241). Delano, unable to grasp what the ghostly profile of the wavering ship might signify, reasons, again in the rationalizing manner of the "Usher" narrator, that its odd movements "might have been but a deception of the vapors." His whaleboat nears the ship, which lies in the still water, "shreds of fog here and there raggedly furring her" (239–40). Cereno's ship is the shrouded, sinister gothic house.

Significantly, disarray, neglect, and apathy are evident everywhere on the ship: Its damaged bell sounds "with a dreary grave-yard toll" (255). "Battered and moldy, the castellated forecastle seemed some ancient turret long ago taken by assault and left to decay." The ship's name, *San Dominick,* appears set in gilt,

on its side "each letter streakingly corroded with tricklings of copper-spike rust
. . . sea-grass similarly swept to and fro over her name" (241–42).. "Her keel
seemed laid, her ribs put together, and she launched, from Ezekiel's Valley of
Dry Bones." Nothing is kept up. The Spanish merchant's pallid, aristocratic master, like the master of the House of Usher, is in "ill-health" evidencing "sleep-
less cares and disquietudes (243), "his pale face twitching and overcast" (259).
He is described, echoing Poe's description of Usher, as "prey to settled dejection
. . . a distempered spirit . . . lodged in a distempered frame . . . his voice like that
of one with lungs half gone" (245). Delano, "wonted to the quiet orderliness
of the sealer's comfortable family of a crew," on boarding the San Dominick,
comes upon, to borrow a phrase from "The House of Usher," a "kingdom of
inorganization" (Poe, Selected 64). Here is the pervasive disintegration and
languishment discussed in the previous chapter—things radically unmade.

Mary Douglas, in Purity and Danger, discussing the disturbing, disorienting nature of conflicting "frames," quotes Marion Milner: "[T]he frame marks
off the different kind of reality that is within it from that which is outside it"
(64). When two frames, two realities, overlap, there can be a species of vertigo triggered by the clash of categories. The frames in "Benito Cereno" are
essentially two—that of the normal, functioning American ship, on the one
hand, and that of the dysfunctional, unheimlich mystery ship, on the other. The
Spanish merchantman under Benito Cereno's command and the American
sealer under Delano's are supposed to stand within a single frame of reference.
They should evidence a shared order—the rules of the high seas, the unambigu-
ous command structure and tradition common to European and American
navies and verified by the economic and social structure of Western culture.
When Delano steps on the San Dominick, however, he encounters disquieting
breaches in the structure of this assumed frame. Still earlier, on his first sighting of the "stranger," he has noted its failure to show its colors—a breach of
nautical custom, a first disturbing note of transgression. Aboard the San
Dominick, maintainance and discipline, the sine qua non of naval operations,
are lacking. Explaining the chaos to Delano, Cereno unconvincingly ascribes
the deplorable condition of his vessel to a series of calamities it has undergone,
but the present prospect the ship presents is anarchic; there is no sign of effort
toward recovery or rehabilitation; there is no practice of the maritime arts in
evidence. Delano enters into this unheimlich frame, one that would suggest,
rather than a functional Spanish merchant ship, a primitive village, and that
in near collapse. Added to the American captain's disorientation is the fact that

all the intelligence he attempts to gather is in fact disinformative. The "world upside down" masquerade scenario that confronts him is, of course, not merely an intellectual puzzle but rather a fundamental disturbance in his whole mapping of reality. Finding himself in this delusional frame and trying to resolve its contradictions, Delano becomes increasingly bewildered: "All this is very queer now," he thinks, and feels "as one experiencing incipient seasickness" (271). He has moved into the realm of the hideous obscure; depths of consternation have opened beneath his feet.

★ ★ ★

Horror literature is built around emergency, the immediate emergency of terror—the Red Death swinging into the hall—or the longer term emergency of horror—Lucy's gradual, mysterious decline in *Dracula*. Conjoined with that terror is typically, as we have noted, a very imperfect image of the nature of the threat. In perilous circumstances, all the senses must be allowed to function at peak efficiency; if one's attention is interfered with in a crisis, it is anxiety provoking in the extreme—for example, children teasing one another in the backseat as one is trying to drive along an icy mountain road—and gothic writers exploit this cybernetic anxiety. Poe, as noted earlier, does so in the final scene of "Usher," when the narrator distressingly commences the reading of "The Mad Trist," a trivial tale he acknowledges is "uncouth" and of "unimaginative prolixity," in order, dubiously enough, to calm Roderick Usher. Poe thereby provides a blaring, incongruous interference with Usher's hearing and attention at a moment when the latter needs them desperately. The reader, too, finds that he or she is suddenly having to process *two* narrative frames, the first of them "real," compelling, and terrifying, and the second, inane and disinformative—ultimately, of course, they merge into a single hallucinatory terror. In "Benito Cereno," one disturbing inanity is Delano's and/ or the narrator's belaboring of racial stereotypes, ones going to the African's docility and happy predisposition toward servile duties—observations maddeningly at odds with the reality of Delano's situation and that of the *San Dominick*. Delano moves along treacherous decks under the command of desperate and deadly Africans, all the while mentally rehearsing reassuring American stereotypes going to the contented harmlessness of Negroes.

An unreliable narrator in horror literature thus serves a purpose he or she does not in ordinary narration—readers are exposed to the horrific through a flawed, distorting intermediary; they therefore lack the essentials of apotropaion, a full and clear realization of that which threatens. They feel incapable of warding off fear, helpless because they lack sufficient command of the facts. Delano is for most of the story as blithely unaware of the danger at hand as is the typical teenaged girl in the typical slasher film who ventures upstairs half-clothed to investigate a noise, and the audience horror-frustration is of the same nature. In opening the "Trist" window, as it were, Poe obfuscates and backgrounds his main window—the one in which the living menace prevails, and thus undermines clear seeing and the readers' sense of how one might deflect the danger. The now familiar tracking shots associated with horror films function similarly in that the viewer shares the viewpoint of the killer rather than of the victim—in effect a dislocated and terribly "wrong" viewpoint from which, as in nightmare, the viewer cannot extricate himself or herself.

William Faulkner employs a disinformational device not unlike Poe's—conflicting frames or windows—with equally great skill and effect in his story "That Evening Sun." The two frames established by the narrative are (1) "Negro Hollow," the region beyond the ditch, as opposed to (2) white, middle-class Jefferson, Mississippi. The father of Quentin, Jason, and Caddy has to negotiate between the two places in dealing with the family's African-American domestic help. Whenever Dilsey, the cook, is sick, Jason and Caddy are dispatched by their father to get Nancy as a substitute, so Nancy is familiar around the house, but her ex-boyfriend, Jesus, is not allowed to come around. He is presently stalking Nancy—or so she is convinced—and determined to kill her, something she is sure he will accomplish in time. She wants desperately to sleep on the floor of the children's room as she has done before, but the children's mother won't permit it. Speaking in the context of the middle-class cultural frame of reference, the mother wants to know why her husband can't *do* something about Jesus: "[W]hat do we have officers for?" (299). The police, of course, are beside the point in the gothic context as well as in the Southern Negro context of the period.

Nancy's uncanny terror is something that falls outside the family's own order and reality, but especially outside the understanding of Caddy and Jason, who are seven and five, respectively. The children's innocent perspective as well, conveyed by Quentin, the narrator, becomes imposed over the tale's beyond-the-ditch horror. As readers of Poe's tale have access to Usher's final terror only through the divided observation of the narrator and the static caused by the pseudo-medieval narrative, Nancy's terror as she awaits Jesus's razor assault is given to the reader through the incongruous field of the children's irrelevant, innocent banter, which conveys their complete failure to understand Nancy's nightmare. (And, shades of "Turn of the Screw," even whether Jesus really *is* lurking out in the ditch is not absolutely established—as readers, the narrative allows, we *might* be entangled, at least partially, in an aspect of Nancy's cocaine paranoia—yet another frame.) This use of overlapping frames to create a confusion within which the horror proceeds is intricately executed in this story to a degree that can only be suggested by one instance of it.

Nancy has gotten the children to go to her cabin with her by promising that they will have fun; she is desperate that they not leave her alone. She must function within her own horrifying reality, awaiting a murderous maniac, and at the same time present an entertaining front to keep the children with her. She makes a fumbling attempt at a story that turns out the be, as in "The House of Usher," a narrative conflated with the larger "reality" narrative:

> "And so this here queen came walking up to the ditch, where the bad man was hiding . . . and she say, "if I can just get past this here ditch. . . ."
> Jason's legs stuck out of his pants where he sat on Nancy's lap. "I don't think that's a good story," he said. "I want to go home. . . ."
> "I know another story," Nancy said. . . .
> "I won't listen to it," Jason said. "I'll bang on the floor." (303)

The irritating obligations a middle-class baby-sitter might be burdened with are terribly incongruous here, belonging to a frame vastly removed from the sordid terror of Nancy's cabin and introducing a disorienting static into the scene—a kind of meta-horror derived from the anxiety-provoking dualism. Horror *cultivates* these layerings, this arabesque narrative of excess and overlap in which rhetorical labyrinth readers have to make their way.

Melville makes use of the same sort of contradictions in characterizing Amasa Delano's distress on Benito Cereno's gothic ship. Driven to seek confirmation of the normal seagoing frame of reference in which his identity is implicit, Delano looks off to where his own familiar ship, with its faithful-dog name, lies in the distance, embodying unambiguously the order and clarity that is missing on the *San Dominick*. He sees his ship "not as before half blended with the haze, but with *outline defined,* so that its individuality was *manifest*" (italics added):

> That boat, *Rover* by name, which, though now in strange seas, had often pressed the beach of Captain Delano's home and, brought to its

threshold for repairs, had familiarly lain there, as a Newfoundland dog;
the sight of that household boat evoked a thousand trustful associations. (*Short Works* 271)

This is an effort by Delano toward that warding off, that *apotropaion* referred
to previously. He seeks to break the spell of the *unheimlich San Dominick* frame,
to undo its disintegrative power and reassert the conclusiveness of his own
reality frame, one in which outline is clearly defined.

Mess and squalor are an affront to clarity and Apollonian ordering, and
Delano is faced with trying to solve the mystery of the *San Dominick* in a context of profound mess. Melville's gothic rendering of the original Amasa Delano
nonfiction narrative is largely a matter of sounding again and again disturbing
notes of confusion, dereliction, dysfunction, and lethargy—privileging the debris, corrosion, mold, slime, and so forth, that characterize the ghost ship and
all of which are outrages in terms of naval ordering, not to mention ordinary
maintenance of place. The oxidation implicated in our organic decline is not a
different process from the one involved in the rust and decay of external inor-
ganic things such as metals, for example, which points up what the gothic has
long recognized, the fact that our own deterioration is not different in kind from
that of the things around us. Our selves, our lives, our families, our environment—as has been stressed before here—are maintained by an essential, indeed
spiritual, upkeep. A repulsive sense of decline and dissipation, on the other hand,
dominates "Benito Cereno," augmented by the tale's antiquarian gothic iconography and other sinister loci themes. The deterioration noted earlier as central to the horror of *Invasion of the Body Snatchers* is central as well to "Benito
Cereno." Here too inroads of squalor speak to us of the collapse of our civilized front, our critical, personal, and communal warding off of the abject.

★ ★ ★

The gothic tale's preoccupation with disorientation and mortal messiness extends into moral areas as well; there too, comfortable orientation is subverted;
moral compasses are placed in doubt. Faulkner's use of "Jesus" as the name
of the menacing, razor-wielding killer in "Evening Sun," for example, sets
things slightly askew, as do the racial pronouncements of Delano and the narrator in "Benito Cereno," adding a sense of moral derangement to the tale's
already squalid landscape. Moral compasses prove undependable in the gothic
context; horror, like comedy, is essentially an amoral mode. Langer remarks
regarding comedy that "even the most civilized products of this art . . . do not

present moral distinctions and issues. . . . Aristophanes, Menander, Moliere . . . are not moralists . . . they have, literally 'no use' for moral principles—that is, they do not use them" (*Feeling* 345). In one of the earliest inquiries into the nature of gothic literature, their eighteenth-century essay on horror, John Aiken and Anna Barbauld remark the fact that in horror literature "our moral feelings are not in the least concerned" (120).[2] At the very least, it might be asserted that ordinary, *familiar* morality is not typically part of horror's main thrust, that horror seeks to collapse as many of the reader's assurances and as much of his or her grounding as possible.

In *Love and Death in the American Novel,* Leslie Fiedler discusses the two literary directions that tend to sometimes become confused in this regard. He emphasizes the difference between "analytical" and the "projective" literature, the second of which characterizes the gothic mode. Fiedler notes as well that in some gothic authors, Melville among them, the realistic-analytical and the symbolic-projective "are mingled confusedly":

> Such authors are the heirs of a confusion at the heart of the gothic about its own method and meaning. Precisely because the early practitioners of the tale of terror were only half aware of the symbolic nature of the genre, they did not know what kind of credence to ask of their protagonists—presenting them sometimes as fully motivated characters in the analytic sense, and at others as mere projections of unconscious guilt or fear. Such an heir of the gothicists, for instance, as Melville was betrayed into giving his symbolic Captain Ahab (who stands for "sultanic" hybris, i.e., for one aspect of the mind) a mind of his own; though the Parsee, who plays Satan to Ahab's Faust, is treated as a simple projection with an inner logic rather than a psychology . . . this confusion of modes and levels of credibility becomes a vexing problem. (141)

Melville's work thus serves as a useful example of the moral-ethical awkwardness typical of the horror species. The hybrid nature of "Benito Cereno," its mixing of analytical and projective-amoral modes, arguably makes it the kind of problematical case Fiedler feels *Moby Dick* is. Historical and moral issues related to slavery intrude in "Benito Cereno" and are arguably never adequately resolved; rather they become lost in the hallucinatory field of the narrative. The story's delusional, nightmare essence belies the documentary appearances that characterize its surface. Babo and the other African slaves emerge more as shad-

owy "projections," nightmare figures, than as fully motivated characters acting in historical time. They work in the service of the story's surreal momentum. Babo, a classic vice figure in the tradition of Iago, Shylock, or Edmund in
Lear, clings to Cereno like an incubus, a cloying, malign presence insinuating
itself at every turn. The hatchet polishers with their chant and their wildly incongruous attention to cleaning and maintaining their hatchets, as if there were
not more pressing maintenance chores given the ship's general condition, are
part of the nightmare masquerade the *San Dominick* presents to the visiting
Captain Delano, and they embody, clearly, the generic dread of alien takeover,
misrule, and disestablishment rather than any actual historical specification.

There is nothing romantically attractive about the revolutionary black
government of the *San Dominick.* An analytic-discursive critique would ask,
where are the sympathetic Africans the reader might expect? Where are reminders of the plight of the slaves, of the evils of slavery, and so on, to balance the reader's repulsion at the ugly, dissipated situation prevailing on the
Spanish vessel? There is a "blank" in "Benito Cereno" as readers wait for a voice
to sort through the ambiguity and racist vulgarity and set things right, to af-
firm a familiar moral position and assuage their unease, but no such voice is
forthcoming. No such voice comes forth in nightmare either, nor in the stories of Flannery O'Connor, for instance, where readers also ask themselves,
who is in charge here, and where is the author's and the tale's moral base? Is
this narrative running on its own? It is even conceivable that Melville—as
O'Connor would later do—throughout his work cultivated the conflicted
middle ground between the two rhetorical practices that Fiedler describes,
strategically exploiting the dissonance and disturbance that ambiguity gives
rise to.

It might be tempting to try, as is so often done, to explain away the problem involved through recourse to Melville's ironic portrayal of Delano, as if
Delano's account were merely one reader response to the *San Dominick* text
and as if the horrifying portrayal of Babo were to be somehow ascribed to the
American captain's misperceptions—as a commentary on Delano's naive or
unconscious racism. In terms of this interpretation, readers can comfortably
consume the tale at arm's length, enjoying their enlightened superiority to
Delano. It is questionable, however, that Melville in fact provides this ironic
buffer. Nor are all the demeaning racial characterizations in the piece clearly
attributable to Delano. Some of the most disagreeable material—for example,
the observation that the Negro's cheerfulness owes to the "unaspiring content-

ment of a limited mind"—appears to be the *narrator's* observations or elements of a double-voiced, hybrid discourse (278–79). In any event, the confusion is unsettling as readers find themselves apparently being oriented by a politically dubious and even offensive reportorial voice. The tale arguably defies any logic except the delusional nightmare logic of the gothic.

In its undermining of familiar moral-psychological orientation, "Benito Cereno" works in the *unheimlich* shadows, apart from ordinary *Uncle Tom's Cabin* liberalism, turning up the raw, demonic reality of slavery, withholding the assurances familiar to the nineteenth-century northern liberal mind. A presumably white middle-class readership is lured into and captive in a disordered context where no safe, familiar path is evident; they in effect find themselves perforce and distressingly *with* the white slave ship crew. One demonism overthrown, not sanity, but another demonism comes forward—darkness at noon. Babo and company are undeniably horror elements, the usurpers in this amorally rendered dark tale. The "problem" with "Benito Cereno" is real and generic—the story is not a humanistic exemplum of some sort; it is a macabre narrative and as such resists, as dream does, the intrusion of ordinary historical and morally complex light of day. It is the dark, elemental tale it is because it offers no escape; it will not be caught, classified, and tamed. The story's disturbing effect, its fright, is its last word.

What Paglia says of Coleridge's classic would apply here: "The problem with moral . . . readings of *The Ancient Mariner* is that they can make no sense of the compulsive or delusional frame of the poem" (*Personae* 326–27). Attempts to justify works of gothic horror through moral or ethical readings derive, no doubt, from the continued sense that there is nothing self-justifying about the horror modality. That attitude surfaces even in the criticism of a gothic specialist such as Chris Baldick, who, in an introduction to *Melmoth the Wanderer,* ascribes its "furious intensity" to the financial urgency that led Charles Maturin to write it. Had it not been for that necessity, Baldick suggests, this "dungeon of a book" might have been a realist novel faulting poverty and not the devil. But the book "never manages to break out of its Gothic bastille" (xix). The implication would seem to be that authors strapped for money write the likes of *Melmoth,* but had they the time to think, they would write something more socially redeeming and meritorious.[3] It is arguable that, on the contrary, the "furious intensity" in horror literature, the uncanny "compulsive and delusional" elements, its to all appearances erratic and confusing moral course, are all part of its strategy and, finally, its power. Like comedy, it cannot be a predictable mode. Some lines from a Dean Koontz novel would serve to characterize the trend of horror literature aesthetically, morally, through and through: "It was a side street without lampposts. There the reign of the night was undisputed" (4).

Gothic moralizing, if it can be called that, is of the primitive, cautionary kind noted in an earlier discussion of teen "slasher" movies—uncodified, and exploiting Apollonian dread of the consequences of Dionysian intemperance. Sex, for example, "needs ritual binding to control its daemonism" (Paglia, *Personae* 36). The demonic power of Eros is thoroughly explored in *The Monk*, both in terms of the force's power when frustrated or when incautiously liberated. The sanctimonious psychiatrist and werewolf-cult guru in the film *The Howling,* as a guest on talk shows, traffics in Dionysian clichés about freeing primitive impulses, and so on. And Carl Dreyer's Danish classic *Day of Wrath* (1942) lures its viewers into identification with the illicit lovers and their Edenic rambles among the birches, but disintegrative consequences broaching witchcraft and patricide follow upon those diverting treks. This kind of "moralizing" really addresses something more in the line of restraint and personal discipline; it privileges an existential-social imperative, the need of a certain amount of deference to social-communal realities, lacking which things may go terribly amiss. The conservatism horror privileges is rooted in something deeper than political positions. The following recognition on Victor Frankenstein's part arguably addresses the matter:

> A human being . . . ought always to preserve a calm and peaceful mind.
> . . . If the study to which you apply yourself has a tendency to . . .
> destroy your taste for . . . simple pleasures . . . then that study is certainly
> unlawful, that is to say, not befitting the human mind. (Shelley 33)

He is referring to the need for moderation, modesty, restraint, humility—the Apollonian ethical complex the opposite of which is the orgiastic, the Faustian, the obsessional. An instance of the latter is the wicked priest Schedoni in Radcliffe's *The Italian* whose intemperate intellectualism the other priests are rather awed by, though they "observed that he seldom perceived truth when it lay on the surface; he could follow it through all the labyrinths of disquisition, but overlooked it when it was undisguised before him" (34). Gothic literary invention seems to seek a moderating foil to its own rhetorical indulgence in excess. Benito Cereno, as noted, has that balancing factor in the form of Delano's well-functioning ship, against which we view the prostrate *San*

Dominick. But such Apollonian notes, negatively underscoring dissolution and dysfunction, reflect a conservative ethos that needs to be distinguished from, say, Toryism or direct Christian moralizing.

In the introduction to Lovecraft's *The Shadow over Innsmouth,* Joshi and Schultz speculate that the designation of Gloucester, Massachusetts, was removed by the author from later drafts of the story because Lovecraft "did not wish to make too obvious a tip of the hat to the real location of his imaginary town" (14). This concern marks another aspect of gothic insularity and obscurity, its Dracula-like disavowal of full daylight reality. Their point remarks an important aspect of one version of horror rhetorical practice, the author's efforts to introduce the realistic gravitas of actual locations in order to then subvert that reality as its solidity is undermined and the assurance afforded by real place dissolves into the hallucinatory. This interweaving of provisionally realistic elements with phantasmic ones is something at which writers such as Stephen King and Clive Barker are extraordinarily accomplished and Poe arguably was not. Poe's tales, characteristically short and impatient, tend to plunge into dreamscape straight away. The superiority of *The Shadow over Innsmouth* among Lovecraft's stories derives, I think, from the tale's situation of the uncanny in a context of a fairly realistic rendering of the Massachusetts north shore area of the 1920s and 1930s. Newburyport, Rowley, and Plum Island, all real locations, are identified in the narrative. But Gloucester, a largish and well-known port, may have seemed to Lovecraft, as Joshi and Schultz imply, to have too much real-world resonance compared to the other then rural backwaters. With the actual landmarks that *are* provided, however, one can pretty certainly locate the hideous Innsmouth south of Newburyport along Route 1-A in the marshlands east of the highway—which realism serves to make the story's dissolution into madness all the more disturbing.[4]

Even *Invasion of the Body Snatchers* is perhaps diminished slightly as horror if one entertains the notion often advanced that it is a 1950s anticommunist allegory or even, as has also been suggested, an anti-McCarthy one. Those references orient one, offering a familiar quotidian framing. *Night of the Living Dead,* however, seems to have fared better, escaping such sublimation. Thomas Ligotti sees that film as "admirably incorruptible. . . . It hasn't sold out to the kindergarten moral codes . . . and it has no particular message to deliver: its only news is nightmare" (*Nightmare* xiv). In a real sense, the gothic author, like the narrator of "Ligeia," is engaged in a study the nature of which is "more than all else adapted to deaden impressions of the outside world"

(Poe, *Selected* 38). This is not to say, however, that in gothic dark imaginings, the mode's reconnoitering of pathological psychic areas, various detritus, including elements of social and cultural morbidity, may not emerge. At worst, horror tracks into the kind of unsavory paranoia and xenophobia that characterized H. P. Lovecraft's life. Indeed, the Nazi nocturnal rallies in the twentieth century, as well as KKK ones, have arguably been expressions of malevolent folk-cultural impulses, and their operatic rites and night fires suggested all too recognizable gothic idioms.

★ ★ ★

Like "Benito Cereno," Melville's "The Tartarus of Maids" is rendered unsettling by a seeming conflation of a social-critical project with a hallucinatory, gothic one. The story's suggestion of a proletarian thematic, its focus on the appalling working conditions in a particular mill, suggests an engagement with ordinary political reality, but that reality, as the tale progresses, becomes increasingly the "reality" of dream. We are again in the realm of the hideous obscure and, as it turns out, caught again in the anxiety of organism. In the end, as Camille Paglia maintains, "Tartarus" evokes horror rather than the empathy toward which it seemed to strive (*Personae* 592). As I have argued above, "Benito Cereno" does something much the same, evoking horror and not empathy from its images of the slave mutiny. Warner Berthoff sees "Tartarus" as "something less—and more—than a piece of social commentary," noting that it "vibrates with imaginative obsession" (202). Joyce Carol Oates views the story as "informed by a political vision, the writer's appalled sympathy with the fates of girls and women condemned to factory work in New England mills." She adds, however—and here the gothic signature appears—that "somehow the paper-mill to which the girls are condemned to work like slaves is also the female body" (3–4). "Somehow" is a marker of the polymorphic perverse character of the projective mode, situating the refusal, as in dream, of things to maintain their discrete borders—"Tartarus" is as gynecologically preoccupied as David Cronenberg's film *Dead Ringers* (1988). Paglia's reading of "Tartarus" is appropriately surreal. Leaving the story's political-proletarian dimension largely unremarked, she goes directly to its obsessional dynamic, its "nightmare condensation of *Moby Dick*'s chthonian theme." The tale unveils, she argues, a *physiological* mystery: "[W]e have penetrated into a female realm" (*Personae* 276). Though sympathetic to the women worker's plight, she observes, the story "is a somewhat nauseating tour of the physiological waterworks" (286). The "pulpy mass" in the factory "represents the non-stop fertility of woman" (585). Whereas "The Paradise of Bachelors," part one of a pair with "Tartarus," is comparatively naturalistic, "Tartarus" is, and I quoted this phrase in an earlier chapter, "grotesque with bio-morphic allegories" (*Personae* 590). It has been my argument that the horror modality *itself* constitutes an elaborate and extended bio-morphic symbolism, but Paglia is correct that the bio-morphism of "Tartarus" is extraordinarily insistent and that the tale is pervaded by a mystique of female biology:

> *Tartarus of Maids* is a descent into a sexual underworld, both inferno and Venusberg. We are seeing the dark underbelly of High Romantic landscape. Melville surely takes his genital topography from Poe: Pym enters "a narrow gorge" with an "excessively slippery" cleft. Melville's gorge contracts into a clitoral "Black Notch," then expands into a labial purple hollow amid "shaggy" pubic mountains. From vaginal "Devil's Dungeon" springs menstrual "Blood River." (*Personae* 590)

This is what Paglia elsewhere characterizes as "the daemonism of the sexual imagination" (*Personae* 264). She offers ample textual evidence from other Melville works of his Freudian-gothic obsession with female physiology and its mythic implications. She quotes, for instance, from *Moby Dick,* where Man searching for the secrets of nature is compared to "an Ohio honey-hunter, who seeking honey in the crotch of a hollow tree, found such exceeding store of it, that leaning too far over, it sucked him in, so that he died embalmed" (590). This is a fall into the hideous obscure of our female biological origins.

Melville's perception of femaleness reflects an anxiety of organism suggestive of the formless fertile swamp, pre-theological, and inconceivably generative. This is another variety of messiness, a blurring of masculine, Apollonian categories whereby we ward off defilement. Woman as vehicle of organic process is provocative of nausea, Paglia argues, "disgust is reason's proper response to the grossness of procreative nature" (12). The narrator's venture into the paper mill—"stifling with a strange, blood-like abominable heat"—represents a gothic journey into the female body (*Personae* 590). "Women have borne the symbolic burden of man's imperfections, his grounding in nature":

> Menstrual blood is the stain, the birthmark of original sin, the filth that transcendental religion must wash from man. Is this identification merely phobic, merely misogynistic? Or is it possible there *is* something

uncanny about menstrual blood, justifying its attachment to taboo? I will argue that it is not menstrual blood per se which disturbs the imagination—unstaunchable as that red flood may be—but rather the albumen in the blood, the uterine shreds, placental jellyfish of the female sea . . . the chthonian matrix from which we rose. We have an evolutionary revulsion from slime. (*Personae* 11)

While emphasizing its concern with menstruation and the queasy desire to staunch the frightening primordial flow, Paglia surprisingly does not note in "The Tartarus of Maids" its considerable preoccupation with rags, the sanitary napkins of the day. This usage is harkened back to in the still current vulgarity "to be on the rag" and even in the name of a commercial napkin presently marketed as "Glad Rags." The stifling "rag-room" in the paper mill holds "hosts of rags" gathered from the nearby country and from overseas; some of them, the narrator points out, possibly from the shirts of the men in "Paradise of Bachelors" (Melville, *Short Works* 217).

The relationship of "Tartarus" to "Bachelors," though Melville conjoined them, is sometimes difficult to grasp, while the gothic affinity of "Tartarus" to "Bartleby" is striking. A sense of decline and demoralization is dominant in both, as is the death-dealing workplace. Unlike "Tartarus," however, in "Bartleby"—and much of Melville—the feminine, the fertile, exists only through its absence. Edward Said describes the world in *Moby Dick* as

so remarkably unproductive, so unregenerate and so bachelorlike, so studiously, unforgivingly *male*. Wives and families are left behind. Whaling is an industry kept going entirely by men. . . . All of Melville's allusions to the Orient—and the presence of such people as Fedallah and his Parsee associates—are also all masculine; there are no harems, no gardens of sensual delight here. If Ahab shares somewhat in the Faustian quest, his Gretchen is no Helen but a roughly, boyishly named male animal. (xxvii)

It is all the more strangely atypical of Melville then, that in "Tartarus of Maids" women are the predominant focus: "At rows of blank-looking counters sat rows of blank-looking girls, with blank, white folders in their blank hands, all blankly folding blank paper" (*Short Works* 215). This is akin to the horror that overwhelms Bartleby—not the speculative dead-letter-office scenario Melville attached as a coda but rather the papery white exhaustion of scrivener work.

"The girl's blankness is the great whale's 'appalling' (literally pale-making) whiteness" (Paglia, *Personae* 592). Melville writes: "So through the consumptive pallors of this blank raggy life, go these white girls to death" (*Short Works* 218). The gothic pattern of insidious physical decline prevails—the "girls," as surely as did Lucy Westenra in *Dracula,* have their life force drained away by a beast seeking its own selfish sustenance. If Melville intended social criticism in "Bartleby" and "Tartarus," that criticism is overwhelmed by demonic gothicism—the demons in both stories and in "Benito Cereno" are ones more awful and more uncanny than any nineteenth-century reform movement can readily locate and fix.

In *'Salem's Lot,* Father Callahan's uneasiness with the postmodern, social-activist Catholic Church, as remarked in an earlier chapter, can be seen as at the same time expressing the long-term gothic distrust of liberal progressiveness and social ideology generally. Ideologies, with their supposed answers, would attenuate the nihilism horror invention broaches—ideologies temporize, denying horror's hideous obscure and its hopeless walls. Father Callahan's reactionary brand of Catholicism, abjuring social answers, thus complements the gothicism of King's novel. Like the traditional Catholic Church, horror literature credits there being evils abroad not to be neutralized by counseling nor by agendas addressed to rehabilitating the world through more finely tuned social strategies. Callahan sees a contradiction in the fabric of a neo-Catholicism, with its ancient sense of evil surviving only vestigially in some ritual forms, but with a revisionist dogmatic structure reflecting "a church more concerned with *social* evils" (italics added). The priest is alienated from the mentality reassured by a faith that "better prisons will cure this. Better cops. Better social services agencies" (King 231). Gothic readers suspend what everyday liberal optimism they have when they enter into the horror frame of reference—"the work of horror is not interested in the civilized surface of our lives" (King, *Danse* 4). We journey to places such as the world on the dark side of the ditch in Faulkner's "That Evening Sun," where there is no 9-1-1, no police on call. In *Nightmare on Elm Street,* Nancy's father in fact *is* a cop, for all the good it does. One of 'Salem's Lot's two policemen is easily sucked into Barlow's vampire novitiate, and the other, paralyzed by the events unfolding in the town, falls helplessly passive.

The reform notes in a gothic narrative such as "Tartarus," like the moral notes Paglia finds unconvincing in "The Rime of The Ancient Mariner," may represent gestures back toward the conventional world by authors who find themselves having journeyed farther into darkness than they are comfortable with. Criticism sometimes takes a likewise conventionalizing stance, one that would dilute horror literature's grim power. Tony Magistrale misinterprets Stephen King, I think, along these lines, using an inappropriately moral-humanistic measure in terms of horror transcendence:

> The audience is provided with the opportunity to gain deep insights into its fear and . . . to acquire an array of coping skills. . . . We are often pained by the loss of human life in the horror story. . . . Moreover, the horror story, like classical tragedy, frequently educates us morally. (24)

The phrase "coping skills" would raise Father Callahan's hackles and I should think Stephen King's. This modeling arguably ignores horror's profound negations, its *no-in-thunder*. It fails to recognize what Ellen Moers notes in a quotation cited in the present book's introduction, that horror does not seek to "reach down into the depths of the soul and purge it . . . (as we say tragedy does), but to get to the body itself, its glands, epidermis, muscles and circulatory system" (214). If there is a horror therapeutic, it is situated in this physicality, not over and above it.

A recent film version of the analytical fallacy Fiedler describes occurs, though in a fairly minor way, in *Stigmata,* a movie discussed earlier. A phantasmagorical adventuring in the symbolic, projective mode entirely—saints, the wounds of Christ, relics, Satanic assault, Vatican intrigues—the film concludes, however, with a jarring element of the analytic-realistic. Another part of the mind is addressed, as if a Red Cross appeal were to intrude, but in this case, it is a brief propaganda message in which the viewer is invited to share some obscure group's indignation that the Vatican, as in the film, is keeping the lid on a scroll found in 1945 and written by Christ himself without the intermediary bother the gospels involve. This scroll offers us the rather traditional bromide that the kingdom of God is within and suggests we not have anything to do with institutionalized religion. While this intrusion occurs only in the last seconds of the film, it still constitutes a flaw in terms of horror rhetoric. The audience arguably is taken out of the hallucinatory frame the film has created by being asked now to link its excessive, uncanny gothicism to an alleged real-world issue of the Roswell, grassy knoll kind. A viewer looks, most ungothically, for a petition to be circulated in the theater, perhaps to be sent to the Papal Nunzio.

In horror, such reform social action is out of place. Fiedler remarks a defining point in the career of Brockden Brown, one which arguably undermined the author's former social optimism: the Philadelphia and New York yellow fever epidemics referred to in a previous chapter here. The epidemics determine a divide in Brown's work, Fiedler argues, "suggesting a new image for human misery, which casts doubt on man's ability to cope with it successfully." He quotes Brown's remarks in the preface to *Arthur Mervyn* concerning the "evils of pestilence" with which Philadelphia has recently been afflicted and that will no doubt give rise to various preventive reforms. Brown then adds that *"if no efforts of human wisdom can avail,"* the civic changes involved might be for the good anyway. Fiedler points to the conditional phrase I have italicized, seeing it as "the first shadow of the doubt which will eventually black out in the heart of this gothic writer his youthful faith in 'schemes of reformation and improvement'" (Fiedler 151). What it would have done to Brown's Enlightenment optimism to know that in the twenty-first century, political factions and nation states would be laboring to *reestablish* conquered plagues can only be speculated upon. But for that matter, not many decades earlier, the British had infected blankets with smallpox and distributed them to American Indians (O'Connell 171).

The most potent of horror invention cultivates such dark realities and disallows the apotropaion, the prophylactic charm afforded by the illusion of social progress and reformation. Captain Delano cannot understand why Benito Cereno will not rebound after his rescue. "You are saved," he reasons. "[Y]ou are saved: what has cast such a shadow upon you?" (*Short Works* 314). But Delano speaks across a divide, to one viscerally terrified and beyond deliverance. In the true dark tale, as the bike racer observes in Hemingway's "A Pursuit Race," they haven't got a cure for anything.

The Soul at Zero:
Dark Epiphanies

These games will be the death of me yet . . . or else salvation. . . .
games pared down to the blazing bare bones, to the beautiful,
terrible core of it all.

—ROB SCHULTHEIS, *Bone Games*

Here in this supreme menace of the will, there approaches a
redeeming, healing, enchantress—art. She alone can turn these
thoughts of repulsion at the horror and absurdity of existence into
ideas compatible with life: these are the sublime—the taming of
horror through art; and comedy—the artistic release from the
repellence of the absurd.

—FRIEDRICH NIETZSCHE, *The Birth of Tragedy*

The gothic flame is capable of tempering the soul to a purity
beyond the range of our dingy realism.

—HERBERT READ

IN CONCLUSION, I WOULD LIKE TO RETURN TO TWO IN-
fluential remarks noted in the introduction—C. L. Barber's that mortality is
implicit in vitality, and Owen Barfield's that human consciousness is something
correlative to a physical organism. Those perceptions defined a direction for
a venture into the landscape of the gothic, one that has privileged horror's
shared roots with comedy in the realm of the biological. The point of view
advanced here has viewed the art expressed in horror fiction and film as, like
art generally, an aspect of human intelligence, not as mimetic but rather as a
generative force enabling essential conceptualizations—"not an imitation, but
a discovery of reality" (Cassirer, *Essay* 143). Like music, horror literature is not
a redundancy; it enacts something not to be found elsewhere and contemplated
complete in an "original" form of its own. An actual dreadful car accident is
by no means beside the point, of course, but horror as something considered

and contemplated is a feature of the human symbolic terrain. To paraphrase
Georges Bataille, it is horror's legendary aspects alone, its literary expressions,
that have ordained the truth of horror (*Trial* 13).

Macabre narratives are symbolic forms bearing the configuration of the
life—Life—that generated them, as dance and verse are presumably not unrelated to the turning of night and day or of the tides and so on—the whole
"cradle endlessly rocking." It has been Julia Kristeva's recent contribution—
significantly indebted to Mary Douglas—to galvanize the analysis of gothic
literature, seeing that literature as very important in the scheme of things and
as horror's "privileged signifier" (208). She addresses horror in terms of its
purifying of the abject within the embrace of an art that embodies "the essential component of religiosity," and that is "rooted in the abject it utters and
by the same token purifies" (17). Emily Dickinson describes such a ritual process in poem 532:

> I tried to think a lonelier Thing
> Than any I had seen—
> Some Polar Expiation—An Omen in the Bone
> Of Death's tremendous nearness. . . .
>
> (260)

This is poetry as extreme sport—bone games; it seeks to slip out of the sys-
tematized repression that characterizes ordinary living and dive to the grim-
mest of psychic depths. The attempt is to touch upon inconsolable darkness,
to summon the worst. Dickinson's work is an extended exercise in the gathering of dark intelligence, a journey like Celine's, to the end of the night. We
are brought round again, however, by that journey, because there is no stopping at the end of the night; we are impelled back from death and abjection—
thus horror's regenerative effect. Through the literature of horror, Kristeva
believes, the dreadful is ritually conjured and an appeasement, an expiation
accomplished. The consolation of horror, its subtle lift, issues from horror as
such, the biological reaction to it, and not from the genre's educating us in such
a way that we are finally "one up" on fear. I once heard the Australian novel-
ist Morris L. West argue that literature has two themes: the presence of God
or the terror of his absence. Metaphorically, at least, I think that formulation
complements Kristeva's, allowing as it arguably does for God's or the sacred's
mythic emergence from the dark power of his or its very absence. Horror
reduces the world, to borrow phrasing from Norman O. Brown in another

context, "to a fluctuating chaos, as in schizophrenia, the chaos which is the eternal ground of creation" (248).

Stephen King's analysis in *Danse Macabre* is in its own way also cognate to Kristeva's. Having, as previously noted, remarked that terror seems to arise from a sense of "things in the unmaking" (9), he argues that "the melodies of the horror tale . . . are melodies of disestablishment and disintegration . . . but another paradox is that the ritual out-letting of these emotions seems to bring things back to a more stable and constructive state again" (13). To reference some examples dealt with in the present work, in "The Yellow Wallpaper," for instance, the bare places showing through where the paper has been ripped off reveal *wall,* that adamancy against which Bartleby curled up in fetal position and died and against which the cabinet ministers are shot in Hemingway's *In Our Time.* What shows through where the wallpaper is missing is the uncanny—the negation of all enhancement, art, culture and civilization, the horror beyond the horror of the wallpaper itself. Yossarian in *Catch-22* is subject to that terror when he sees Snowden's insides, normally discretely out of sight and elegantly arranged within the body, fall out into the public sphere in a confused, horrifying pile—an abomination. "The corpse, seen without God and outside science," Kristeva writes, "is the utmost of abjection" (4). The dead body as its mere contents is defilement, that which is "jettisoned from the *'symbolic system.'* . . . what escapes that social rationality" (65).

This abjection, this experience of the dreadfully unmade, triggers art, civilization, and the self. This is the defilement theme that so much of gothic invention turns on; the genre privileges the lethargic squalor and hopeless unhealth that is civilization's antithesis and nemesis, its horror. The individual and the society, Kristeva argues, define themselves, in effect come into being, through the rejection of what is "rank and vile" as intolerable, through the drawing of a line in the sand as a margin excluding filth and defilement (65). Horror's sickening descent into ashes defines an end point and a beginning; disintegration can entail in and of itself a negative power that is therapeutic in that it impels toward reintegration. Drug addicts and alcoholics often re-form in response to nothing more than the powerful *fact* of their own deterioration—their *deformed* condition becoming manifest and undeniable. Some symbolical version of this effect arguably surfaces in horror invention. When Carys in Clive Barker's *The Damnation Game* languishes in the lair of Mamoulian and his agent Greer, her life reduced to heroin and empty drowsing, she becomes, as Mamoulian wishes, mere death in life. When Marty breaks in and offers a chance of es-

THE SOUL AT ZERO

cape, the assertion escape would call for is not there—her body no longer understands the language of life. Mamoulian has infected her, she sees, with world-weariness, so that every possibility appears to her in the shadow of its own dissolution. "She saw that now in Marty whose face she'd dreamed, whose body she'd wanted. Saw how he would age, would wind down and die, as everything wound down and died. Why stand up at all." (299). Her question articulates ultimate despair, the point where one disintegrates or pulls oneself together. She will die unless, by way of this very null and voidness, an epiphany occurs and the life force kicks in. For Carys, the catalyst to that end is the abhorrent fact that Marty himself, likewise in the sway of Mamoulian's dark magic, falls into a demoralization mirroring her own, when, like her, he is "only certain that to lie down [is] easiest, in this, the emptiest of all possible worlds" (312).

This is a long way from the fertile and phallic celebration enacted by comedy. But it suggests the arguable ritual therapeutic potential in horror, the way in which horror may bring things round to a kind of affirmation negatively provoked—to the more stable and constructive state King refers to. The therapeutic would seem to function on different levels. Langer, for instance, mentions "gallows humor," the lift of which she ascribes to "a flash of self-assertion" (*Feeling* 341). A kind of gallows humor—her existential spunk—is a central energy in Dickinson's poetry: "I lived on Dread," she writes, noting the stimulus there is in danger, compared to which other impetus "is numb and vitalless" (376–77). She writes elsewhere of the frisson following upon terror, "That reaches to our utmost Hair / Its Tentacles divine" (522). We crave emergency. It unifies our consciousness, sweeping away the neurotic dross of our lives; we are secretly disappointed when the predicted hurricane turns out to sea. "The central nervous system needs a certain amount of stimulation. To a dynamic organism, monotony is unbearable" (Ackerman 5). In literature, we look to horror to provide an energizing extremis mundane life does not afford.

But the horror therapeutic arguably runs deeper than this; its effect might be framed homeopathically. A small quantity of morbid material—dilute smallpox vaccine for instance—provokes the body's healthy energies to muster themselves, and thereby tones them. Small doses of arsenic and similar substances, according to homeopathic theory, can have the effect of invigorating the body's immune responses, awakening listless organic functions. Analogously, horror literature involves "not resistance to but an unveiling of the abject" (Kristeva 208). We are exposed to a kind of ritualized confrontation with terror through the gothic tale. The virtual claustrophobic, for example, revives our awareness of space in actuality; of good, well-oxygenated air in actuality; of our freedom and movement in space. "Yet here we are all abroad once more! All at Liberty! And may run, if we will . . . from one end of the earth to the other, and back again without being stopped!" (414). Radcliffe's *The Italian* concludes in these images of joy, but they are come to by a different way than the comic one. These idioms of physical unbinding are part of a narrative that has wound its way through convoluted paths of evil, morbidity, and tyranny—through various scenarios of sinister constraint, confinement, and enclosure, concluding in this energized sense of being-in-the-world. Whether or not the relief occurs in the narrative itself, there is a process in gothic literature of disorientation and reorientation in which the demarcation between things life-beneficial and things morbid is clarified and refreshed for us. The nature and character of transgression are vivified as we ritually revisit situations of defilement, schizophrenia, and repulsion that are an impetus back toward order and identity. The spirit and conviction of Father Karras in *The Exorcist,* as mentioned earlier, is marshaled and invigorated, pulled out of its new-age doldrums, by the diabolical horrors of the possession.

Captive in Dracula's castle, Jonathan Harker writes in his journal: "No man knows till he has suffered from the night how sweet and how dear to his heart and eye the morning can be" (B. Stoker 64). Stephen King recalls the effect 1950s horror films had on him: "There was that magic moment of reintegration and safety at the end. . . . I believe it's this feeling of reintegration, arising from a field specializing in death, fear and monstrosity that makes the danse macabre so rewarding and magical" (*Danse* 14). This dark-epiphanic sense of reprieve and return to order is conveyed in chapter 16 of *Dracula,* when Dr. Seward and company have filed out of the vault of the Un-Dead Lucy, leaving behind the vile, *disintegrative* atmosphere of the tomb. Dr. Seward records his reintegrative physical exhilaration and refreshment:

> Oh! But it seemed fresh and clear in the night air after the terror of the vault. How sweet it was to see the clouds rush by, and the passing gleams of the moonlight between the scudding clouds crossing and passing . . . how sweet it was to breathe the fresh air, that had no taint of death and decay; how humanizing to see the red lightning of the sky beyond the hill. (269)

Horror texts, filmic or literary, would thus seem to present these benign possibilities, this arrival at a reawakened sense of fertility and vitality. Much of the horror in films such as *The Exorcist, Rosemary's Baby, The Stand,* and *Stigmata,* as noted before, derives from the dread of evil inroads to the heart of human fertility—the body of a young woman. The violation of these women may appear lurid and prurient, may in fact *be* so in any given case, but to a viewer of reasonably healthy instincts, a deep aversion response is arguably triggered by the sacrilege involved, the pollution implied. Through its interrogation of sacrilege, literary horror may awaken awareness of the sacramental. The virtual space of art indeed *is* sacramental: "It is ritually clean, a swept floor, the threshing floor that was the first sight of theater." The pathologies of the gothic are thus enacted in a "sacred precinct," the frame of art where contemplation and not action is called for and we are subject to "that hieratic ceremony ritually replayed through time. The blood that is shed will always be shed. The ritual of art is the cruel law of pain made pleasure" (Paglia, *Personae* 29–30).

Real world pollutions and horrors and the memory of them can evidence a related reactive effect, provoking art.[1] A scourge can occasion a social, communal epiphany, activating a renewed sense of the clean and proper individual and civic body, an awareness that systems of preventive maintenance, for example, are not to be taken for granted. The public *Orders* issued during the 1665 plague year in London reflect such an invigorated response emergent from a morbid context, rulings such as these:

> THAT . . . every Householder do cause the Street be prepared before his Door, and so to keep it clean swept all the Week long. THAT the Sweeping and Filth of Houses be daily carry'd away. . . . THAT special care be taken, that no stinking Fish, or unwholesome Flesh . . . of what Sort soever . . . be sold about the City. . . . THAT the Brewers . . . be looked unto, for musty and unwholesome Casks

and so forth (DeFoe 41). Similarly, the Black Death in the fourteenth century led to the abandonment of an outmoded epidemiology and begot a better grounded and more sophisticated medical structure: "In 1347 the members of Europe's medical community were rigid and generally inept. . . . The response of doctors to the new medical problems resulted in a series of changes that led to the evolution of modern clinical medicine in the seventeenth century" (Gottfried 104).

In this regard, the Kristeva-Douglas argument referred to often in this book, that the sense of horror provokes rational, ordered civilization, will be indispensable, I think, to future work addressing the aesthetics of terror. Civilization, Kristeva maintains, is everywhere a response to its own opposite, a reactive creativity issuing from abject, disordering, and disturbing images of defilement. "Defilement is an element connected with the boundary, the margin, etc., of an order" (66).[2] Horror literature comes at fertility from below in effect—we ritually revisit elements of abjection, the place "where all ladders start," where the housekeeping that is civilization begins. Anne Rice in fact testifies to how she has valued that very line from Yeats's "The Circus Animals Desertion": "I must lie down where all ladders start, / In the foul rag and bone shop of the heart" (Riley, *Conversations* 19).

The human infant must lie helpless in its own urine and feces, and I would return here to Wittgenstein's observation quoted in the introduction, that a child's crying "harbours dormant psychic forces, terrible forces. . . . Profound rage, pain, and lust for destruction." I am not at all sure but that the baby, helpless but to lie in its own waste, does not experience the primal sinister locus and that later morbid fear reactions relate to the terror of regression to some version of that helpless and defiled state. Civilization, the ladder up and out of dejection and abomination, in such a paradigm would come with a parent's terribly significant act of picking the child up, cleaning it, powdering it, renewing it, and putting it down in a refreshed, clean place. This act speaks of care, system, and order—of a world that might be respected and ventured out into. Kristeva in effect posits a primordial rag and bone shop whose foulness is a triggering horror that "pushed aside, begets purification and systematization, a horror that civilizations seize on in order to build themselves up and function" (210).

This hypothesis does not of course impute such power to every given instance of horror literature, any more than every exposure to the comic is deeply exhilarating. We are referring to a subtle, aesthetic-somatic complex, and the salient point is that horror literature's final effect is not in keeping with the morbid events it sets forth but can be stabilizing and reintegrative. Referring to the fascination that tales of horror exert on us, Kristeva notes that "far from being a minor, marginal activity in our culture, as a general consensus seems to have it, this kind of literature . . . represents the ultimate coding of our crises. . . . Hence its nocturnal power" (208).

The genre is just now eliciting the full critical attention that it has long merited, and the discussion in the present book, one hopes, may contribute to an energized examination of this vital, eccentric literary species. It seems a certainty, in any case, that the popular consumption of film and literary gothic works will continue apace. We will presumably continue to be drawn by the alluring spell of these weird narratives, by their insistent, sinister imagination and—with a paradoxical undercurrent of thrill even—be lured again and again back to horror's Desolation Row and to the things that inhabit the ominous shadows out that way.

NOTES

WORKS CITED

INDEX

NOTES

Introduction: "The Body Is His Book"

1. I think the passive voice is appropriate here, rather than saying "we" ignore and repress physicality. Our cognitive construction encourages this, as any number of analysts from Bergson to Lacan have in one way or another noted. To be less than fully aware of immediate physical life is a given of our mental design, its default mode.

2. I will be using the term *gothic* in an admittedly very broad, generic sense in this book— hence my use of the lowercase *g*.

3. See Francisco J. Varela, Evan Thompson, and Eleanor Rosch, eds., *The Embodied Mind: Cognitive Science and Human Experience* (Cambridge: MIT Press, 1991); and George Lakoff and Mark Johnson, *Philosophy in the Flesh: The Embodied Mind and Its Challenge to Western Thought* (New York: Basic, 1999).

4. As an example of the tendency for gender and gothic-body elements to converge, see, for example, Kristine Swenson, "The Menopausal Vampire: Arabella Kenealy and the Boundaries of True Womanhood," *Woman's Writing* 9.3 (2002). Much recent analysis of horror, such as Carol J. Clover's *Men, Women, and Chain Saws* (1992) and Susanne Becker's *Gothic Forms of Feminine Fictions* (1999), has of course addressed its gender relevance. Some has been literary-historical; see the essays in *American Gothic: New Interventions in a National Narrative,* Ed. Robert K. Martin and Eric Savoy (Iowa City: Iowa UP, 1998). Mariana Warner's *No Go Bogeyman* interrogates popular fear images, mostly psychologically. Mark Edmundson's *Nightmare on Main Street* analyzes the pervasiveness of gothic elements in contemporary American life.

5. See Owen Barfield's chapter "Meaning and Myth," notably page 80, in his *Poetic Diction* (Middletown: Wesleyan UP, 1973).

6. The brain, Bergson argues, has the image "brain" and the image "physical world." Were it somehow to erase the image "physical world," the image "brain" would disappear with it. Were it to erase the image "brain," on the other hand, the image "physical world" would lose merely "an insignificant detail from an immense picture" (*Matter and Memory* 19).

7. Fritz Hippler was credited as the movie's director, but the introduction to four papers on the film by the Danish historian Stig Hornsoj-Moller, published on the *Holocaust History Project* Web site, notes that *The Eternal Jew* "was produced at the insistence of Joseph Goebbels, under such active supervision that it is effectively his work."

8. This is not, of course, to fault Murnau or certainly Lang, who was by choice an exile from Nazi Germany, for the fact that the Nazis may have capitalized on morbid angles of their work. On the other hand, Alfred Hitchcock, who apprenticed in the German film industry during the 1920s, later gratuitously introduced an anti-Semitic element into his film version of Sean

O'Casey's *Juno and the Paycock*. The Shylockian character he created and inserted into O'Casey's play is arguably sinisterized using expressionist film techniques. I discuss the case in my article "Alfred Hitchcock's *Juno and the Paycock*" in the *Irish University Review* (Autumn/Winter 1994). The article has since been expanded.

1. Mortal Coils: The Comic-Horror Double Helix

1. Part of the original manuscript of Wharton's autobiography *A Backward Glance*, the typhoid episode is included in the 1973 Scribner edition of Wharton's ghost stories.

2. Unless otherwise indicated, numbers relative to Dickinson's poems refer to the page in *The Complete Poems*, not to the individual poem number.

3. Compare Eleanor's first reaction to Hill House in Shirley Jackson's *The Haunting of Hill House;* it is somatic-primordial; the house: "caught her with an atavistic turn in the pit of the stomach" (33–35).

4. Victor Frankenstein's work is technically in electrical reanimation, but its contemporary descendant would be human cloning.

5. A treatise might be written, however, on the question of nausea, for example, which, along with pornography, would seem to mark a kind of aesthetic special case in that the representation can come close to triggering the actual thing. Film, as distinct from written literature, can trigger actual nausea in the viewer, or come close, though mainline movies have shied away from exploiting this power. Vomiting represented in mainline films has up to now always been a greatly understated rendering of the real thing.

6. Emma McEvoy, in her introduction to the Oxford University Press edition on Matthew Lewis's *The Monk* (1998), sees contagion functioning metaphorically in high gothic literary expression: "The fates of the characters seem to spread over and through them, as if they are communicated from one to another, and characters repeat patterns set up by their ancestors" (xviii).

7. Since transhistoricalness is as a rule somewhat suspect currently, I should probably at least acknowledge the issue as it might arise in terms of a generic view of horror tradition. Chris Baldick is one of many who argue that "Gothic fiction is neither immemorial nor global, but belongs specifically to the modern age of Europe and the Americas since the end of the nineteenth century" (*Oxford* xx). This is so, of course, as far as it goes—the same could be said for the specification "Restoration comedy," but that does not deny comedy's existence outside the Restoration period nor the latter's debt to earlier comic invention. It does not do, I think, to assume reductively that gothic literature historically situated is the modality more or less accounted for. The full costume high gothic prototype with its exotic pattern of contrivances in fact had a very brief career involving mainly a few novels of Radcliffe's and one of Lewis's and running roughly from *Otranto* (1764) through *Melmoth the Wanderer* (1820). And Ann Radcliffe's malevolent monk Schedoni, for instance, is not created from whole eighteenth-century cloth but rather recapitulates Shakespearean vice figures such as Iago, Richard III, and Edmund, who themselves owe to earlier medieval models, and so on. Victor Sage remarks the Marquis de Sade's historicizing of the novels of Lewis and Radcliffe in terms of their reaction to the political trauma of the French Revolution, a view that held sway for quite a while and that still has its spokespersons. Sage questions, however, why the modality survived in nineteenth-century fiction long after the revolution (xii). The flourishing of a related macabre literature entering upon the twenty-first century only reinforces the point. The Age of Reason provided a historical special case particularly amenable to horror literature for a while, but in 1973, *The Exorcist*, for example, subverts not an

Enlightenment rationalist model but rather a contemporary psychoanalytical one. The possessed girl's mother exhausts the promise of the psychiatric field, becomes disillusioned with its pretense to the power of ordering, and finds herself negotiating an older, occult landscape. Horror's project turns on the subversion of assurance, order, reality, not on a protracted argument with a specific eighteenth- or nineteenth-century *weltanschauung;* it passes beyond that argument as it long preceded it. (Even in historical terms, I would argue, reverberations of the political-cultural trauma of the 1605 Gunpowder Plot in England are more discernable in and more important to the classic gothic novels in English than are the events of 1789 in France.)

The argument for horror's emanation from physiological reality need not imply, however, an entirely natural and transhistorical energy manifested in time but much more significant than its merely historical-cultural expressions. The modality's biological anxieties necessarily express themselves in concrete historical forms. An analogy might be made to sports and games that around the world are idiosyncratic, historical, and culturally specific, but which more elementally are so many expressions of an underlying mammalian play impulse.

8. Camille Paglia emphasizes the sado-masochistic in Dickinson's work, something akin to the gothic, in *Sexual Personae*. See as well Daneen Wardrop, *Emily Dickinson's Gothic* (Iowa City: Iowa UP, 1996).

9. A caveat of Reid's would hold as well for the present study. He notes as regards generalizations about the ritual, myth, and art of antiquity that we are dependent on "the solid anthropological researches" of scholars such as Jane Harrison, Gilbert Murray, and F. M. Cornford—the "Cambridge Ritualists" who followed J. G. Frazer. Arguably critics such as C. L. Barber, Stanley Edgar Hymans, Northrop Frye, Harold Bloom, and Camille Paglia are later Frazierians, affirming a significant linkage of ritual, myth, and literature. But the underpinnings of much of the Cambridge work, Reid points out, tend to consist of some inspired intuitions of Nietzsche's: "the origin of Greek tragedy in Dionysian ritual, and the general interdependence of myth and ritual in primitive cultures" (Reid 25). Much of my analysis obviously assumes the essential validity of the work referred to.

10. Miquel de Unamuno, for instance, contrasts the impaled, agonized, but still living Jesus favored in popular Spanish iconography to the more resolved, placid representations of the body of Christ in the sepulcher, its torment done. He cites the suffering "Christ of Velasquez who is forever dying but never dead" (xxii). "Terribly tragic are our crucifixes, our Spanish Christs. They are indicative of a Christ not dead, but in agony. . . . A Christ whom one adores on the Cross is a Christ in agony. . . . the Christ who exclaims: 'My God, My God, why hast Thou forsaken me?'" (19). But wouldn't this agonized, carnal iconography—a Christ that writhes, sweats, bleeds, and cries out—be more accurately described aesthetically and stylistically as at least marginally *gothic,* in the macabre tradition of Goya and Mantegna? In any event, the graphic crucifixion icon he describes has long since become an important, even ubiquitous gothic motif. It occurs, for example, in Clive Barker's *The Damnation Game,* wherein the depraved Joseph Whitehead's inner sanctum, for all its sparseness of furnishings, "did boast one treasure. An altarpiece stood against one of the bare walls. . . . Its central panel was a crucifixion of sublime sadism; all gold and blood" (19).

2. The Muse of Horror: Traditions of Dreadful Imagining

1. This is my reason for employing, as I noted in the introduction, the lowercase *g* gothic to refer to horror literature in general as well as to the classic eighteenth- and nineteenth-century body of work.

2. Freeman's short story "The Wind in the Rose Bush" would serve as an example of the stark dreadfulness that the accomplished ghost story can bring forth. Harold Bloom seems to privilege the ghost tale rather than bloody horror literature when he distinguishes Henry James and Robert Louis Stevenson, for instance, from the "rougher storytellers" such as Lewis, Maturin, Stoker, and Mary Shelley, all of whose canonical status he sees as problematical. He considers James "the best writer in the mode" (*Classic Horror* xi). If that means the best writer ever to take up the mode, I would not argue. If it means the best practitioner *of* the mode, however, I am less sure. At the very least, it is arguable that horror has been critically enriched by its "rougher storytellers," running from Maturin to Stephen King and Anne Rice; horror literature's essential grain is a rough one. The species can work powerfully without poltergeist elements and the like, but it needs its earthy, vulgar power.

3. See Angela Bourke's nonfiction account of surviving folk beliefs—including witchcraft and demon possession—in the putatively Catholic western Ireland of 1895, in *The Burning of Bridget Cleary* (New York: Viking, 1999).

4. Regarding the unsettling liminality of the threshold, compare Edith Wharton's threshold anxiety described at the start of chapter 1. Etymologically, liminal of course *means* "at the threshold."

5. "It is no accident," Chris Baldick observes,

> that Gothic fiction first emerged and established itself within the British and Anglo-Irish middle class, in a society which had, through generations of warfare, political scares, and popular martyrology persuaded itself that its hard-won liberties could at any moment be snatched from it by Papal tyranny. . . . At the foundation of Gothic literature's anti-Gothic sentiment lies this nightmare of being dragged back to the persecutions of the anti-reformation. (*Oxford* xiv)

Without arguing with this in fact precise formulation, however, it might be pointed out by way of caveat that it is descriptive of a historical situation, not prescriptive. If it were the latter, one would expect Northern Ireland to have been an absolute seedbed of gothic literature lo these many years, especially so since its Presbyterian imagination is farther yet removed from Catholicism, and even more suspicious of it, than is the Anglican, and more prone to cherishing memories of Papist transgressions and anti-reformational excesses.

Relevant to the political scare element mentioned by Baldick, see Gary Wills's *Witches and Jesuits: Shakespeare's* Macbeth (New York: Oxford UP, 1995), which analyzes *Macbeth* in the light of, or darkness of, the Gunpowder Plot. Based on Wills's historical construction of the play, we might view *Macbeth,* in its subtextual compounding of magic, necromancy, witchcraft, and fears of Jesuitical conspiracy, as a prototypical anticipation of later high gothic novelistic expression. Radcliffe's epigraph to chapter 10 of *The Mystery of Udolpho,* for instance, would seem to register the chill that swept through Protestant England in reaction to the events of 1605: "Can such things be, / And overcome us like a summer's cloud, / Without our special wonder?" (*Macbeth* 3.4.109–11). However, the same atavistic dreads of siege and social undermining are explored in *'Salem's Lot,* for instance, long afterward and within a very different historical and religious framing.

3. Macabre Aesthetics

1. Bynum sees ramifications of this in the anxiety extensive organ transplants give rise to— "it is . . . significant not only that religious groups differ in their responses to organ transplants

but also that they consider the matter a deeply fraught ethical issue, not merely a medical matter" (9). Perhaps implicit here as well is the point E. W. F. Tomlin and others argue, that natural *structure* presupposes value, that "the dissolution of a thing into its elements [indicates] the absence of value, or rather the prolapsus to a level of lesser value" (201). After vampire or pod impact, the body has devolved to something of lesser value; it has become a matter of its uninspired material elements functioning in the service of an alien dictate. *The Malleus Maleficarum* (The Witch Hammer) (1484) interrogates the intricacies of incubus and succubus invasion of the body, a succubus's taking over of a man's semen, for instance, and using it for its own ends— "they absorb the seed of other things (Kramer and Sprenger 26). (I recently heard a TV evangelist arguing that a bio-replication of this kind will be involved in the coming of the anti-Christ, that the beast will come through cloning, appearing as a doppelganger babe, the double of Christ.)

2. In the 1929 surrealist film *Un Chien Andalou,* a recurrent motif is a man gazing at his own hand over which ants are crawling, seemingly out of a hole in the hand's center. There is an apparent disconnect—no suggestion that he has control of the hand or that the hand can throw off the insects. A process is underway within him over which he has no control; he is the unwilling host to something awful. Hands embody will—it is with our hands that we actually and symbolically *ward off* and exclude. If the hand is incapable of that action, it is a gratuitous appendage bespeaking helplessness, a paralysis of the will. In a later *Un Chien Andalou* scene, the hand that was insect ridden is severed, lying on the ground. The hand as soul is a trope played out in many films, from *Hands of Orlac* (1923) to Oliver Stone's *The Hand* (1983). See the discussion of Sartre's *Nausea* in the next chapter.

3. This of course marks the origin of now mean and empty "traditions" of initiation and hazing.

4. It may be, in fact, I will be arguing so, that horror is not without its therapeutic effects; the point here, however, is that resurgence is not implicit in the very structure of horror as it is in comedy—the banana peel fall, for example, has degradation and transcendent laughter implicit in it at one and the same time.

5. This formality too occurred in the traditional Odd Fellowship ritual wherein the initiate was invited to contemplate a skeleton in a coffin (Carnes 20–21).

6. See Stephen King, quoted in chapter 8, regarding the absence of an aesthetic sense in the victims in *Invasion of the Body Snatchers.*

7. Whether Melville had read Douglass's biography, I have been so far unable to determine. Likely he had, and if so, the reversal of black and white roles, the reverse panoptic surveillance, would be an ironic devise. It is ironic even if unintentional.

8. In terms of pathologically relentless pursuit, a related trope, one thinks of the small boy, in the film *Night of the Hunter,* who, seeing the mad preacher (played by Robert Mitchum) who has been tracking him and his sister down river, says to the girl, "Don't he *ever* sleep?"

4. The Anxiety of Organism

1. It must be reiterated, of course, that there are two "real" horror dimensions—the one in which, for example, the airliners are flown into the twin towers, and the one in which imagination extrapolates that terror, considers it, dwells upon it.

2. The same motif occurs in the grotesque pavilion dance of the dead in the cult film *Carnival of Souls*—the stilted, hopeless bodies "dancing."

3. Chris Baldick discusses the role played by the original Frankenstein film (1931) in reshap-

ing the myth, Karloff's interpretation supplanting Shelley's original and becoming in effect "authoritative" as regards the monster's appearance and distorted physical movement (*Frankenstein's Shadow* 5). This film also introduced the trope of the dwarf assistant to Victor Frankenstein, the Igor figure that has begotten a convention—the physically stunted, grotesque shadow to the overreaching scientist. A marvelous comical version of the Igor figure was of course performed by Marty Feldman in *Young Frankenstein* (1973).

4. This quotation is from Byron's *The Giaour*. It is quoted in Stoker's *Dracula,* 213.

5. In this pathological sense of intimacy, Jon Hinkley Jr. achieved an extraordinary intimacy with Jody Foster—he is forever a part of her biography. One of his calls to her while she was at Yale was recorded. It is evident on the tape the *he,* sickeningly enough, perceives the conversation—in which she tells him emphatically not to call any more, and so forth—as a lover's quarrel. This is no doubt why people being stalked are advised to avoid *any* form of communication with the pursuer.

6. The Soviet scientific community, for instance, notoriously allowed its research in genetics to be hijacked and compromised from 1937 to 1964 by the charlatan T. D. Lysenko; it is very doubtful that it would have allowed such a turn of events in its physics and engineering research. See Zhores A. Medvedev, *The Rise and Fall of T. D. Lysenko* (New York: Columbia UP, 1969). Even as of 2000, Russia has notably not been a significant player in recent genome research—arguably evidence of the depth of damage done by Lysenko.

7. An exception to the physics-dominated trend in the seventeenth century, Whitehead notes, was the biological work at the University of Padua. Hawthorne significantly situates his gothic tale "Rappaccini's Daughter" there.

8. The word *comparatively* here is mine. Like many of Bakhtin's critics, I would not necessarily follow him all the way to positing a perfect peasant ease with all aspects of biological being, if indeed Bakhtin would argue that.

9. Sometime after writing this, I came upon a new book on the Coen brothers, Ronald Bergan's *The Coen Brothers* (2000), in which it is mentioned that O'Connor is indeed one of the pair's favorite authors.

6. Dark Carnival: The Esoterics of Celebration

1. I think it is significant that Terry Heller and Julia Kristeva, both to some extent Bakhtinian analysts, have written horror-related studies though Bakhtin's project was addressed to the comic.

2. The prostitute in the film *Klute,* the Jane Fonda character, uses "party" in this illicit sense, counseling her clients that it will be healthy to let go their inhibitions, to "let it all hang out." Unwittingly, she thereby unleashes a monster and murderous forces.

3. Debate is an important carnival element. Bakhtin refers to the "folk-carnival 'debates'" between life and death, darkness and light, winter and summer, etc., permeated with the pathos of change and joyous relativity of all things, debates which did not permit thought to stop and congeal in one sided seriousness" (*Poetics* 132).

4. The fact that there is no *there* there adds to the elusive dreadfulness of gothic serial killers such as "Mr. Blank" in *The First Deadly Sin* or "John Doe" in *Seven.* Their characterlessness is akin to the horror of whiteness Melville defines in chapter 42 of *Moby Dick,* a whiteness that can "heighten . . . terror to the furthest bounds" (224).

5. But another possible interpretation suggests itself, one that would question whether the comic pattern in which Youth comes to the fore replacing recalcitrant Age and its justifiably

bygone values (*The Graduate,* for example) is any longer relevant to a postmodern American culture that is notoriously youth centered. Do contemporary American teenagers in fact represent the traditional image of the young capable of refreshing the aging social order? Not in *Friday the 13th,* and certainly not in *Halloween* or *Carrie.* Do they themselves now constitute a hegemony in which youth culture reigns supreme? It is arguable that contemporary American and European society secretly yearns for an element of the Apollonian, of decorum and restraint, and that the seminal films in the teen horror genre constitute an inversion of the New Comic pattern, a reactionary imagination of a society where the spoiled, self-indulgent young are violently reined in. It is a vision that might, on a symbolic and unconscious level, be attractive even to the young horror moviegoers themselves. Might even anorexia nervosa be a syndrome enacting a purification ritual (laxatives), the rejection of defilement that Kristeva argues yields identity? Anorexia may gesture toward a kind of ascetic sanctification impossible to negotiate in the undisciplined secular frame of teenage American life and a warding off of taboo elements—indulgence, sloth, obesity, uncontrol.

7. Languishment: The Wounded Hero

1. "Bartleby," "Benito Cereno," and numerous other American literary pieces, especially ones of a gothic disposition, have for decades suffered from the New Critical bias Camille Paglia notes, that of foregrounding *irony* in texts wherever possible (*Sex and Art* 103). My characterization of the "Bartleby" narrator here, for example, viewing him as an eminently decent man, runs counter to the common tendency to merely emphasize his "ironic" foolishness. I think the bizarre depths of "Benito Cereno" have been covered over by passing off all too much in that story as ironically reflecting Captain Delano's denseness (see chapter 9).

2. It should be noted that the bringing of provisions to the faltered ship occurs in Captain Delano's true account. Melville's retention of the detail, however, I would ascribe to his recognition of the motifs mythic resonance.

3. I'm of course aware that such characterizations related to gender are open to objection, to say the least, but one is talking mythically here and not politically, sociologically, or even "realistically." The question is what resonance the Annie Wilkes character has in the unconscious, in mythscape. The inappropriateness of a light of day measure applied to the demonic spirit of gothic horror will be considered in chapter 9.

4. The story's ambiguity is such that one of the common interpretations—thanks to Edmund Wilson—is that the governess is projecting the diabolical upon the circumstances at the Bly estate. Camille Paglia's discussion of the story in *Sexual Personae* seems to entertain this projective reading—"[t]he ghosts may be emanations of her own double-sexed imagination" (613)—and the objective one at the same time. I have chosen not to take up this other interpretation in my discussion.

9. Apotropaion and the Hideous Obscure

1. See Murray Melbin, "Night as Frontier," *American Sociology Review* 43.1 (Feb. 1978): 3–22.

2. Moral content can of course be imposed on horror as it can on comedy. Contemporary films such as *The Crow* and *Spawn,* for example, derive from a comic strip genre that blends horror and superhero conventions. The latter tradition introduces a righteous element, but at root revenge horror is arguably the dynamic. Further regarding amorality in the gothic context, see Louis A. Renza's article "Poe's King: Playing It Close to the Pest," *Edgar Allan Poe Review* 2.2 (Fall

2001): 3–18. While the article's theoretical tact is far removed from what I am arguing here, at one point Renza notes, regarding "King Pest," that the tale "amounts to a preemptive strike against those whom [Poe] imagines will finally encounter a text without any socially redeeming value" (4). Renza notes the story's resistance to the middle-class "market-inflected public sphere," to "contemporary American political agendas" and "proliferating systems of knowledge" (5), and to a "pestilential criterion of literature as a carrier of public truths" (14), which criterion would denature Poe's dark imaginative project.

3. Baldick's point may not be as flat as I suggest here, but in any event, it serves to suggest a not uncommon attitude toward horror fiction's moral vacuity.

4. Lovecraft buffs seek to rigorously establish the author's mythical towns in terms of real locations, something that probably cannot be done with exactitude. But I think Joshi and Schultz place Innsmouth too far south. They maintain that "if the narrator's bus trip from Newburyport to Arkham is duplicated today, one would actually end up in the town of Gloucester" (14). But the narrator doesn't go from Newburyport to Arkham—that is the bus's full run; he goes only as far as Innsmouth. The story does not suggest a journey anything like as long as the one to Gloucester would be. After Plum Island is lost sight of, no major towns—Ipswich, for instance— are passed through, and Rowley, much closer to Newburyport than to Gloucester, would seem to be Innsmouth's nearest neighbor.

10. The Soul at Zero: Dark Epiphanies

1. I don't think it would be inaccurate, for instance, to view the impressive political-military tonicity and social cohesion of post-World War II Israel as issuing from a prior horror.

2. She is of course discussing Mary Douglas's work here. I think, however, Kristeva's analysis in the long run transcends Douglas's, which is arguably too intellectual, too narrowly confined to remarking category transgressions that violate a given culture's conceptual-classificational paradigm and thereby provoke aversion responses to "impurity."

WORKS CITED

Abrams, M. H. *Natural Supernaturalism: Tradition and Revolution in Romantic Literature.* New York: Norton, 1971.

Ackerman, Diane. *Deep Play.* New York: Vintage, 1999.

Aiken, John, and Anna Barbauld. "On the Pleasure Derived from Objects of Terror." *Miscellaneous Pieces in Prose.* London: J. Johnson, 1775. 119–27.

An American Werewolf in London. Dir. John Landis. Universal, 1981.

Angel Heart. Dir. Alan Parker. Carolco, 1987.

Arlen, Michael J. "The Cold Bright Charms of Immortality." *The Contemporary Essay.* Ed. Donald Hall. New York: St. Martin's, 1984. 273–80.

Auden, W. H. *The Dyer's Hand and Other Essays.* New York: Vintage, 1968.

Auerbach, Nina. *Our Vampires, Our Selves.* Chicago: U of Chicago P, 1995.

Bachelard, Gaston. *The Poetics of Space.* Boston: Beacon, 1994.

Badley, Linda. *Film, Horror, and the Body Fantastic.* Westport, CT: Greenwood, 1995.

The Bad Seed. Dir. Mervin Leroy. Warner, 1956.

Baker, Carlos. *Hemingway: The Writer as Artist.* Princeton: Princeton UP, 1952.

Bakhtin, Mikhail. *The Dialogic Imagination.* Ed. Michael Holquist. Trans. Caryl Emerson and Michael Holquist. Austin: U of Texas P, 1981.

———. *Problems of Dostoevsky's Poetics.* Ed. and Trans. Caryl Emerson. Minneapolis: U of Minnesota P, 1984.

———. *Rabelais and His World.* Trans. Helene Iswolsky. Bloomington: Indiana UP, 1984.

Baldick, Chris. *In Frankenstein's Shadow.* Oxford: Clarendon, 1987.

———. Introduction. Maturin vii–xix.

———, ed. *The Oxford Book of Gothic Tales.* New York: Oxford UP, 1992.

Ballard, J. G. *Concrete Island.* New York: Farrar, 1974.

Barber, C. L. *Shakespeare's Festive Comedy: A Study of Dramatic Form and Its Relation to Social Custom.* New York: Meridian, 1959.

Barfield, Owen. "Meaning and Myth." In *Poetic Diction.* Middletown: Wesleyan UP, 1973.

———. *The Rediscovery of Meaning and Other Essays.* Middletown: Wesleyan UP, 1977.

Barker, Clive. *Books of Blood.* New York: Berkley, 1998.

———. *The Damnation Game.* New York: Berkley, 1990.

———. *The Great and Secret Show.* New York: Harper, 1989.

Bataille, Georges. *The Accursed Share: An Essay on General Economy.* New York: Zone, 1991.

———. *The Trial of Gilles De Rais.* Los Angeles: Amok, 1991.

Beaver, Harold. Introduction. Poe, *The Narrative of Gordon Pym of Nantucket,* 7–30.

Becker, Susanne. *Gothic Forms of Feminine Fictions.* New York: Manchester UP, 1999.

Beowulf. Trans. Seamus Heaney. London: Faber, 1999.

Bergan, Ronald. *The Coen Brothers.* New York: Thunder's Mouth, 2000.

Bergson, Henri. *Creative Evolution.* 1911. Mineola, NY: Dover, 1998.

———. *Matter and Memory.* New York: Zone, 1991.

Beroul. *The Romance of Tristan.* London: Penguin, 1970.

Berthoff, Warner, ed. Introduction. Melville, *Great Short Works of Herman Melville* 9–18.

The Big Sleep. Dir. Howard Hawks. Warner, 1946.

The Blair Witch Project. Dir. Daniel Myrick. Haxan, 1999.

Bleiler, E. F. Introduction. Le Fanu, *Best Ghost Stories* v–xi.

Bloom, Harold. *Bloom's Reviews: The Sun Also Rises.* Broomall, PA: Chelsea House, 1996.

———, ed. *Classic Horror Writers.* New York: Chelsea House, 1994.

Blowout. Dir. Brian DePalma. Filmways, 1981.

Bly, Robert. *The Light Around the Body.* New York: Harper and Row, 1967.

Boase, T. S. R. "King Death: Mortality, Judgement, and Remembrance." Evans 203–45.

Booe, Martin. "Deliciously Terrifying." Interview with Clive Barker. *U.S.A. Weekend* 26–28 Jan. 1990: 8.

Bourke, Angela. *The Burning of Bridget Cleary.* New York: Viking, 1999.

Bradbury, Ray. *Something Wicked This Way Comes.* New York: Bantam, 1963.

Bradford, William. *Of Plymouth Plantation 1620–1647.* New York: Modern Library, 1981.

Brooks, Van Wyck. *New England: Indian Summer 1865–1915.* Chicago: U of Chicago P, 1984.

Brown, Charles Brockden. *Ormond.* Ed. Mary Chapman. Ontario: Broadview, 1999.

———. *Three Gothic Novels: Wieland, Arthur Mervyn, Edgar Huntley.* New York: Library of America, 1998.

Brown, Norman O. *Love's Body.* New York: Random, 1966.

Browne, Sir Thomas. *The Major Works.* New York: Penguin, 1977.

Bruhm, Stephen. *Gothic Bodies: The Politics of Pain in Romantic Fiction.* Philadelphia: Pennsylvania UP, 1994.

Bryant, William Cullen. "Thanatopsis." *American Poetry: The Nineteenth Century.* New York: Library of America, 1996.

Burke, Edmund, *A Philosophical Enquiry.* New York: Oxford UP, 1990.

Burke, Kenneth. *The Philosophy of Literary Form.* New York: Vintage, 1957.

Bynum, Caroline Walker. "Why All the Fuss about the Body? A Medievalist's Perspective." *Critical Inquiry* 22.1 (Autumn 1995): 1–33.

The Cabinet of Dr. Caligari. Dir. Robert Wiene. Germany, 1919.

Caillois, Roger. *Man, Play, and Games.* Urbana: U of Illinois P, 2001.

Cain, James M. *Cain x 3.* New York: Knopf, 1969.

Caldwell, Patricia, ed. Introduction. C. Williams xi–xxii.

Capote, Truman. *In Cold Blood.* New York: Vintage, 1994.

Carnes, Mark C. *Secret Ritual and Manhood in Victorian America.* New Haven: Yale UP, 1989.

Carnival of Souls. Dir. Hark Harvey. Harcourt, 1962.

Carroll, Noel. *The Philosophy of Horror or Paradoxes of The Heart.* New York: Routledge, 1990.

Cassirer, Ernst. *An Essay on Man.* New Haven: Yale UP, 1972.

———. *The Philosophy of Ernst Cassirer.* Ed. Paul Schilpp. New York: Tudor, 1958.

Castle, Terry. *Masquerade and Civilization: The Carnivalesque in Eighteenth-Century English Culture and Fiction*. Stanford: Stanford UP, 1986.

Cawson, Frank. *The Monsters in the Mind: The Face of Evil in Myth, Literature, and Contemporary Life*. Sussex, Eng.: Book Guild, 1995.

Chandler, Raymond. *The Big Sleep*. New York: Vintage, 1992.

Chapman, Mary. Introduction. Brown, *Ormond* 9–31.

Cheever, John. *The Stories of John Cheever*. New York: Knopf, 1978.

Chien Andalou, Un. Dir. Louis Bunuel. France, 1929.

Chrétien. *The Complete Romances of Chrétien de Troyes*, Trans. David Staines. Bloomington: Indiana UP, 1993.

Cohen, Leonard. *Stranger Music: Selected Poems and Songs*. New York: Pantheon, 1993.

Coma. Dir. Michael Crichton. MGM, 1978.

Cook, Robin. *Mortal Fear*. New York: Berkley, 1989.

Copjec, Joan. *Read My Desire: Lacan Against the Historicists*. Cambridge: MIT UP, 1995.

Cornford, Francis M. *The Origin of Attic Comedy*. 1912. Ann Arbor: U of Michigan P, 1993.

Creature from the Black Lagoon. Dir. Jack Arnold. Universal, 1954.

Davidson, Cathy N. *Revolution and the Word: The Rise of the Novel in America*. New York: Oxford UP, 1986.

Dead Ringers. Dir. David Cronenberg. Mantle Clinic II, 1988.

DeFoe, Daniel. *A Journal of the Plague Years*. Ed. Paula R. Backscheider. New York: Norton, 1992.

Dekker, Thomas. "From *The Wonderful Year*." DeFoe 237–41.

Dickens, Charles. *Bleak House*. New York: Norton, 1977.

Dickinson, Emily. *The Complete Poems of Emily Dickinson*. Ed. Thomas H. Johnson. Boston: Little, 1960.

Dinesen, Isak. *Carnival: Entertainments and Posthumous Tales*. Chicago: U of Chicago P, 1979.

Donne, John. *The Complete Poetry of John Donne*. Ed. John T. Shawcross. New York: Anchor, 1967.

Donoghue, Denis. *Walter Pater: Lover of Strange Souls*. New York: Knopf, 1995.

———. *We Irish: Essays on Irish Literature and Society*. Berkeley: U of California P, 1986.

Double Indemnity. Dir. Billy Wilder. Paramount, 1944.

Douglas, Mary. *Purity and Danger: An Analysis of the Concepts of Pollution and Taboo*. New York: Routledge, 1996.

Douglass, Frederick. *Autobiographies*. New York: Library of America, 1994.

Eagleton, Terry. *Crazy Jane and the Bishop and Other Essays on Irish Culture*. Notre Dame, IN: Notre Dame UP, 1998.

Edmundson, Mark. *Nightmare on Main Street*. Cambridge: Harvard UP, 1997.

Eliot, T. S. *The Complete Poems and Plays, 1909–1950*. New York: Harcourt, 1958.

Emerson, Ralph Waldo. *Collected Poems and Translations*. New York: Library of America, 1994.

The Eternal Jew. (International Historic Films, Chicago). Germany, 1940.

Evans, Joan, ed. *The Flowering of the Middle Ages*. New York: McGraw-Hill, 1966.

Fantasia 2000. Dir. Eric Goldberg, Hendel Butoy. Disney, 2000.

Fatal Attraction. Dir. Adrian Lyne. Paramount, 1987.

Faulkner, William. *Collected Stories of William Faulkner*. New York: Vintage, 1995.

Fiedler, Leslie A. *Love and Death in the American Novel*. 1960. Normal, IL: Dalkey, 1997.

Fieldsend, Andrew. "The Sweet Tongues of Cannibals: The Grotesque Pacific in *Moby Dick*." <www.otago.ac.nz/deepsouth/vol1no3/fieldsend_issue3.html>.

The First Deadly Sin. Dir. Brian G. Hutton. Kastner/Artanis, 1980.

Fitch, Janet. *White Oleander.* Boston: Little, 2001.

Fitzgerald, F. Scott. *The Crack-Up.* New York: New Directions, 1993.

The Fly. Dir. David Cronenburg. Brooksfilms, 1986.

The Fly. Dir. Kurt Neumann. Twentieth Century–Fox, 1958.

Foote, Timothy. *The World of Bruegel.* New York: Time, 1968.

Fort, Charles. *The Book of the Damned.* New York: Ace, 1972.

Foucault, Michel. *Discipline and Punish: The Birth of the Prison.* New York: Vintage, 1995.

Freeman, Mary Wilkins. *The Wind in the Rosebush and Other Stories.* Chicago: Academy Chicago, 1986.

Freneau, Philip. *Poems of Freneau.* New York: Hafner, 1968.

Freud, Sigmund. *Studies in Parapsychology.* New York: Collier, 1963.

Friday the 13th. Dir. Sean Cunningham. Cunningham, 1980.

Frye, Northrop. *Anatomy of Criticism: Four Essays.* Princeton: Princeton UP, 1971.

———. *Fables of Identity: Studies in Poetic Mythology.* New York: Harcourt, 1963.

Gilman, Charlotte Perkins. "The Yellow Wallpaper." *American Gothic Tales.* Ed. Joyce Carol Oates. New York: Plume, 1996.

The Gold Rush. Dir. Charles Chaplin. Chaplin Productions, 1925.

Gottfried, Robert S. *The Black Death: Natural and Human Disaster in Medieval Europe.* New York: Free Press, 1985.

Greenblatt Stephen. "Mutilation and Meaning." Hillman and Mazzio 221–41.

Halloween. Dir. John Carpenter. Falcon, 1978.

The Hand. Dir. Oliver Stone. Orion, 1981.

Hands of Orloc. Dir. Robert Wiene. Austria, 1925.

Hardy, Thomas. *The Mayor of Casterbridge.* New York: Knopf, 1993.

———. *The Return of the Native.* New York: Oxford UP, 1990.

Harris, Thomas. *The Silence of the Lambs.* New York: St. Martin's, 1988.

Hartman, Robert S. "Cassirer's Philosophy of Symbolic Forms." Schilpp 291–333.

Hawthorne, Nathaniel. *The Complete Short Stories of Nathaniel Hawthorne.* Garden City, NY: Hanover, 1959.

———. *Hawthorne's Short Stories.* Ed. Newton Arvin. New York: Knopf, 1946.

Hayles, N. Katherine. *How We Became Post Human.* Chicago: U of Chicago P, 1999.

Heaney, Seamus. *Beowulf: A New Verse Translation.* New York: Farrar, 2000.

———. *Death of a Naturalist.* New York: Oxford UP, 1966.

Heller, Joseph. *Catch-22.* New York: Scribner's, 1996.

Heller, Terry. *The Delights of Terror: An Aesthetics of the Tale of Terror.* Urbana: U of Illinois P, 1987.

Hemingway, Ernest. *In Our Time.* New York: Collier, 1986.

———. *The Short Stories of Ernest Hemingway.* New York: Scribner's, 1966.

———. *The Sun Also Rises.* New York: Scribner's, 1954.

Herriman, George. *Krazy Kat: The Comic Art of George Herriman.* Ed. Patrick McDonnell, Karen O'Connell, and Georgia Riley DeHavenon. New York: Abrams, 1986.

Hillman, David, and Carla Mazzio, eds. *The Body in Parts: Fantasies of Corporeality in Early Modern Europe.* New York: Routledge, 1997.

Hindle, Maurice. Introduction. Bram Stoker vii–xxx.

Hornsoj-Moller, Stig. Introduction. *Holocaust History Project.* 2 Dec. 2000. <http://www.holocaust-history.org/>.

The Howling. Dir. Joe Dante. MGM, 1981.

Huizinga, J. *The Waning of the Middle Ages:* New York: Anchor, 1989.

Invasion of the Body Snatchers. Dir. Dan Siegel. Allied, 1956.

Invasion of the Body Snatchers. Dir. Philip Kaufman. United, 1978.

Jackson, Shirley. *The Haunting of Hill House.* New York: Penguin, 1959.

———. "The Lovely House." Oates 204–25.

Jacob's Ladder. Dir. Adrian Lyne. Carolco, 1990.

James, Henry. *The Turn of the Screw and The Lesson of the Master.* Amherst, NY: Prometheus, 1996.

Johnson, Mark. *The Body in the Mind: The Bodily Basis of Meaning, Imagination, and Reason.* Chicago: U Chicago P, 1987.

Joshi, S. T. *The Weird Tale.* Austin: U of Texas P, 1990.

Joshi, S. T., and David E. Schultz, eds. Introduction. Lovecraft, *The Shadow over Innsmouth* 9–24.

Joyce, James. *A Portrait of the Artist as a Young Man.* Ed. Chester G. Anderson. New York: Penguin, 1977.

Kauffman, Stuart. *At Home in the Universe: The Search for the Laws of Self-Organization and Complexity.* New York: Oxford UP, 1995.

Kilgour, Maggie, *The Rise of the Gothic Novel.* New York: Routledge, 1995.

King, Stephen. *Carrie.* New York: Signet, 1974.

———. *Danse Macabre.* New York: Berkley, 1983.

———. *It.* New York: Signet, 1987.

———. *'Salem's Lot.* New York: Pocket, 1999.

———. *The Shining.* New York: Signet, 1978.

———. *The Stand.* New York: Signet, 1991.

Kipling, Rudyard. *Something of Myself and Other Autobiographical Writings.* New York: Cambridge UP, 1990.

Koontz, Dean. *The Bad Place.* New York: Berkley, 1990.

Kramer, Heinrich, and James Sprenger. *The Malleus Maleficarum of Heinrich Kramer and James Sprenger.* Trans. Montague Summers. New York: Dover, 1971.

Kristeva, Julia, *Powers of Horror: An Essay on Abjection.* New York: Columbia UP, 1982.

Lakoff, George, and Mark Johnson. *Philosophy in the Flesh: The Embodied Mind and Its Challenge to Western Thought.* New York: Basic, 1999.

Langer, Suzanne K. *Feeling and Form: A Theory of Art.* New York: Scribner's, 1953.

———. *Philosophy in a New Key: A Study in the Symbolism of Reason, Rite, and Art.* New York: Mentor, 1962.

Lawrence, D. H. *Complete Poems.* New York: Penguin, 1993.

———. *Studies in Classic American Literature.* New York: Penguin, 1977.

Le Fanu, J. S. *Best Ghost Stories of J. S. Le Fanu.* Ed. E. F. Bleiler. New York: Dover, 1964.

———. *Uncle Silas.* Ed. Frederick Shroyer. New York: Dover, 1966.

Lévy, Maurice. *Lovecraft: A Study in the Fantastic.* Detroit: Wayne State UP, 1988.

Lewis, Matthew. *The Monk.* New York: Oxford UP, 1998.

Ligotti, Thomas. "The Last Feast of Harlequin." Oates 420–54.

———. *The Nightmare Factory.* New York: Carroll and Graf, 1996.

———. *Noctuary.* New York: Carroll and Graf, 1994.

Lovecraft, H. P. *The Shadow over Innsmouth.* Ed. S. T. Joshi and David E. Schultz. West Warwick, RI: Necronomicon, 1997.

————. *Supernatural Horror in Literature.* New York: Abramson, 1945.

Lumley, Brian. *Necroscope.* New York: Doherty, 1986.

M. Dir. Fritz Lang. Germany, 1931.

Mack, John E., M.D. *Nightmares and Human Conflict.* Boston: Houghton, 1974.

Magistrale, Tony. *Stephen King: The Second Decade, Danse Macabre to the Dark Half.* New York: Twayne, 1992.

Maturin, Charles Robert. *Melmoth the Wanderer.* Ed. William Axton. Lincoln: U of Nebraska P, 1961.

McCarthy, Mary. *Memories of a Catholic Girlhood.* New York: Harcourt, 1974.

McCourt, Frank. *Angela's Ashes.* New York: Scribner's, 1996.

McDonald, Patrick, et al., eds. *Krazy Kat: The Comic Art of George Harriman.* New York: Abrams, 1986.

McDonald, Russ. *The Bedford Companion to Shakespeare: An Introduction with Documents,* Boston: Bedford, 1996.

McEvoy, Emma. Introduction. Lewis vii–xxx.

McGrath, Patrick. "Blood Disease." Baldick, *Oxford* 502–18.

Medvedev, Zhores A. *The Rise and Fall of T. D. Lysenko.* New York: Columbia UP, 1969.

Melbin, Murray. "Night as Frontier." *American Sociology Review* 43.1 (Feb. 1978): 3–22.

Melville, Herman. *Collected Poems.* Ed. Howard P. Vincent. Chicago: Packard, 1947.

————. *Great Short Works of Herman Melville.* Ed. Warner Berthoff. New York: Harper, 1969.

————. *Moby Dick.* New York: Library of America, 1991.

Milton, John. *Complete Poems and Major Prose.* Ed. Merrit Y. Hughes. New York: Odyssey, 1957.

Mimic. Dir. Guillermo Del Toro. Dimension, 1997.

Misery. Dir. Rob Reiner. Castle Rock, 1990.

Moers, Ellen. "Female Gothic: 'The Monster's Mother.'" *Frankenstein.* By Mary Shelley. 1818. Ed. J. Paul Hunter. New York: Norton, 1996. 214–24.

Morrison, Toni. *Beloved.* New York: Knopf, 1998.

A Nightmare on Elm Street. Dir. Wes Craven. New Line / Media, 1984.

The Night of the Hunter. Dir. Charles Laughton. United, 1955.

Night of the Living Dead. Dir. George A. Romero. Image 10, 1968.

Nosferatu the Vampyre. Dir. F. W. Murnau. Germany, 1922.

Nosferatu the Vampyre. Dir. Werner Herzog. Germany, 1979.

Oates, Joyce Carol. *American Gothic Tales.* New York: Plume, 1996.

O'Connell, Robert L. *Of Arms and Men: A History of War, Weapons, and Aggression.* New York: Oxford UP, 1989.

O'Connor, Flannery. *The Complete Stories.* New York: Farrar, 1974.

Olson, Charles. *Archeologist of Morning.* New York: Grossman, 1973.

O'Nan, Stewart. *A Prayer for the Dying.* New York: Holt, 1999.

Paglia, Camille. *Sex, Art, and American Culture.* New York: Vintage, 1992.

————. *Sexual Personae: Art and Decadence from Nefertiti to Emily Dickinson.* New York: Vintage, 1991.

Panic in the Streets. Dir. Elia Kazan. Twentieth Century-Fox, 1950.

Perez, Gilberto. *The Material Ghost: Films and Their Medium.* Baltimore: Johns Hopkins UP, 1998.

Perillo, Lucia. "'I, With No Rights in This Matter': an Elegy." *The Chronicle of Higher Education* 30 Mar. 2001: B24.

Phantom of the Opera. Dir. Robert Julian. Universal, 1925.

Play Misty for Me. Dir. Clint Eastwood. Universal, 1971.

Poe, Edgar Allan. *The Complete Poems and Stories of Edgar Allan Poe.* Ed. Arthur Hobson Quinn and Edward H. O'Neill. New York: Knopf, 1973.

———. *The Narrative of Arthur Gordon Pym of Nantucket.* Ed. Harold Beaver. New York: Penguin, 1982.

———. *Poetry and Tales.* New York: Library of America, 1984.

———. *Selected Tales.* New York: Library of America, 1991.

Porter, Katherine, Anne. *Pale Horse, Pale Rider: Three Short Novels.* New York: Modern Library, 1998.

Pound, Ezra. *The Spirit of Romance.* New York: New Directions, 1968.

Praz, Mario. *The Romantic Agony.* New York: Meridian, 1965.

Preston, Richard. *The Hot Zone.* New York: Anchor, 1994.

Psycho. Dir. Alfred Hitchcock. Paramount 1960.

Rabelais, Francois. *Gargantua and Pantagruel.* Trans. Burton Raffel. New York: Norton, 1990.

Rabid. Dir. David Cronenberg. Cinema Entertainment, 1977.

Radcliffe, Ann. *The Italian.* New York: Oxford UP, 1981.

———. *The Mysteries of Udolpho.* New York: Oxford UP, 1998.

Regan, Robert, ed. *Poe: A Collection of Critical Essays.* Englewood Cliffs, NJ: Prentice Hall, 1967.

Reid, B. L. *William Butler Yeats: The Lyric of Tragedy.* Norman: U of Oklahoma P, 1961.

Renza, Louis A. "Poe's King: Playing It Close to the Pest." *Edgar Allan Poe Review* 2.2 (Fall 2001): 3–18.

Rice, Anne. *Interview with the Vampire.* New York: Ballantine, 1977.

Riley, Michael. *Conversations with Anne Rice.* New York: Ballantine, 1996.

Roethke, Theodore. *The Collected Poems of Theodore Roethke.* New York: Doubleday, 1966.

Rosemary's Baby. Dir. Roman Polanski. Paramount, 1968.

Rukeyser, Muriel. *The Orgy.* Ashfield, MA: Paris, 1997.

Sage, Victor. *Horror Fiction in the Protestant Tradition.* New York: St. Martin's, 1988.

Said, Edward. Introduction. Melville, *Moby Dick* viii–xxix.

Saliba, David R. *The Psychology of Fear.* Boston: UP of America, 1980.

Sartre, Jean-Paul. *Nausea.* 1959. Trans. Lloyd Alexander. New York: New Directions, 1964.

———. *What Is Literature?* Trans. Bernard Frechtman. New York: Harper, 1965.

Scanners. Dir. David Cronenberg. Filmplan, 1981.

Scarry, Elaine, ed. *Literature and the Body: Essays on Populations and Persons.* Baltimore: Johns Hopkins UP, 1988.

Schilpp, Paul Arthur, ed. *The Philosophy of Ernst Cassirer.* New York: Tudor, 1958.

Schmitt, Jean-Claude. *Ghosts in the Middle Ages: The Living and the Dead in Medieval Society.* Chicago: U of Chicago P, 1998.

Scream. Dir. Wes Craven. Woods/Dimension, 1996.

Scudder, Harold C. "Melville's 'Benito Cereno' and Captain Delano's *Voyages.*" *PMLA* 43.2 (June 1928): 502–32.

Seven. Dir. David Fincher. New Line, 1995.

Shakespeare, William. *The Complete Works of Shakespeare.* Ed. Hardin Craig and David Bevington. New York: Foresman, 1979.

Shelley, Mary. *Frankenstein.* New York: Norton, 1992.

The Shining. Dir. Stanley Kubrick. Warner, 1980.

Shroyer, Frederick. Introduction. Le Fanu, *Uncle Silas* viii–xxviii.

Siddons, Anne Rivers. *The House Next Door.* New York: Harper, 1978.

Simpson, Philip L. *Psycho Paths: Tracking the Serial Killer Through Contemporary American Film and Fiction.* Carbondale: Southern Illinois UP, 2000.

Smith-Rosenburg, Carroll. "Domesticating Virtue: Coquettes and Revolutionaries in Young America." Scarry 160–84.

Something Wicked This Way Comes. Dir. Jack Clayton. Disney / Bryna, 1983.

Stallybrass, Peter, and Allon White. *The Politics and Poetics of Transgression.* Ithaca: Cornell UP, 1986.

The Stand. Dir. Mike Garris. 1994.

St. Armand, Barton Levi. "The 'Mysteries' of Edgar Poe: The Quest for a Monomyth in Gothic Literature." Thompson 65–93.

Steinbeck, John. *The Long Valley.* New York: Viking, 1956.

Steiner, George. *The Death of Tragedy.* New Haven: Yale UP, 1961.

Sterne, Laurence. *The Life and Opinions of Tristram Shandy, Gentleman.* New York: Penguin, 1997.

Stigmata. Dir. Rupert Wainwright. FGM / MGM, 1999.

Stoker, Bram. *Dracula.* Ed. Maurice Hindle. New York: Penguin, 1993.

Stoker, Charlotte. "The Cholera Epidemic" (in letter to Bram Stoker, c. 1875). Bram Stoker 498–506.

Strangers on a Train. Dir. Alfred Hitchcock. Warner, 1951.

Straub, Peter. *If You Could See Me Now.* New York: Ballantine, 1977.

Suspiria. Dir. Dario Argento. Italy, 1977.

Swenson, Kristine. "The Menopausal Vampire: Arabella Kenealy and the Boundaries of True Womanhood." *Woman's Writing* 9.3 (2002).

The Tenant. Dir. Roman Polanski. France, 1976.

Thompson, G. R. *The Gothic Imagination: Essays in Dark Romanticism.* Pullman: Washington State UP, 1974.

Thucydides. "The Plague at Athens" (excerpt from *The History of the Peloponnesian War*). DeFoe 233–35.

Tightrope. Dir. Richard Tuggle. Malpaso / Warner, 1984.

Tomlin, E. W. F. *Living and Knowing.* London: Faber, 1955.

True Confessions. Dir. Ulu Grosbard. United Artists, 1981.

Tuchman, Barbara. *A Distant Mirror: The Calamitous 14th Century.* New York: Ballantine, 1978.

Twain, Mark. *Adventures of Huckleberry Finn.* New York: Oxford UP, 1999.

Unamuno, Miguel de. *The Agony of Christianity.* Ed. Kurt F. Reinhardt. New York: Ungar, 1969.

Vampires. Dir. John Carpenter. Storm King / Largo, 1998.

Vampyr. Dir. Carl Dreyer. Germany, 1932.

Varela, Francisco J., Evan Thompson, and Eleanor Rosch, eds. *The Embodied Mind: Cognitive Science and Human Experience.* Cambridge: MIT UP, 1991.

Variety Portable Movie Guide. Berkley Boulevard, 2000.

Varma, Devendra P. *The Gothic Flame.* Metuchen, NJ: Scarecrow, 1987.

Vincent, Thomas. "From *God's Terrible Voice in the City.*" DeFoe 211–14.

Wardrop, Daneen. *Emily Dickinson's Gothic.* Iowa City: U of Iowa P, 1996.

Warner, Mariana. *No Go the Bogeyman: Scaring, Lulling, and Making Mock.* New York: Farrar, 1998.

Watson, E. L. Grant. *The Mystery of Physical Life.* Hudson, NY: Lindisfarne, 1992.

Welsford, Enid. *The Fool: His Social and Literary History.* Gloucester, MA: Peter Smith, 1966.

Weston, Jessie L. *From Ritual to Romance*. 1920. Princeton: Princeton UP, 1993.

Wharton, Edith. *The Ghost Stories of Edith Wharton*. New York: Scribner's, 1973.

Whitehead, Alfred North. *Science and the Modern World*. New York, Macmillan, 1967.

Whitman, Walt. *Leaves of Grass: A Textual Variorum of the Printed Poems*. Ed. Scully Bradley, et al. Vol. 1. New York: New York UP, 1980.

———. *The Works of Walt Whitman*. Vol. 1, *The Collected Poetry*. New York: Minerva, 1969.

Wiener, Norbert. *The Human Use of Human Beings*. Boston: Da Capo, 1954.

Wilbur, Richard. "The House of Poe." Regan 98–120.

Williams, Catherine. *Fall River: An Authentic Narrative*. Ed. Patricia Caldwell. New York: Oxford UP, 1993.

Williams, Tennessee. *Four Plays*. New York: Signet, 1976.

Williams, William Carlos. *Selected Poems*. Ed. Charles Tomlinson. New York: New Directions, 1985.

Wills, Gary. *Witches and Jesuits: Shakespeare's* Macbeth. New York: Oxford UP, 1995.

Wittgenstein, Ludwig. *Culture and Value*. Chicago: U of Chicago P, 1984.

Wolfen. Dir. Michael Wadleigh. Orion, 1981.

INDEX

abjection (*see also* depletion), 70, 79, 81–82, 172, 186–87, 225–27, 230
Abrams, M. H., 6
Acts and Monuments (Foxe), 56
aesthetic, body-horror, 80–82
"Afterward" (Wharton), 181
age, *versus* youth, 152
Aiken, John, 20, 213
"Algerine Captives, The," 119
alien aggression, 68–69
alienation, from organic life, 109–10
America: crime films in, 126–27, 129; culture of, 113–16, 125; gothicism in, 113, 120–21; horror literature of, 111, 113–17, 119, 217
American Werewolf in London, An (film), 45
Andersen, Hans Christian, 134
Angela's Ashes (McCourt), 33
Angel Heart (film), 20, 65, 128, 129, 130, 134
antiquarianism, 121, 182–83
anxiety, 51–52, 70–71, 147–48, 194, 211; of languishment, 172–73; of organism, 10, 90–94, 197, 218–19; and reality, 2–3, 11, 21, 41, 203; of vagueness, 172–73
Apollonian myth, 141, 154, 156–57, 212, 216, 217
apotropaion, 201, 205, 223
Archeologist of Morning (Olson), 118
architecture (*see also* loci, sinister), 183, 188, 192
Argento, Dario, 191
Aristotle, 22, 24
art, horror (*see also* culture; films, horror; literature, horror), 17, 28, 48–50, 70, 90–91, 108, 152, 229; biological life in, 40–41; as discovery, 224–25; of housekeeping, 186; of tragedy, 23
Arthur Mervyn (Brown), 51, 223
As You Like It (Shakespeare), 25
Auden, W. H., 34

baby-sitting, neglect of, 154–57
Bachelard, Gaston, 189, 196, 197
Badley, Linda, 20, 37–38, 43, 90–91, 96, 129
bad places (*see also* loci, sinister), 159, 184, 186–87, 191
Baker, Carlos, 166, 170
Bakhtin, Mikhail, 46–47, 49, 106, 110, 144; on carnival, 25, 28, 108, 135, 137–38, 146; on comic, 132, 139–40, 148; on pageantry, 166; works, 8, 141
Bakley, Linda, 10
Baldick, Chris, 37, 63, 79, 215, 240n 3
Ballard, J. G., 20, 195
Barbauld, Anna, 4, 20, 213
Barber, C. L., 7–8, 27, 89, 97, 158, 224; on comic, 31, 132–33; on folk dynamic, 44, 140–41
Barfield, Owen, 2, 224
Barker, Clive, 10–11, 13, 20, 136, 185, 217; works, 9, 34–35, 75, 196, 226, 237n 10
"Bartlesby the Scrivener" (Melville), 160–63, 220–21, 241n 1
Bataille, Georges, 58, 81, 225
Batman (film), 134
Beaver, Harold, 207
"Because I Could Not Stop for Death" (Dickenson), 193
Beloved (Morrison), 83
"Benito Cereno" (Melville), 7, 84, 115, 163, 241n 1 (chap. 7); obscurity in, 205–10, 211–12, 213–16, 218, 221, 223
Beowulf, 37, 183, 185
Bergson, Henri, 2, 8, 67–68, 92, 107, 235n 6
Beroul, 69
Berthoff, Warner, 218
bestiality, 118
Bible: Job, 71; Judges, 47, 182; Revelation, 179
Bierce, Ambrose, 166

Jack Morgan teaches in the Department of English at the University of Missouri-Rolla. He has published widely in American and Irish literature and is a coeditor, with Louis A. Renza, of *The Irish Stories of Sarah Orne Jewett*, Southern Illinois University Press, 1996.